PAINTED in BLOOD

PIP VAUGHAN-HUGHES

First published in Great Britain in 2008 by Orion Books,
an imprint of The Orion Publishing Group Ltd
Orion House, 5 Upper Saint Martin's Lane
London WC2H 9EA

An Hachette Livre UK Company

1 3 5 7 9 10 8 6 4 2

A CIP catalogue record for this book is
available from the British Library.

ISBN (Hardback) 978 0 7528 9197 2
ISBN (Export Trade Paperback) 978 0 7528 9198 9

Typeset at The Spartan Press Ltd,
Lymington, Hants

Printed and bound in Great Britain by
Clays Ltd, St Ives plc

The Orion Publishing Group's policy is to use papers that
are natural, renewable and recyclable products and made
from wood grown in sustainable forests. The logging and
manufacturing processes are expected to conform to the
environmental regulations of the country of origin.

www.orionbooks.co.uk

For Flora
patient daughter

Acknowledgements

My thanks go to Jon Wood, for editing like a friend; to Christopher Little and to Emma Schlesinger, for love and aid; to Angela McMahon; to my father for his perfect advice; to my family, and especially and always to Tara.

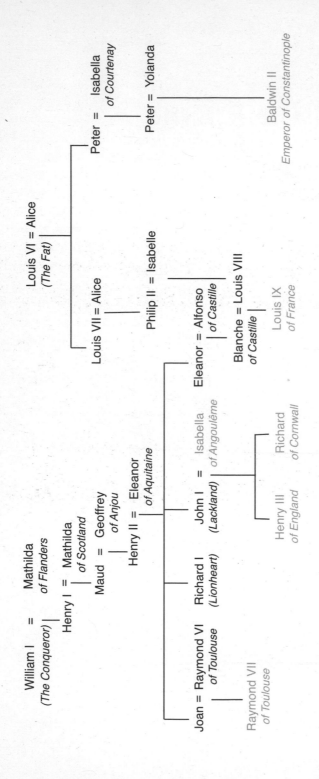

William I = Mathilda
(The Conqueror) | of Flanders

Henry I = Mathilda
| of Scotland

Maud = Geoffrey
| of Anjou

Henry II = Eleanor
| of Aquitaine

Louis VI = Alice
(The Fat)

Louis VII = Alice

Peter = Isabella
of Courtenay

Philip II = Isabelle

Peter = Yolanda

Eleanor = Alfonso
of Castille

Baldwin II
Emperor of Constantinople

Blanche = Louis VIII
of Castille |

Louis IX
of France

Joan = Raymond VI
of Toulouse

Richard I
(Lionheart)

John I = Isabella
(Lackland) of Angoulême

Raymond VII
of Toulouse

Henry III
of England

Richard
of Cornwall

Very simplified family trees of the Plantagenets and Capetians, showing that they were all each others' cousins; characters who figure in *Painted In Blood* are noted in grey.

ETROC'S FRANCE

CHERBOURG

★PARIS

•TAILLEBOURG
•SAINTES
ROYAN

•BORDEAUX

LYON

ALBI•

TOULOUSE•

•MONTPELLIER
CARCASSONNE•
•MONTSEGUR

•MARSEILLES

MILES

0   50   100   200   300

Prologue

Venice, August 1239

The blood was drying, caking on my top lip and setting hard across my mouth. My eyelashes were smarting as it began to clot and knit them together, and a burning line ran across my eyeballs from the blood trying to seep between my tight-shut lids. Cooling blood tightened the skin on my chest and itched and stung in every scratch and flea-bite. The air cracked and soughed above me, and with a gentle sigh of air the cloth settled over me.

I dared not twitch an eyelid, though the salt was stinging horribly. There was a panicked scream growing under my breast-bone, but I dared not let it out, dared do nothing but let my breath creep in and out of my nose, softly, panic growing each time the blood-soaked cloth stuck to my nostrils and cut off the tiny stream of air. The cloth began to bind itself against me, the blood sucking it tight to my skin. I was goose-flesh from my scalp to my toes. As the wet linen moulded itself to the dips of my face, as the pooled blood drew it into the sockets of my eyes, the distant red glow of torchlight that had been filtering through my lids went out.

'Just a bit longer, Patch,' said Gilles de Peyrolles, softly. I flinched as hands began to smooth the scratchy linen against the length of my body. At least they had had the courtesy to heat the blood first, but it was beginning to cool now, in the chill of a rainy Venetian evening, made more frigid – even in August – by the ancient stones of the palace known as Ca'Kanzir, in the kitchen of which we were conducting what it pleased Captain de Montalhac to call an *experiment*.

'Is that enough time, do you think?' It was Gilles again.

'I think so. Any longer and the blood will come off in flakes, won't it?' Captain de Montalhac didn't sound too certain, so I tried a series of small twitches and pathetic noises in my throat to let my two friends know that it most certainly was time to peel the shroud off me. And peel it they did, starting at my feet and pulling the linen taut so that it snapped away from my skin all at once. And suddenly I was very cold, and very relieved. My eyes were still gummed shut, but I opened my mouth, lips straining against the salty glue until they came apart with a sticky kiss.

'Sit up, quickly,' said the Captain, gingerly taking hold of my shoulders. 'Gilles, do you have hold of it?'

I sat up, and the Captain put the knotted end of a rope into my hands. It was slung across the main ceiling beam, and as we had planned I used it to pull myself sharply off the table on which I had been lying, so that the shroud beneath would not be smudged. Still blind, I swung myself to one side and let go, hoping not to land on anything sharp.

'Oh, fuck,' I gasped. 'For mercy's sake, get me some water.'

The image on our shroud was pitiful. We hung it up to dry from the ceiling, and there was my outline, head down and then head up again, as if I had been sliced in half and arranged end to end. I had been growing a beard, and so the face on the shroud should have been that of a young, long-haired, bearded man. But it was nothing more than a clotted daub of darkening pig's blood, and indeed the whole affair looked like nothing better than a child's gigantic finger painting.

'So that isn't how they did it either,' I said at last. I was standing in a tub of hot water that I had insisted be ready for me, sluicing away the last of the gore with a ewer of more water. I smelled like a blood pudding. It would take days to get it out of my hair, though, and as for my beard . . .

'I still think it was some sort of . . . you said honey, didn't you, Michel? But I think caramel,' said Gilles.

'I am *not* painting myself with honey, nor caramel either,' I said flatly. 'But it isn't right anyway. The face, for instance. Can you get . . . can you get *it* out? To compare.'

None of us wanted to, but in the end Gilles, wrinkling his nose with unease, opened the slim wooden case that lay at the far end of the room, well out of the way of sloshing water and spattering blood. He drew out a wide strip of thin, brownish cloth and hung it over a broom handle that we had suspended from the ceiling. I felt the air change, imperceptibly, as I always did when the *Mandylion* of Edessa was brought out. For now we were in the presence of something, of – I could not quite bring myself to say it, now or at any time – of *someone*. For the

2

ancient linen bore the image of a man, a naked, bearded man, his hands crossed to hide his manhood, his brow and side spotted and streaked with what had once been blood. All this somehow seemed to shine from what, if you got close enough, was nothing more than a faint, very faint arrangement of stains. But what the *Mandylion* exuded, what changed the temperature in any room where it was displayed, was suffering.

Now it hung next to my own image, but compared to that, the new-made shroud was nothing more than a butcher's apron or a torturer's memento. To call it crude would have honoured it far beyond what it deserved. But why? The *Mandylion* was reputed by legends reaching far back into the murky past to be nothing less than the burial shroud of Jesus Christ, and the image was that of his body, conveyed miraculously to the cloth in the hours before His resurrection. But if it was not a bloody imprint – and the three of us in that kitchen all agreed, with our silence, that our experiment had demonstrated that it was not – what, then, could it possibly be?

Michel de Montalhac, captain of the ship *Cormaran*, was the greatest dealer of holy relics the world has ever known, although he was too modest a soul to brag of it. Gilles de Peyrolles was his oldest companion and lieutenant of our company, and I was their partner. It was I who had stolen the *Mandylion* from its home in the Pharos Chapel in far away Constantinople, and in the five years since I had joined the company of the *Cormaran*, I had learned from these two masters everything that could be learned about holy relics: how to find them, how to sell them, and above all, how to make them to order. But Gilles and the Captain, let alone my own modest intellect, could not work out how the ancient forger had made the *Mandylion*. For it had to be a forgery.

It had to be.

'The cloth is ancient, agreed?' Gilles said quietly. We nodded. 'So who worked out how to do this, a thousand years ago?'

'Someone cleverer than us,' said the Captain. We always did this, studiously avoided the real question posed by the *Mandylion*. Perhaps the three of us were daring each other to say it first:

'What if?'

But we never did. 'We've all seen the painted mummy boards in the bazaars of Cairo,' said Gilles instead. 'The ancients knew how to paint a face – far better than our painters today.'

'Yes, but they used encaustic – we tried that, remember? It looked like a . . . like a bad mummy board, except cloth.'

'I still think it looks like scorching,' said the Captain. 'Perhaps an iron statue, heated until it was red hot, and the cloth just *touched* to it . . .'

3

'There would be burns,' I pointed out. 'It would have singed right through somewhere.'

We had told each other many times of the great coffers of silver awaiting us if we could make a decent copy of this thing. But we were hiding behind our professional interest, for there was one thing the three of us agreed upon. The *Mandylion* of Edessa was no forgery.

But if not, what was it? In the world that turned outside the Ca'Kanzir, our dilemma would have been no dilemma at all. Kings were waiting to pay the worth of their kingdoms for the thing that dangled from our kitchen ceiling, if they but knew it existed; cardinals would poison each other, bishops would risk excommunication. For here was Christ's image, made by nothing less than the emanations of His dead flesh. But none of us believed in Him. I was godless, faithless; and Captain de Montalhac was, with Gilles, a heretic of the sort they call *Albigense* and *Cathari*. An erstwhile monk who had lost his faith years before, and two men who believed Christ had been either a phantom or a lie told by the Church to bind men to its rule: such were the guardians of the *Mandylion*.

'Put it away,' said the Captain at last. With the help of Gilles I folded it up and closed the lid of the plain reliquary. The sun seemed to have come out, though the mists of Venice still hovered outside. 'I will take it tomorrow, for the brothers must leave, and Bishop Marty is waiting for it.'

'Are you sure your people need it?' I asked. 'It does not seem . . .' I put the box carefully on a side table and stepped quickly away from it. 'It tells us of nothing but pain and death.' That was the truth, to me at least. A thin murmur seemed to come from the shroud, a whispered agony and a seeping coldness. Not malevolent, not evil: simply the absence of hope. I did not believe it had witnessed a resurrection. It was empty, like all graves are empty: their occupants, though they lie within, are not there. When I looked into the shadowy eyes of the man on the shroud, that is what I saw.

'Marty will teach the people with it,' said the Captain, finding his own strong voice again, for we had all been whispering. 'It proves Christ was a man, that he suffered, and because of that was not the son of God. The Church has lied, she has always lied, and here is the proof. Besides, do you want to keep it?'

'I do not,' said Gilles.

'I am sorry I ever found it,' I said.

'Perhaps it was waiting for you,' said the Captain, and he levelled his eyes at me for a moment. Then he smiled. 'There's blood in your beard,' he said.

'I know.' And at that moment the cook walked in, and at the sight of all the gore that was growing hard upon her table let out a shriek of outrage, and as for the bloody two-headed figure suspended from the rafters . . .

'We were cooking,' Gilles explained, gathering her up in his arms and steering her away from the carnage.

'What in God's name were you making?' she breathed, fanning herself.

'We don't know,' said Captain de Montalhac. 'We do not know.'

Chapter One

'Do you understand heretics, Monsieur Petroc?' asked Louis Capet, King of France, rolling an acorn absently between slender fingers. It was last year's fruit, and winter had polished it until it shone, fat and brown against Louis' white skin.

Overhead, in the great canopy of the oak tree, a squirrel was chittering and a family of blackbirds were screaming at a magpie. A horsefly was attacking my neck. I grabbed for it and caught it in my fist, feeling the tiny crunch as it paid for its boldness. Opening my hand, I watched as the bright stained glass of its tiny eyes faded.

'Understand them in what sense?' I replied, scraping the bloody gut-smear of the fly from my palm. Looking up, I met the king's gaze. Somewhere above me a baby blackbird was perhaps about to become a magpie's dinner.

'Their inner workings, if you will.' He held up the acorn's smooth brown oval, turning it so that it gleamed in the dappled sunlight. 'One might consider this thing,' he went on. 'Flawless, simple, even beautiful, for are not all God's creations beautiful? But within . . .' His thumbnail whitened for an instant, and the acorn burst, raining shards of dust into the king's lap. 'Within, it is rotten.'

'So I see, Your Majesty,' I said, carefully.

'It seemed so perfect, did it not? And so how did I know of the rottenness within? A hole, a tiny hole no bigger than a pinprick. The canker had wormed inside and laid it to waste. So it is with heretics.'

'Your Majesty,' I said, 'I understand rottenness, but my experience of corruption . . .' I paused and licked my lips. They were very dry. 'I know more than enough of the corruption of matter. Things go bad. They rot. In a tree, a gardener might allay a canker, and in a person, a surgeon

6

might be of use – or not.' I glanced at the king to gauge the effect of that feeble wit, but he was staring up at the shifting leaves. 'But you speak of an invisible canker. I believe the diagnosis and cure of that should be left to the doctors of Holy Mother Church. Indeed I would fear to understand it, in case it corrupted me in turn.'

The king chuckled, and I let myself relax a little, a very little. 'Wisely said. But such a subtle poison. How many acorns hang from my tree? A thousand, more? Into how many of them will the canker burrow?'

'It is a city of acorns, Your Majesty. How long would it take to examine each one, do you suppose?'

'Do you know, Monsieur Petroc, if they were human souls I would do it, I would, no matter how long it might take. I love God so well that I would look inside every one of my subjects for signs that evil had corrupted their innocent souls. But, lo!' He flung the last of the ruined acorn away. 'There is no need. Happily the Holy Father in Rome has created the Inquisition to do it for me.'

'And for that blessing Christendom should be truly thankful,' I said hurriedly. I wiped the broken body of the horsefly onto the grass. A tiny green and red stain remained on my finger.

'If this tree were France, I could tell you where the canker lies,' he said. 'Those lower branches. Do you see that fat crop of nuts hanging there? The lands of Toulouse are the lower branches of my kingdom, and there the heretics cluster just as thickly.'

'So one has heard,' I said.

The king sighed and rose to his feet. As was his custom he held out a hand to me and I took it and let him haul me upright. The gold of his rings had grown warm in the sunlight.

'Enough of this gloom,' he said, brushing the dust from his robe. 'We were talking of my chapel, and what might be found to adorn it. As to my acorns, before they ripen there is hope. But one day the wind will shake the branches and they shall fall, pure and rotten alike.' He slapped the trunk lovingly.

'And then the hogs will eat them all,' I said quietly, but Louis did not hear me.

Chapter Two

Paris, March 1242

It was the last week of March, and the sun was drifting lazily in through the windows of King Louis Capet's chamber. Outside, the park of Vincennes stretched away, legions of oak and elm and beech just beginning to flush out in the first colours of spring. Inside, the king was spreading big sheets of parchment across a writing table.

'Look at this, my dear fellow,' he called, and I obediently stepped over from the window and peered deferentially over his silk-robed shoulder.

'My Sainte Chapelle,' he told me, unnecessarily.

A succession of narrow pointed arches, tall and severe as archangels ascending to the heavens, rose up to a roof crowned by a spire as light and graceful as a unicorn's horn. Even as this, a dream scratched out in ink, it was breathtaking. I wondered how stone and glass could be made to do such things, to form a delicate bower for a treasure beyond worth.

'Your Majesty,' I replied, 'This is magnificent beyond belief.'

Louis turned and gave me a smile of such genuine warmth and gratitude that, disarmed for a moment, I almost reached out and patted his shoulder. But I had trained myself well, and resisted. In truth, my mind had turned to another chapel, small and ancient, clinging to a rocky shore against the sea that would, one day soon, devour it. The Chapel of Pharos in Constantinople had given up its last treasure now, and had no more value than any other place in that great, dead city. That was why I was here, to deliver the final pieces in its inventory. I had come to Paris bearing heads, three of them. I wondered if Saints Simeon, Blas and Clement had been lonely in that dark, damp place after the other relics had been taken away. I felt a coldness fluttering through my bones, as I always did when I thought of that place. I winced inside, and turned my thoughts back to the plan. As one city died, so another burst into life.

'The Crown shall rest here,' Louis was saying, tapping the plan, 'and the other treasures here and here. And these shall be the finest windows in the world, for they must light what Our Lord Himself touched and gave forth his own blood upon.'

'It shall be the finest reliquary the world has ever seen, and will ever see,' I said piously.

And so it should be, I thought. Christ alone knew what he was spending on this chapel, but I knew what he had paid for the treasures he was placing there, for he had paid me. One hundred and thirty five pounds of gold for one thing alone, the Crown of Thorns. And then he had proceeded to buy up everything else on the shopping list my company had given him – no, not buy, but receive as tokens of gratitude, for Louis would not commit the sin of Simony, and thanks to the company of the *Cormaran* he did not need to.

Louis was lost in his plans, no doubt seeing the ink turning to stone and glass and lead and rising from the parchment before him. But my mind had turned again to those three heads. I had looked inside their boxes – of course I had looked, for one always checked the merchandise – and lifted each head, light as balls of stale bread. I had unwrapped the brittle linen from them and seen the black skin clinging to yellow bone, seen the shrunken, bitter leer of each mouth, the dry blindness of the eye sockets. Saint Simeon was no more than a skull, but the others let me have a glimpse of what they must have looked like before their flesh met with such ruin: men, at least, with mouths that let in the sweet air and let it out again, eyes . . . God's wind, enough of this! It was no more than the ruin that comes to us all. Three heads, twelve pounds of gold. The blessings of the saints indeed.

Louis always got a strange look on his face when he beheld a relic – I had seen it often enough, for in the three years since I signed over the Crown of Thorns to him at Troyes I had brought him another twenty-one items, and for each he had paid far above the going rate. I had conveyed these things as gifts from Louis' cousin Baldwin of Constantinople, the sad and desperate youth who perched upon Constantine's throne much as a crippled seagull clings to storm-blown flotsam. And I had conveyed to Baldwin the expressions of Louis' gratitude, which had so far kept the dispossessed Greeks from taking back their beloved city from the Frankish occupiers, the Latins who had conquered in the name of the Church of Rome, although in this year of 1242 the Greeks were almost at its walls and Baldwin had opened his holy treasure-house for the last time. He had no more relics to sell, now, and there was nothing else that could be stripped from his Empire, if a ruined city populated by unpaid soldiers and ghosts could be called that.

But Louis was happy. He had done all he could to shore up the Church of Rome's pitiful bastion in the east, and now he could turn to the enjoyment of his treasures with a clear conscience. When I had said farewell to Baldwin, standing on a freezing quay on the Golden Horn three months ago, he looked like a man left to die on a lonely shore, despite the Frankish banners that waved bravely above him, and perhaps he was. But here in France, with its oak trees, its plump, blushing girls and its bottomless treasury, his cousin was happy.

'How, by the by, is your employer? How is dear Monsieur de Sol?'

'The last time we saw each other, he was well,' I replied.

'That is good,' said Louis, picking up a goblet of wine and strolling lazily towards the window. 'He is in Venice, I suppose?'

'In Florence, Your Majesty,' I told him. 'Our company has founded a bank there, as you know. He divides his time between Florence and the Serenissima these days.'

'He was always a wandering soul,' said the king, resting a long finger pensively against his cheek as he leaned on the window ledge. 'And you, my dear Monsieur Petrus, have inherited his travelling cloak.'

I bowed. 'Would that I were fit to wear it,' I said.

'Oh, come come. You are a worthy protégé. De Sol swears it was you who foiled that Venetian scoundrel . . .' He clicked his fingers, brow furrowed.

'Querini.'

'Querini! Exactly so.' The king turned his face to the sunshine. He loved this story that he had bought his way into: the relic beyond price, the failing empire, the Venetian adventurer who had stolen his prize, and the English lad who had mended all. It was a good story, a king's story, and he was welcome to it. For my part in it had been as nothing more than a creature of fate, pulled hither and yon by the schemes of great men as I saw my friends die around me. And I had lost someone . . . but no, I did not think of that any more. If I had triumphed, it was because in the end I had used the greed of one side to pull down the other, nothing more. If Louis knew how much blood was on my hands and on his Crown of Thorns – fresh blood, mind, not the ineffable stuff that gave that horrible tangle of black sticks and spikes its value – he might not like his story half as much. But then again, he probably would. Blood, greed and betrayal: a king's story after all.

Food was brought in, and we gossiped a little more about Jean de Sol and Constantinople, and Venice, and old Pope Gregory, who had died last year, and his successor Clementine, who had lasted a mere three weeks on the throne of Saint Peter before he too had keeled over from the shock of it all. I had become accustomed to these royal chats, for Louis had made me his relic-finder, and to a king prepared to pay half of everything in his kingdom's treasury for one frail coronet of twisted wood, that was a not unimportant title. And besides, Louis Capet was a strange sort of king. He did not care for the pomp and trappings of kingship, but liked to deal plainly with his courtiers and subjects. His favourite place to conduct the business of state was where we had lately been sitting, underneath his oak tree in the park of Vincennes. While I still found it strange and not a little terrifying to be chit-chatting with the king of France as if we were two burghers in a tavern, he did not. So I nibbled at the food, which was the simple stuff Louis preferred: bread, cheese and garlic sausage; sipped the wine, and offered token suggestions for the Sainte Chapelle, until all of a sudden there came a curt rap at the door and a young man entered, a disturbed look upon his exquisitely barbered face.

'Your Majesty, I humbly beg pardon for this disturbance, but there is some news I thought it best to bring.' He paused, and shot a meaningful glance in my direction, but Louis leaned across the table and patted my hand to let the man know that I was a confidante.

The man – scarcely a man, for he could have been no more than eighteen summers old, and his beard was still soft and innocently curled – drew himself up and placed one foot before the other. When he was satisfied that he had struck an impressive enough pose, he cleared his throat.

'Your Majesty, the news is from the south,' he said. Louis raised his chin.

'Oh, yes?' he said, evenly.

'Two messengers arrived today, one from Poitou, one from Languedoc,' said the youth. 'Count Raymond of Toulouse has been taken ill at Penne and is not expected to live. From Poitou news comes that Hughues de Lusignan has renounced his ties of fealty to Your Majesty.'

'That, at least, is not unexpected,' said Louis, calmly. He sighed, sounding more disappointed than angry. 'Lusignan is a viper, but we have always known it. He wishes to go to war with us. No doubt his appalling wife will bring the English across to help him. If Raymond is dying . . .' He rubbed his brow and frowned. I realised that he had forgotten I was in the room. 'The alliance Raymond has been trying to make with Aragon against us will be forfeit, but how strong is Lusignan?'

He set down the goblet he held, taking care not to spill anything on the plans. Then he turned to me, and I saw his eyebrows flicker with surprise before he remembered who I was. I hastily formed my features into an appropriate display of outrage.

'This is most vexing news, Your Majesty,' I said. 'I will leave you, if I may, with the humblest thanks for your kindness and generosity to your most lowly servant.' I thought I might have overdone it – the honeyed words demanded by other princes were wasted on Louis, or so he at least pretended – but he gave me a smile of gratitude and patted my shoulder.

'We will talk tomorrow, Petrus,' he said. 'There is much . . .' But he had lost his train of thought, and the courtier was watching me with ill-concealed impatience, so I bowed my way from Louis, turned elegantly in front of the bearer of ill news, and removed myself from the royal presence.

It was a three-mile ride back to Paris, and I let my horse trot when she wanted to, and walk when it suited her. The sun was shining on the river away to my left, and up ahead, the smoke of numberless cooking fires rose straight up, for the breeze that had ruffled the king's oak had faded away, and it had become sultry. I should have been happy. I *was* happy, for I had concluded the company's business with Louis and received the papers which would authorise a gift of twelve pounds of gold to be paid to Baldwin de Courtenay, Emperor of Constantinople. And I would carve off a fat slice of that gold as commission and send it hurrying to the coffers of the Banco da Corvo Marino in Florence. Monsieur Jean de Sol would be happy with that. Baldwin would be ecstatic, if only for a month or so, before his money bled away through one of the many severed veins of his realm. Louis would be happy, playing holy families with his new heads. So why was I not utterly content? I was twenty-five years old with most of my teeth still in my head. I was on shoulder-slapping terms with the king of France, and I had the confidence of the wisest and most extraordinary man I knew, Monsieur Jean de Sol, otherwise known as Michel Corvus Marinus, and to a very few as Michel de Montalhac.

De Montalhac. There it was. A name of Languedoc. And Michel de Montalhac was a Cathar. Had he heard the news in Florence? He would be there with his deputy, Gilles de Peyrolles, also a Cathar. These two men had done business with almost every prince, spiritual or worldly, in Christendom, and had kept this deadly secret all through the long years. I had seen Captain de Montalhac treated as a friend by a pope, by countless bishops and cardinals. And Louis Capet loved to sit beneath his tree and speak of holy things with him. I wondered, not for the first time, what canker the king might fear to find in his own soul if he knew how many hours he had passed in discourse with a heretic?

And now this matter in the south, the lands of Raymond, Count of Toulouse. Everyone knew how much Louis hated the heretics who the rulers of Toulouse had let flourish, and likewise even the peddler pushing his creaking, jingling barrow on the road beside me knew that Count Raymond had been humbled, humiliated by the French, who had invaded his lands, all but usurped his patrimony, and now imposed the terrors of the Inquisition on his people. He had rebelled before, and it had only been a matter of time before he did so again, even if he was the king's cousin. But now, perhaps, he was dying, and it seemed as if his last act would be to bring war down upon his country.

The South. You could not lift a cup in a tavern here in Paris without some young buck wearing his father's stained silk cast-offs bragging about how he was going south to take some land from the heretics. Down there, where the wine flowed in the streams, corn grew in the winter and the girls . . . I put my horse into a canter and kicked up the dust for a mile, until the Templar's marsh came in sight. I had been in Venice with the Captain when the last round of troubles had broken out. The young lord of Carcassonne – a lord without land, for the French had stolen it – had tried to take back his city, but had failed and had been forced to sign his birthright over to Louis. Now there was no pope on the throne to call a crusade, Raymond had plainly tried to sieze his chance. He was getting old, and he might not have another. The news had meant something to Louis, without a doubt. But even more certain was that it boded evil times for the people of Occitania, or I had misread the look on the saintly king's face. I decided to send a note along with the commission. The Captain rarely spoke of his homeland, but he still sought out the news, although it was never good. This would not cheer him, but he would appreciate it.

Inside the walls, Paris closed in around me. Sometimes in this teeming, vast city I felt as if I were a tiny adventurer on the scalp of a giant, pushing through the dense, stinking forest – and this particular giant was mightily infested with lice, the people who seethed every-where, in everything. Or perhaps I was just another louse.

My lodgings, though, were not bad at all, for I could afford the best, and as the king's provider of relics I had a reputation to uphold. So I had taken a set of rooms in the Cité near the palace: not far, in fact, from where Louis was planning to raise his astonishing chapel. I was in with the quality folk, the lords and ladies, and the truth was you could not have told me apart from them.

Petroc of Auneford, the farmer's son, the outlaw monk and penniless fugitive, was a rich man. I still found it hard to believe sometimes, when something in the air reminded me of Dartmoor and my boyhood, or when hunger grabbed at me and I found that I had money enough in my purse to buy myself whatever I desired. But mostly I found that I was quite comfortable, for I had grown used to this new life. And I had fought for it. In many ways I was no different from the nobles who strutted around me, noses on high, paying no mind to the scuttling masses of the struggling, the ordinary. But I was different, of course. I was Petrus Zennorius, official of the company of the *Cormaran*, toast of Venetian society. To become this creature I had seen my dearest love die in my arms. I had dragged myself through sewers, and pilfered things that most men would fear to touch lest they be struck dead on the spot by their furious God. And I had killed a man in cold blood, to save my own life but also to make myself who I was now: someone who was known, who garnered respect and even fear. Petroc of Auneford was dead as far as the world knew, for he had not been seen in England since the night, seven years ago, when Captain de Montalhac had found him bleeding on the wharf at Dartmouth and carried him aboard his ship, the *Cormaran*. In England I was an ogre, for it was believed I had cut open a priest's throat in the cathedral of the town where I was a novice monk, and drunk his blood upon the altar. The Gurt Dog, they called me, the Devil's hound, and I could scare a child beneath the blankets as well as any witch or hobgoblin.

I had been innocent then, but I was not innocent now. That is to say, I had been shown the world from every side, and had peered into every dark corner, or so it seemed. It was as if the Captain, in the seven years I had known him, had held up the world and turned it for me in his hand – for like Ptolemy he believed our world is a great ball hanging in the void – and revealed that it was like nothing more than one of the saintly heads I had just sold Louis Capet, full of corruption and sadness. I had not wished to believe him, but the paths I had taken, some of my choosing, others not, had shown me that he had at least touched on the truth. So I was not innocent, as the Captain was not. But I had tried to remain true to myself, to Petroc of Auneford as he had been that night in the city of Balecester, just before he stepped through the Cathedral doors.

And the world *is* still beautiful, I thought now as the swallows swooped below me through the wooden span of the bridge. I was crossing the Seine just as the sun was beginning to sink below the rooftops, and the lovely knife-winged birds had come out to feast upon flies, and dance in the evening air. It would be a fine night, I was thinking as I stepped into the courtyard of the building where I had taken a set of rooms. The doorkeeper stepped out of his alcove and bowed respectfully, holding out a folded note.

'Gentleman left this for you, sir,' he said, touching his hand to his forehead. I bid him thanks with a nod and a coin, and climbed the tiled stairs to my rooms. The doorman had alerted the servant, and he was already there, lighting the candles and pouring water into a basin. I gave him my dusty riding cloak and washed my hands and face. I had not asked for food, but here was a tray of country cheese, sweet butter, ham and sour, peppery pickles. A silver ewer held dark Cahors wine, and there was a silver goblet with a gold-washed bowl from which to enjoy it. I dismissed the servant and he bowed deeply as he left. Pouring myself a draught of wine I sank down onto the bed. The smell of clean straw and sun-bleached linen rose up to meet me.

The evening sang through the open window, and I wondered what I would do with it. I had been in Paris for a week, and would be here for another, before starting back to Venice. There was the king's business to be concluded – all but done really, save for tomorrow's audience. I had some bank business to do with the Commander of the Paris Temple, and a bishop in need of a relic to justify the new altar he had added to his personal chapel. Then an easy ride south, to Lyons where there were more bankers to meet, and then across the mountains. I would be home before the apples ripened.

Then I remembered the note. No doubt a dinner invitation. I looked around for it, and found it under my breeches on the floor. Tearing off a chunk of ham I broke the plain black seal and carried it over to the window, holding it up to the last beam of rosy light.

Greetings to Petrus Zennorius,
From a friend of the Cormaran.
I carry instructions and words from Sol *that must needs be delivered in person. Pray forgive my insistence, but I would meet you with all urgency. Today being Tuesday, I will be at the market of Les Halles by the pump where the andouillette makers wash their tripes, at the fifth*

hour after noon, or at the same place on Wednesday at Prime if you do
not come today.
Fear not. I shall know you.
Peace be upon you.

Chapter Three

I set my goblet down on the window-ledge without looking, and it found an angle and fell with a loud ring. Wine splashed cold onto my bare feet and I cursed, kicking away the goblet. It rolled under the bed, clinking its protest of a precious thing scorned. I could not see properly, so I leaned out of the window to catch the last of the sunlight. The note was written in a strong, precise hand using good ink and a well-trimmed pen. I did not recognise it, though.

Sol. That was clear enough: Jean de Sol. All well and good: a message from my employer, and nothing unusual about that. It was in Occitan, which made it seem authentic, for the language of the Captain's homeland was the common tongue of the *Cormaran*. But why all this secrecy? The Captain was a prolific writer of instructions, and so was Gilles. We had a cipher that we used if secrecy was called for, but nowadays it was rarely needed and besides, as the Captain often said, when the world is unschooled a plain-writ word is cipher enough. But who was this stranger who wished peace upon me? And why did he wish me to meet with him in such an unwholesome place? I considered. He knew where I lodged – easy enough. I had made no secret of my presence here, for I did not need to. He knew my name . . . ach, this was vexing, I decided, but only that. Either the writer bore a message from Captain de Montalhac or he was some trickster looking to gull some money or perhaps some business from me. But we would be meeting in a place where a thousand people could be found at any hour of the day, the most public place in the city. I would meet him, and then ride out to Vincennes.

I studied the letter once more. Black ink, yellow vellum. An everyday note. My eyes followed the lines to the bottom of the little page: peace be upon you. The language, the words . . . They were Cathar words. Of course. Suddenly I had no doubt that this person had been sent by the Captain, and that I could trust him. It was instinct, nothing more, a confidence no stronger than the vellum in my hand, but somehow it was enough. Whoever he was, I would meet this man tomorrow by the pump. *Là*. It was decided. Breakfast with a heretic, luncheon with the most Christian king. All in a day's work.

I rose early the next morning and put on my court clothes. I buckled on my fine belt of tooled and gilded leather, and arranged it so that my Moorish dagger hung across my left thigh. She was called Thorn, and her hilt was of pale jade that curved over like a frozen wave to form a smooth pommel. She had done for her former master, and so I treated her with a deal of respect. Then I drew on my travelling cloak. It was long, faded and stained with many months' worth of travel, and when I fastened a simple black belt around it my finery was hidden. I stretched, sighing, and cracked a bad night's sleep from my backbone and shoulder blades.

I should not have gone out, but the evening had grown distressingly empty in my apartments and at last, far too late, I had wandered out to a house of entertainment that more than one bravo at court had recommended to me. I had drunk far too much and had forgotten to eat, but drink takes a man in many a strange way, and as the madam had begun to tempt me with the flowers of her establishment I had begun to feel that my dignity was somehow at stake, this despite the fact that I had entered her door with every intention of swiving the tiles from the roof. The more lovely the proffered candidates, the flimsier their raiments, the greater grew my sense of a dim, puzzling affront to my person, until at last I had staggered to my feet, paid my bill with icy politeness (or so it seemed to me then: God alone knows what absurd figure I had cut in reality) and strutted out into the street, banging my shoulder painfully on the door-jamb as I left. I remembered climbing the stairs, and stopping half way to rest my forehead upon their cool tiles; shouting for water and bringing forth a muddled, barely civil serving-man; and then, no more until I woke, my mouth as dry as a fillet of salt cod. It gave me no pleasure to spend my nights thus, but more often than not I seemed to do so. But if I lacked the appetite for this aimless life, in equal measure I lacked any reason to avoid it. For I was a young man, wealthy beyond the dreams of most men, and I was alone.

It had not always been so. After my return from Constantinople and those first days in Venice when the fortunes of the *Cormaran* had been won, I had had a companion. Letice Londeneyse, she was called: Letitia of Smooth Field, sometimes known as Magpie or Pyefote. If I had stolen victory from the darkness of certain failure, it had been she who had lighted my way. I had fallen in love with her, slowly and even, one might say, carefully, for she was not a mannerly noblewoman or a shy, chaste maiden. No, and no again. The first time I had seen her, her eye had just been blacked by her lover in a busy Roman square. The second time she had been scrubbing a man's blood from a boarding-house floor. The third time I had been in her power, and she could have had me killed with a twitch of her eyebrow. That she chose to spare me might be seen as an auspicious beginning to our tryst, but it was not until much later that we came together after pain and the spilling of blood. No, she was not a mannerly woman, my Letice, but she was like no other, and I had loved her as a man alone in the night time wilderness loves the spark and flare of flint upon iron as it lights his lantern.

We had lived, for a time, as man and wife in the Captain's palace in Venice – the Ca'Kanzir – an ancient, half-forgotten refuge on the Rio Morto that was closest thing I had to a home – but we had been betrothed and planned to wed in earnest, for with the sudden rise in our fortunes had come the urge in both of us for . . . what, exactly, I could not have said, but although I would not have admitted to a desire for respectability, I wanted that which I had not had since leaving Balecester – and that was peace. In Letice's yellow hair, the colour of primroses in springtime; in her cool blue eyes, which read words and people with equal subtlety; in her pale skin, the arch of her eyebrows, the swoop of her too-long nose, the way her wide mouth fell into a pout when she was thinking: in all this I did find a strange, profound peace. She must have found something of the like in me, for when I had first known her she had seemed to burn inside with a trembling heat, as if she had foxfire in her soul. She was free, for Nicholas Querini, a rogue of terrifying wealth and power and the man who had called her his lover though she was nothing more than his slave, was ruined, and would soon vanish from this world. She had helped destroy him, but victory had not made her crow: instead it had revealed the girl she had once been before life had made her a whore and a thief. We were thieves together, of course, but we were carefree, for we had just picked the pockets of Christendom and been thanked into the bargain.

I had seen this gentle change in her, but she had seen something else happen to me, for the Captain had been paid his commission from King Louis for the Crown of Thorns, and though I will not divulge an exact sum, suffice to say that Christ at Cana did not perform so great a transformation as that which then came over the company of the *Cormaran*. The *Cormaran* was Captain de Montalhac's ship, our ship, that had sailed for many years, roving far and wide across the face of the waters, from Alexandria to Skraelingland, or so the stories went; and the company had been her crew. Like a petrel she had crossed from land to land, kingdom to kingdom, bearing the Captain's stock-in-trade, for in her hold she carried miracles.

Michel de Montalhac, as he wandered, had made himself the greatest dealer in holy relics in all the lands of Christendom and indeed beyond, for the Captain did not care who bought his wares, and the Mahometans give reverence to relics just as we do. He counted popes and kings as his customers and even his friends, but though his wares brought him an odd kind of power over them, they had no claim to him, for he bowed his knee to nothing but the wind in his ship's sail.

Like their master, the crew were outcasts and outlaws, wanderers and exiles and malcontents from every land. Their only home, their country – if Herodotus was right, and countries can float upon the sea – was the *Cormaran*, and they loved her. Strange, then, or perhaps not so very strange, that as soon as the wealth of Louis rained down on them, those men of the sea suddenly regained their taste for the land. They took their shares and straight away found that all along they had longed to marry and buy an inn in Thuringia, or invest in a company of mercenaries, or go into the wool trade. Some were close by: Zianni had bought himself a pardon for the killing which had got him exiled from Venice many years before and now lived in outlandishly lavish style across the Grand Canal in San Marco, married, no less, to a sweetly rounded, giggling cousin of the Doge. Istvan the Dalmatian had bought a palazzo off the Riva degli Sciavoni where his fellow Croats had made their home, and Dimitri the ferocious Bulgar Master at Arms had moved in with him. They had already set up a nice little business selling arms and ammunition to the government of the Serenissima, and we saw them often.

But mostly the crew had scattered to the four winds. Nizam the helmsman had sailed for Cairo to find the Sufi master he longed to study with. Latchna the sail maker had gone back to Dublin, Carlo to Rome, Mirko to Genoa. Even the Cathars – and there were still a few of them, though once they had been the backbone of the crew – even they drifted away, to risk their lives in Languedoc or just to find peace in some country where the hounds of the Inquisition were not so numerous. Of the old company, suddenly only the Captain, Gilles de Peyrolles, Roussel and Isaac of Toledo remained – and myself, of course. We had to do something with all the silver and gold that King Louis kept giving us, and so we followed the fashion of the day and started a bank.

It was startlingly lucrative almost at once. Fortune had caused us to batten on to the great artery that pumps silver and gold from Venice and Florence up to Lyons, Bruges, London and beyond, just as it had started to flow. It was not exciting business, and I did not care for the short-sighted, long-fingered coin-counters who peopled it, or the vast ledgers, for those were the oceans we sailed now, endless pages ruffled by the winds of greed and commerce into rolling waves of inky numbers. But the life it brought us made up for the boredom, for a time at least. It was a world we had regarded from the outside with the eyes of thieves, but it was exciting to learn the many ways one could rob a man with a few strokes of a quill and win the acclaim of respectable men for it, and so we settled, slowly, and the *Cormaran* became a company of bankers, though the ship herself was still berthed out on the Molo, and the Captain would go and sit in his old cabin often, when the ink and the numbers became too numbing.

And in the midst of all this change, Letice and I were engaged to be married. When we had first met I had been, if not a boy, then not exactly a man. I had been in my twenty-first year, but although I had seen things, done things that many an old man could not claim to have experienced in the longest of lives, I was – I will admit it now – somehow unformed. In many ways I believed my life was already at an end, for I had just suffered the loss of my beloved, my Anna, murdered in the muddy streets of London, and my own life, shaped as it had been by violence and death, had turned itself inward. Letice was the same: she had fought against the world her whole life and it had not destroyed her, but made her very hard. But in the end it was she who changed, and I who did not. Because when she found herself loved and admired, not just by me but by the Captain and Gilles, and discovered that the in-finitely mutable society of Venice accepted her without question now that she was wealthy, though she had been a rich man's whore, she began to shed her armour and to find that ease and pleasure could be had without suffering.

I, meanwhile, had eagerly taken on the responsibilities that the Captain had given me, for I was now a full partner in the company of the *Cormaran*, and the man whom Louis of France trusted to bring him more relics from Constantinople, and so I started, by slow degrees, to be seduced by the world I had learned to despise, and Letice could not bear the change it brought to me. One day she left the Ca'Kanzir for good, a month before our wedding. I had just returned from a brief journey, a quick dash down the coast to Zara to outbid a rival on a cargo of silk. It was nothing, but in my hurry to beat everyone else to the prize I had forgotten to tell Letice I was leaving, and when I returned I had lost her. She told me that I was becoming like the men who had used her in the past, so seduced by power that they felt nothing but the desire for it, and their lust, as it could never be satisfied, had to content itself with causing pain. I was not there yet, but, she told me, red-eyed but not crying, she could not bear to see the rot begin to work in me. And then she was gone, on a ship bound for London, and I was left alone with my money.

She had been right. I had seen it clearly myself in the weeks and months after she left. I tried to claw back something of the man I had once been, and found release in travel, for Venice, with its endless layers of seduction which a man might never exhaust in two lifetimes, began to trouble me. I spent my time criss-crossing the lands between Paris and Constantinople, bringing one relic after another from the Pharos Chapel to King Louis, who dug more deeply into his kingdom's treasury for each new holy morsel. I tried not to stay in one place for too long. I drank too much, and when I thought of the love I had squandered I would take myself off to the Rose Street or the Gropecunt Lane of whatever town I was in, for they all have them; or seduce some maiden of the court who wanted me only for my wealth. Two years went by, and though I was Purveyor of Relics to the King of France, and equal part-ner in the Banco di Marangone, which is how one says *Cormaran* in the dialect of the Florentines, I found that I could not find any stillness in me. Perhaps I had not become what Letice had feared, but I was nothing but a finely dressed vagabond with a bottomless purse and a heart that I kept locked up tight inside me.

I crossed the river and rode north through the narrowest of streets. Even this early they were stiff with people going to and from the market: servants lugging baskets out of which lolled blank-eyed goose-heads or hares' legs, barrows piled high with cages of nervous pullets, stolid mud-booted men carrying staves hung with quail, thrushes, partridge. A countrywoman and her daughters were pushing a barrow on which lay a gigantic hog, trussed up and watching the world resignedly through its little red eyes; and next to them a funeral procession passed, an old cleric in a threadbare surplice ringing a hand bell while four men bore the sheet-wrapped corpse. The city's burial ground was ahead, the walls of its charnel house blocking out the light. I rode past it, wrinkling my nose at the stench. I guessed they had opened a tract of old graves and dug out the bones, for there was a dolorous odour of rot and wet clay, something like old mushrooms, save far worse. I pushed the mare through the crowds and was cursed from all sides, but I ignored the words as I ignored the flies that were already filling the air. At last the street gave way to the great market square. I dismounted and led the mare over to an inn I had spied over by the church of Saint Eustache, and found a stable-boy who agreed to watch the beast. I gave him copper and showed him the silver he would get when I returned.

My feet slapped and slopped in puddles of blood as I wove my way through a press of market-goers. The pungencies of cheese, spices, spring onions, and the rust and shit stink of animal insides almost overpowered the cemetery's exhalations of decay, until I could not tell quite what I was smelling. A fat game seller was busily skinning rabbits, jerking the glistening pink bodies from their furry cocoons like a grotesque midwife, his great bare arms matted with hair and slime. I asked him where the tripe butchers might be found. He pursed his fleshy lips and pointed across the market. Then he held up a slick, flayed coney and waved it alluringly at me. I shook my head and ducked back into the crowd.

There was the pump, and there were the tripe butchers, washing their tripes. It was not a sight I found myself relishing at that hour of the morning. Like a gaggle of blasphemous washerwomen, four or five burly men in crusted leather aprons were gathered around a plain stone column, from the side of which jutted a green-stained bronze pipe and a crude iron handle. There was a sort of shallow marble basin at the pump's foot. The marble was worn, the colour of old tallow veined with bluish-green. The men flopped pallid festoons of corrugated stomach lining around on the stone of the basin while a boy, no doubt an apprentice, worked the handle and kept a steady pulse of water falling. The water that flowed from the basin was grey and flecked with chewed grass. The smell, wafting from great wooden trays of flaccid tripe, was brutal, and I felt my eyes begin to sting. One of the butchers caught my eye and gave me a look both pitiful and pitying, the look reserved for the rich and idle by those who toil in filth and reek. There was a secret knowledge there as well, though. I was on the outside, being regarded from within some place of pride, of belonging. I shrugged, suddenly uncomfortable, for I knew that look of old; and at that moment a hand tapped at my sleeve.

A grey man stood an arm's length from me, in front of a curtain of split hogs. His cloak was grey and dusty, his beard was grey and his skin was the colour of wood ash, and all was rendered more grey by the contrast with the pinks and purples of the pig-flesh behind him.

He regarded me levelly from beneath unkempt eyebrows that seemed sprinkled with moth dust, but his eyes were bright and filbert green.

'Señor Petrus.' He spoke quietly, but I heard the two words clearly above the clamour of the market. I cocked my head, searched his eyes for a moment while I waited for my instincts to tell me whether or not to trust him. They did.

'You have words for me,' I said.

'I do. This way, please.' He turned and, skirting the split hogs, wandered calmly into the nearest aisle of stalls. I followed him, down one aisle and up another, and as he paused here and there to inspect an offering of spring onions or a quaking basket of snails I began to wonder if I had found my man after all. At last he stopped in front of a sausage-maker's stall and ran his eyes over the bunched and stacked goods. He caught the attention of the woman, asked her a question, nodded at her reply and fished in his purse for some change. Meanwhile the woman had gathered up a fistful of black blood sausages, wrapped them in chestnut leaves and bound them with twine. She handed them to the grey man and to my surprise he passed the little package to me.

'Here, Señor Petrus: the butifarra of Carcassonne.' He closed my hand around the package, then looked me straight in the eyes. 'It is unmannerly to take back a gift once given, but I should love to try one of these, for I am homesick for the south,' he said, and an eyebrow twitched fractionally. 'There is a man over by Saint Eustachius' church who will grill a couple for us. Shall we go?' And without waiting for my reply he plunged back into the throng, even thicker now that the morning was growing older. I glanced down at the sausages in my hand: I could already smell the wine and garlic in them, and my stomach gave a cautious rumble. Breakfast, at least. Then I noted something white among the brown leaves. It looked like a little roll of parchment. I looked up again. The buyer of sausages was waiting for me, peering around a pair of portly Franciscans who were buying duck eggs. I started after him.

There was a line of braziers glowing under the wall of the church, where sooty men were cooking up food for the folk who were too hungry to get their purchases home. My grey friend walked up to the first cook who hailed him.

'Here,' he said over his shoulder to me. 'Let us have two each. Be careful with the package – look how well they are wrapped.'

I loosened the twine and pulled out a sausage, palming the tube of parchment as I did so. The sausages were tied together, and the cook leaned over with his knife and cut four away from the chain. He threw them on his griddle and at once a pungent, spicy smoke rose up. Pretending to wipe my eyes, I unrolled the parchment, and hiding it in the shadow of my sleeve, scanned it quickly.

> Patch,
> Trust the bearer of this. On the subject of religion, he is as good a
> Christian as any in the lands of Mother Church. He has words for you.
> Once you have heard them, you are free to decide. Know, my friend,
> that I would not ask this of any other man. It can be done by another,
> but not well, I think.
> De M, ex Cormaranus

I let the message roll itself back into a tube, and slipped it through the bars of the grill. It flared briefly and shrivelled into a black twig. The cook did not notice, but my companion did, and gave the smallest of nods. Another funeral procession was coming down the Rue Montorgueil, and I pretended to watch it as I pondered what I had just read.

'As good a Christian.' That was clear: the bearer of the message was a Cathar, for that was what they called themselves – Good Christians. But why the secrecy? We were distressingly legitimate businessmen these days. And who was this strange, faded man? Someone the Captain trusted, plainly, but I had never seen him before, and I had been close to the centre of the company's business these past three years. Not from Venice, not from Florence, nor Bruges, nor . . . well, he was from the south, from the Languedoc, for he had told me so himself. I looked up, to where the kites were wheeling in the blue sky. Could this be some return to the work we used to do, with its deceptions and secrecy? But we had no need for that any more. What if, though . . . I had found, lately, that I missed those days, for there had been a kind of desperate joy to them, a thieves' comradeship. That was why I recognised the look the tripe washer had given me: I had been inside the secret, guarded world of our company and our trade, and now I could not help feeling that I was just another rich passer-by come to amuse himself among lives he would never have to live.

The cook had speared our sausages and was holding them out to us on buckled plates of rough bread. I took mine, lifted it to my mouth without thinking and singed my lips. The good Christian had paid the cook and was watching me solemnly.

'Shall we mourn?' he said, inclining his head towards the funeral, still struggling with its coffin through the crowds of shoppers. And without waiting for a reply he strolled off, nibbling at the edge of his bread. The coffin – plain quarter-sawn oak, but nicely done, so its occupant had, I guessed, been a burgher of the middling rank – bobbed and swayed down the aisles of the market, brushing against hanging meat and herbs. Every now and again a stallholder swore at the pallbearers, but others crossed themselves or spat noisily. At last we had followed it beyond the market's roof and were kicking through the debris of vegetable trimmings, feathers and all the other leavings of the day's business towards the gate of the Cemetery of the Innocents. I thought my companion would turn aside, but to my dismay he passed inside. With a muttered curse I did the same.

The cemetery was a wide square of churned earth and patchy grass mounded everywhere with the humped pillows of graves. My earlier guess had been right: a band of sextons were digging in the raddled soil, pitching up bones with their shovels. The odour of earworms and decaying mushrooms was cloyingly heavy in the air. Around the burial ground towered high walls which were roofed to form cloisters, and there in the shadows were piled the bones of countless Parisians. A sexton was taking more from the jumble in his barrow and arranging them with scant care, pausing now and then to knock the earth from a leg-bone, or from the eye-sockets of a skull. In a far corner, a pitiful little funeral party was standing around an open grave, a small shape wrapped in sacking lying at their feet.

'Over here,' said the grey man. 'The bones are oldest. They do not stink.' I let him lead me into the far corner of the cemetery. He was right, after a fashion: the smell was not so bad here, nothing worse than a dry mineral breath that spoke, nonetheless, quite eloquently of the despair and finality of death. Ignoring the serried ranks of dismembered skeletons behind us, he leaned against a pillar and took a careful bite of a sausage.

'Delicious – really,' he said, eyes closed with pleasure.

'I'm not all that hungry, somehow,' I told him. The stench of the place, and all the bared teeth around me, had somewhat taken my appetite away.

'Dear man: what better place to eat a blood pudding?' he answered with a shy grin. There was something of the Captain in that, and I knew I had been right to trust him, as the Captain had told me I should. 'Go on, señor: tasting the simplest pleasure in a charnel house – is that not like life?'

Reluctantly I bit into one of my sausages. A rich spurt of warm liquid filled my mouth, salty and hot. I chewed, watching the funeral party lower their burden to the ground. A priest began to shake holy water into the grave, and a professional mourner began to wail out a psalm in a cracked old voice.

'Delicious,' I agreed, grimly. 'Shall we talk, then?'

'Certainly.' He chased a cube of white fat from his moustache with the tip of his tongue. 'You may call me Matheus. I have come from Michel de Montalhac in Toulouse. We travelled together from Florence. That is where I live – you might know that there are many of us in Italy, Good Christians, that is. I am from Michel's own country, though, and we were comrades in arms once, a very long time ago. But never mind that. Michel has a task that he wonders whether you would care to undertake for him. It is somewhat . . .' He licked a finger. '. . . weighty.'

'I would welcome something like that,' I said, finding, as I said the words, that I meant them with all my heart.

'Michel was sure that you would. And that you would like to go home.'

'Home?' I blinked at him. Out in the burying ground, the coffin was sinking into the earth.

'England. I can see he was right. Well then. Listen carefully.' He stepped closer to me and leant on the pillar. 'Michel de Montalhac is . . . perhaps you will be surprised, but he is still joined, in many ways, to our land. I will call that land Toulouse, for that is what it is today, I am afraid. The good Christians are being scattered, those who are not burned by the black-cloaks, and many have gone to seek shelter with their brothers and sisters in Italy, for is it not amusing that in the pope's own garden, if you will, his challengers find greater safety than they do in Toulouse? Michel has become, since he settled down, something of a leader for those scattered souls, myself included, and through his business he keeps news flowing to us, and money, and a little hope along with that.'

'Settled down?' I said, with a laugh. 'Well, I suppose he has.'

'Ah. Perhaps not, after all. Do you know anything of Count Raymond of Toulouse?'

'I know a fair amount, thanks to the gossip and complaints I have been listening to at court in Vincennes.'

'Complaints?'

'A thorn in the flesh, is how he is usually described.'

'Hmm. Well, here is Michel's message to you.' He took another bite of his sausage, chewed for a moment, eyes closed. Then he drew himself up and stepped into the shadows of the cloister, beckoning me with a flutter of his hand. The bones were indeed ancient here, dry and white, and stacked to the roof with some care, so that skulls and pelvises formed a kind of crude pattern facing outward, keeping watch on the burying-ground. I noticed that the floor was thick with dust and the leavings of pigeons and bats, and that ours were the only human footprints. There had been a doorway in the wall once, long ago. I could still its outline in the stained, mossy stones. But the bones had been stacked when the door still functioned and had been piled into knobbed pillars formed of skulls, jaws, scapulars, that jutted out into the cloister like the gateway to some minor Hades, and between them there was a little space, a thumbprint of shadow upon the implacable white of the bone-wall. Matheus stepped into it and all but vanished. My flesh crawling, I followed him. The shadows swallowed us, cool and sharply dry. There was no odour of death here. The smell was of nothingness.

'There is a war coming,' said Matheus. 'The people of Languedoc have waited long enough, and now they will rise up and drive off the French wolves for good. Count Raymond has made a secret treaty with the English king, with the king of Aragon, the king of Castile and of Navarre. He has the word of the Emperor Frederick himself. There is no pope in Rome. The time is upon us.' He paused, and picked something from between his front teeth with a thumb nail. 'Treason – are you thinking that?'

I shook my head. 'No. I am no Frenchman. Are you?'

'Oho, no, my friend.'

'My loyalty is to Captain de Montalhac,' I said. 'But as I am taking luncheon with the king of France in a short while, you might explain the Captain's part in this.' He was silent, and studied me with eyes that were no more than smears of shadow. The shadows in a score of empty sockets joined in this bland scrutiny, until I bowed my head in reluctant surrender.

'Good Matheus, I mean that seeing as I *am* dining with the king this very noontime, it might be useful for me to know the manner in which I am to undermine his authority.' I tested him with the hint of a smile, and got one in return. 'But how . . .' I would have unleashed a juicy oath here, but bit it off short, for one of the many peculiarities dear to the Good Christians was that they did not swear, and there was little point in doing so in front of them unless you wished to receive a mild, faintly pitying look in reply. 'But how is Captain de Montalhac involved in this? He is – we are – bankers now.'

'Who else pays for wars?' shrugged Matheus. He leaned back against the wall of bones, and they creaked faintly, the susurrus of the dead that the living try not to hear, although the dead have much to teach us if we would but listen.

Chapter Four

As soon as the gates of Paris were behind me I kicked the mare into a gallop. At first the lurch and shock of her motion made my head ache and my stomach roil, but she was a good horse with a smooth gait, and soon I was enjoying myself, kicking up dust and speeding past the cursing foot traffic. I could not afford to be late for King Louis, and I needed to clear my head after my morning's work. For I had agreed to do what Matheus had asked. It was nothing so very complicated, and the Captain had known, of course, how I would jump at a chance to relieve the boredom of my present employment. And known, somehow, that I had been suffering from a thirst to see my homeland again, for I was a foreigner everywhere, and while I had learned to be at home wherever I found myself, that is an exile's skill, and I was growing weary of exile.

Nothing complicated about my task: it would be simple, in fact. I was to deposit the gold that Louis had paid for the heads of the three saints with our agents in Paris, deduct our commission – Matheus was most clear on that – draw up letters of credit for the balance, and ride with all speed to the coast. I was to take ship for London, hasten to court and sign over the letters of credit to Richard, Earl of Cornwall and the king of England's brother. Matheus had given me a sealed letter from the Captain to the earl which would explain matters for me. After that I was to make my way back to Venice at my leisure and take over the offices of the *Cormaran* there. So much for the *what*. As to the *why*, Matheus had leaned out into the cloister and casually glanced up and down to make sure we were quite alone before he told me.

Count Raymond of Toulouse had, as King Louis guessed, been promised the support of England. Even better, Henry Plantagenet had an excuse for war, for his brother Richard was not only Earl of Cornwall but also Count of Poitou, that lush, sunny land that stretches down the coast of France from Brittany to Bordeaux, and there the trouble lay.

For last year Louis of France had decided that he was the overlord of Poitou, and to that end had dismissed Richard's claim and made his brother Alphonse count in his stead. Richard must surely be upset, went the gossip at court, but it was his mother, Isabella, who felt the insult most keenly and had pushed her sons into winning back the county. The whole world knew Isabella for a proud and vengeful schemer. She had survived her marriage to King John Lackland, after all, and kept her little son Henry on a shaky throne until he came of age. Now her husband Count Hughues de Lusignan was itching to rebel against Louis, and no doubt Isabella had made the itch unbearable. Hughues and Raymond had made a treaty, and the Count of Toulouse was now looking forward to the landing of a great English army on Louis' western flank.

But things were not proceeding quite as the anxious Raymond had planned, and it was because of this that I had reluctantly been eating blood sausage with a stranger in a Paris charnel house. For though King Henry of England, not the most resolute of monarchs at the best of times, was to everyone's surprise ready for war, his brother was not. From the intelligence gathered by the Captain, it seemed that Richard did not see things quite so starkly as his mercurial dam. Richard, it seemed, was not convinced that the prize was worth the cost of another war and the displeasure of the English barons. More intelligent than his pious brother, he was also more cautious, and his skills at diplomacy, not with the sword, had made him a hero in the recent crusade to Jerusalem. But meanwhile the English army was in place and could be aboard their transports within a week, if the earl would make up his mind. Some well-placed gold would surely do the trick, the Captain felt, for Richard, despite his caution, was as avaricious as any king.

Simple. I had my excuse to visit London, for Earl Richard was a sometime customer of the company, and he had brought a number of items from us over the years – nothing very grand, but connoisseurs' things, always expensive, always with good provenance. 'He competes with his brother,' I had heard the Captain say once, 'but Henry is the pious one. Richard likes to collect things that will impress his dinner guests, and that means he is the more difficult customer, for he does not revere his relics, but enjoys them. We cannot sell him trash – his brother, mind you, would buy the pizzle of an ass if it were styled *membrum virile Sanctus Christophorus* – so we offer the good stuff, and he is happy to pay.' Which meant that Richard would be pleased to receive me. As for my mission, I was to call my present *a token of earnest intent and of steadfast alliance,* or some such flowery nonsense, from his cousin Raymond. Dear God, all these cousins who rule over us.

Dusty and breathless, but punctual, I arrived at the palace of Vincennes a little before noon. The young courtier who had brought yesterday's unwelcome news was waiting to escort me to the king's chambers. He was as stiff-necked as he had been yesterday, but he greeted me with effusive politesse – indeed with all the careful enthusiasm of a schoolboy showing off a skill recently learned – and I allowed myself to be charmed, a little, by his youth and zeal.

'His Majesty is expecting you, monsieur Petrus,' he said with a perfectly executed bow.

'And are you to accompany me?' I asked, forcing back a smile.

'With your permission,' he said.

'My dear sir, I am at a disadvantage . . .' I told him, as we set off.

'Jean de Joinville, at your humble service,' he said, turning and favouring me with a tooth-white smile.

'I have not had the pleasure of seeing you before,' I said.

'No, indeed! I am lately come from the court of Champagne,' he said. 'I was with the king just lately at Poitiers, where he was treating with the Comte de la Marche.'

'Hughues de Lusignan?' I asked, surprised.

'The very same. There was some matter between him and the Count of Poitiers that needed to be put right, and King Louis brought his wisdom to heal things. But there are some upon whom kindness is thrown away.'

'The people of France are blessed to have such a wise and just king,' I said, agreeably. 'And you are newly at court?'

'Yes, but for a little while only, to my regret. I am Seneschal of Champagne, and ought, by rights, to be back in Troyes, but my lord the count graciously allowed me to accompany His Majesty back to Paris for a few weeks, and I am so happy – nay, *overwhelmed,* if you will allow me – to have been providing my king with some meagre service.'

I knew the ways of courtiers, and this Jean would no doubt rattle on in this obsequious vein for hours if I let him. I decided, for the sake of my ears, not to do so.

'Such trying news from the Languedoc,' I put in.

'The swine,' he spat, turning to me again. There was the taut anger of yesterday. His lips were tight amongst the fledgling curls of his beard. 'The south is rotten with heretics and Jews . . . like . . . like . . .' he stopped, blinking. Evidently his schooling in bows and posturing had been flawless, but in metaphorical discourse, not as thorough.

'Like smoke before the face of the sun?' I ventured. 'For surely the heretics will soon be exactly that, if they lift their hand against the crown of France.'

'Yes, exactly,' said young Jean, gratefully. 'The king will have to crush them now. My father – God rest his kind soul – took the cross against the Albigenses when he was a young man, and when I hear of such . . . such outrages, I burn, I truly burn to follow his example.'

'Is it simply the heretics, though? Who would have thought they would be so bold? Surely it is more the quarrelling of princes?'

'No, no. It is heresy that has brought this matter to pass. Just as in my father's time. There should be another crusade . . . I should dearly love to serve my king, and Our Lord, by taking up my sword against His enemies.'

'Well, there is no pope at Rome just now,' I pointed out, 'So there can be no crusade. Most probably Count Raymond will die of his sickness and save everybody the bother, eh?'

Jean de Joinville was still wriggling his shoulders with a child's desperation to find the right words to answer this when we came to the door of the king's chambers. Within I found King Louis; his brother Alphonse; a man I recognised as the Count of Soissons, and Enguerrand, lord of Coucy, the most powerful baron in all of France. They were talking excitedly, and the king waved a casual hand at me.

'Dear Petrus, our business is finished. Wait for me a minute, dear man.'

I bowed gratefully, for I found Count Enguerrand, with his stern face corrugated by years of war, and his shock of dirty white hair, somewhat terrifying. He had small, pale eyes that probed like gimlets, and though I had never exchanged more than a few courtly words with him, I had no wish to make his acquaintance any further than that, and certainly not today. And what was Alphonse, of all people, doing here? I had not seen him at Vincennes at all on this visit, and here he was, two hours after I had first heard of his new title of Comte de Poitou and the difficulties that had come with it. Well, this must be a council of war, I thought to myself. Had Henry already moved against France? Perhaps my little trip to England was not needed after all. Well, if this was a council of war, I ought to be relieved, for now I could get back to Venice. And yet I found myself hoping that it was not what it seemed, for since I had left the Cemetery of the Innocents I had felt something inside me, a faint, secret agitation, like blood returning to a sleeping limb but deeper, in my soul, if indeed I still had one of those. Something was happening. I was going to *make* something happen.

At last Louis dismissed his brother and the nobles. When they had left, and young Joinville with them, Louis clapped his hands.

'And now, dear Petrus, there is something I wish you to see before we take our luncheon. I think it will – nay, I am certain it will delight you.'

We left the chamber, a pair of palace guards falling in behind us. Joinville was waiting in the passageway, and when Louis beckoned to him his face went slack with joy. We left the royal quarters and soon our footsteps were echoing down halls I had not seen before. This was the older part of the palace, what remained of the old hunting lodge. The kitchens seemed to be nearby, and no doubt this was where the lowliest servants lived. It was draughty, the walls exhaling the damp chill of old places. I wondered why this king, who was spending a fortune on planning his Sainte Chapelle, surely the most astonishing building of this age, was content to live here. But then I considered his back, clothed in plain taffeta with the lilies of France embroidered upon it in silk with only a touch of gold thread here and there. The chapel was for his subjects, I supposed. One heard a lot about the modesty of Louis, but I had to admit that it was true. He did not care that his palace was his grandfather's hunting lodge with a new coat of whitewash, for he would rather be outside under his favourite oak tree. Accustomed as I was to seeking out the lies and artifice in every man I dealt with – and the higher the office, the filthier the soul – I could find very little in Louis Capet, and while that made me inclined to like him, it made me uneasy. He was a modest, gentle, even kind man, and to my way of thinking he had no right to be any of those things.

We had come to a heavily banded door. The king paused and seemed to be considering. Then he turned to young Jean.

'De Joinville, would you seek out the chamberlain and have the table readied? And await us there? We shall not keep you long.' The young man blushed, no doubt at the notion that his king was concerned that he should not wait for his luncheon, and hurried away giving another of his exquisite bows.

'A sweet child – he shows considerable promise,' Louis told me, opening the door. Beyond was a flight of stairs and we descended into musty torchlight. The cellars below were clean-swept, the stone of their high vaulted ceilings hardly touched by spider webs. A scullion was filling silver pitchers from one of the great tuns of wine that lined the walls. We passed her and entered a narrower passage. The palace's winter fruit and vegetables were stored here, and there was a wholesome smell of apples, onions and earth. The king paused to pat the head of a little serving boy who was digging carrots from a box of sand. I followed

Louis as he turned down another corridor and stopped in front of a plain door. Three royal guards stood against the wall, looking as if they were resting from some labour. Louis struck the door with the flat of his hand and at once it was opened from within.

I saw a big room with walls of ashlar, lit by torches and an ugly wrought iron candleholder upon which trembled twenty or so candle flames. Clean rushes on the floor. Against the far wall, two women and a man were sitting. Another figure was slumped amongst the rushes. Between them and the candles a bench had been set and on this sat a priest and a black-robed Dominican friar. Hearing the door, they turned and rose hurriedly to their feet. Over the green scent of the rushes and the warm fug of the lights crept the reek of fear and piss. The king waved away the fawnings of the two clerics and leant to engage them in earnest mutterings. I stood as close to the door as I could. Pleasant as this room seemed to be, there is no mistaking a torture chamber, or its victims. Louis turned back to me at last. My sinews were tensed. It was all so obvious: why else would I have been brought here? But instead his brow was furrowed with honest concern.

'My dear Petrus,' he said. 'You were there yesterday, when de Joinville brought the news from the south.' *Dear God*, I thought with a horrid uncoiling of my bowels, *He knows. Matheus . . . a trap . . .* But Louis was still talking, heedless. 'I saw right away, as you must have done, that the heretics of Toulouse have decided that they are a power in this land. They are not. You know my feelings on the matter – you *share* them, of course.'

'I will not forget our conversation last year under the oak tree,' I said, earnestly. The stench of the huddled creatures' terror was stifling me, but I summoned up every grain of false piety I could, and crossed myself twice over. 'But surely these are not the murderers, unless . . .'

'Alas, alas! That would be a miracle indeed! No, there is no better place to seek out your Enemy than at home.'

'Albigenses in Paris? I did not think it possible.'

'These are not Albigenses, my son.' It was the friar. He had very black hair and skin of fish-belly whiteness, and his stubble-shadowed face was running to fat. 'They are Leonistae – not from Albi, do you see, but Lyons. They call themselves the Poor, or Waldenses.'

'But they are . . .' I searched my mind for words that would not implicate me. 'They suffer from the same detestable errors as their brethren in the south?'

'No. They do not – although they call their priests *perfecti*, as do the Albigenses, and do not take oaths or lie . . .'

'And their particular error?' I enquired, adding a note of prurience that I saw strike home with the pallid friar.

'Dear oh dear, my son.' He lowered his voice to a mock whisper. 'They deny the existence of purgatory!' He shook his head and crossed himself. 'They deny the efficacy of prayers for the dead, and indulgences!' He held his hands up beseechingly to the ceiling. 'Appalling. And they teach the absolute need for poverty. They hold worldly goods to be sinful, and go about the land prating and chastising our mother Church for what they regard as worldliness.'

'The shame of it!' I breathed, pointedly stroking the fine brocade of my tunic. 'And they were spreading these errors in this great city?'

'They were living in the Temple marshes,' said the friar. 'I cannot tell you the squalor . . .'

'Well, Your Majesty,' I said, turning to Louis, who stood regarding the heretics with a brow ridged in discomfort. 'Your words to me last year were truer than I could have brought myself to imagine.'

'The canker must be stopped,' he said quietly. 'The Enemy is always – *always* – nearer than we believe.'

Nearer even than that, I thought. Aloud I said: 'What will become of these wretches?'

'Two have recanted,' said the friar. 'They have confessed their errors and wish to come back to the bosom of the Church. The others . . . That one there—' and he nodded at the still figure in the rushes '—could not be budged, even when the stones were crushing his limbs.' He spread his arms helplessly. Over his shoulder I noticed an orderly stack of big granite blocks, each with an iron ring set in its top. How neat it was in here.

'He will be burnt,' said Louis, sadly. He turned to me and laid a hand on my shoulder. 'If a limb of my dear oak tree began to wither, I would have it cut off to save the others. So it is with these . . . these fools. They are denying themselves the Kingdom of Heaven. Nothing that befalls them can be worse than that. And I must save the others. Men such as yourself, Petrus, carry out such great labours to glorify our Lord and Saviour. I wanted you to see, to reassure you that we will not tolerate your work, yours and others, being undermined by these cankerous worms.'

'Your Majesty, I am humbled,' I said. 'I do the Lord's work, it is true, but I am just a servant. I require no proof of Your Majesty's piety. It is as evident as the sun that warms the earth.'

'Nonsense,' said Louis, smiling wryly. 'Good brother Umbertus, we will leave these wretches to your tender care. Try and bring that last fool back to Christ, I pray you.'

'As you command me, Majesty,' said the friar, bowing his glossy head. He followed us from the room, and as we left I heard him giving curt orders to the soldiers outside.

Luncheon was a sunny, pleasant affair, and I ate the king's meat and drank his wine as if a man's joints were not being splintered a few yards below our feet for believing . . . in what? As it happened, I knew a little about these Waldenses. Their error was one of the gravest in the eyes of the Church: the belief that Christ's teachings, as laid out in the Gospels, should be heeded by Christian men – and women too, for the Waldenses saw no need to bar women from their priesthood. The teachings of Christ – preposterous! Where would the Church be then? And how could honest men such as Captain de Montalhac hope to make a living if that holiest of institutions abjured wealth and worldliness? I allowed myself a grim little laugh, for of all the absurdities rife in the great cesspool of Christendom, that was the bitterest. I had trained for the priesthood. As a novice monk I had lain on cold stone floors and risen when the puddles were frozen in the cloisters to say the night office, and fancied myself an honest imitator of Our Lord and his apostles, but all that I had seen and heard since, all that I had done, had taught me that the Dominicans and their Inquisition would have spared the Pharisees the trouble of crucifying Jesus Christ, for they would have had him crackling on one of their pyres long before he rode into Jerusalem.

King Louis was listening intently to the Archbishop of Saint Denis, who was rumbling, sonorously but ominously, like a distant storm cloud, about the detestable presence of heretics amongst his flock. To my right sat a stocky, slab-faced man, who was laying into his meat as if he had just been plucked from the desert. I had been amazed to learn that this was none other than Pierre de Montreuil, architect of the king's Sainte Chapelle, for he seemed more like a dull-witted stone-cutter than someone capable of drawing, let alone imagining, such a delicate vision. I never heard him speak, save to answer, with curt yeas and nays, the questions the king now and again loosed at him. When he heard that I was the man who had brought the relics of the Pharos Chapel to Paris, he raised his eyebrows at me as if to scold me for causing him so much trouble. I did not have much appetite, for the morning's revelations, and then the goings-on in the royal cellars, had left my spirits turbid. So I was glad when the last crumbs of bread had been swept up and the lute-player waved away, and Louis had risen, giving us leave to do the same. We all made to leave the royal presence, but the king stayed me with a raised finger.

'You are leaving Paris tomorrow, I believe?' he asked. 'Perhaps you would care for one more walk outside.'

In a few minutes we were sitting on the warm grass beneath the high shade of the king's oak. A pigeon was soothing the still air with her call.

'Your Majesty knew, yesterday, about the Waldenses?' I asked. Louis' lack of guile was legendary, and I was fairly sure that I would have sniffed out a trap by now if one had been laid for me; but it would not hurt to probe a little.

'Alas, yes,' he sighed. 'They have been wandering into the city from Lyons for several years now. They are few, and often the folk whom they dwell amongst drive them out, so . . . but after the news we heard yesterday, an example must be made. We will not tolerate heretics in Paris, as we will not tolerate them in the lands of Toulouse. They grow bold because there is no pope on the saint's throne, so it falls to the Christian monarchs of the world to do the Lord's work. And I for one will not shrink from it.'

'The more innocent the error, the greater is its danger,' I agreed.

'There you have it, Petrus!' sighed the king. 'To tell the truth, I feel a little beset. My cousin Isabella is trying to stir up a rebellion in Poitou for her Lusignan husband, and she will try and enlist her son Henry, *your* king Henry . . . now, is he as much in thrall to the Poitevins at his court as the talk would have it? Will he go to war for Hughues de Lusignan? If his mother tells him to?'

'I do not know, Sire,' I said, wondering again if I had been spied upon. My instincts told me no: Louis was not cunning, and I was certain he would consider any sort of subterfuge beneath his dignity. 'I am hardly an Englishman any more, sad to say,' I added, for it was the truth, and when you are filled to the brim with falsehoods it is good to be able to speak the truth.

'Mothers . . .' Louis let out a mighty sigh. 'But let us talk of happier things!' he went on brightly, plucking a blade of grass and putting it between his lips. 'Will you be returning to Constantinople?'

'There is no need, Your Majesty,' I said. 'The Pharos Chapel is empty. You have everything.'

'Ah, but do I?' said Louis, and for the first time I saw something furtive in his open face. It did not belong there, and indeed in an instant it was gone, and the young man looked almost sheepish.

'You do, Your Majesty, I can assure you of that,' I said kindly.

'Aha. Everything in the Chapel, yes. And for that . . .'

'And *with* that you have enriched your kingdom more than Charlemagne himself,' I put in.

The king winced. 'I *have* spent rather a lot of money,' he admitted. 'I hope my wretched cousin . . . nay, that is unfair. Baldwin is a stout rock standing against a sea of infidels and schismatics. But I should hope he has put his . . . his gifts from me to good use.'

'You can be certain of it,' I told him. In fact, the last time I had been in that dismal city, Baldwin had himself taken me up to the roof of the palace of Constantine and showed me how he was mining the lead from it to pay his starving, resentful troops. The Greek army was a mile beyond the walls, their cooking fires rising into the low clouds that seemed to hang permanently over the Bosphorus. 'Thanks to you, the Emperor is Christ's champion in the east, as you are in the west.'

'Well, that is good,' said Louis, sounding less than convinced. I could not blame him. Baldwin de Courtenay had been sniffing round Vincennes off and on for years, kissing hands, putting on airs and treating the court to petulant outbursts that only made it more plain that he was callow and desperate. Louis might be guileless but he was no fool – not in any way save his faith, and in that he was by no means alone in this world – far from it. We both knew what Baldwin was, and if we danced around the matter, that was because I was a merchant and he was King of France. He did not pay me to tell him the truth; he paid me to understand what he wanted, and to get it for him. I suddenly hoped with all my heart that I was not about to be sent off to Constantinople once more, to poke amongst the bones and the burnt and desecrated ruins for some fabled but chimerical treasure.

'Have you heard . . .' he paused. 'Petrus, this is between ourselves, if you do not mind. You of all people know what has passed from the treasury of France to Venice, and Constantinople . . .' I closed my eyes and nodded gravely, a gesture I had learned from the Captain. 'My mother does not approve,' he said flatly. He caught my eye, and there was that furtive look again, like a child caught climbing into a stranger's orchard. Then he smiled, and I remembered that he was only a little older than me, for while life had been somewhat careless with my face, leaving me with a fine collection of lines and scars and a crooked snout, Louis still had a boy's countenance. And he had been a boy-king, just eleven years old when his father died, and for another eight years his mother had been regent. A terrifying woman, old Blanche. She had fought the English and beat them, and then had been forced to crush a rebellion of her own barons. Louis might rule France now, but Blanche had never ceased to rule Louis.

'The Queen Mother need have no fear,' I told him. 'There is nothing left in Constantinople.'

'Ah, but listen, Petrus. Have you heard of Robert de Clari?'

'I have, Sire. You yourself gave his book as a gift to Monsieur de Sol.' De Clari had been one of the Crusaders who had sacked Constantinople, and being, I suppose, somewhat less of a brute than his Frankish brethren, he wrote down what he had seen of the greatest city the world has ever seen, before it was destroyed. It was de Clari who had itemised the treasures of the Pharos Chapel and, in so doing, had given Louis Capet his shopping list.

'The *Mandylion* of Edessa.' Louis was biting his lower lip. That was guilt, not guile. He was not testing me; he was wondering if his mother was spying on us. 'Is it . . .'

'The *Mandylion*! Oh, of course,' I chuckled, although I did not feel in the slightest bit amused: in truth, the terror I had felt in the dungeons had once again taken hold of my tripes. 'It was not in the Pharos Chapel, but de Clari saw it in Blachernae, which is in a different part of the city. So far as I know, the palace of Blachernae and its church were completely pillaged. It is abandoned now, certainly.'

'Was it real, do you think?'

'Real, sire? Do you mean, did it exist, or was it . . .'

'Was it – *is* it – the true imprint of Our Lord's body?'

'Ah.' I thought carefully, or pretended to. The memory of lukewarm pig's blood and clinging, stifling cloth binding to my mouth and nose welled up like vomit, and I shoved it to the very back of my mind. 'The Greeks thought it was real. But, sire, it is possible that you already possess it, for I have always thought that de Clari was writing about the burial cloths in the Pharos Chapel – the *sudarii*, the shrouds.'

'But they bear no image,' said the king, raising a pedantic finger.

'Just so. But it is possible that the chroniclers were talking of a . . . an imagined image, if you will, or a miraculous one, not ordinarily visible? I do not honestly know, Your Majesty. But I would be terribly dishonest if I said I have not been extremely curious.'

'I rely on your honesty, good Petrus,' said Louis. 'So you think it never existed?'

'In point of fact, Your Majesty—' God's guts, how I hated speaking like this! 'It is my belief that the *Mandylion* of Edessa *did* exist, and every piece of evidence I have found indicates, to your humble servant at least, that it was a miraculous image, not made by human hands. While you possess the burial clothes, this *Mandylion* is reputed to have been some sort of sheet on which Our Lord appeared at his full length.' I forced myself to purse my lips like a matron and cross myself delicately. 'But it has gone, and left no trace save in rumour. My Lord, Constantinople must have been a place of wonders such as the mind of man cannot begin to imagine. No longer. What you have saved from the ruins is, I fear, all that was left when the Crusaders and their Venetian friends sacked it. There is nothing left save bones, of the ordinary variety. My unpleasant conclusion is that the *Mandylion* left Constantinople in the satchel of some man-at-arms from Flanders or Burgundy who had no clue as to what he had stolen, and in the way of delicate things that are not valued by their owners it has since faded from this world.'

'So it has disappeared.'

'I fear so, Your Majesty.'

'For good.'

'I cannot truly imagine it otherwise, Sire.'

'Lost.' The king pressed his hands together as if in prayer, and rested his chin upon his finger-ends. I sighed, and nodded.

'What is lost can be found, if one knows where to look.'

My blood froze. 'Sometimes, Your Majesty, sometimes,' I agreed, keeping a croak from my voice with difficulty.

'I cannot think of a living man better suited . . .' he began. Then he pointed his clasped hands straight at me. 'Petrus, if it could be found, you would find it.'

'You . . . you wish me to look for the Shroud of Edessa?' I stuttered, unable to keep the panic from my voice any longer.

'I do, truly I do. Will you accept this mission? I can see in your face that you will. Excellent! My dear man, it is settled. But . . .' and his voice sank to a whisper. 'Do not tell my mother.'

Chapter Five

I stepped ashore on London Bridge, snatching at an iron ring that hung against the grey and slimy face of the pier. The wherry that had brought me up from Tilbury was bucking and scraping against the pier even though it was slack tide, and the Thames was slumbering. I heaved up my valise and paid the wherryman, and started up the worn and treacherous steps towards the tumult above.

I had not wanted to come to London. I had been here only once before, and that occassion had left a stain on my memory that time had not scoured away. As I stepped out onto the carriageway of the bridge, I did not see the shops, the yelling barrow boys, the servants running on their errands, the knights and ladies riding by with their noses pointed at the unrepentant tedium of the English sky. I only saw the dung-crusted stones of the road, and as I stepped onto them I felt a lurch inside. This bridge crossed the river and became a street, and that street in turn led to the place where, five years ago, I had seen a horse rear up and kick a woman to death. Anna had been destroyed there in the mud of Cheapside while idlers stared and market-goers stepped over her body. I looked at the mud of London, spread across the foot-smoothed cobbles by countless boots and hooves and wheels, and saw Anna's black hair flung against it, and the terrible brightness of her blood, and her fading eye.

Enough of this. I had dreaded coming here, had felt a gathering unease in my belly as I had ridden across Normandy, and as my fat little ship had carried me over the Channel and up the Thames. Now here I was. I made myself look up. There, in a gap between two buildings, were the great shoulders of Saint Paul's, and out of sight in its shadow lay the little church where Anna rested. I closed my eyes and stood there, feeling the crowds move around me. Someone knocked against my side and cursed me evilly. My eyes opened in time to see a fat arse lurching towards the north bank. Here I was, then, not alone at all, but blocking the roadway and being someone else's nuisance in a city of fifty thousand souls. Someone was dying as I stood here. Someone was being born.

Perhaps I had imagined the air to be thick and stale, like a tomb. It was not. It stank, all right, but it was alive with stench: fish from Billingsgate just alongside, horse-shit, man-shit, pigeons, beef pies, beer, clary wine, the fetid waft of filthy men and the sharp, sweat-and-flowers savour of pretty women. Anna was nowhere here. She was where she had been these five years: in her grave, and in my heart. I watched the raddled, magnificent mountebank's parade of the city for a moment streaming like a flood tide, a second river above the Thames. Then I slung my valise over my shoulder, stepped into the roadway and let it carry me away into London town.

I walked to my lodgings, for they were not far. The company had an interest in a hostelry close to Baynard's Castle called the Three Coneys, and I found a set of rooms for myself, paid the landlord to be discreet, and went upstairs to change. I had thought to go straight away to the palace at Westminster, for I had heard that the king was there with his brother, but the tide had delayed me, and by the time I had washed the day's travel from my face and eaten a late luncheon it was well past the ninth hour. The morning would do just as well, and I would be the fresher for a night's sleep, so I went out and wandered the streets for a little while. At first I skirted around the city walls, but the huge escarpment of Saint Paul's drew me, the tower like a spindle pulling the confusion of London to it, and at last I surrendered and allowed myself to be pulled in to the happy din of the booksellers and clerics who bantered in its shadow. They had still been building the tower when I had last been here, and we had heard the pulleys creaking and the hammers tapping as we buried Anna. I did not remember much of that day, except that as the nervous priest had chanted the requiem mass, the voice of a mason had risen in song to bless someone's mighty cock and balls and the merry fur his lady sported below. He had been high above us, but his words had fallen down and slipped through the windows, and to me they had made no more or less sense than the priest's as he called for the chains of Anna's sins to be forgiven.

Something drew me round the buttresses of the great church to little Saint Faith nestling beneath its northern flanks. The door was open and I went inside. It was empty but some candles were flickering. I found Anna's tomb easily, for the marble slab glowed bravely from the floor of the aisle. I knelt beside it.

Anna Komnena Doukaina
A Ω

I pressed my palm against the cold, grainy stone. She had once asked me if the dead can dream. I had not known the answer then. But I had picked through enough graves since then to know the truth. There is no peace in the tomb, only the busy work of decay, the seething haste of death as it transforms beauty into its opposite. The alpha melting into omega. Anna was no longer Anna, except where I had carved her beneath my ribs, and painted her behind my eyes. I did not have to say goodbye. A tombstone is a farewell already said, so I added nothing to the silence, but kissed my fingers and touched the alpha of her name, and left.

Outside, the bells of London were pealing five, and the clouds were fragmenting into mackerel skin. I ambled back through the emptying streets to my hostelry, climbed into bed and fell asleep with the dying sun across my face.

The palace at Westminster is nothing like Vincennes, I discovered the next morning. It is a vast old building onto which each new king had daubed his own vanity as a swift in spring daubs mud upon last year's nest. That day the halls belonged to strutting men with silk upon their backs and red meat in their bellies, casually seeking out their friends and far less casually circling their enemies. People had enemies here, it was plain: they all pranced and circled like bantams in a cockpit, from the squires and pages up to the formidable creatures I took to be earls and counts, and barely restrained violence hung in the air. It was interesting, though, and not unlike certain places in Venice, where a friendly gathering can end with one man's sweetbreads on the end of another's dagger without anyone finding it amiss. It suited me, in any case. This swarm of popinjays were so intent upon each other that I passed through them like a ghost.

At last I came to a large chamber thronged with men of all sorts, whom I took to be supplicants for royal favour. Most were commoners of the better sort, merchants and ship-owners, and they all looked as though they expected their wait to be a long one. I thanked my good fortune that I had papers from the Captain which I knew would at least bring me to the king's door-keeper, and to my relief, when I presented them to the bored clerk who was supervising the room, I was admitted to a smaller, empty antechamber that had one large door in the back wall and another to the side, and after an hour of mapping the cracks in

44

the ceiling, that personage did indeed come to investigate. I explained that I had come from Venice on a pressing matter, and that Earl Richard would receive me. The door-keeper, a thin-lipped fellow with sandy eyebrows and red-rimmed eyes, squinted at me and scratched his beard.

'I am afraid not,' he said at last.

'Is His Highness not in London?' I asked, puzzled. The man twirled a finger through a curl of his hair and tugged.

'It is not our custom, sirrah, to bandy explanations to tradesmen,' he said. 'You have my answer. Now get yourself gone.'

'My lord—' I assumed he was a lord, for did not the nobility get all the best jobs at court? Doormen, sniffers of the piss-pot royal and the rest? '—The head of my company is a fond acquaintance of Earl Richard, and I am his lieutenant. I hope that these papers will be a sufficient introduction.'

The door-keeper was holding my letter. He narrowed his eyes and held the paper first close to and then away from the tip of his nose, and I wondered if he could read at all.

'Petrus Zennorius. A Devon name.' It was not a question. So he could read after all.

'Cornish,' I told him.

'Yes – you *do* sound foreign. A Cornishman from Venice: we live in wondrous times,' he said. There was no trace of friendliness in his voice. 'Should I call the guards, or will that not be necessary?'

It was not. I took my letter and went back to the waiting room. I was furious, but a room full of bored merchants is the greatest place to collect gossip and information, so I mastered myself and looked around at the crowd. I chose a portly fellow with a cloak of heavy wine-coloured velvet, much too heavy for the season, but new and expensive.

'Is the king indisposed today?' I asked, after a little small-talk. 'I had thought he was here with his brother.'

'Not indisposed, no,' said the man. 'But he's shut in with his damn French relatives.'

'Really?' I asked.

'Yes, his bloody in-laws.' He lowered his voice. 'And *their* relations. Bad for business. Not English at all.'

'I should think not,' I agreed. 'By the way, who is the door-keeper?'

'Today? That is Sir Edward. Bloody man. He's got pink-eye: can't get rid of it, and it does his temper no good.'

'So Sir Edward is today's doorman.' My new friend chuckled and gave me a knowing wink. 'And tomorrow?'

'Sir Edward again.' He shrugged. 'Or some other bugger. What is your business here, my friend?' It was professional curiosity, nothing more, I decided.

'In fact, I came to see the king's brother, Earl Richard,' I said. 'But he isn't receiving either.'

'Aha! Our great Crusader,' said the man, with the merest touch of mockery. 'Well, you must be in someone's good graces if you got as far as Sir Edward. Try again tomorrow – no doubt you'll see me here.'

I said my farewells and stalked back through the palace. Angry as I was, I took care not to rub shoulders with anyone, for the whole building looked as if it was about to ignite with rage like the bush on Mount Horeb. My temper was not improved when I found I had missed the tide, and that I would have walk back into the city. It took me the better part of two hours, and I had to suffer the contempt of mounted gentlemen and ladies, and the rough curiosity of a swarm of peasants and poor townsfolk, for the road was crowded. I had just come in sight of Lud Gate when it began to rain, and my day was complete.

The next day was dim under lowering skies. I bought the use of a handsome gelding from the landlord, who also maintained a stable, and spent extra coin on a noble-looking saddle of tooled and gilded leather. Now I would not be dependent upon the Thames, at least. I hoped this would be my last day in London, for I did not feel at ease here, and I was beginning to yearn for Venice and blue skies.

But although the door-keeper was a different gentleman, more polite and free from pink-eye, his answer was the same. I returned the next day, and the next, until the surly cleric in the waiting room began to greet me rudely by my name. Even my friend with the burdensome cloak must have received more satisfaction, for I only saw him on that second day, and then no more. On the third day I fell to chatting with a gaunt soldier, a Templar Preceptor from Suffolk. He turned out to have a capacious if eccentric knowledge of holy relics and told me of a set of Saint Christopher's undergarments he had been offered in the bazaar of Jaffa. Vast, they had been, and as sails they might have propelled a small boat. But too new, and too little soiled . . . From there the conversation turned to undergarments in general, and his own painful experiences in the itchy heat of the Holy Land, and how the finest breech-clout he had ever worn had been woven by a cloister of nuns in Bury Saint Edmunds . . . Before our talk could take a more unsavoury turn, as I saw it might by the heat that had risen in his face, I excused myself and left for the City.

The weather was refusing to cheer up, and although my lodgings were pleasant, I left early and came back late, and never in the mood to go out and enjoy what the town had to offer. Instead I kept to my rooms and tried to work out how I could break through the seemingly impenetrable door to the inner chambers of Westminster. It was well known, as the merchant had said, that Henry was dominated by his French relations. These were in the main from Poitou, the family of his father-in-law Hughues de Lusignan, on whose behalf Henry was supposed to be invading France. I told myself that if the king was listening to Poitevin counsel, he might not need any encouragement to launch his invasion. But I did not see any preparations for war in London. I asked about for rumours and speculation, for merchants and especially financiers are full of that, but although I heard that an army had been raised in the West Country, it was not thought to be very large. The king might be planning to fight in France, but there again, weren't they always? I thought myself that the impatient and choleric mood at court was due to a battle promised but not forthcoming, and that could be a good sign or a bad one: I had no way of knowing which.

Richard of Cornwall was supposed to be at court: my information had been right about that. But no one had seen him or indeed the king for days, and gossip had it that he had had one of his frequent quarrels with his brother. I cursed my luck by the hour. It was supposed to have been as simple as delivering a package, this mission, and instead it was becoming a frustrating, time-devouring burden. And as the days threat-ened to become a week, I began to think more and more about the Captain far away in Venice, and the great plot slowly grinding into motion like a mill-wheel after a long drought has broken, the vast net of alliances and promises that were spreading out to snare Louis Capet. I had no loyalties in this affair save to the Captain, and so I supposed that my loyalties were his. Was I, then, an agent of Raymond of Toulouse? Of the Cathars? Was my part in all this very small, or did the whole enterprise hinge upon my success or failure? The more I pondered, the less comfortable I felt.

And then – it was Wednesday evening – I went out to a tavern and came back too full of beef and beer, and was met by the landlord, wringing his hands.

'I am so sorry, dear sir, so very sorry!' he cried.

'About what?'

'A thief, in your room.'

'Good Christ! How do you know?' The beer gave a nasty lurch in my belly.

'Oh, we have him, sir. The fool slipped on the stairs and turned his ankle. Sitting there moaning, he was, so we put him in the scullery. Would you care to see him?'

'Of course I would!' I snapped. I followed the landlord through the kitchen and there, in the middle of a little stone room, on a chair brought in from the dining room, sat a thin little man in black clothing, a black coif tight around his head, his unshaven face twitching in discomfort. He was tied hand and foot to the chair, and he was pouring with sweat, even though the room was cold. I could smell him from the doorway.

'Was anything taken?' I asked the landlord.

'Nothing, funnily enough. He made a bloody mess, though. I'll send someone up to tidy.'

'No, don't do that!' I said. 'And leave us alone, would you? I want to ask this fellow something.'

'I'm sure you do, sir,' he leered. The thief watched him leave, and then watched me as I began to pace in front of him.

'Who are you?' I asked.

'Nobody,' he said. 'My ankle hurts something horrible. Will you turn me over to the watch?'

'Not if you fuck me about,' I said. Drawing back my cape I showed him the green hilt of my knife. 'I have enough money that I could put your head on a spike and stick it out of my window, and the watch would say nothing. Now then. If you weren't after my silver, what were you after?'

'Oh.' He screwed up his bristly face in pain. 'I *was* after your scratch, mate. I heard a noise and ran for it. Bit careless on the stairs.'

I knew thieves. I was once a thief myself. And I had been robbed more than once since I began to roam across Christendom. So I was neither impressed nor surprised by the idiot who sat before me. The only problem, as he had taken nothing, was what to do with him. I could turn him over to the night watch, who would lock him away or string him up according to how they felt, or I could let him go. Old habits die very slowly, and I did not like the thought of the night watch poking through my affairs, respectable as they were, so I caught him by the ear and twisted it until it would stretch no further.

'Where do you live?'

'Ebbgate Street,' he squealed. Too quick. I pulled out my knife.

'Listen. I'm going to let you go. But I want to be able to find you again if we need to discuss things further. Tell me where you live.' I laid the watered steel blade against his cheek. 'Because it's easy to find a man without a nose,' I said. The knife bit ever so gently into the bulge of his nostril.

'Oh, Christ!' he yelled. 'Christ almighty! It's Candlewyck Street, right by the church! Don't do it, your lordship! 'Tweren't my idea, I fucking swear!' He cast his eyes desperately around the room and winced horribly, as if I had already sliced him. 'He . . . he paid me to do it!'

'Oh, come on, damn you! D'you expect me to believe that?'

'No, I swear, my lord! I was put up to it . . . by the Frenchman, the wineseller in my street . . .'

'Jesus.' I sighed, and rubbed my forehead with exasperation. Suddenly I was more infuriated by his pathetic lying than by his botched thievery.

'Right.' I stepped back and sliced through the cords at his wrists, and then his ankles. 'What's your name? Your real name, mind?'

'Stevin, sir. Honest.'

'Honest, is it? Get out. I'll be here for a few more days. If I see you in the street anywhere near here, or if the landlord's boys see you, I will kill you. Do you understand?' He nodded earnestly.

'Thank you, your lordship,' he said, levering himself upright. He limped to the door and I watched him go, knowing that the landlord's three sons would give him a kicking to remember before he finally left this place. Wiping Thorn on my cape I felt a little upset that I had convinced the fool quite so easily of my savagery, for whatever else I had done in my life I had never been intentionally cruel. By God, I had scared him, though. Reluctantly I climbed the stairs to my chambers. The landlord was right: the thief had made a bloody awful mess. My satchel had been shaken out and my papers strewn about the floor, and my saddlebags treated the same way. By the way the papers were scattered I knew that the thief could not read, and as I had my purse with me, and the rest of my money safe in the landlord's muniment chest, the only thing of value in the room had been information. Nothing was missing. But curiously, every item of clothing I had with me had been shaken out and thrown into a corner as if the thief had been sorting it. All the linens from the chest had been taken out and unfolded, and the bed had been stripped and the pallet turned over and ripped open. Cursing volubly, I retrieved my papers and clothes and stamped downstairs again, there to drink off a jug of the landlord's Rhennish wine while the sleepy chambermaid put my room back together.

I was out of my bed the next day as the first cockerel of the morning was clearing his throat. I would be going to Westminster, of course, but first I had it in mind to see whether my burglar had been telling the truth, for after I had seen the curious damage he had done to my room I had begun to wonder what exactly he had been looking to steal, and it had woken me much too early with a headache that was probing the inside of my skull with a thin blade as sharp as spoiled wine. Something was not as it should be if the wretched Stevin was as clumsy and inept a burglar as he seemed to be. His tale about the Frenchman was, I reckoned, nothing more than a fool's attempt to steer blame away from himself, but . . . but what *had* he been up to?

The bastard had woken me up early, and I resolved to return the favour. So I wrapped my cloak about me and slipped out past one of the landlord's sons dozing by the embers in the fireplace, out into the bone-gnawing chill of dawn mist. The frigid vapour swirled lazily around me as I hurried up towards Saint Paul's. I let the grey whisps play around my nostrils like the fumes of a fine wine: cat piss, nightsoil, chicken dung, rotten fruit and damp plaster, the rich, foul breath of London.

There were a couple of people up and about in Candlewyck Street: a newly-wakened drunkard flopping like a beached fish in a doorway, and a peddler-woman setting off on her day's rounds. Thinking her a more likely guide, I hailed her and, as she began to scowl, slipped her a brace of coins.

'Is there a Frenchman in this street, mother?' I asked her. 'He'd be a rich man.'

She squinted at me and at the money in her hard, creased palm, and licked speculatively at a large coldsore on her upper lip.

'The wineseller,' she said at last. 'Master Thybaut. Up there, the 'ouse that's new-painted. 'E's French, and e's fucking rich an' all.'

'Well, then he's who I want,' I told her, and gave her another penny. She looked at me grimly, shugged her pack higher on her shoulders and stumped off in the direction of the Bridge. I peered in the other direction, and through the mist, rising like smoke from the kennel now that the noxious waters were growing warm, I saw the looming gables of a freshly whitewashed house. Walking closer I saw it was quite a grand building, not just newly painted but studded with bright coats of arms, carved heads of dogs and bearded men. Stevin, as I guessed, had picked the name of his street's most conspicuous inhabitant. I should have known better. I spat out the taste of the city, which had worked its way, as it always did, up my nose and down my throat. Thybaut the unpopular Frenchman. Perhaps that ought to have been good enough for me, but I had come this far without breakfast and still felt a lingering fury over last night's intrusion, so without really thinking I jumped across the kennel and stalked up to the Frenchman's door. I knocked once, twice, and as I was raising the bronze mermaid for a third knock the latch rattled and the door opened a hand's breadth. A pale face peered out.

'What do you want?' The servant demanded rudely.

'Is your master at home?'

'He is not. He is at the palace.' The man placed an extra emphasis on the last word, and narrowed his eyes at me, as if he had uttered the spell that would make me vanish.

'Ah. Where I shall be in a hour or so. Tell me: what does Monsieur Thybaut do for a living? Is he a wineseller?'

The servant's eyes widened at my impertinence.

'A *wineseller*? Monsieur Thybaut de Fouras is no wineseller, sirrah! My master is *purveyor* of wines to Her Majesty Queen Isabella . . .'

'Fouras – your master is a Poitevin, I take it.'

'What business of yours could that possibly be?' The man was almost choking with indignation, but stepping back from the door I flicked a silver coin through the dark slot between his upraised arm and the door-jamb and we both listened to it tinkle on the flagstones inside.

'For your trouble,' I told him brightly, and left him to his grand airs. No wonder Thybaut the Wineseller was not a popular man on Candle-wyck Street. If I were a wretch like Stevin, I would have named him too. A simple burglary then, no more, and Stevin a more than usually simple burglar. What a waste of time – and on an empty stomach, to boot.

Even in the short while I had been distracted, Candlewyck Street had come to life. Folk were trudging out to work, or to market or, in the case of the two crones who leant upon each other, the folds of their grimy black dresses blended into one shadowy garment, doubtless on their way to some empty chapel. There was a growing thud and clatter and here came a huddle of bullocks, wide-eyed, heads down, bound for Smooth-Field and the chopper. I stepped into a doorway to let them pass, and turned towards my hostelry and breakfast, but I had not gone twenty paces when I heard loud voices raised in a mix of sorrow and irritation – a curiously Londonish sound – and peering down a shadowy and damp-looking alley, I saw a group of men struggling to lift something from the ground. Something long and awkward. With a wobble and a heave they hoisted it up onto their shoulders. An arm fell slackly onto one man's back and he cursed vehemently, trying to shrug away the pale hand, its fingers already beginning to curl around whatever it is that Death puts into the hands of those he has taken. The men came towards me, and the bare feet of their burden passed through a shaft of tentative sunlight, which striped across toes and then ankles, and showed me that one of them, the left, was swollen and bruised reddish-blue.

'Do you know this man?' I asked the nearest fellow. He was red-faced, sweating even though the morning was still cool, his thin black hair plastered to his forehead.

'Stevin,' he said shortly.

'What happened to him?'

'Listen, I don't mean to be rude, brother, but fuck off out of it, will you?' It was the man on the other side of Stevin's knees who spoke, taller and younger than his mates, his face a welter of pimples, a fresh scar from a knife or a ring on his jaw.

'Not rude in the slightest, brother, I replied easily, stepping in front of them and making them halt, clumsily, in the mouth of the alley. The three men behind muttered something foul. 'Listen to me,' I went on. 'Here's two farthings for the sexton, and two more for the innkeeper of your choice.' I tucked the four coins under the legging band on the corpse's right leg. 'And all I want to know is what happened to poor old Stevin here. What about it, lads?'

'Waste of your time and money, mate,' said the spotty young man. 'As you know him, you'll know he's always been a waster. And what would a gent like yourself be wanting with a mudlark like Stevin, any-way?'

'Shall I ask the questions?' I said. 'Or shall I pay for the sexton's beer instead of yours? I just want to know how he ended up dead.'

'Got pissed and fell out the window,' said one of the men at the back. 'Broke 'is back. Now 'e folds the wrong way in the middle. Hinged like a fucking door. Want to feel?'

'So he lived down there?' I went on, ignoring the offer. A forlorn reek of stale beer and fresher piss was beginning to rise from the corpse, and the men were wrinkling their noses.

'I rented out a corner to him,' said the sweaty man. 'Nice pile of rags, and away from the damp spot. He was out most nights anyway, so I never saw him.'

'And when you did 'e was pissed,' added the spotty one.

'Up your pipe, Daniel,' chimed the man at Stevin's head. 'He was a good shit. And what he was doing to fall out the windy, I can't imagine.'

'Bothering a tart, I expect,' said Daniel.

'The sill might have been rotted,' muttered the sweaty man, 'but not badly, not badly. Should 'ave put his weight on it, should he?'

'So you saw him fall?' I said.

'No, no. Spend the night . . . elsewhere, if you get me. Came back to find him on the front step. And it gave me a bit of a turn.'

'What time?'

'Oh, before sun-up. The brothers were starting their racket over in the chantry. Can we be off now, mate? He was a skinny bastard, but death puts lead into 'em, if you know what I mean?'

'On your way, lads, and I thank you.' I turned to go, but another thought struck me. 'By the by, what do you think of Master Thybaut the Wineseller?'

'Who?' scowled the young man, wincing as he adjusted Stevin's weight on his skinny shoulder.

'Thybaut de Fouras. He lives in that big house yonder.' I pointed, and they looked, and shook their heads.

'The Frenchie?' said the man who had defended Stevin's memory. 'Don't know nothing about him.'

'Seems a decent enough soul,' said the red-faced one. 'Gave my sister a groat at Christmastide.'

'Did Stevin know him?'

'Fucked if I know,' said the mudlark's friend. 'But I'd doubt it. Stevin was at the river, or about his night's work, or in the ale-house when he wasn't sleeping. What would he want with a Frenchie, save to rob him? And as to that, he wouldn't 'ave dared. A villain, God rest him, but he didn't 'ave great daring in him. And that . . .' and he dipped his head towards the Frenchman's house, new whitewash beginning to gleam in the sunlight. 'That would have been shitting on his own doorstep, wouldn't it? He wasn't the brightest spark, but he wasn't stupid.' A drop of sweat was beading on his beer-veined nose, and the look in his eyes was almost pleading. The dead are heavy.

I let them stumble off, and made my own way back west, to my lodgings and, after I had broken my fast, to Westminster. I almost wished that I had not gone to Candlewyck Street, for instead of a simple answer I had more questions – or did I? Men fall out of windows and break their backs, and a man would be more apt to do it drunk than sober, perhaps. He would have been lame from that twisted ankle, and I could imagine him dejected or angry at the painful humiliation his adventure had brought him that night. That there was a wealthy French merchant in Candlewyck Street did not surprise me: there might be twenty more of them for all I knew. A wretch like Stevin would have harboured many grudges against rich men, those who lived in nice houses, and perhaps he had some reason to hate the French. One thing was certain: I could not picture that whey-faced popinjay of a servant admitting a mudlark to the house of Monsieur Thybaut under any circumstances whatsoever.

By the time I had drawn near to Westminster the whole thing had shrunk to yet another of the inconveniences of city life, and I was resigned to my tedious routine, though in a much worsened mood than yesterday. But when I had made my way to the antechamber, following a path through the halls that had become all too familiar, I was greeted with something like a smile from Sir Edward.

'This way,' he said graciously, with a twitch that might have been a grudging bow. Amazed, I followed him into the inner room that I had penetrated on my first day at the palace, and with a tremble of excitement watched him turn the handle of the smaller door. But instead of the king's chamber, or a great hall, or whatever else I had expected, I followed Sir Edward down a wide corridor hung with old but still bright tapestries that I knew must have cost a small fortune a hundred years ago. We came to a door, and with an obsquious smile daubed, I thought, unwillingly across his livid features, Sir Edward opened it and ushered me into a large room with a long window of leaded glass that looked out over the watermeadows of Thorney Island. Many racks of candles added warmth to the watery spring light, and a fire burned in the hearth. Around it sat five or six people, most of them court ladies in the finest clothes I had seen at Westminster. As I stepped over the threshold, they turned to me, and a tall man stood up and strode over to me, hand outstretched.

'Monsieur Petrus? I bid you welcome! I am so sorry that you have been marooned in the waiting room – when we heard that such a distinguished and *interesting* guest was being neglected, it seemed plain that we must put matters to rights! Come, sit with us.'

This was more like it, I thought, though it was not the audience I wanted, and still counted, in truth, as more buggering about. I could not deny, however, that the four ladies, who I now saw were nothing less than royal ladies-in-waiting, were comely. By their dress and braided hair I guessed they were Queen Eleanor's companions, and the young man sitting with them looked to be a royal equerry, as did the fellow who had greeted me. It was too late to politely refuse their hospitality anyway, for the doorman had shut the door behind me. So I bowed my finest court bow and allowed myself to be led to a bench close to the fire, where I settled myself onto a fine cushion of purple India silk. This was, certainly, better than the waiting room, for instead of my usual sort of companion – bored or angry merchants, nervous petty noblemen, all of them twitching, sniffing and spluttering their impatience – a pale young woman with red hair and a lovely oval face gently brushed with freckles was leaning towards me.

'You are the famous hunter of relics, aren't you?' she breathed.

I shrugged, making a show of modesty. 'I'm not sure if I am famous,' I replied. 'I merely serve the Lord.'

'Oh, we all serve the Lord!' cried another woman. She had a large bow-shaped mouth and green eyes, and her chestnut hair curled out from under a cloth-of-gold mantle. 'But few of us get to be so bold, or to see such treasures, as you have.'

'Dear ladies, who have you been listening to?' I laughed. 'My life is no more interesting than that of a counting-house clerk.'

'So it was not you who brought the Crown of Thorns out of Constantinople?' said the redhead, pouting in a most charming manner.

'Oh! Well, yes, it was, it was,' I said, allowing myself to be charmed. Another of the ladies had thrown a cushion at my feet and sunk down upon it. I glanced over at the two men, who were leaning against the hearth. They gave me an encouraging smile. Earl Richard had laid this on for me, I guessed. How nice of him, and how surprising. No doubt there would be an invitation to luncheon, and there the earl would make his appearance. Meanwhile I decided to enjoy myself. A gilt ewer of malmsey wine had appeared, and dishes of honey cakes. The sunlight beaming through the glass was warm, and the fire purred like a great orange cat curled in the hearth. I knew that these lovely women were not really flirting with me, but I had come to appreciate the courtly arts and my new companions were delightfully expert. I let myself be drawn out, and told them the stock of tales that I kept for such occasions. Some of them were even true.

They were good tales, and I had a polite audience. The men were even kind enough to interrupt every now and again and make me repeat some of the bloodier details, and I was glad to oblige them. The two of them, I guessed, were too young to have seen a battle; but like all of their kind they had been trained in nothing else but the arts of war since they could stand upright, and so life held no meaning to them beyond fighting, swiving and honour. Hard times for men like this, the slack tide between crusades and wars, and the frustration was part of what I felt when I walked through the palace. It makes barons fight kings or each other, and squires liable to attack anything that moves. The common folk have their football games to shake out the demons in their blood, but the knightly classes, when they are bored, tend to reach for their blades. Pope Urban, so I had been taught many years ago, had preached the first crusade just to keep the noblemen of Christendom from killing each other and anyone else who happened to get in their way. Much better to vent one's anger against the benighted infidels. But England had been at peace for more than twenty years, and that was downright unhealthy. So while I was glad I had gained the respect of these fellows, I was also wondering if it would be so very hard to send this country to war.

The dark-haired woman, Lady Blanche, was making a great show of concentration, seeming to pluck my words from the air as if each were a rare gem, and though she was overdoing it I let myself be seduced. She was beautiful, and I was alone in a city that does not favour the lonely. I took a sip of wine and let my eyes dally with hers over the lip of the goblet.

'. . . and you have come to England because . . . ?'

One of the young men, whose name was Rocelin, had let that question hang in the air. He looked innocent enough, leaning to refill my goblet.

'I have matters to discuss with Earl Richard,' I told him. He was a good enough courtier not to press me, and I turned back to the ladies.

'Surely you have more entertaining things to do here in this great palace than bandy words with a road-stained traveller?' I asked the dark-haired girl.

'It is *so* dull here,' she protested, and the others all agreed with her.

'How long are you in London?' asked Lady Alicia, prettily plump and blushing from the heat of the fire. 'Say it is for a while – we feel so abandoned in this old place!'

I was just assuring them that I indeed meant to stay a while longer – a barefaced lie – when the doorlatch clacked. Lady Blanche glanced over my shoulder and her face changed. The corners of her mouth tightened, and her face seemed to harden, as if an icy wind had caught it. I turned to see who had come in, and saw, in the doorway, a tall woman wearing a plain dress of fine grey linen. Her hair was long and silver grey, with the burnish that can only come from hours of brushing, and it hung like spider-silk around her shoulders. She wore no adornment save for a wedding band on her finger and a thin circlet of pale gold around her temples. She was not young, not even in the mid span of her years, but her face was quite unlined, and hauntingly beautiful. It was very pale and quite long, and her mouth was still a young girl's curving rosebud. Only her lips, once full and now beginning to wither; and her skin, finely stretched across the bones of her face, betrayed her age. I realised that the room had gone utterly quiet save for the low hissing of a damp log in the hearth. The woman raised a long white hand and at her silent command my companions rose in one movement and padded to the door, heads bowed. None of them gave me so much as a sideways glance. One by one they filed past the old woman until we were alone. I saw Sir Edward's hand reach out of the shadows for the handle of the door. It swung to, and the two of us were alone in the chamber.

I stood, not knowing who this personage might be but realising at once that she held a deal of importance, and bowed gravely. She said nothing, but her eyes, hazel-green, fixed themselves on mine. She walked towards me, and her back was so straight and her steps so precised that she seemed to glide. There was a high-backed chair near the window that I had not noticed before. The woman lowered herself into it and settled her long hands on the curved armrests. She gave me no sign, and I dared not move a muscle.

'You are the relic dealer,' she said at last.

'Yes, madam. I am, indeed, a finder of relics,' I said carefully. I had no idea who this beautiful but terrifying person might be, but every nerve in my body was telling me not to make even the tiniest mistake in front of her. 'Certainly not a dealer. Holy Mother Church does not allow . . .'

'Simony. A mortal sin. You must tread a very fine line, Master Petrus Zennorius.'

'If one serves the Lord, the line one must follow is clear,' I replied, as piously as I could.

'And you serve the Lord.' The green eyes blinked cooly. 'Which lord?' she demanded, abruptly. A pale oval fingernail tapped sharply on the wood of the chair.

'Our Lord . . .'

'Of France. Tell me, what is your business here, and why is it with Earl Richard and not the king himself?'

'Madam, I do not know what you mean. King Louis has concluded his business with my company. My errand to the Earl of Cornwall is a private matter, and just as I do not buy and sell holy relics as if they were turnips, nor do I betray the confidence and privacy of my company's clientele.' I was bristling now. Who was this woman? A mad old countess, perhaps, hoping to scare a complimentary relic out of me? I drew myself up to show her I did not care for her tone.

'You are impatient, sir. Are you keen to unburden yourself? Of something you have *found*?' She narrowed her eyes. Then she smiled. The change in her face was startling. 'Tell me, how did you like your wine?' she asked.

'It was very good,' I said, caught off guard.

'Yes. My supplier finds me the best barrels,' she said. 'Monsieur de

Fouras is a very clever man. He lives near your lodgings, I believe. In Candlewyck Street.'

The world did an odd dance before my eyes, and the sunlight gleaming through the leaded panes seemed to flicker. I must have been blinking like an owl as I realised that I was talking to the king's mother. The Queen Mother. This ageless, silvery creature was Isabella of Angoulême.

'I humbly beg forgiveness, Your Majesty,' I stammered, dropping to one knee, my blood sinking into my boots.

'For what? You have nothing to hide, do you? You are a famous man, Master Petrus Zennorius: a famous relic finder. Doubtless you have come to *find* something for us. There are things that we should be most sorry to see found by – found *for* – anyone else.'

So that was it. Queen Isabella thought I had come to spy for King Louis. That was why she had had my room searched. Well, poor Stevin had found nothing, for there was nothing to find.

'Your Majesty, please believe me when I say that I have nothing but matters of finance to discuss with your noble son. King Louis has been a customer, as, I might add, has His Holiness the pope, among others. I can offer you credentials and references if you wish . . .'

'Do not trouble yourself.' She was studying me from under her silvery lashes. 'You have been useful to our noble cousin Louis. But we are not in France now, sir. To begin your business here you must break your ties with France. It would be such a shame if it were not so, don't you agree? As an Englishman yourself? Of course you do.' She raised her hand, palm down, fingers straight, and rested her chin upon it. 'My sons are not here today. You may go. But any business you conclude with my sons, either one of them, will reach my eyes and ears. I have no such scruples about confidentiality, and I expect you to bring them no less a prize than you would fetch for Louis Capet. *No less a prize.* Do you understand me? Now go, and tread your fine line.'

Without truly remembering how I had arrived there, I found myself back in the corridor, back to a closed door, Sir Edward regarding me as if I were a dead cat he had found on his doorstep. I brushed past him and stamped back down the passageway, kicking through the rushes, heedless of what the man behind me thought of my manners. May God take Westminster and all who reside within and cast it down into the fissures of Hell, I was thinking, and I was still calling down fire and smoke as I reached Lud Gate, for I found myself tangled in a snare I had not anticipated, I seemed to have made an enemy of the Queen Mother though I was no nearer to fulfilling my mission for the company, and ahead stretched another empty night to fill in this city that seemed to have rejected me.

But when I got back to my lodgings I found that a letter had arrived for me. It bore the Captain's hand, and the stamps of the company's offices in Lyon and Paris.

Petroc,

I am writing this in haste, although the matters I wish to explain deserve time and care. Alas, I have neither. I earnestly hope that these words reach you before you leave Paris. You will, I expect, have met with Matheus, for he is a swift and doughty traveller. The task he offers you is well within your capabilities, indeed it could have been done by any promising clerk. I wanted you, though, for there might be difficulties and in any event I desire you to learn as much as you can about the English court and about the money marts of London. It is not about this that I am writing, for I have no doubt that you will manage things.

No, it is to make a confession. From Matheus you will have learned what is going on. As you are no fool, you will also have divined that this matter is personal to me. Please do not be dismayed when I explain how personal!

Count Raymond has built an alliance that can, without any doubt, tear his lands out of the grasp of the French. Louis Capet's southern vassals are itching to revolt against him. The Count has been two years at preparing this. Louis is strong, but Toulouse, with his new allies, will beat him. Why do I – why do we care, for as you will have gathered, the company is involved in this? At last I can tell you. The time for which I have waited and prayed has come. I have returned to my home.

Gilles left before me. He will be at Montségur by now, and perhaps he has found his heart's desire and taken the Consolamentum. I will join him soon. I am putting my share of the company's treasury, and that of Gilles, at the disposal of Toulouse. It is a hazard, but I earnestly hope you will see it as a business opportunity, as an investment, if you will, for I do not believe that Toulouse will fail.

As I wrote those words I thought of you reading them, and trust that you are not discomfited too greatly. My dear Patch, this need not concern you at all. Your share of the business is yours to do with what you will. In the event that I am wrong about what lies ahead, you will not be implicated, for I have taken care that no blame will attach itself to you. I would ask this, though: when you are done in London, make your way to the city of Toulouse and seek me out. If you are quick you will be ahead of the storm. I will explain things more fully and hope that I may set your mind at rest, for if I know you at all, you are brimming over with questions, and my letter not even done.

There is one more thing, and perhaps this will shock you most of all. I can tell you in one word why I have taken this road, and that word is faith. *The faith of my father and mother, my brother and sisters, my uncles, my friends and my land. That it should come to this: I rejoice that I have lived long enough to see the great wrong done to my people avenged, and to play my part. I cannot ask for your understanding, but if I must have your forgiveness, I earnestly beg you for that.*

Until we meet in Toulouse,

Michel de Montalhac, ex Cormaranus

I read the Captain's words again, and then again, and forgot all about the palace until the bells of London began to tell the tenth hour of the morning. I studied the curling sheet of vellum, black with its dense burden of ink, and at first I wondered if the Captain had written it at all. It did not sound like him. It sounded like a much younger man, a Christian, if that were possible, all wide-eyed and pious. A *fool*. Dear God. After I had admitted that to myself I threw myself on the letter and read it again, scanning each curlicue and flourish, each dot. I divined it, I dowsed it for any clue at all, for it made no sense to me.

The Captain's affection for his homeland was no surprise, for he and Gilles had often told me little things about it. The lands of Toulouse, in their telling, were a paradise of waving corn and vines heavy with grapes that burst in the mouth already transformed into the finest wine. The roads were full of poets, and even the thrushes sang brave songs of love from the olive trees. But that was all past. That world had ended, and at its ending had sent men like Gilles and the Captain spinning into chaos and the unknowable future, like the embers that fly up when a burning house falls in upon itself. There had never been any going back for them save as something wished for but impossible, as the Jews long for Jerusalem in their Sabbath prayers. Exile had held us all together, and even when the *Cormaran*'s crew had dissolved, Gilles, the Captain and I had remained, for our home was where we were. And now this.

The Captain had been right. It was the word *faith* that shocked me most of all. I had never heard it on his lips save to explain the reason why some new fool had been gulled into buying a preposterous and vastly expensive relic. No, that was not true: he had spoken of his Cathar faith to me twice: the first time in Greenland, in Gardar, that cursed town dying of the cold that rose over the edge of the world; and the second time in the pope's own palace. That was all. He freely admitted neither he nor Gilles were diligent in their practice, and Gilles had certainly not been, for he swore with relish and had a twinkle in his eye that I would not have expected to find on the face of a Cathar *perfect*. Jesus. I stood up and paced about the room, cursing bitterly. All this slack-jawed nonsense about faith. Gilles taking the *Consolamentum*? Impossible and grotesque! I paused and tried to calm myself by looking out of the window. Below me in Knight Rider Street a trio of prostitutes walked arm in arm, doing their best to look respectable. A black pig, very hairy and with one broken tusk, rooted about in the muck of the kennel that ran down the middle of the street. The whores brushed past a young cleric – he could have been me seven years ago, in his Benedictine habit and his raw, newly-scraped tonsure – and he turned his face pointedly to the wall. *There's faith*, I thought. *You sniff in disgust at the tarts that you long to swive, but doubtless you are off on an errand from some priestly master who has each hand up a different apron every night except Sunday. Much good it will do you, my son. Much good it did me.*

'Follow them back to Gropecunt Lane,' I called, but no one heard me save the pig, who eyed me contemptuously and went back to rootling for turds. The whores swayed out of sight, no doubt on their way back to the brothels of Fleet Street beyond the wall. A tinner came by with his barrow, and a rag picker and his son. A gang of children chased a hoop, angering the pig, who scolded them with a shriek. Then an old woman came in sight, leaning on a staff, white curls spilling out from a badly tied coif. The children came back with their hoop, and she leaned back against the wall of a house to give them room. When they had passed she gazed after them, and I thought I could see a smile. Then she looked down. At her feet lay something round: a turnip, perhaps, or a beet. She prodded it with her staff. The pig stopped rooting and stared at the thing. With a surprisingly energetic kick the old woman sent the turnip spinning at the beast. It splashed into the filth of the kennel and ran up against its front trotters. The hog gave a squeal of joy and fell upon the turnip, nosing it out of the gutter and onto the flagstones, and out of my sight. The old woman looked after it for a moment, then lifted her head. Over the distance our eyes met and she smiled at me. Then she leant on her staff and shuffled away. I stared at the place where she had stood long after she had gone, remembering her smile. She had not been addled, or any of those slanders the young heap upon grey heads. But she was no longer bound by the desires that made the children chase, the whores shake their arses and the young monk quiver,

I realised. She was not really walking down the same Knight Rider Street that they had been. And then I saw the truth. The Captain was not a fool. No, he had opened his eyes and taken a step outside the world. He had simply grown old.

Chapter Six

It took me until luncheon, which I snatched from an eel-seller near Queen Hithe Wharf, to work out what I should do next. I ate, and watched the gulls hopping up and down the steps where Anna and I had come ashore years ago. The Captain had told me not to worry, but it seemed all too clear that a great deal depended on getting King Henry to fight. I had read the letter a last time and saw that the Captain had not taken leave of his senses, as I had feared, but was instead setting out on another adventure. Only this time, the goal was not to find some arcane thing, some hidden remnant of the past with which to trick a prince or a cardinal. My master was off to win back his lost life. Spitting out an inch of eel-spine for the gulls to fight over, I decided that was a good thing after all. Did I want anything more, when all was said and done, than to lie back on the rough grass of Dartmoor and watch the larks rise and fall above me, and be sure that no hunting party was out seeking the Gurt Dog of Balecester? I did not. Well then, I needed to find Richard of Cornwall, and there was someone in this city who might be induced to help me.

I would not find Letice Londeneyse by that name. She had returned to the city of her birth with a fortune, for the Captain had been as good as his word and given her a partner's share of the Pharos Chapel commission. She had arrived in London as the Lady Agnes, just returned from the Holy Land. Her husband, a knight from Essex, had won a trading concession from one of the ports there – I had heard these details from the Captain, and had feigned an indifference I did not, in my heart, really feel – and the couple had been returning with a company of ships laden with the wonders of Outremer when her poor husband had caught sick and died. Being his sole heir, she had put in at Venice and sold the lot, and with the proceeds had come back to London and bought herself a warehouse and the controlling interest in several trading ships. Thus she had managed to conjure a thriving business from thin air. Her cruel master, Nicholas Querini, had amused himself by letting his whore, for so Letice had been, advise him on his many schemes to turn gold into power, and vice versa; and so Letice had turned misery into profit, for during those years she had kept her eyes and ears open, and many of her former master's trading allies were stored up in her prodigious memory. In no more than a brace of years she had set up a web of trade that stretched from Hamburg to Constantinople. It was modest – for if I knew Letice, she would not wish to draw attention to herself, and she knew better than to take too much money away from powerful men, lest they turn around and crush the upstart woman out of spiteful pride. She even did business with the company of the *Cormaran*, for we were happy to serve as bankers to the Lady Agnes. I say *we*, but I did not interest myself in her affairs. I saw the letters come and go, and the entries in our ledgers, but that was all. It would have been easy to send a letter of my own, but I was angry and proud, and as I always told myself, I was much too busy with my own magnificent life.

Now, though, it was time to choke down a dry and gristly mouthful of pride and seek out my erstwhile betrothed. But first I needed to get rid of the man who had been following me since I had left the hostelry. Queen Isabella had not been convinced, then. The man, early middle age, nondescript and balding, dressed in the neat but dull clothes of a well-to-do artisan or a guild member, had been trailing me with some expertise, but I had learned this craft from true masters, and he had not been hard to discover. At least he did not look like a killer, but you could never be sure. So I threw the rest of my eels into the river and set off north, idling through the streets as if I were a bored sightseer. My path took me past Saint Paul's and through streets that grew narrower and meaner until I had reached Saint Martin's-le-Grand, where I let myself be carried along by the crowd passing through Aldersgate. As I passed underneath the great arch I made sure the bald pate of my follower was still behind. It was, and so I stuck my thumbs into my belt and turned left towards the steeple of Saint Bartholomew's Church.

Even blindfolded I would have known Smooth Field by the stench. The ground was open here, with a litter of shanties and crooked houses around the edge of the churned meadow that stretched north of the priory of Saint Bartholomew. I struck out from the priory lane and soon I was walking through rutted mud still reeking with the blood and ordure of the cattle that had died here last market day, and as I had hoped, packs of emaciated, shock-haired children were circling me. I ignored them and made for the nearest huddle of shanties, my follower in plain sight now, trying to hide among a knot of country folk on their way home. As soon as I was among the hovels I stopped and let the children catch up with me. They swarmed around me, their small faces streaked with dirt and scabby with ringworm, hands tugging at my clothes, little fingers scrabbling at the strings of my purse.

'All right,' I said, squatting down. They were so surprised that they drew back, alarmed and angry. I pulled out a handful of pennies and one cut piece of silver. 'Do you want this? Then look over there. See that man in grey, with the shiny head? He's come to Smooth Field looking for little chaps like you to roger. Now I don't like that, and I'm sure you don't either. So here's some coin if you make sure he doesn't play his game around here any more, eh?' I selected the tallest child and poured the coins into his cupped hands, pausing long enough to see his eyes widen. As I turned away I heard their feral voices raised in something like a hunting cry, and glancing back I saw the whole pack of them, twenty or more, racing across the field towards Queen Isabella's spy. I ran the other way, through the squalid maze of huts towards the Fleet River. Following the stream brought me down to Lud Gate. Making sure that no one else was following me I passed back into the city and hurried east towards the bridge.

The warehouse that Letice owned was downstream, just beyond Billingsgate wharf, that much I remembered. She now rejoiced in the name of Agnes de Wharram, and I did not think it would be hard to find her. I was half-right, at least. The de Wharram warehouse lay between the river and an ancient little church that was slowly being swallowed by the new buildings going up around it. Letice's building was new as well, a fine stone barn of a place, looking well-swept and prosperous. It was locked up, as I had expected, but round the corner was a little counting-house, and inside, in the shadows that smelled of tallow and scraped parchment, a young clerk laboured amidst towers of accounting ledgers.

'Is your mistress available?' I asked him.

'Lady de Wharram? She is not,' he said, surprised.

'Where might I find her?'

'She is down here every day in the morning. You have missed her by not even an hour,' was my answer.

'I have urgent business with her. Where might she be now?'

The clerk rubbed his spotty cheeks and studied me. I probably looked like one of her investors, I supposed, all done up in my Venetian stuff. I let him take in the quality of my tunic, the gold upon my fingers, and the sea-green glint of Thorn at my belt. He blinked, and stood up, wincing. He had been sitting since before dawn, I guessed, scratching entries and poring over spider-scrabble handwriting in the bad light. I wondered if Letice was a kindly employer, and realised that if I were in this pale young fellow's place I would probably be scared half to death of her.

'She will have gone home,' he said, unhelpfully.

'Good sir,' I said, and he lifted his chin a little at the compliment. 'I have come a long way to see Lady Agnes. I would certainly be welcomed at her home, and would have gone there, but during my voyage – and it was a lengthy one – I had the misfortune to lose much of my baggage, including the particulars of everyone in London with whom I have business. It is a little mortifying to have come two hundred leagues only to arrive as helpless as a blind man, but at least I still have life. Now, if you could direct me?'

I pulled out a small gold bezant and laid it on the leather face of a book, where it glinted, inches from the boy's nose. I could see him gazing at the worn head of a Byzantine emperor and the Greek writing. He had counted gold coins before, no doubt, but had he ever possessed one? I guessed that he had not. I was right. He caught my eye and I nodded, and the coin disappeared. A shy grin revealed an unhappy set of teeth.

'Don't tell your mistress I gave you that,' I said dryly. 'Now, where might she be?'

'Two Dogs Court, off Aldersgate Street,' said the clerk. 'Shall I draw you a map?'

He did so, and as he did I looked about the place. She was doing well, judging from the piles of accounting this poor boy was saddled with. I peered at an open book.

Saffron
Ginger
Grains of Paradise
Pepper
Canel
Galyntyne

'How is the Lady Agnes?' I asked absently.

'She is . . . very well, master,' said the clerk, looking up from the neat hatchmarks of his map.

'Does she treat you well?'

There was a suppressed snort. The boy wiped his nose and leaned close over the map.

'Well, does she?'

'We . . . we call her Agnes Peuerel – not to her face, master, but . . .'

'Peuerel. So she is fiery, like pepper?'

'She's hot all right,' said the clerk. 'I mean . . .' I did not have to see his face. His ears were burning red. 'That is to say, she does not suffer fools gladly, and when her blood is up . . .'

'Indeed. That I know. Well, young man, thank you for this fine map. And a word of advice: your mistress' temper may burn like pepper, but she will heat the blood as well. Resist the temptation of hot-blooded women, boy. They will lure you to a doom your worst dreams could not imagine.'

'As to that I wouldn't know, sir,' said the clerk, an eyebrow rising. 'I meant no dishonour to the Lady Agnes. She is a widow, and has suffered much.' Fine words, but the knave was blushing to his roots.

'Your mistress has suffered more than most,' I agreed. 'But I can assure you that she has given as good as she's got. You have my word on it.'

'And who might you be, sir, if you don't mind me asking?' I was beginning to make the poor boy uncomfortable. No doubt swarthy, scar-faced strangers making mock of his mistress did not cross his path very often.

'Since I have my directions and you have your bezant, it hardly matters, does it?' I told him. 'But in terms of your lady's hard life I would call myself a phantom, of sorts.' A frown twitched at the corners of the boy's pustular brow. 'Nay,' I said, with a cheery wink, 'I am from her bank in Venice. Don't dream about Lady Agnes so much, and maybe those spots will go away.'

I left him gawping and set off to find Letice. I hoped he would take my advice. Everyone in my abbey had known that spots came from interfering with yourself – God knows that I had come by mine that way. I hoped, though, that I was not begrudging him his sweaty dreams simply because they involved my almost-wife. He had drawn me a nice map, after all. It was sending me crab-wise to the north-west, and soon enough I found myself on the broad thoroughfare of Cheapside, hurrying along with the flood-tide of market-goers. It was the one place in London that I had determined to avoid, but I was in a hurry. I tried to keep my eyes on the ground, but there were too many obstacles – filth, dogs, a dead chicken, a lost child – and instead I fixed my eyes on the filthy kennel, the stream of ordure that divided the street in two. I set my shoulders and barged my way forward, one hand on my knife, the other on my purse. Then something fluttered very close to my face: it was a live goose hanging by its feet from a pole that was slung across a serf's shoulder. I flinched, and as I did so I saw, across the way, the sign of the Blue Falcon. So I had come here after all. This was the place where four lives had met for less than a minute, and of those four, only I remained. I swallowed, gritted my teeth and climbed onto the stepping stone that bridged the kennel. There was the spot where Anna had fallen. I do not know what I expected to see, but I saw nothing, and all of a sudden I was glad of that. The tide of flesh and toil had washed it all away. I let it carry me.

Up Blowbladder Street I went, and into Aldersgate Street. The wind was blowing from the north-west, bringing to my nose the gifts of Smooth Field – animal dung and man-shit, and all the rotting waste of the great business of butchery that went on there, day in and day out. I wondered why Letice had chosen to live so close to her old home. 'I grew up on a dung-heap,' she would say, and here she was, back again and downwind. I was starting to feel nervous, if truth be told, for I had not seen the woman in almost two years, and while part of me looked forward, with a happy tremble in the lower quarters of my person, to our reunion, another part – and it included my head – trembled with less pleasant anticipation. Well, here was Two Dogs Court.

I paused at the entrance to the narrow street. Houses pressed very close together over the passage, which was marshy with nightsoil. At the end was a small court that allowed a little sunlight to fall upon the broad face of a large house. That must have been the Two Dogs Tavern, I supposed, or had a knight lived there, who wore a brace of hounds upon his shield? The former, I supposed, for this place had the look of a Grope Alley about it, and smelled like one into the bargain. Letice had bought the tavern, or knocking shop, or whatever it had been. Christ's mother! Could she not have found herself a better place to live? And then it occurred to me that perhaps it was still a knocking shop. That was a trade my Letice knew more than a little about. Not a bad investment, either. I knew her old madam in Venice well – there was no information whispered in the Republic that did not reach Mother Zanetta's ears, and no thread of the weave of power that was Venice that she did not hold an end of – and she was less a brothel-keeper than the queen of the San Polo quarter. Letice would make an excellent madam, I realised. Then I shook that thought from me and plunged into the alley.

The door had a bronze knocker upon it, and I banged three times. The door was sound, and new, I saw: good oak with finely worked wrought iron bands and hinges. I half expected a half-naked sylph to answer my knocking, but instead an older man dressed soberly in fustian the colour of sea-coal opened the door carefully, blinked deliberately, and drew back his shoulders.

'Yes?' he inquired, any note of curiosity wiped from his voice.

'I should like to see the Lady Agnes de Wharram, my good fellow,' I replied, trying as best I could to sound English. I did not succeed, I guessed, for he ran his eyes over my get-up for a moment and tightened his grip on the door. She had chosen this one well, had Letice, but I was at least glad that he did not look like the doorkeeper to a brothel.

'Is she within?' I asked politely. Nothing.

'Perhaps you would tell her that Messer Cane – *Caa neh* – is without?' That had been her jesting name for me, Master Dog in Venetian, in honour of Gurt Dog, the name I had left behind me in England. The servant stepped back and beckoned me inside with a small, elegant turn of his hand. I followed him into a short but wide stone hall with a dark, ugly Venetian bench on each side. They were polished so that they glowed like new chestnuts, and the air was sweet with lavender and beeswax. The servant indicated that I should sit, and disappeared through an inner door. Not a knocking shop, then. Letice was free to live her life as she pleased, but I was a little bit relieved all the same.

I waited for some time, scuffling my feet in the fresh rushes on the floor and enjoying their spicy fragrance. But I was still nervous, and when a female form stepped into the hall I jumped up with clumsy haste. But it was not Letice, just another servant, a young woman in dove-grey linen, who gave a nice curtsey and asked wouldn't I follow her, please?

The de Wharram residence was spotless and furnished sparingly with the finest things a trading ship could bring. There were Flanders hangings, Damascus curtains, lustreware jugs and bowls from Al Andalus, candleholders fit for a cardinal's palace. The girl showed me into the solar. It was a neat room with narrow windows that let in enough thin London light to show off the quality of its furnishings. Venetian chairs. An Egyptian carpet, of the kind that Mussulmen kneel on to pray, graced a new oak table, and on it rested a pair of tall silver candlesticks.

'You take me by surprise, sir.' The voice was light and as polished as honed marble. I turned, gracelessly. Agnes de Wharram stood there, hands loose at her sides, head very high, yellow braids falling onto a plain dress that looked as if it had been spun from cobwebs gathered on the moon. For more than a moment I believed that I was looking at a sister, some lost twin of Letice, for this Agnes seemed to possess the woman I knew, as I had once seen a holy man entered by the ghost of a saint, one night in Alexandria.

'My lady,' I said. I almost bowed, and felt myself wincing with the effort to stop myself. She noticed, and the suggestion of a smile appeared on the face I thought I would have known but did not. 'It . . . It's me,' I added, feebly.

'I know,' said the apparition, flatly. She glided past me and stood behind the table so that the light surrounded her. 'What is it that you want with me?'

'Agnes . . . Oh, for fuck's sake!' I could not keep myself in check a moment longer. 'Letice, I am sorry that I have come here, and even sorrier that I must . . .'

'Must what?'

'I need your help.'

'Of course you do.' The words were Letice, but the voice was not. A fingernail tapped imperiously upon the foot of a candlestick. 'How long have you been in London, Messer Petrus?'

'For God's sake, Letice, do not make me stand here like a bloody pilgrim! I have been here a week. On business – unexpected business, and unwelcome, at that. And I have reluctantly tracked you down, through the good offices of your clerk who, by the way, abuses himself mightily in your honour, to ask you a very small favour. Grant it, and I shall show my gratitude by leaving on the very next tide, and that I swear on my mother's bones.'

'Sit down, Patch,' she said, with a sigh. I did so, and she did as well. We faced each other across the alien colours of the prayer rug: her control and elegance, my twitchy, street-soiled impatience.

'What do you want?' The finger had ceased to tap, and the room was very quiet.

'I should like you to be yourself. Please.'

'And who might that be?' I could not see her face, but it did not sound as if she was smiling.

'The woman who . . .' I paused, mouth stoppered by the surge of memories I had let out of their gaol. Christ, what a terrible mistake I had made, coming here. 'The woman who used to be about to marry me – how about that?' There was silence. I thought I heard myself blink, a tiny wet snap, but perhaps I was mistaken. 'I did not come here to ask you that – to marry me,' I said at last. 'I am not sure that this Agnes de Wharram, whoever she might be, would have me.' I took a deep breath and let it out slowly through my nose, feeling my heart slow to where it would not make my voice tremble. I had not meant to get angry, but there again, it had not really been anger. 'I thought you might be able to get me an audience with the Earl of Cornwall,' I told her, and leant back, finished, in my beautifully polished chair.

'I might,' said Lady de Wharram. 'Mightn't I?' added someone else.

'Jesus! So you are in there!' I cried. 'I am sorry,' I said hastily, seeing her back stiffen. 'I am innocent of . . . of any sort of romantic guile, honestly. You see that, don't you?'

'Yes. You've been here a week,' she said icily.

'And I would not have blighted your lovely house, nor bribed your clerk, had I not been . . .'

'. . . Desperate. You are *desperate*, Patch, aren't you? This is more like it. I might end up liking this.'

'All right, I am. I need to see Earl Richard, I do not like this city, and I wish to get myself back on to the Continent as soon as I possibly can. I'm sure you'd like to speed me on my way.'

'Not really, Patch.' Letice sighed, and smoothed the nap of the prayer rug with her palm. 'I've wondered, every now and again, if you would come here. I thought: he'll come looking for me. I didn't – *don't* – want that, you understand. It is the looking and not the finding that is important in these thoughts, which are idle, and get me nowhere. And besides, I am a respectable widow.' She picked a teardrop of wax from one of the candlesticks, and sighed again. 'It is nice to see you, Patch, and I say that in spite of myself.'

'In spite of Lady Agnes, you mean.'

'Oh God. Agnes.' She rubbed the tip of her nose with her fingertip. 'Toly – my clerk – what exactly did he say about me?'

'About *her*. That's what you were going to say, wasn't it? 'Twas not what he said, rather the way he twitched.'

'Workers,' she said bitterly. 'Well, since you are here, have you dined yet?'

Chapter Seven

As it turned out, neither of us were hungry. Letice picked at a cold pheasant and I sipped some excellent claret. We studied each other for a while. Finally, Letice broke the silence.

'Why do you need to see Earl Richard?' she asked, abruptly.

That was a good question. I had not decided what to tell Letice about my mission. It was not her business any more, and I did not want to involve her in even a small corner of the great plot against Louis of France, for I had realised, as I had made my way to her house, that I could not predict what side she might be on. Not that Letice was likely to have any loyalties based on birth or blood, but she well might have some commercial interest to protect or, God knew, some ideas of her own. So I lied.

'The Captain has it in mind to sell Richard something very choice,' I said. That was the obvious answer, was it not? Letice rolled a leg bone between finger and thumb and looked at me down her nose.

'Oh, yes? What?' she said, brightly. Her eyes were narrow, intent. Not a good sign.

'Something . . . choice. I found some other things in Constantinople, you know. Especially when I was there last. The bloody Franks are so hard up that they started to bring me all sorts of stuff – bits and pieces that their fathers had looted, that sort of thing. Most of it was rubbish, but some wasn't.'

'And the something for Earl Richard?' She was not taking my vagueness as a hint.

'Ah. Well. Not quite in the same league as the Pharos treasures. Not *quite.*'

'So, what? An arm, a leg? A holy pizzle? Saint Peter's loincloth?'

'Ahh . . . yes, something like that.' There was silence.

'You're lying to me, Petroc,' said Letice.

'I am not!' But my protests were useless, I knew already. Letice could

72

see into people. She was as good a liar as I have ever met, and found out the lies of others as easily as a dowser finds hidden water. I sighed.

'Very well then. The truth – all I can tell you – is that the Captain does have something for Earl Richard, that it will please him, and that I should like to get it to him as soon as I can. It is just business, Letice, and I really do want to leave here as soon as I can.'

'Thank you, Petroc. It wasn't very nice of you, bringing me fibs after all these years.'

'Not even two years,' I muttered into my wine.

'Well, it seems longer. And I am glad to see you, actually.'

'Really?'

'For what it is worth. I have found that I am a stranger here, in my own town.'

I put down my wine and leant my elbows on the table. She leant away from me, but easily, and raised the bare leg-bone in front of me like a little grey sceptre. 'I am sorry for that,' I told her. 'I wondered why you had chosen to live so close to . . .' I inclined my head in the direction of Smooth Field.

'For the smell, of course. Reminds me of my girlhood.' She dropped the bone and reached for a towel. 'I don't know, Petroc. These streets are what I used to see before I went to sleep. When I was sad I would close my eyes and walk around here in my mind. Of course I came back here. But . . .'

'But it isn't the same. I know.'

'How do you know?' She said sharply. Then she dropped her head and smiled, warm and sad all at once, for the first time. 'Oh, Patch. I had forgotten. I'm not angry with you now. I never was, if you want to know.'

'I do,' I said.

'I could not live like that any more,' she said. 'You understand Venice. It worms itself inside you. The smell of the water . . . Christ above, it was stifling me.'

'But we were happy!' I protested.

'I wasn't. Were you?' She gave a great sigh and leaned her arms on the table, so that her clasped hands were almost touching mine. 'Listen. Mother Zanetta saw it better than I did. She said that if I did not leave you, I would end up a suicide, or else a whore again. Would you have wished that?'

'You know I would not.'

'And you. Are you happy? Are you brim-full of content?'

It was my turn to sigh. 'Happy, perhaps. I *should* be happy, with all my money and respect and whatnot, so I tell myself that I am. That would seem to imply that I'm not content either, wouldn't it? My life has changed, Letice. I'm not a child – I do not do things just because they make me happy.'

'Nor me. Shame, though, isn't it?' She stood up, and her lovely robe swung and shimmered. 'I am neither happy nor unhappy, but I am rich, and in London that is almost the same thing. Like in Venice.'

'So what are we complaining about?' I said, leaning back and looking at her properly. She was as lovely as she had ever been, her face still dancing on the rope between beautiful and homely.

'I don't know, love,' she said, and held out her hand to me. It was the gesture of a lady to a courtly stranger, but I took it gladly, and rose. 'I know a man at court – you knew I would. Let us go and see him. You can tell me all the gossip from San Polo in the meantime.'

Letice's friend at court lived a fair distance away, in the ward of Bishopsgate. I wondered if he would be at home, and whether it was worthwhile trudging through the streets just to find him gone, but Letice had decided that we would go, and we did.

'We could ride, but I'd rather walk, and I know you would,' she said as we stepped outside into the dingy passageway. She was right. It was the first time I had been in the city with someone who knew it as well as I had known my small corner of Dartmoor, and I let myself be led, although she put her arm in mine and allowed me to squire her. It was plain that, although Lady Agnes de Wharram had only appeared two years ago, she had the respect of her neighbours, for she received many nods and curtseys, and had parted with a good handful of coppers to the urchins that tugged at her skirts and my tunic before we had even reached Broad Street.

'You seem quite at home,' I told her. Then I noticed her sour expression. 'What is wrong?'

She shrugged. 'Nothing,' she said at last. 'The weather. I'd forgotten how low the bloody sky is.'

I did not think she had been talking about the weather earlier, but I let it go, glad to be with her. We chatted, like the old friends we almost were, about business: hers and mine, the company. The house of de Wharram was doing well. It had gone into partnership with a Jewish company in Genoa that was well respected on the wharfs of Alexandria, and so the spices I had seen itemised were flowing into the Billingsgate warehouse.

'But things have to flow the other way, too,' she said, as we passed St Benet's church. 'I have bought estates in the Weald, you know.'

'Iron?'

'And timber. I buy spices from the traders in Egypt, and sell them iron and good Wealden oak.'

'I don't believe it!' I stopped in the middle of the tailors' street and laughed aloud. An old rabbi from the synagogue across the road eyed me curiously. 'Does the Church know about it?'

'That I provide the Mussulmen with stuff to make swords and warships? Of course.'

'And?'

'I bribe them. They call it a penance, but we all know that it is a bribe. It isn't just me, you know.'

She was right. I was not surprised that Christians were selling arms to the Saracens, simply that Letice had managed to carve out a piece of that excellent and lucrative trade for herself, and so quickly. I told her so, and she snapped her fingers. 'Silver opens every door and cleanses the filthiest soul, my dear,' she said, and led me out of the path of a bullock cart.

John Curtesmains lived in a large, newly whitewashed house in a court behind the church of Saint Adelburga-the-Virgin. Fortunately he was at home, and we were shown into the hall. This John was very well-to-do, with a new-looking coat of arms that graced hangings, ceiling bosses and a large and dazzlingly bright shield that hung on the wall.

'Is he a knight, this John?' I asked Letice under my breath, as we waited for our host to appear.

'Just, as of last year,' she said. 'His son will be a baron if John lends King Henry enough silver, though.'

Sir John was a thin, balding little man with a sparse beard, who did not look as if he would ever have been able to heft his gaudy shield, even in his youth, which was long ago spent. He was friendly enough, though, and did not press us too hard as to my reasons for needing an audience with Earl Richard. Letice introduced me as a sort of diplomat – she kept it hazy – with friends in Venice and Constantinople. John seemed to find it perfectly natural that such a person should need to see the earl, and that Richard would want to see me.

'If you could arrange an audience, I would be most grateful,' I told him. 'And without a doubt the interests whom I represent would share my gratitude.' This was a language he understood very well, apparently, for he grinned and rubbed his hands. Then his face fell.

'Alas! I know why you have had such a frosty time of it at West-minster,' he said. 'Henry and his brother . . . well, they are brothers, and like brothers they quarrel on occasion.'

'Come now, John, they fight like two cats in a sack!' said Letice.

'Oh, well, Agnes. But you are right. Richard has never got used to Henry's Poitevins – his in-laws and all those bloody hangers-on. My dear Petrus, I have no side in this, you understand, except the king's, so please do not misunderstand me. Have you heard, though, what the Poitevins are up to now?'

'You mean the war?' said Letice. John gave her a pained look.

'Our guest is perhaps . . .'

'Oh, do not fear. I have heard of Earl Richard's troubles in Poitou, and the Lusignans, of course. That is not my concern. Why, though, are Richard and Henry at odds about this, of all things? Surely Henry would love to defend English rights against the French.'

'Henry is not like his brother,' said John, with what might have been a hint of regret. 'Richard is a martial lord, of course – most puissant, most puissant indeed. He just returned from the Crusade, you know.' I nodded. 'He has taken up arms against Henry three times,' he went on, 'and he loathes de Montfort, his brother in law, especially now that he is Earl of Leicester. They went to the Holy Land together, and rumour has it that they did not speak a single word to each other the entire time they were away. But it is Richard who does not want to go to war.' He raised his eyebrows at me, inviting surprise. I obliged.

'Why not?'

'Unlike the king, Earl Richard . . .' He stopped himself, and held a finger to his lips. 'Richard is a clever man – a good business man, actually, and he prefers to use sense and influence whenever he can. He knows that wars cost money, and the barons are already furious that Henry has levied their purses to fight this one. Richard does not like nor trust his father in law Hughues de Lusignan, and he resents being ordered around by his mother. That is the short answer. He was only Count of Poitou in name, and he has always had his eye on what one might call an actual throne – not his brother's,' he added hastily, 'but some rich, foreign kingdom. Who can blame him? It is difficult to be a second son, especially when the eldest is . . . innocent.' Apparently content with his choice of words, he nodded to himself. 'Is that, perhaps, why you are here?' The question was left dangling in the air between us.

'No, not at all,' I said firmly. 'I am here on a business matter, really; not unconnected with Mother Church, but that is, alas, all that I can tell you now. I know that Earl Richard would be glad to receive me, though.'

'I am sure he would. But that is just the problem, you see. The earl is not *at* Westminster.'

'Oh! Where is he, then?' asked Letice.

'Devon, when last I heard, Lady Agnes. At his manor of Lydford, no doubt.'

'But the king is at court,' I said.

'No, he is not. He is going about the countryside, trying to talk the barons into war. No, the only royal personage at Westminster – ' he smacked his lips over *personage*, as though it were a luscious sweetmeat – 'is Queen Isabella, lately arrived from France.'

'Devon, then,' I muttered.

'Oh, dear! Good master Petrus! It seems you have a long journey ahead of you!' Letice cried, with all the subtlety of a village mummer. 'You must ride to . . . to Devonshire, wherever that is!'

'You're here because of this war, aren't you?' asked Letice as soon as we were out in the noise of Blackfriars Street. She squinted at me accusingly, shielding her eyes against the slanting light of the sun.

'What makes you say so?'

'Oh, come off it, Patch! I saw you cock your head like a fucking papagallo when old John brought it up. Why did you not tell me? Are you . . . you've come from Louis, haven't you? You spend half your life at Vincennes these days, so I hear.'

'Language, *Lady* Agnes. And from whom do you hear it?'

'From the Man in the Moon. From Gilles and dear Michel, obviously, or have you forgotten that *they* still write to me?'

'No, I can assure you, absolutely and on my life's blood, that I am not here on behalf of Louis Capet. Can we change the subject, please?'

'Hmm. I believe you, oddly enough. But it is about Poitou. I'll stake one of my ships on it – nay, a ship and a cargo.' She clapped her hands. 'La! Captain Michel has some stake in this – but what? He . . . Richard has borrowed money from him. Am I right? Or is it Lusignan?'

'No.'

'Yes. I am right. Admit it! Admit I'm right, and I won't mention it again, I promise. I don't care, you know. War with France doesn't affect my business.' She pulled me across the street and into an alley. 'Tell me!'

'No, Letice. It's not your business. It isn't mine either, come to that. I'm trying to run a fucking errand, and when it is done I will never think about it again. You know all you need to: you are English, you live in London, unlike me; and I won't put you in danger.'

'So there *is* danger, then?' said Letice triumphantly.

'There's absolutely no danger. My lady, thank you for luncheon, and for your assistance. I am glad we saw each other once more. And now I must say goodbye.' I leant in and kissed her very quickly on her cheek. It was flushed, and warm. Her eyes flashed as I pulled away. 'Goodbye, Letice!' I gave her a courtier's bow, and she shook her head resignedly.

'Goodbye to you, Patch,' she said, and with her hands on her hips she watched me as I strode away up the alley.

Back at the hostelry I took stock. My trip so far had been an inventory of nuisances. I had wasted a week at the palace. I had seen Letice, although I had sworn I would not, and made a great buffoon of myself into the bargain. And now I had to ride all the way to Devon. I should not have left Letice that way. It had been a joy to see her, though it seemed plain that there would always be a coolness between us now. She had not seemed angry with me – God, she had even helped me. And like a mountebank I had left her in the street. I had not known what else to do. I did not want to tell her why I had come to England. But . . . I could have told her, I supposed. What harm would there have been in that? She had guessed it, in a way. The Captain was sending aid to Richard, but it was not a loan, and it was not, alas, business. I thought of going back to her house and giving her this almost-truth just to redeem myself in her eyes, though that did not seem very likely to work, I decided. And why did I care what she thought in any case? There was nothing between us any more. Lady Agnes, forsooth.

But I did not have a restful night. I was excited, of course, overjoyed, even, to be returning at last to Devon. And not just Devon, but Dartmoor, *my* moor, for Lydford is on the western edge of those hills, and I could, if I chose, ride there by way of my old home at Auneford. But would that be wise? I was not known in London. The Gurt Dog of Balecester was just a legend these days if anyone remembered at all. No doubt in Balecester itself the memory was still raw and vivid, but I was not going anywhere near that godforsaken place. Devon, though: there I might be recognised. I doubted anyone would know me at Auneford, for I had been a child when I lived there. But had I changed very much since leaving the abbey at Buckfast? I was older, with a broken nose and skin darkened by southern skies, and I had hair on the top of my head. But monks are observant in more ways than one. Their life is a dull one without variety, and to compensate they often develop keen powers of observation, if only to entertain minds that would otherwise wizen from lack of use. And they did leave the abbey, to sell wine or corn, or to buy provisions, and if I met someone upon the road, someone who had known me when I was Brother Petroc . . . Well, they would have to prove it. I laid my head down long after the bells of midnight had bullied the air, but I did not sleep until much later, and then only to dream fitfully of the moors, and of a hall full of Benedictines who all had my face, but were sitting in judgement against me. In my dream I leapt up and found I could fly, and floated out of a narrow window and out into the sky above the river Dart, but as happens in dreams I could not control my actions and stopped there, hanging in the air, while the brothers filed out and solemnly shot at me with arrows. They struck my flesh with hollow thuds which did not hurt, but the more I flapped my arms and struggled to rise and fly away, the louder the thudding became, until I awoke to find my door being hammered upon.

'There's a bloke downstairs,' said the innkeeper's son, blearily.

It was Letice, dressed like a man in traveller's clothes, face all but hidden by the heavy serge of her riding hood. She did not look as if she had slept at all. 'I am coming with you,' she said at once, before I could open my mouth.

'No, you are not!' I told her. 'How did you find me, for God's sake?'

'Silver,' she said, as if to a child. 'How d'you think? Right. When are we off?'

'I'm off when the sun rises,' I said. 'You'll be safely back in Two Dogs Court by then.'

'No, I won't. Where's your room? I'll explain while you get dressed.'

The innkeeper's boy and a couple of other shock-haired servants were ogling us, and so as not to argue in public I clenched my teeth and ushered her upstairs. She dropped down on to my bed with a groan.

'Don't mind me,' she said. 'Go on: get dressed.'

'No. I have a long day's ride, and I haven't had anything that you might call rest. Go home, Letice. I am sorry that I came looking for you, and I did not mean to cause you any upset. Can we . . . can you please accept my apologies, and leave me be?'

'Ah. Not so simple. When you throw stones into a pond, you must expect to have things stirred up, yes? Don't worry, though. I'm not here because of you. I need to leave London, and you've given me a good excuse.'

'Excuse? I don't think so!'

'But yes. You turned up at my storehouse yesterday, causing a fuss. No doubt the court will be all a-murmuring about you and the Lady Agnes tomorrow – today, beg pardon – thanks to old John Jabberchops. I've been called away on an urgent matter of business to, ahh . . . Plymouth. One of my ships and the customs men. Absolutely perfect.'

'Why?' I said, too tired to argue, groping for my clothes and wondering, vaguely, if I were still dreaming. Maybe Letice would start shooting at me next.

'The king's customs men are about to find some, oh, irregularities in the duties I have paid over the past year.'

'They'll fine you. Pay them, Letice, they'll go away.'

'No they won't. It's this bloody war, you see. Henry is having trouble raising money for it. The barons don't want to pay, and why should they? So he is taxing like a madman, and he has sent his tax collectors and customs men out to chisel everything that may be chiselled.'

'Like I said, pay them.'

'Do you remember I told you about my other business?'

'Timber and iron? That is not the king's concern.'

'No, but it is the Church's. They have been sticking their fingers in too often of late. Henry is a terrible God-botherer, you know. It takes him a day to get from Westminster to the Tower because he has to stop and pray at every bloody shrine along the way. The bishop of London has decided to turn all of us who trade with the Saracens – there's more than me in London doing it – over to the Crown, so that Henry can confiscate everything we own and fund his bloody fight with cousin Louis.'

'Well, what does the Church get out of it?' I asked, hopping about as I drew on a stiff boot.

'A lot. Henry is going to rebuild Westminster Abbey. Did you know that? His mother has been pushing him to do it, as she pushes him to do everything *she* wants. I thought that was why you were here, at first: to find Henry something miraculous for the high altar.'

'But why come with me? Get your silver and take a ship over to Bruges or Ghent. It will blow over soon enough. Henry never stays on the same course for very long anyway, or so I hear.'

'Richard.' She put her hands behind her head and fell back onto the pillow, and her yellow braids fell out of their prison. 'Richard is the steady hand in the kingdom. And he is interested in trade and most particularly in finance.' She sniffed, and kicked her legs out on the pallet. She was exhausted, I saw, but all stirred up inside. I knew this mood well, and it would have to play itself out.

'How, though, could he help you?' I asked, finally, when I could bear her impatience no longer.

'Aha. I thought you would never ask. It's time I told you about my husband.'

80

'Don't mock me, Letice,' I said, stiffening. 'It was you who left me in Venice, and I have not forgotten that.'

'Not you, Patch. My real husband. The one who died at sea.'

'De Wharram? He's a fiction, Letice. You made him up.'

'Now there's the thing of it. I didn't.'

Chapter Eight

'Godwyn de Wharram was a rich young knight who went to seek his fortune in the Holy Land about nine years ago. He was probably twenty or so years old. He arrived in Jaffa and soon decided that he preferred trade to fighting. So he found himself a partner and bought an interest – a large interest – in a spice ship bound for London. His partner was Nicholas Querini, of course. Now, unlike in my version of things, Godwyn did make it to Venice alive – I met him, actually. Don't look at me like that, Patch. Yes, I *met* him in that way. Nicholas lent me to him for a night. That was before they fell out, though. About a week later he had Facio knife him and bury him out in the Lagoon. Now during our tryst, as I will call it, I found out all about him, for he was a talker and not much of anything else. He had no parents and no brothers or sisters. He had a nice fortune – all tied up with Nicholas by then, as you might imagine – and an estate in Northamptonshire. His father, though, had held a fief for Richard, brother of the king, and he was Richard's vassal too – very proud of it. He had some deeds with him, and Richard had given him some letters of introduction. Anyway, he died, and I forgot about him, until I decided to come back to London. Nicholas had kept all his papers – he kept records of everything he did, because he liked to gloat over them, and that's how I learned to read, by the way, poring over Nicholas' records.

'So I resurrected Godwyn. When I . . . after I had made up my mind, I had Mother Zaneta get the papers for me. There was a palace clerk, an important one, who spent half his life in the *Bisato Beccato*. All the Querini stuff had been confiscated by the state, and this little man knew where it was, and for an extra bit of tongue, or some free Greek-style, he filched it. So I arrived in London as official as could be. And as far as Earl Richard knows, I am his vassal's widow, and he can never prove it otherwise.'

We were riding past Turneham. It was just past nine, and the rain was coming down as a thin mizzle. But it was sweet on the eye and the ear, as only a May morning in England can be, and when we had left the village piggeries behind, our noses could take delight as well.

I had given in to Letice after the bells of Saint Paul's had rung the fourth hour of the day. I could not find within me the resolve to send her away, and besides that I was still feeling guilty and foolish for having left her in so ungentlemanly a fashion the day before. It would be pleasant to have some company on the long ride, and I could leave her, with a clear conscience, with Earl Richard when we found him.

'So you will put yourself under his protection?'

'Why not? He is the coming man in England, you know. And besides, I am sure I can interest him in a few things I have going on.'

'So you have met him before, then.'

'Actually I haven't. He only got back from his Crusade in February, and there was all that fuss with the barons dissolving Parliament . . . And besides, I didn't need him. I have been keeping that particular card in reserve.'

'Incredible. So you feel perfectly all right about passing yourself off as this Godwyn's wife?'

'Patch, love, I can tell him things about that poor man that he could not possibly know, and they'd be true and all.'

'From one night in Venice.'

'He was about the place longer than that. And I told you: he was a talker, and I'm a listener.'

'Meanwhile, you have fled London in the dead of night with a strange foreigner. That is going to look interesting.'

'Not a stranger, dear one.' Letice looked at me and pouted fetchingly. There was a mist-drip on the end of her nose. 'After you left me so hurriedly—' she put a charming accent on the word, and I groaned silently. 'I went around to my various places of work – and told everyone that my gentleman cousin was returned from Outremer and was squiring me down to his country estates for a month, with the idea of marrying me off. You can imagine how happy everyone was.'

'Glad to be rid of you?' I meant to annoy, but failed.

'Absolutely. A rich and competent woman is no one's friend. They all hope that I will find some overbearing man who will take over my business or put an end to it, thus sparing them the shame of having to compete with me on losing terms. I cannot wait to see their faces when I return with the Earl of Cornwall in my purse.'

'I'm not sure how I feel about being your cousin. Though I suppose I should be grateful that you've made me a gentleman.'

'As well you should, Patch; as well you should.'

It took us five days to reach Dorchester along muddy roads that the rain had turned for long stretches into sluggish brown streams. The wild wood pressed about the feeble excuse for a track, and we kept our hands close to our hilts, though we had no sniff of trouble. Letice seemed in all respects a man, her hair tucked up out of sight, her clothing dark and purposeful. I knew she could fight, but my anxiety simmered nevertheless. I had not intended to be anyone's protector, no matter that the person in question did not believe she needed one. The inns were crowded and all seemed to have the same smell of mildew and rotting thatch. There seemed to be a couple of other riders headed south and west, for three times we saw the same faces at dinner. By the third night Letice began to worry.

'Those two men are following us,' she said. I looked over to where they were sitting closer to the fire.

'What makes you think so?'

'Don't know. Something about them. Don't they have a tax-collector look about them? I think King Henry has sent them to spy on me.'

'You're giving yourself airs, my dear,' I told her, and to prove my point I raised my beer mug and nodded in the men's direction. They gave me a smile of recognition, the old travellers' appreciation of shared coincidence.

'Don't worry, Letice,' I told her. 'Tax-collectors do not spy, they collect. Have you felt any fingers in your purse? No. And I don't think those two are spies, really, do you?' She was not mollified, but I thought no more about it, especially as we seemed to have taken different roads after that, for we did not see their faces again.

For propriety's sake Letice and I had to take separate rooms and twice I found myself sharing a bed with three other men who filled the chamber with beery farts. The beer, it must be said, was good, and as I had missed the taste of it for many long years I perhaps had more than my share. Every night, Letice watched me primly over the scrubbed and stained tables, her face unreadable. I returned her gaze from the snug warmth of a bellyful of ale. She was, alas, the same woman I had ached to marry. I had hoped to find her changed, but she was not, and all the feelings I had packed down at the very bottom of my heart began to stir. I could not help the warmth that stole into my eyes and my words, though I felt nothing from her by way of an answer. She was not cold to me, not at all; and nor was she unduly warm. I did not know my cousins well as a child and had forgotten even what they looked like long before I ever went aboard the *Cormaran*, but there was something unmistakeably cousin-ish about Letice – not quite sisterly, thank Christ, but not quite anything else. But I knew very well – and that knowledge pained me – that I could do nothing. Our time as lovers was past. Letice did not want me in her bed, and I no longer disliked her enough to make a nuisance of myself. Far from it, for to my relief I was discovering that I enjoyed Letice's friendship for its own sake. And so every night I drank my beer and we kept each other company until it was time to go to our separate beds.

By daylight we bowled along merrily. After Sherborne the weather improved, strangely enough, and so we passed through the sweet round-topped hills of Somerset in the green glory of late spring. The dog roses were in bloom, and fat bullfinches rollicked among the whitethorn buds. We picked up the Fosse Way west of Yeovil, and on the hard-packed road we began to make better time, daring to trot or even canter from time to time without fear that our horses would break an ankle or vanish into some bottomless, muddy sink-hole. Somewhere up on the Black-down hills, the breeze coming strong and salty from the west, we passed over into Devon. A night at Honiton, then across the marshy levels of the Otter River to Exeter. One night in that city's finest inn, where we dined on Exmoor roebuck and plump thrushes, and then on into the west. We climbed the steep slope of the Exe valley and there in the distance was the brown back of Dartmoor, the crag of Haytor stark and grey in the sun.

Suddenly, everything seemed familiar, although I had never been hereabouts so far as I could recall. The brambles were lush and bristling with red spines. Ferns and harts-tongue spilled from the hedgerows like green flames. Moss grew thick on tree and stone, and buzzards wheeled, screeling above the oaks. I could find my way now, but I had not decided what that should be. To reach Lydford it might have been more sensible to skirt the northern brows of the moor and drop down past Okehampton, but I had felt my heart clamouring ever more insistently since we had left Exeter, and I let myself be led past the southern slopes of Haytor towards Ashburton. Letice was deferring to me and I had not let her know why I had chosen this particular route. I told myself that we would take the monks' track from Buckfast and over the moor to Tavistock, being a way that I knew and so, of course, safer than the northern one. It made good sense, except that we would ride past the gates of Buckfast Abbey, and that would be the sheerest folly.

But perhaps not. Time passes, and the mind of man cannot hold anything for very long. The Gurt Dog must have been the talk of the whole valley when the blood was still wet in Balecester, but perhaps he had been forgotten. Maybe some new ogre had supplanted me in songs and the threats of wet-nurses. I was starting to feel completely free for the first time in years, and it was filling me with strange thoughts and feelings. It was as if I had been carrying two souls within my flesh since I had fled from Hugh de Kervezey: that of the man I had become, Petrus Zennorius or whatever title of convenience fit my errand or scheme; and poor Petroc of Auneford, who had disgraced his abbey and disappeared into some appalling reckoning with the demons who had corrupted him. It was Petroc who was coming alive again, like apple juice turning to cider, a great golden head of foamy joy rising up inside me. And if I passed through Buckfast unrecognised, I would be as free as any man.

We slept a night in Ashburton, full of sullen miners drunk in the street, and left before sunup, passing beneath where the stannery gibbets were serving up the bodies of dishonest tinners for the ravens, and in an hour the tower of Buckfast Abbey came into sight. I was shaking as we splashed through the ale-brown waters of the Dart and started up the track on the left bank. Some brothers were walking towards us in a loose group, spades and rakes in hand, on their way to the fishponds, no doubt. I searched their faces as we passed. How familiar, all of them: monks' visages, smoothed by their interior certainties as rocks are polished by a river. Healthy and well-fed, and off to do a few hours' easy work on a sunny day. Then with a shock, I saw that one of them was more than familiar. It was Stephen of Cornwood. We had been novices together. We had sat side by side in the refectory for years, cleaned out the pigeon coops, fed the pigs. Taking a deep breath I stared him straight in the eyes. He smiled, a little startled perhaps, and mistaking my intent he gave me a quick blessing, a murmured *pax vobiscum*, and carried on, the strangers on horseback forgotten already. I was a stranger. I was a free man again.

We rode on, past the high gates of the abbey. They were open, and I slowed and looked inside. Nothing had changed, as I had known it would not. There were the stables. There was the old cart I had hidden under, all those years ago, nothing more now than a heap of nettles and briars. There was the pigsty, and the edge of the garden where I had spoken to Adso the librarian. Letice rode up alongside and gave me a quizzical look, so I shrugged and set heel to horse, and up the track we went.

I knew that, if we were early enough upon our way, we could cross the moor and reach Tavistock long before nightfall, and put up in the abbey hostelry there. So we followed the trackway across the river Mardle, past Button and Bowerdon and Bowden until we had passed the last field and our horses had stepped out onto Dartmoor. The sound of their hooves changed in an instant: where before they had clattered on the stony bed of the track, now they were muffled and hollow, as if the moor were a giant drum, or the vast, distended belly of a sleeping giant: Gog, or Magog. The hedgerows had been loud with songbirds, but now silence came down on us: only the whistle of the breeze through last year's sedge, and the faraway call of a lark, disturbed the hush. Letice reached over and caught my bridle.

'We're not really going in to this place, are we?' she asked, plaintively. Her voice sounded little and faint, dwarfed by the great sweep of the hillside above us.

'My lady, you are safer here with me than any London soul who leaves his house on a morning to buy a dozen eggs. This was my garden when I was a boy.'

'It is a desert. It is dead.'

'Nonsense. It is Dean Moor,' I said, and whistled my horse into a trot. With a pleading look, Letice set off after me.

It was as if I were riding through my own dreams. Here were the hills I saw when I closed my eyes at night. The tumbled grey rocks with their orange blazes of lichen, the mossy, grassy, sheep-dung tang of the air, the hunched, wind-crippled blackthorn trees – all this I knew as well as the lines on the palm of my hand. The swelling joy returned ten-fold, until I thought it would burst my skull apart like a flower bud. We crossed the Aune, just a brook here, so close to its source, on the granite slabs of the tinners' bridge. This was the river I had swum in as a boy, where I had tickled the quick, leopard-flanked trout from under rocks. This was the river that ran past my home. I looked downstream to where the valley lost itself in the piled domes of White Barrow and Gripper's Hill and Dockwell Ridge. Beyond, under Black Tor, where the river ran over golden sheets of granite and dived down ravines whose sides were the knotted roots of oaks that were old when Brutus came to Totnes-town, was my parents' house. And further, the little village of Auneford, and the church where they lay. The hills shut all of it off from me, a curtain wall half as high as the sky, and I found myself glad of that. So I did not linger there, but let a prayer fall into the stream and rode on.

The track we followed had been made by the monks of Buckfast and Tavistock and Buckland as a safe way across the moors a long time ago. My father ran his sheep up here, and many times I had sat upon a rock, watching the flock idle around me, and observed the folk coming and going upon the pathway. I saw an abbot once, and a knight and his lady.

But mostly I saw tinners and pack-trains of tin on their way to Ashburton or Lydford, and most often I saw no one at all. Today we were alone, and as we came up onto the High Moor I sensed that Letice was as uncomfortable as I was at home. The middle of Dartmoor is a vast, wet plain that gives birth to many rivers: the Dart, the Aune, the Erme, and a score more of them. It is an odd place where the shadows of the clouds moving overhead can sometimes be the only thing that tells the traveller he has not stepped over the threshold of some place where time has no power. But time does pass upon the High Moor, and if night catches you there unawares, you will find it quite as sinister as you could ever imagine.

'There,' I said to Letice, pointing to the south. 'That's the sea.'

Beyond the hazy billow of the South Hams a crescent of pure blue gleamed. There was something she would recognise, I knew, and indeed she took a deep breath and loosened her shoulders.

'Is it far?' she asked.

'Lydford? Yes, it's far. We will be there as the sun is setting. If you don't fall into a quagmire, that is.'

'What the fuck is a quagmire?'

'Keep to the path and you won't find out.'

Ahead of us, smoke rose from a dozen blowing houses as tinners smelted the ore they had streamed from the bed of the Erme. We rode past, and a couple of tinners knee-deep in the stream straightened up and waved. Then we struck out across the wastes of Great Gnat's Head to Nun's Cross. I pointed out the dun plateau of Fox Tor Mire to our right.

'That is a quagmire,' I said. 'If we strayed in there, we would never come out again.'

'Your affection for this place is . . .' Letice shook her head. 'I have heard you rattle on about your precious moors a thousand times. I expected the Hanging Gardens of bloody Babylon, not this vile desolation.' She wrinkled her nose, for we were passing the melting corpse of a pack-horse, and the bones of sheep and ponies that the winter had killed were scattered far and wide.

I tried to change her mind all the way across Hessary Tor, showing her the beauty of the little brooks as they hurried, all green and golden, across their beds of pillowy stones. The larks, how they sang as they rose up around us! The blossom of the rowan trees, the call of the ouzel birds. The great stretch of the sky overhead, the freedom all about us, as if we were little ships passing across an inland sea. Look, there: the fields and woods of Cornwall, and the cuckoos calling. But my words made no impression on her, and at last I gave up. Letice was a child of the city, and the wildness of the moors must have been quite terrifying for her. I tried to sympathise, but found I could not, so I decided to keep all the moor's wonders for myself.

Leaving the monks' path behind us we turned north, stopped for luncheon on Hessary Tor, and then set out again. We had made good time, and we would be at Earl Richard's gate well before sundown. Great Mis Tor rose to our left as I led us north down one brook and up another, until we came to a well-worn track that cut across our path. I allowed myself a small sigh of relief, for what I had not told Letice was that I had never been north of Nun's Cross, and for the last couple of hours had been steering us by hearsay and by the faintly remembered words of old moorsmen I had known as a boy. In any case, by luck or by judgement we had found the Lychway, and it would take us to Lydford.

This Lychway is the road by which any man, woman or child who dies in one of the moorland farmhouses is carried to their rest, for the whole moor lies in the parish of Lydford, and the Church will not allow any moor-dweller to be buried in any other churchyard. I did not think that this information would have a happy effect on Letice, so I kept quiet about it. It was a good track, though: much scored by cart-wheels but straight and level. We were riding along easily, and as our faces were now towards the green lands and away from the emptiness of the High Moor, Letice suddenly grew much more cheerful. When a pair of riders appeared in the distance, she brightened even more.

'Look, Patch,' she called, 'Horsemen! So we cannot be too far . . .'

'From polite company? I told you we were not,' I said, a little grumpily. We rode on, and through the heat-shimmer the two horsemen became three.

'Who are these folk?' I was talking to myself.

'Not your sheep-shaggers and tin-grubbers, at any rate,' said Letice, sounding almost cheerful. 'We must be getting close to the earl.'

As we drew closer, Letice was proved right. The three were plainly gentlemen, or knights, rather, for even from a distance I could see that they wore emblazoned surcoats, and swords knocked against their legs. Their faces had just formed out of the haze when they reined in and spread themselves across the path. They did not look like cut-purses, so I led us on. The three leaned together for a moment, and pulled out their swords. With an oath I tugged on my reins and grabbed the bridle of Letice's horse.

'Christ's blood!' I yelled. 'Turn! Turn!'

But it was too late. Letice was a competent rider but her horse was a stolid beast who merely grew confused at our tuggings and shouts. He set his feet and bared his teeth. Letice was pulling at her sword, her hand tangled in her sleeve. Letting go of the bridle I drew my own sword and kicked hard at my mount. She was a livelier animal than her companion, and did what my hands and heels commanded, plunging forward with a clatter of stones. Too late: the three men were upon us. Remembering something my riding instructor, my dead friend Horst the German, had taught me, I pulled back and up on the reins with all my strength. The horse stopped with a shriek and reared just as the first horseman came up. I threw myself sideways, hauling on the reins, and my horse, tottering on her hind legs, fell sideways against the other's mount, knocking it off balance. Thank Christ, my horse found her feet, and the other, deflected, hurtled off to the side, her rider screaming commands in vain.

I kicked my beast into motion again just as the other two men reached me, wheeling her across the path. One horse baulked, seeing the stamping hooves of mine, but the other kept on. The man had mistimed his sword-stroke, I saw, and I easily leant back out of its arc, heaving my own blade over my left shoulder for a back-handed cut. My arm was already straightening, sinews thrumming, when the man's face came into focus. His eyes were wide with amazement or horror, mouth open. But all at once I saw that his hair was fine and there was hardly a beard on his chin, and his pink cheeks were marred by pimples. With a desperate yell I turned my wrist at the last second so that the flat of my sword caught him across the right ear. He dropped to the path with a ripe thud as I followed through with my stroke. With another shout I halted the steel point a hand's breadth from the other man's throat. He had let his sword arm drop as he tried to control his horse, and now he found he could not raise it, for it was a long-sword, and a touch too heavy for him, for like his companion he was little more than a boy.

'Yield!' I screamed. Then, mastering my voice as well as I could: 'I am bearing urgent letters for the Earl of Cornwall, and this lady is a Crusader's widow under the earl's protection!'

The third rider had stopped his horse a hundred paces off into the heather and was cantering back to his friends' aid. He must have heard my words, for he slowed and walked up alongside. To my shock he was laughing.

'Lady?' he cried. 'Have we frightened a lady, my lads?'

'Shut up, Gervais,' hissed the boy at the point of my sword. He still held his own blade, and I told him to put it away. He did, and after a hard look at Gervais, I turned my attention to the lad on the ground, who was crawling gingerly away from the skittish hooves that surrounded him. He did not look badly hurt, although his nose was bloody and dripping.

'What is the meaning of this?' I asked in my court voice.

'Your pardon, sir,' said Gervais, the only one of this sorry trio to have a working tongue in his head. 'We came up to pass the time, and to look for robbers. 'Tis said the moor is infested with them.'

'No such thing,' I said, offended by this more, almost, than by what had just happened. 'The tinners prevent any such nonsense. Who are you? You are not from these parts.'

'We do beg your most earnest pardon, sir. I am Gervais Bolam, this is Edmund of Wykham, and my friend in the dust is William Maynet. We are knights in the service of our lord Richard, Earl of Cornwall and staying, at the moment, in Lydford Castle. Which does get rather dull,' he added, as if this were excuse enough.

'Dull?' Letice had finally found her voice. 'You young rogues,' she shrilled, and the icy rage of Lady Agnes drove the roses from Gervais' cheeks.

'This is Lady Agnes de Wharram, young sirs. Widow of a brave crusading knight. Should she be used thus? For shame – and you are knights at that!' I raged, but everything was becoming clear. Three bored knights waiting for a battle that kept being postponed, cooped up far from home. They had been out looking for sport, and found us.

William Maynet had struggled to his feet and was rubbing his arse, wincing. 'We are most awfully sorry, sir,' he said, as if I had caught him pulling carrots from my garden. 'We had been hearing tales of a foul villain who haunts these moors, and we fancied . . . our fancies ran away with us, sir. Unless you are the Gurt Dog, that is?' He was jesting. But I flinched for a moment. No, this child could not know what he was speaking of.

'You have been listening to ghost stories,' I said, wearily. 'The Gurt Dog is the Devil's hound, who chases lost souls across the moor. A huge black dog with flaming eyes. If you see him you will likely be dead by morning. I can assure you that we are not hounds, and further, I would counsel you not to meddle in the affairs of the Devil. But the folk in these parts say that the Wisht Hound, as they call him, hunts away over there by Whistman's Wood.' I turned and pointed to the south-west. 'Why don't you try your luck. I will escort this lady to your lord, and be assured I will tell him all about you.'

'We are heartily sorry, sir,' piped up Edmund. 'But, Christ's guts, you made a good account of yourself! Please let us escort you back to

Lydford. It will be dark soon, and we would dearly like to make amends. Wouldn't we, lads?'

They would, and indeed they were all so young and so cheerful that, despite that they would quite happily have killed us both for a prank, I found myself softening a little. Letice's mouth was a white line, but I could tell that rage was changing to exasperation in her eyes, so I nodded, coldly. The boys fell in around us, William looking a bit stiff in his saddle and Edmund somewhat hangdog – but by no means as penitent as I would have wished.

'So, you are bound for the war in Poitou?' I asked him. 'If you plan to face the knights of France, you would do well to practice your skills. I am no horseman, and no swordsman either, and yet . . .'

'Nonsense, sir! You are indeed. By the by, we were out for sport,' said Gervais. 'Had we been in the lists or on the field, it might have gone ill for you. And Our Lord is to be thanked it did not,' he added, hastily. But I understood. These boys had played at war since they could crawl, and fighting was their work, their love and their sport. They would have killed us for fun and thought no more about it. It was the Frankish way. I had seen their fellows swagger through a thousand towns, lording it over the Greeks in Constantinople, kicking beggars on the docks at Jaffa. These three lads had the whole world spread out before them. They were the cream of England. And God help us.

It was not unpleasant, to tell the truth. The boys chattered amongst themselves and made the politest of conversation with me. Letice they gawped at as if she were some image of the Virgin carved out of ivory, but no doubt their brain-boxes were seething with the confused, energetic and fleshy desires of the young and spotty. Lydford was further than I had thought, and the shadows were very long on the ground as we began the climb down into the gorge of the River Lyd. By the time we had crossed the granite bridge, coaxed our tired horses up the far slope and passed through the village to the gates of the castle, the sun had dropped below Bodmin Moor and the castle seemed, for a moment, to be nothing more than a great cloud, like those that boil up over the land in the failing days of August. Then the light changed, and we had arrived.

Chapter Nine

Lydford Castle is a dour, four-square bastion of cut stone staring down the challenge of the ancient stones of the moor. It is man's attempt to take all the wildness, all the ugly, terrible splendour of those hills and squeeze it into a form his feeble mind can understand. It is a fortress and more particularly a gaol feared by the tinners and moorsmen, for the moor has its own laws and those that break them do not find mercy. We had seen the hanged corpses at Ashburton, but that was nothing to what a man might see at Lydford on hanging day. There was no welcome for us from its gateway. Our companions hailed the men at arms who guarded the door, we all dismounted and went in.

The castle was no friendlier inside. Some attempt had been made to pretty the walls with hangings, but there is little one can do to cheer up a prison. The earl's steward, a Londoner in court dress who looked as out of place inside the castle as he would have done in a tinner's hut, met us with evident relief, for plainly he was suffering from the same malady that had afflicted Letice as we crossed the hills. He heard my story with polite interest, and bowed his head respectfully as Letice told hers. A bed would be arranged for each of us, of course – dry, warm, a rarity in this barbarous place! – and hot food sent. The earl would see us in the morning, but first we should rest ourselves. I was crestfallen, for I wanted to get my business done right away. As we had journeyed that day I had decided to award myself a few days to roam the moors on my own before I took ship for France, and I was suddenly very keen to start. If we were to be caught up in protocol, we might be here for a while. A prison, indeed. My shoulders drooped.

'Albin, who are these people?' It was a very clear voice that rang like a bell of the finest bronze, not loud, but like the insistent pulse of a bell's chiming the words filled the room. There is no mistaking the voice of royalty once you have heard it, and I dropped onto one knee at once and pressed my hand to my heart. From moorsman back to courtier at the snap of a finger – dear God, my training had prepared me for moments such as these, but my head was swimming. Albin was explaining matters, and then the voice bid us rise, and I took my first look at Richard of Cornwall.

He was quite tall, and very fair. His hair was long and curled in the fashion of the day, but his beard was fuller than most courtly men preferred, and golden. He wore a tunic of dark blue velvet on which golden leopards twined through crimson vines. His eyes were blue and his lips were red and finely curved, like a woman's. But there was nothing else effete about this man. He stood like a soldier, feet apart, fists on hips, ready.

'You have come all the way from Venice to see me,' he said, as if this were the most natural thing in the world: be sought out in one's prison-castle at the edge of nowhere by emissaries from the other end of Christendom. And of course for such as the Earl of Cornwall it was nothing, a commonplace.

'I have words for you alone, my lord, from a man you know well,' I told him. 'Jean de Sol, of the company of the *Cormaran*, sends humble greetings.'

'How very nice!' Richard chimed. 'Would you care to deliver them now, and then we can dine together? I think that would be the best idea, don't you? And this dear lady is the widow of young de Wharram, so Albin tells me. I was not aware that he had died, but at least, madam, you may take comfort in the knowledge that his soul rests in Paradise. He was *returning* from the Holy Land, was he not?'

'He was, my lord,' said Letice, or rather Agnes de Wharram, for Agnes had reappeared, a little hoarse from having been silent since she had left London.

'Exactly. A Crusader – and a crusader's widow. You are fortunate, madam – not in your loss, but in your family's gain. We will talk at dinner, if that suits you.'

Of course it did, and Letice followed a maid-in-waiting off to her quarters. Richard gave some curt instructions to Albin, and beckoned to me.

'We won't stand on ceremony, if you don't mind, Messer Petrus. This place is a bloody gaol, and I would much rather have jollier surroundings in which to receive guests.'

'The moor is a barbarous place, my lord,' I agreed, tactfully.

'Oh, dear me, no!' said Richard. 'Dartmoor is a wondrous place. I would ride across her from dawn till dusk if I had no cares to attend to. I would rather be in this manor of mine than in the finest palace in

London. I do not care for *this* place, mind, but Devon has other lodgings.'

'I am surprised that you find the moor pleasant,' I said, following him down a short, narrow corridor with walls that breathed cold moisture. 'In my own experience, most find it terrifying.'

'And you, Messer Petrus?' Richard turned before a doorway. His eyes, blue even in the dimness of the corridor, fixed themselves upon mine.

'I must confess that I feel as you do, my lord,' I said. I had been asked for the truth, and for once there was no need to be sparing with it. 'I . . . I was raised in Cornwall – Zennor is a day's ride from here, at the mouth of the Fal – but my father bought tin at Plympton, and he would take me up to the workings at Plym Head, and so . . .'

'You know the moor, then?'

'The southern part. We had a wet-nurse from Buckfastleigh and I would visit her when my father went abroad on business. I have roamed most of it, I daresay, from Hexworthy farm across to Tavistock. I live very far from these hills now, my lord, but I carry them with me wherever I am.'

The earl paused, and regarded me from under his golden eyebrows. Then he turned and opened the door, and I followed him inside. When we were seated on a pair of uncomfortable stools, more suitable for milkmaids – or prisoners, I thought to myself – the earl held out his hand and I passed him the letter from Captain De Montalhac. He read intently and, I noticed, quickly, unusual in my experience for a noble-man. When he looked up, his face was expressionless.

'Do you know what is written here?'

'In substance, yes, my lord.' I took the letters of credit from my satchel. 'I believe these are relevant.'

Earl Richard studied them carefully.

'How does one know that things like this are genuine?' he asked, casually.

'You may take them to Messer Milot Presson of Saint Nicholas Lane in London and exchange ink for gold that very hour,' I said. Earl Richard knew full well what letters of credit were. I had found out enough about him during my long hours at Westminster to know that he was a modern man in this as well as other ways. He dealt with banks and credit often. So I added: 'Messer Milot speaks well of your own financier – Wymer of Berwick, I believe?'

'Indeed, Messer Petrus.' He seemed to relax, minutely. At least one part of a tedious game did not need playing further. 'Well, I am amazed. Your master . . .'

95

'Your pardon, my lord, but I am a partner in the company,' I put in, politely.

'Well then. Your *colleague* does not specify, exactly, whom this largesse is from. Should one know?'

I held his stare, which was polite but had me feeling like a plump snail being eyed by a hungry thrush. What, I was asking myself frenziedly, had the Captain put in that letter? Some cryptic riddle about faith? Dear God, not that! I made a point of adjusting my satchel. What could I say?

'My lord,' I found myself saying, 'You will have been upon the moor when the wind blows up from the south? It brings the taste of the sea, and sultry heat, and sometimes strange birds and butterflies are borne upon it. This comes as those wonders do: from the warm lands of the south, made warmer at this moment by injustice.'

'From Hughues de Lusignan?' said the earl in disbelief. 'Is my father-in-law throwing money to the four winds now?' I shook my head, about to launch into another desperate bit of wind-imagery, but the earl cut me off. 'Toulouse. The wily old Count Raymond.'

I steepled my fingers. 'Not specifically. But Toulouse has gathered a great legion of . . . of well-wishers to his cause, as you know: your royal brother, for one. But from Aragon to Sicily and Swabia come support. Toulouse, in turn, supports Lusignan and indeed your own claim to Poitou.'

'Wait a minute, my good sir. This letter . . . You have been an ad-mirable messenger and have not spied. As your reward, you may read it now.' With a look I could not fathom he handed it to me poised between two fingers. I opened it. There was the Captain's writing, a lot of it. I read carefully. Much was diplomatic jargon and aristocratic nicety, but at last I came to the passage that had made Earl Richard raise his eyebrows. It was not written by the Captain, but was a codicil attached to the original letter and stamped with an impressive seal:

Further, in return for your bringing the strength of England to our aid, on the successful conclusion of said expedition we solemnly vow to relinquish all and every claim, design, transaction, and promise relating to the Lady Sanchia of Provence, daughter of His Lordship Ramon Berenguer, styled Count of Provence, to whom we are at this time betrothed, and furthermore will place no impediment or argument against any match you conclude with the said Lady Sanchia.

There were more rambling promises of loyalty and mutual aid, and the letter ended with the signature of Raymond de Saint-Gilles, Count of Toulouse, Duke of Narbonne, Marquis of Provence.

'My lord, I must reveal my ignorance. The Lady Sanchia of Provence – she is the sister of your brother the king's wife, is she not?'

'She is,' said Richard, looking almost sheepish. Something had come over him, a flutter of nervous energy which I had not noticed before. 'The most lovely woman in the wide world.'

The earl drew in his breath. I found myself clutching the letter against my chest. He was staring hard into my eyes, and it took all my will not to look away, though I was so dumbstruck I was sure it must be clearly written on my face. Then he let out a great laugh, slapped his knees and stood up.

'Good Christ, the face of honesty! I hardly recognised it! Now then. I have been tardy – is that it? Poor old Hughues is champing at the bit, and no doubt my dear mother is digging her spurs into his rump. Never fear, then, my dear Messer Petrus from the *Cormaran*. I take it this gift—' and he tapped the letters of credit '—is intended to cover certain expenses, such as one might incur in launching an expedition across the Channel? Christ. Well, I have waited as long as I could. If my brother, my mother and her husband, and all the lords of your balmy south wish me to go to war, I shall.'

During supper the earl paid far more attention to Letice than to me, and I was grateful, for it let me sink into a pleasant reverie that had been lapping at me since we had left Ashburton. Why, I had begun to ask myself, should I go back to Venice at all? The Captain and Gilles seemed to have left the company, if I understood the Captain's letter. Was I really going to sit in Florence or Venice, running a bank, of all things? I had come to know the trade in holy relics as well as any living man, but our new venture held no real interest for me and I had been happy to avoid it as much as I could. What was to stop me, then, from taking my share as a partner and . . . I could hardly articulate the thought, even inside my own skull. There were plenty of manor houses hereabouts. Cornwood, or Lustleigh, or Ugborough – I could buy myself a handsome estate, some tinning interests, and settle down as some mysterious gentleman from Outremer. By Bartholomew's hide, I could purchase a knighthood, nay, make myself a baron, and still die a wealthy man. I began to dream of my house: a grange, with a gatehouse and a view down some valley to the south. Fields for my corn and my beef. Sheep, of course. And a green lawn where my children would play.

Children? The dream grew hazy. I frowned, and found myself gazing at Letice, deep in conversation with Earl Richard, all Lady Agnes and none of the woman I had known in our other life together. Where had these ghost-children of mine sprung from, then? There is nothing so vexing as a daydream over which one loses control. I tried to sweep the skipping children from my lawn – replace them with sheep, with yew trees, anything at all – but they would not go, and . . .

'Messer Petrus, are you tired after your ride today?' It was Albin the steward, filling my goblet solicitously. 'I think you were nodding. My lord has invited you to join his retinue for the expedition to Poitou.'

The grange vanished. Earl Richard was smiling at me, and tapping his fingers lightly upon the table. I understood very clearly what had happened. I, who had been on the watch for snares these many years, had walked into a trap as plain as the side of a barn. Here I was, in a prison-castle, with a bored prince. It had not quite sunk in earlier that Letice and I were the only guests at the earl's table, but now it did. We had become Richard's amusements, his trifles. And if I refused his offer, which was of course an enormous compliment, I would cause dangerous offence and even jeopardise the Captain's plan. Chilly sweat rolled down between my shoulder blades.

'My lord is far too kind,' I croaked. 'I would be honoured to accept, and I pray that I may be of some small use, although I am not skilled at war.'

'Nonsense!' said the earl. 'That is not what I have heard from my intemperate young friends over there.' He pointed with a lamb-leg to where the three knights lolled, blind drunk in the glow of the fire. 'Tell me, how did a soldier come to find employment with the worthy Jean de Sol?'

So I trotted out the tale of Petrus Zennorius, how the young merchant's son from Cornwall had been sent for his studies to Oxford, had joined the household of a Flemish bishop and followed him to Outremer, where he had died, leaving Petrus to fend for himself. He had learned to fight in the meanwhile, for as the late bishop had said, 'one may serve God with the sword as well as the pen.' Petrus had met the Captain seven years ago while serving as a mercenary in Athens, and had joined the crew of the *Cormaran*. An adventuresome tale, more wholesome than my own, but it had served me well. Now, at last, it had landed me in the shit.

'We will arm you, sir, and you will ride against the French and bring honour to Cornwall,' the earl told me.

'On condition that I might represent Dartmoor,' I conceded, weakly. It was done. I was, more than likely, doomed.

Albin had hit the mark: I was exhausted, in both body and spirit, for being in Devon at last had drained me, and I dearly wished to lay down my head, even in this drafty prison, and sleep until noon. But Earl Richard was not so inclined.

'You must be aware, sir, that I know Monsieur de Sol tolerably well,' he said. I agreed that I was. 'I understand that the *Cormaran* now interests itself in the world of finance,' he went on, 'and that is something I understand: it is the future of the world, alas: directing invisible rivers of silver and gold with the wave of a quill. But de Sol knows me from his original business.'

'My lord is a collector,' I said, at last finding my professional feet. And so ensued a long conversation about relics: those he had, those he desired. The whereabouts of this, the veracity of that. Richard was, as the Captain had said, a man of exquisite taste. He also had a mind as keen as any that sat on the Council of Venice or wore a cardinal's hat, and I found myself enjoying our talk, despite my exhaustion. I began to wonder what item in the company's inventory might interest him. The shin-bone of Saint Christopher, a bone as long as a child is tall which we had found in Alexandria and bought from a blackamoor from the upper reaches of the Nile, perhaps? Lavish, but too crude. Various fingers and toes? Trifling. King Louis had taken everything from the Pharos Chapel, alas, and those had been relics truly fit for a prince. Ah, but not *everything*. There had been four things in the chapel that Louis had never known about, for although he possessed an inventory of the treasures and bought from it like a marketer's list, I had had an older list, and had done some shopping of my own. The *Maphorion*: the mantle of the Virgin. The Captain and I had been holding that in reserve. Something for a pope, or an emperor. Maybe a little too rich for the earl's blood. But as I was pondering, the earl let one of his carbuncled rings tap against his goblet.

'A miraculous image – Our Lord's image on a winding sheet. One has heard of such a thing. My mother the Queen is very taken with the idea. What do *you* think, Master Petroc?'

Wearily I trotted out what I had told Louis Capet: that legend and the word of one long-dead Crusader did not mean the holy shroud of Edessa was still in this world, or indeed ever had been. It did not seem to matter to Earl Richard all that much, and we dived back into our idle conversation. There were always Christ's sandals, I was thinking to myself, and the holy lance – one of two I had found, that is, and with authenticating documents to boot. When the time was right I would float one of these, I decided, and see if Earl Richard was tempted. And perhaps I would recoup the Captain's bribe into the bargain. It was with these thoughts that I took myself off to bed at last, and though my room was as sparse and cold as I had known it would be, and as comfortable as if I were sleeping out on the moor, I slept deeply, and if I dreamed of a manor house and a sheep-nibbled lawn danced upon by laughing children, I did not quite remember them when I awoke the next day.

Lydford Castle was in an uproar when I came downstairs. It was quite early, but the hangings were being taken down and chests and bags carried out. Letice was drinking milk in the great hall.

'What is going on, Lady Agnes?' I asked her.

'We are leaving,' she said, wiping a white moustache from her lip. 'The earl sent riders to London last night, after you went to bed. The king is to march down to join the fleet at Portsmouth and we will meet him there. Earl Richard's army is mustering. We will be off in an hour. You'd better have some breakfast.'

'We?' I queried, cutting myself a slice of cold rabbit pie.

'Earl Richard has invited me to join his retinue – just like you.' She gave a quick flounce – pleased with herself, then. 'The ladies of the court are all going. 'Tis a great honour. And my lord—'

'You mean Agnes' lord.'

'*My* lord has promised to deal with my worries in the meantime. A spell abroad should do the trick, he says.'

'*My* lord?'

'Good Christ, Patch, but you have a filthy mind,' she said merrily. 'I'm not the lass I once was, and the earl is not that sort of man. He's in love, you know.'

'Strangely enough, I had guessed,' I said, supping at some breakfast beer. 'But, hey ho, it will be delightful to have you along. You can watch me get chopped to pieces by the French.'

'Oh, you will acquit yourself, my dear. And who knows? Maybe you will be rewarded.'

I doubted that. But I brooded on the future as we rode out of Lydford and down to Plymouth, where the earl received a party of vassals and inspected a company of ships. The next day we set out for Portsmouth, and before long we were retracing our steps across the Exe. We took the southern fork of the Fosse Way to Axminster and then pressed on to Dorchester. In a week we were riding across the downs above Portsmouth, the waters of the Solent like scoured pewter below us. It had been a merry journey, for our party was full of young men going to war for the first time. William, Gervais and Edmund had appointed themselves our escort, and they rarely shut their mouths, but yapped and cawed and brayed from sunup until long past sundown. I had kept a politely amused smile pasted to my face for so long that my muscles had begun to twitch and cramp. For I had not felt like smiling as we rode from Plymouth under the southern slopes of Dartmoor, past the bastions of Ugborough Hill and Brent Hill. I did not want to leave – not just yet, perhaps never. I gazed up each wooded valley that climbed up towards the brown tops and imagined my house there, my life. Instead I was being dragged away by pure inconsequentiality. I had done my job. Why, now, was I going off to war with this band of fools?

Because Earl Richard was anything but a fool. My simple errand was never going to have been simple, I could see now. Richard had a glamour about him, and he used it to ensnare those who might be useful to his various causes. I interested him, and my trade even more, therefore I had been conscripted. I thought more than once of simply leaving in the night, for who would follow me? But Richard might be suspicious. He might guess, rightly of course, that I was the agent of a vast scheme that did not have him at its centre, and withdraw. For Richard was ambitious. He should have been king, there was no doubt about that. He had friends all over Christendom, as I learned from many evenings at his table. And he commanded a respect outside the kingdom of England that his callow brother could only envy. He would be a powerful friend: that was easy to see, for the earl had proved himself a negotiator and not a fighter, although no one had ever called him a coward. If I made it through whatever nightmare awaited me in Poitou, he might well put some of his influence at my disposal, or so I told myself. And while I was thus engaged in self-appeasement, I also assured my frustrated soul that of course I could return to Devon whenever I wished. The manor in the valley was postponed, nothing more. No, I only had to ride against Louis of France, my best customer; survive, and make my way through another war to discover whether or not my friend and protector had lost his senses. Then I could get back to the moors. Nothing easier, my friend, nothing in the world.

Our party rode through the gates of Portsmouth and it began to rain almost at once, the rain sheeting down, turning the lanes into gurgling little brooks awash with bobbing, spinning filth. It had been dry for a while and so the air became heavy with the smell of wet thatch, an English smell if ever there was one. The knights, gentry and men-at-arms began to drift away in search of lodgings, but Albin the steward let us know that the Lady Agnes and I were to be guests of the court, for brother Henry was already here at the Kings Hall. This was favour indeed. The Captain would chuckle wickedly if he knew, I thought –

but then again, maybe he would not. In truth I was no longer sure what he would think of anything, and that thought nagged at me as we followed the Earl of Cornwall into the great Hall.

Letice was enveloped within minutes by a pack of court ladies. They had been in Portsmouth for two days and by the looks of things that had been long enough, for they fell upon the poor woman as if they had not seen a new face in years. I soon found out that although the honour of lodging in the Kings Hall was to be mine, I would be sleeping on the floor with the other gentry. But I would be dining that night with Richard at the king's table, so I found a promising corner to stow my bags and changed into my finest Venetian silks – much wrinkled by travel they were, but I stepped out into the rain with them and then stood by a fire for a bit – a fire that seemed to be lit only for the use of a small pack of deerhounds who lay before it, grey and silent and twined through one another's long limbs – and soon my clothes were presentable again, though I felt damp and bothered.

Chapter Ten

That night I sat within speaking distance of Earl Richard, who in turn had the king at his right hand. Between Richard and I sat a young knight who proved to be Guy de Lusignan, son of the Count of Poitou, and next to him another older nobleman who spent the night complaining about his teeth. The place next to me was empty, but not for long. A strong hand landed upon my shoulder and steadied its owner as he climbed over the bench and settled next me, apologising as he did so in a deep and steely voice.

'Think nothing of it,' I began to say, turning to greet my new neighbour. But the words lodged in my throat as I saw a thick crop of almost white hair cut close like a helmet spilling out from under the purple biretta of a bishop, a pair of close-set eyes the colour of the sea in February, a peregrine's beak of a nose and a tight, sickle mouth.

'Who are you?' he said, a trifle shortly, when he found he did not know his dinner companion.

'Petrus Zennorius, sir, of Venice,' I uttered through a windpipe that could not have been more frozen if it had been packed with snow. 'I am delighted to make your acquaintance, sir, although you have the advantage of me . . .'

'Ranulph,' said the man, as I knew he would. I bowed my head, reached out my hand and kissed the cold amethyst of the Bishop of Balecester's ring.

'Zennorius . . . Zennorius?' said the bishop, a slight frown upon his brow. 'Devon?'

'Cornwall, my lord,' I said hurriedly.

'The name is familiar. Might I ask as to your presence here?'

'He came with me, Ranulph,' Earl Richard called down the table. 'I put him next to you on purpose, dear man. You will see why.'

'Will I?' The bishop turned to me, eyebrows raised sceptically. I found it hard not to cringe from his eyes, but instead I inclined my head modestly.

'If my memory serves me right, my company assisted with the translation of a most holy relic to your cathedral, my lord.'

'Oh, by God's throne! You are of the . . . what was it called? The company of Jean de Sol!' He struck the table and the platters hopped obediently.

The company you sent your bastard son to destroy, I agreed in the silent place behind my eyes. The company you plotted to usurp, using a young nobody as bait after turning him into a monster in the eyes of the whole country. Yes indeed, my lord bishop.

'The translation of Saint Exuperius of blessed memory was a little before my time,' I said out loud. 'But I understand that he has blessed your cathedral and your city.'

'Indeed he has, *indeed* he has,' nodded the bishop, greed turning his face even more into the likeness of a baited hawk. I winced, and pretended to chase a thread of meat about my mouth with my thickened tongue.

'For I believe there were some unpleasant circumstances attendant to that translation,' I said at last. 'Appalling sacrilege of some kind – a murder in the cathedral?'

'You are well acquainted with our city,' said the bishop. He accepted a goblet of wine, never taking his eyes off me. Could he possibly know me? It seemed impossible. He had met me once, long ago in a candlelit room, and I was not the innocent young fellow I had been then. Life had put its marks on me, and there was not much innocence left.

'I studied at Oxford under Magister Jens, who had just come from the cathedral school in Balecester,' I said. 'And who has not heard of the Gurt Dog?' I shrugged. 'For myself, I give no credence to tavern hysterics,' I went on, taking a moment's refuge behind my own goblet. 'It gets in the way of business.'

'Ah. Business,' said the bishop. 'Your master . . .'

'I am a partner in the company, my lord,' I said, as firmly as I dared. His brow furrowed momentarily, and his eyes focussed yet more closely upon me.

'Well, well. And what brings you to court?'

'Business, naturally,' I said with a smile. 'Very minor business, but it appears I have garnered some unlooked-for but most welcome favour. I am to ride against the French with Earl Richard.'

The grey eyebrows went up even further, fluttering like martens under the eaves of the bishop's berretta.

'Then we will ride together, my son,' he said. 'How very interesting.'

'You are going to the wars, my lord?' I asked in disbelief.

'Of course. One may serve the Lord with the mace as well as with the crosier,' he said, contentedly. 'Now, as my lord Richard has brought you to us, there are one or two matters that you might be able to advise me upon . . .'

The bishop had lost none of his avarice, it seemed. He probed me for the next hour, trying to tease out as much as he could about Jean de Sol and the *Cormaran*. I treated him as I would any powerful customer: with friendly respect and extreme caution. Words that the Captain had spoken to me a thousand times – 'Patch, *pay attention!*' – sounded in my head like an orison. But how often does a man confront a demon from his nightmares made flesh, and discover that he is no worse than a score of other men of his acquaintance? For compared to Nicholas Querini, or the departed pope Gregory, or even to his own bastard son Hugh de Kervezey, I found Bishop Ranulph to be a lesser species of monster. He was older – as old as the Captain, perhaps – and some of the terrifying will and ambition that had cowed me when I had met him on the night of the killing had been sloughed away by the years, but not all. Not by any means: I could never let down my guard with this man. For he still wanted something, *needed* something – and it must have been this need, that maybe had no real goal but was simply a terrible, animal hunger, that had brought him the power he now grasped – and I knew, before the next filling of our goblets, that the lodestone of his need had settled itself upon me.

That was not a comfortable thought to take to my bed, which I made close beside the companionable huddle of deerhounds. I had gathered, from our conversation, that Bishop Ranulph was high in the king's favour and expected a cardinalship when the next pope was elected. He had brought with him a large company of knights and soldiers from the countryside around Balecester and a large sum of silver to place in the king's money chest, for I had learned from the man sitting on my left, a French knight called Pierre de Moings, that Henry was bringing coin as well as soldiers to the Poitevin cause. That was what had upset the barons, and why Westminster had been so angry. I guessed that the gold I had brought to Earl Richard would not be going into Henry's chest. Well, that was no concern of mine.

A hound snuffled me gently and settled his long back against my stomach. Try as I might, I could not drive the bishop's words from my mind. I had been so careful to guard my own tongue that I had not paid the closest attention to what he had said, for there had been much of it, but now that I tried to sleep, something kept troubling me. Balecester had let slip that his great friend at court was a man likely to become the most powerful baron in the kingdom – short of Earl Richard, to be sure – he was the Earl of Leicester, and his name was Simon de Montfort.

It is comforting sleeping with dogs if they are well-behaved, and I was not too stiff when I awoke the next morning. The Earl of Leicester was still on my mind, and so I went in search of Letice. I had first heard of him from her friend John Curtesmains, after all. It was a little embarrassing, but the affairs of England had not been uppermost in my mind for the last few years. I had been shuttling back and forth between Paris, Venice and Constantinople, and the politics I had concerned myself with had been, perforce, those of the lands I passed through and dealt with. The pope – and latterly the lack of one – along with Frederick the Holy Roman Emperor and Louis of France had been my focus. What happened on the edges of this world, in England, the kingdoms of Spain and the principalities of Germany, was a blur that I only paid attention to if and when there was something to be concerned about, and that was rare. Letice was in the great hall, and with some difficulty I drew her away from a party of noblewomen with whom she was gossiping, loudly.

'The Earl of Leicester? De Montfort – you mean you haven't heard of him?'

'He is the son of the Crusader, though?'

'The famous father. Yes, that's him. He is the prodigy of the kingdom. The king's brother in law, no less.'

'Sir John said that Earl Richard hates him – I remember now. Why?'

'Simon is even more ambitious than he is.' She shrugged. I understood completely.

'But he is more favoured by the king than Richard?'

'Ah! No, there was a mighty falling-out between Henry and Simon a few years ago.' She lowered her voice to a fluttering whisper. 'Henry is . . . some call him a simpleton, some a child. He is not soft in the head, really, but he does take a child's view of things. Simon owed a lot of money to the Count of Savoy, and apparently – only *apparently*, mind you – named Henry as security. When our king heard, he went off his head and all sorts of things came out. He even accused Simon of tricking him into giving away his sister's hand. Anyway, Simon took off to France until Henry calmed down, and then went away on crusade with Richard. He's back in France now, and in the meantime Henry's forgotten all about it and is praising Simon up to the heavens. Bloody ridiculous if you ask me.'

'Have you met him?'

'De Montfort? No, he was gone when I got back to London. But he's waiting for us across the Channel, so we'll both make his acquaintance, no doubt.'

'His father . . . you know it was de Montfort the elder who killed the Captain's family?'

'No.' Letice shook her head. 'I did not. I thought Michel was from Toulouse?'

'From Montalhac. A little town and a castle where he was born. His father was a vassal of Toulouse, and a Cathar. Simon de Montfort – this one's father – destroyed Montalhac along with everything else down there.'

'And Michel's parents?'

'Something horrible. He almost told me once.'

'Dear Lord. So what became of Simon the elder?'

'He had his head knocked in by a woman at the siege of Toulouse,' I said. It was my turn to shrug. 'Or that is his legend. A stone from a mangonel worked by ladies on the city walls.'

'There's justice for you.'

'A bit late for justice, my sanguine Lady Agnes. Now, am I not keeping you from your fun?'

'Oh.' She sighed. 'Fucking hell. I am the only widow here, and so every last one of them has sworn to find me a husband.' She was smiling, though. 'I will be wedded and bedded even before the French have surrendered. I've been assured of that.'

'So many eligible men, and who more so than the Earl of Cornwall's new friend from Venice?' It was a joke, and she gave me a sisterly shrug, the kind I had learned to accept with good grace. I left her to it, and went back to where I had left my bags. A young man, freckle-faced and with a mop of flaming ginger hair – a page by the looks of him – was standing over the place where I slept, and he seemed to be fiddling with my gear, but when I came up to him I saw that he was fussing one of the dogs who still lay there. I gave him a warning look nonetheless and he excused himself. The dog looked sad to have been abandoned, so I squatted down and rubbed his soft ears, and made plans to avoid my lord bishop of Balecester if I possibly could.

But the good bishop found me soon enough. I had decided to go out and exercise in the field in front of Kings Hall, where butts for archers and lists for mock-jousts had been set up. I was swinging my sword, trying to loosen my shoulders, when I saw a tall, white-haired figure striding towards me across the grass. He was bareheaded, and walked like a much younger man. I had a sudden and horrible sensation of dread, as when one is feeling inside a bird's nest for eggs, and one's fingers find, not the smooth, warm oval they expect, but spiky bones or crawling maggots. For Bishop Ranulph walked like his son, the same stalking self-control, head up, spine taut with arrogant defiance. A strange gait for a bishop. But then the prelate in question was holding a long, stout, steel-crowned mace. He pointed it at me like a sceptre.

'Zennorius! Let me see your blade.'

Astonished, I handed it to him without a murmur. He inspected it critically – it was an excellent sword of German make, with a watered blade that tapered sharply and balanced back towards the hilt, and I had learned to fence with it and a dagger or little buckler shield in my left hand – and handed it back to me.

'New-fangled. Are you a new-fangled sort of fellow, Zennorius?'

'When it suits my purpose, my lord. I believe that one should use every gift that God provides, the better to thrive and thus praise Him,' I answered, tersely.

'Amen, amen,' muttered the bishop, impatiently. 'Well, let's see you use it.' He whistled to a squire who was leaning against a tree exploring the caverns of his nose with a busy finger, and commanded him to fetch a training shield. Then he stood, leaning a little upon his mace, while I made the poor wretch skip and gasp, feeling, as I knew the lad must also, like a performing ape dancing for the amusement of the hawk-faced priest. He grew tired quite soon, the squire, for I had been schooled over the years by many teachers, some subtle and some vicious but all of them deadly. When I feared that he would drop his guard and cause me to lop off his arm by accident I let him go, and sheathed my sword.

'Have you killed?' It was a bald question, incurious, purposeful. I wiped the sweat from my forehead and bowed my head modestly.

'As I said, I believe one should use the Lord's gifts . . .'

'To suit your purpose. Amen again. Let us walk.'

I could have refused. I could have told him that I had indeed killed, and that one of my first victims was his own son. And while I was about it, I could let slip that his pride and joy, the blessed carrion he knew as Saint Exuperius of the Theban Legion, was that very son, hung and smoked like a ham until he looked a thousand years dead. I could have told him all of that and more, but instead I suffered him to take me by the arm and lead me in the direction of a line of clipped yew trees.

'You are the Constantinople expert, I hear,' he said, when we were away from the men who still went at each other grinning with swords and sticks, and the ladies who watched them, blushing and fanning themselves with their hands.

'If you heard it from Earl Richard, I can hardly quibble,' I replied.

'Well, then. You have heard the rumours, my son. I am curious to know if they are true.'

'Rumours?' I said, properly surprised.

'The burial cloth of Our Lord,' he hissed, suddenly, and his hand on my arm became a hawk's claw for a second, grasping, implacable. Then he let go. 'Was it found in Constantinople?' he said. I flicked my eyes towards the mace, but it hung loose in his other hand. 'Is it real?'

'The king of France has received everything that lay in the Chapel of Pharos,' I said levelly. 'That included diverse burial cloths and what was termed, in the *Inventarium*, the shroud of our Lord Jesus Christ. That is hardly rumour, my lord. It has been trumpeted the length of France and many miles beyond, at that.'

Bishop Ranulph cocked his head at me. His hard mouth puckered up beneath his beak of a nose until I beheld a great, white-haired buzzard, ready to rip, to tear.

'Not those,' he uttered, as if his throat were strangling the words as they escaped. 'The *Mandylion*.'

I fought to keep my face impassive, using an old trick of tightening my calf muscles until they hurt. I managed a very slightly condescending smile that was the very opposite, as the moon is to the sun, of what my face sought to make of its own volition. I was wondering, as I did so, if he had not sent someone, an equerry for instance, to search through my bags.

'That is not a rumour,' I said lightly. 'But it is perhaps a myth. You are talking of the miraculous image seen by many Crusaders in the church at Blachernae? Raised up with poles until the congregation beheld the very image of the standing Christ? From a purely professional standpoint, my lord, I wish as you clearly do that the so-called *Mandylion* existed. In fact I do not doubt that something of the sort did once dwell in Constantinople, for that place was once a storehouse of miracle the like of which our minds can hardly imagine. But like almost everything else it was burned or looted, or destroyed in ignorance or carelessness by the common soldiery. I searched, I assure you.' I paused, and scratched my chin, earnestly. 'But I found nothing. Not a trace. No living man or woman in the city would admit to seeing it. The knight de Clari, who wrote of it, is dead. If it existed it is gone, my lord – as appalling and blasphemous as it sounds, the Crusaders committed many an act of desecration, and although the destruction of the *Mandylion* of

Edessa would count amongst the greatest of those, no doubt it was done heedlessly and without a thought.'

'That is not what one hears.' If the bishop's mace could have spoken, it would have used that voice.

'Then those rumours have not reached my ears, and that in itself troubles me,' I replied. 'What, my lord, has one heard?'

'That the *Mandylion* is at large. That it is in the hands of . . . of . . .' his voice sunk to a whisper that hissed like sleet. '*Heretics*.'

'My lord!' I said, drawing away from him. 'Forgive me, but that sounds . . . I mean, if it were true it would be blasphemy. And what would heretics want with a holy relic? It is a contradiction, surely?'

'The Cathar crucifix,' said the bishop, darkly. 'I have written to young de Montfort about it, for he was raised in those cursed heretic lands that his father gave his life to save from the damnable Albigenses. He has been back there, just this year. The heretics have been parading some ghastly mockery of Our Lord's passion, the painted image of Christ upon cloth. They say it proves He was a man, and therefore not the Son of God – dear Lord, what dupes of Satan these vipers are! Now you know as well as I that Constantinople, before the true Christians saved it, was a nest of Bogomils and Cathars and every other kind of vile schismatic and sodomite. Well, do you see it? One of those vipers conveyed the very *Mandylion* that your Clari saw, to his brothers in error: yes, in the lands of Toulouse.' He was staring at me fixedly, and there was a faint line of white all around the grey irises of his eyes. His son had had his father's eyes. I took a deep breath and smoothed my face into something like acceptance.

'It is not altogether improbable, as to how it might have left Constantinople,' I said at last. 'But Cathars . . . No, my lord, if the *Mandylion* survived at all it became some crossbowman's bed linen or his wife's hosen – forgive me if I speak plainly, but there you have it. In any other matter, however, I would be more than delighted to be of assistance.'

Bishop Ranulph blinked, and the whites of his eyes receded. He hefted his mace and smiled stiffly.

'No doubt you are right,' he said. 'The quickness of youth. It has been an entertaining morning, my son. You fight altogether too well for one whose vocation is the translation of holy relics, but I can hardly disapprove. One may serve God . . .' he paused and studied me intently.

'With the sword as well as the pen,' I finished. 'I prefer to serve Him with the ledger and, if need be, the lantern in dusty old chapels and tombs, for time and ignorance have hidden His greatest wonders in such places. And I insist: I am at your service.'

'And I shall hold you to it, my son,' said the bishop. He smiled benevolently, then without warning hefted and swung his mace in a violent arc that decapitated an old yew stump in a cloud of dun splinters. 'Callings are difficult things, my son. The important thing, the *only* thing, is to serve.'

And with that he turned and stalked away, back towards the sparring knights, head up, eyes already upon another encounter. I found I had nipped the inside of my mouth, and spat a red-streaked gob onto the shattered yew.

Chapter Eleven

It was the twentieth day of May when we landed at Royan, a cosy little port at the mouth of the Gironde. We had had a horrible crossing, first becalmed, then storm-tossed, but after putting in at Finisterre we sailed into the mouth of the Gironde and descended upon the sleepy town. We had been delayed at Portsmouth while the king prayed and fussed over his clothes, and while he had the royal ship painted with scenes to delight him as he crossed over to France. Earl Richard was beside himself with fury, or so Letice told me, for Henry was already squandering the money he had raised from his barons – thirty casks of silver, no less – for no one wanted to fight in this useless war, and Henry was charging three marks in scutage tax for every knight who did not join the army. I was beginning to see why Henry had been besieged at court by angry nobles, indeed I thought it was a wonder that he dared show his face. But I did not care to understand the ways of kings. It was my business to part them from their money, after all, not to wonder where that money might come from. As it was, the ships that left Portsmouth carried near to sixteen hundred knights, twenty thousand foot soldiers and a thousand crossbowmen. We stayed in the port for nearly two months while Henry exchanged barbed letters with Louis. Hughues de Lusignan, the rebel count of Marche – a splenetic-looking fellow with grey hair and a pointed black beard – rode in with his wife Isabella, the king's mother herself, at the head of his own army of Poitevins and swelled our own small army to a great, stinking town that hung off innocent Royan like a canker on a dog's belly. We would trounce the French, said the gentlewomen, and the knights, and the drunkards. So we might, I thought, if we ever got free of the stifling and increasingly panicked gentility of Royan.

I was standing in the street with William and Gervais when the Lusignan party rode in. The common soldiers were pressing in and I had stepped back into a doorway, but still I caught a glimpse of the queen, Isabella, who had been married to King John Lackland. She was tall, slender and sat as straight as a reed in her saddle. Her face was shadowed by the long whimple she wore, kept in place by a simple gold circlet, but I saw her hands: they were long and white as candlewax. Her husband was calling in a hoarse voice to someone on the other side of the street and then they had passed on. I was cupping my hands around my mouth to yell at Gervais, who was looking for me a few yards away, when I caught sight of someone in the queen's retinue. He was an equerry and was wearing a magnificent tabard adorned with the blue and silver device of the Lusignans. His face was oddly familiar, though. I could not place it. He looked . . . he did *not* look like a tax collector. That was it. How very strange: I might have sworn, at that moment, that he was one of the men who had so alarmed Letice as we rode down to Devon, one of the men who had seemed to be following us. I put the thought out of my mind. The man at the inn had not been a tax collector, so why should he have been a royal equerry? And here was Gervais, come to drag me off to some tavern or other. I forgot all about it.

I had but one friend in this place and that was Letice, but I saw precious little of her, for she had made friends with the court ladies who had come over with the army, and they formed a gossipy, giggling clique that had no time for an upstart like myself. I suspected, though, that the good ladies had decided to find Letice a new husband, for they were forever holding little gatherings to which a selection of chinless, thick-necked Norman knights were invited and I was not. God alone knew what tales their new friend was telling about me, but, while I was not party to their gatherings, I began to get some interested looks from two or three of them. One in particular, a lady-in-waiting called Margarete, began to arrange little coincidences by which we would come across each other apparently by accident. I took the hint gladly, and found that Lady Margarete was more than interested in stealing an hour here and there with me, and that her rather dainty appearance and her coyly freckled face hid a much warmer spirit. There is much to be said for bawdiness when it is enjoyed by both lovers for its own sake, and, as is the way of the world, something about my demeanour must have changed, for I suddenly found myself unaccountably popular with the other ladies-in-waiting. I might not have been allowed into their gracious little parties, but I was by no means unwelcome in the bedchamber. Still, I spent my days wandering up and down the beach, avoiding the bishop and wondering what in hell's name I was doing here.

It was almost a week since we had landed at Royan. I was down on the beach, skipping stones across the flat waters of the turning tide, when an officious cleric, sweating in his heavy robes, scuttled out of the dunes and hailed me irritably. It was a summons from my lord the Bishop of Balecester, as I had known it would be, if only because I had, of late, been getting the reverse of what I wished for, and I had been earnestly wishing that the bishop would leave me alone. But I smiled accommodatingly and followed the man back into town.

Balecester had taken over the rectory. I was shown into the parlour, a cosy room whose walls seemed to cringe away from the hard bulk of Bishop Ranulph. He was seated at a table by the largest window, and opposite him sat a man of about thirty-five years, who turned towards me at a nod from the bishop. He was a Norman, with straight, corn-coloured hair and a pleasant, open face, although his nose had been broken badly at some point. He was clean-shaven, and there were dark circles under his eyes as though he had been sleeping poorly. His dress was noble but plain: very pricey cloth cut for a soldier's needs. I bowed and waited for my introduction.

'Simon, this is the fellow I have spoken of: Petrus Zennorius, from the company of the *Cormaran*. Zennorius, the Earl of Leicester honours us with a visit. You will join us.'

Thus I met Simon de Montfort, sixth Earl of Leicester. He gave me a brusque but friendly smile, and gestured to the empty chair next to him. I moved it until I was a polite distance between the two men and sat down.

'Earl Simon has just arrived in Royan,' said Balecester.

'Last night, in fact,' said de Montfort. 'I hear that you have joined our army?'

'I have been so honoured,' I replied. Behind the earl's genial face there was something implacable, I realised, for he was taking my measure coolly and efficiently. I could feel it.

'He has a new-fangled way with a sword,' said Balecester. 'But some skill, for a commoner.'

'My lord is too kind.'

'Skill is always welcome, Master Petrus,' said the earl. 'Nevertheless it is skill of a different kind that has brought you to this table.'

'You recall our talk at Portsmouth,' said Balecester. I nodded. 'I told you that I had inquired of my lord Leicester as to the truth behind these tales of a Cathar crucifix.' Again I nodded, my heart sinking. This above all other things I did not want to discuss with these two dangerous and clever men.

'I should point out straight away that while I share my lord bishop's zeal for the Faith, I do not have his passion for relics – I mean that I am a soldier and not a churchman, and I leave the knowledge of such things to holy men – I seek only to worship,' he added, smoothly. 'But you may know that I spent my youth in the lands of Toulouse, watching as my father battled against the heretics and later joining the battle myself. I have some holdings there, and that is where I have been since returning from the Holy Land.'

I made the appropriate show of respect, but de Montfort held up his hand modestly. 'I am His servant, nothing more,' he said. 'But to the matter in hand: my lord bishop has written to me more than once about a particularly foul blasphemy that has sprung up amongst the Albigensian rabble, this so-called crucifix.'

'My lord Balecester and I have discussed this at some length,' I put in. 'It is my sincere opinion . . .'

'No one is questioning your sincerity,' snapped Balecester. An unsaid 'yet' hung heavy on the air.

'Or your expertise,' said de Montfort, warmly. 'Which is why my lord wanted you here. And I agree: you sound like the very man.'

'My lords, for what?' I asked.

Balecester nodded at the earl and both men rose to their feet. 'Follow,' said Balecester, as if addressing his hound. I obeyed, and we made our way from the parlour and along the corridor to the back of the house. Through the kitchen, where five clearly annoyed French women were preparing lunch, and out into the little walled courtyard. A soldier with a big beer gut stretching his surcoat was sitting against the far wall next to a low door, dozing. A slug-trail of spit shone on his pink, bristly chops. The bishop gave him a hard kick on the thigh and he leapt to his feet, not even quite awake, his breath coming in gasps.

'Open the door,' said de Montfort. The man had been gripping an old key, and its rust had stained his palm. He turned it in the keyhole and pushed the door open. It was the rectory stable barn, empty save for a scattering of hay upon the cobbled floor and a small cart piled with sacks of grain standing in the corner. I guessed the army had taken the hay. So what was in here? Not . . . I blinked my eyes, for the only light inside came in through a slit window, and the air was full of straw dust. No, not the *Mandylion*. That would be blasphemy, I thought with a nervous giggle that did not get further than my windpipe.

It was not the *Mandylion*, but something far worse. Face down beneath the tiny window lay the figure of an emaciated man. His arms were pulled tightly behind his back and bound at the elbows and wrists, and his ankles were also bound.

'Who is that?' I asked carefully.

'A Cathar. I thought it might be interesting to ask one of the vermin in person,' said de Montfort breezily. He knelt beside the man and rolled him over. A grey, sunken face appeared, crusted with old vomit. 'We found this on him.'

De Montfort took a small bundle from the guard and shook it, unfurling the dirty parcel of linen into a long, single sheet. My blood jumped into my ears for a moment, for the dark figure of a bearded man stood before me, but when I looked closer I saw my mistake. It was the figure from the *Mandylion*, all right, but a crude copy done in some dark reddish pigment by someone who could not really draw, but who, it was plain, had been using the shroud itself for his model. This painting seemed to show an act of torture, for Christ's hands were nailed to a single post above his head and there was no cross-bar. But it was the man from the shroud. There were too many likenesses for it to be otherwise: the wounds on the brow, the bearded face. Except that this Christ's eyes were open and he looked, if truth be told, like a farmer who has just walked in on his wife swiving the local tax-collector: rather than the finality of death, there was nothing but an almost comic surprise.

'This is worthless,' I told them. 'No older than last year. What is it?'

'Is it not . . . ?' De Montfort was almost interested. 'No, of course it isn't.'

'It is interesting, though,' I said, thinking how best to turn their attention away from the shroud and the man. 'And it could be some heretical idol from the East. The Bogomili, I think they are called, the heretics who taught your Cathars their creed, copied all sorts of old icons and paintings from the Greeks. I would guess this is some half-remembered portrait of an Emperor or, who knows? The Patriarch of Constantinople. Or it might just be a copy – the face, I mean – of the *Volto Santo* of Lucca – there are heretics in Italy, too, you know.'

'The Holy Face of Lucca? King Henry's favourite relic,' said de Montfort. '*By the Holy Face!* He is apt to shout that out on the slightest pretext.'

'But this is nonsense, that I can assure you,' I said, twitching the painted sheet disdainfully. 'Painted by a fool. Look: they even left out the cross-beam. Not enough space, I suppose.'

The man on the floor twitched and moaned. He seemed to be waking up, and it was bringing him nothing but pain and fear.

'Is he ill?' I asked.

'No. He is one of their priests,' said de Montfort. 'They call themselves *perfect* – the enemy's pride has no bounds, does it? The perfect believe that they can choose when to die. This one is starving himself to death.' He gave the man a mocking pat on the head. 'The sooner he gets himself to Hell the better, so far as I'm concerned. You will not have heard, as I brought the news myself, but the Albigensians have outdone even their own wickedness,' he went on. 'They have murdered the Inquisitors of Toulouse in some wretched town called Avignonet. The two Inquisitors – a Stephen of Saint Thibéry and one William Arnald – three friars, an archdeacon and four servants, all butchered with axes. The killers were all men from the heretic stronghold called Montségur, and led by the lord of Mirepoix.'

I raised my eyebrows and shook my head in the disbelief that was required of me. 'And this wretch?' I enquired. 'Is he one of the murderers?'

'No, no,' chuckled de Montfort. 'This one I found sneaking about my villages, trying to corrupt my serfs. I have managed to keep him breathing long enough for Balecester to ask him a few questions. And then my lord bishop thought you might be able to shed more light. So, shall we?' He looked up at us. Balecester nodded impatiently. The fat soldier muttered 'excuse me, lords,' and stepped past us. De Montfort said something under his breath and the soldier nodded. He grabbed the man and heaved him upright. It was plain that he weighed no more than a bundle of dry sticks. His eyes tightened and flew open. They were green, bright, although the whites were yellow and blood-flecked. For one ghastly moment I had thought that I would know him, but of course he was a stranger. Meanwhile the soldier, supporting him with one arm, was tying one end of a coil of rope to the cord that bound his wrists. When it was done to his liking, he heaved the coil up and over one of the low beams of the ceiling and without ceremony pulled the man's arms up so that he stood, leaning sharply forward, his arms jutting behind him at a vicious angle.

The bishop walked up to the man, whose face had gone white as bone, even his lips, which were crushed together. The muscles of his jaws were bunched like walnuts.

'You worship a mockery of Our Lord's cross, do you not?' snarled Balecester. The man looked at him, expressionless. 'You dare to claim your own heretical crucifix, do you not?' Balecester drew back his hand and slapped the man hard on the cheek. 'You will answer!' But the man did not. He had not taken his green eyes from the bishop's face, who turned to us, his eyes beady, black as a buzzard's.

'Have you got anything out of him, Simon?'

The earl shrugged. 'I have not tried. This is work I would rather leave to the Inquisition, my lord. For myself, I would have burned the swine when I found him, but I thought you might find him useful. I'm afraid you will get nothing but lies in any event – what else, from a heretic?'

'That is why I have invited our friend from the *Cormaran*,' said Balecester, giving me a look of appalling smugness. *Is this the trap you prepared for me, my lord bishop?* I wondered to myself. *To infect me with your cruelty as if it were the red plague?*

'I am no Inquisitor, my lords,' I protested. But they were both staring at me now, and to my horror the Cathar was also looking at me almost curiously. There was nothing for it. The poor bastard was dead anyway, no matter what I did. I could do no good, but maybe I would do no more harm.

'Let him sit,' I said, trying to sound as if I did these things every day. The soldier, pouting his fat lips, let go the rope and the Cathar dropped down onto his arse. Feeling less of a man with every step, I went up to him, indicating to the bishop that he should step back. Then I bent my face close to the Cathar's deathly face.

'Good morning, my friend,' I said. 'I will not ask you to renounce your faith or betray your brothers and sisters. May I ask you some questions?' He regarded me, breathing painfully through his nose, struggling with the pain from his wrenched arms. Then to my surprise he nodded.

'Ah . . .' I hesitated, watching him. He was fifty or so, and he had been strong once, for his flesh hung from him a little. A nobleman, perhaps, from the way he held his head. But he had lived out of doors for many years, for his skin was coarse from sun and wind. He could have been any man out of a dozen I had sailed with on the *Cormaran*, exiled, driven out beyond the light, beyond the warmth of his own hearth.

'These men wish to know about the crucifix of the Good Christians,' I said quietly. His eyebrow twitched. 'I have heard that your people have a cross that you say resembles the one Jesus met his death upon, is that not so?'

The man nodded. 'That is so,' he said in Occitan. They must have been the first words he had spoken in days, and they hissed forth like sand blowing across the dunes.

'Why?'

'It proves . . .' He blinked, and when he went on his voice was stronger. He meant for his tormentors to hear. 'It proves that he who died at Golgotha was a man of flesh and blood. Flesh is of the Devil. Jesus Christ was the son of God, who is not flesh. He who the Romans crucified was not Christ. It is a lie that binds you to the Devil.'

I heard an angry inrush of breath behind me, but I held up my hand sternly. De Montfort grew up in the lands of Toulouse. Of course he would know Occitan.

'They say it is not like . . . like *our* true cross, that has four arms. They say it shows that Jesus was nailed in a different way.'

'With three nails,' he hissed. 'And His hands above His head. His side pierced by a lance.'

'I cannot hear you,' I said loudly. Then I leaned my head so that my face was an inch from his. 'And how do you know this cross is true?' I said in the merest whisper.

'Because we have the blood and body of Christ.' His breath was failing. 'We have it.'

'Have you seen it?' He fixed me with his eyes. The pupils were widening, crushing the green iris against the dying yellow beyond. He gave a little nod, and his mouth stretched into an almost-smile, a last triumph over the rictus of pain.

'Good. I am glad, *Perfectus*,' I whispered in his ear. Pretending to wait for an answer, I stayed there for another moment, then straightened up.

'You heard what he said, my lord Leicester.' I spoke loudly, giving them a touch of swagger, the torturer's pride in his work.

'A blasphemous cross,' said de Montfort. 'Yes, I heard.'

'But the *Mandylion*? You asked him about the *Mandylion*?' snapped Balecester.

'I did, my lord. He only knows of the heretic cross. I am sorry.' I strolled over to where the two lords, of earth and spirit, stood black against the doorway. 'But it was, as you promised, interesting. I did not know the *why* of this so-called heretic crucifix, but now I do. It is barely conceivable to those of us who love God, but these fools actually believe that the fact that Our Lord died as a man upon the cross *disproves* His divinity!' I shook my head in disbelief. 'So thank you, my lord Leicester, and you my lord bishop, for educating me. How many pitfalls the Devil digs for us . . .'

'Amen, amen,' said the bishop crossly. He was looking over my shoulder to where the Cathar knelt, slumped over.

'Is he dead?' he barked.

'Perhaps . . .' I began.

'No he ain't!' the fat soldier sung out. He hauled up on the rope and again the man was jerked to his feet, his arms flexed obscenely behind him. Balecester let out his breath and loosened his shoulders, like a drunk who has decided to pick a fight.

'With your permission, Lord Leicester, he might still talk, and we have our duty as Christians to perform,' he said, showing his teeth. De Montfort blinked and sighed.

'As you say, Ranulph,' he said wearily.

First they hoisted the Good Christian up until he dangled above the floor. The soldier squatted down and hauled on his skinny legs until his shoulders dislocated with a wet pop. His mouth opened wide and his tongue stuck out, but no words came. Then they let him drop. The soldier kicked him flat upon his face. Then Balecester ordered the soldier to pile the grain sacks from the cart on to the heretic's back. The fat man began to heave the heavy sacks off the cart and drop them one by one upon the still, silent body. Balecester knelt by the man's head and lifted it by the hair.

'Is there a real shroud, you heretical wretch?' he yelled. The soldier, sweat pouring down his blotchy meat and tallow face, heaved up another sack and let it fall. The bishop shouted another question. Another sack fell, then another.

Then, in the silence after the leaden whump of one more sack dropped onto the pile, there was a cough, no louder than a child coughing in its sleep. The bound feet rose, tapped the cobbles with painful delicacy once, then slumped sideways.

'Jesus!' The Bishop of Balecester rose stiffly to his feet. 'Damned . . . You.' He pointed at the soldier, who was leaning forward, hands on his thighs and belly wagging between, breathing hard. 'Take this polluted carcass to the square and burn it for all to see. And this rubbish as well.' He flung the painted sheet at the corpse and stamped off in a barely stifled rage.

I turned and walked out into the courtyard. Plainly I needed to be sick, for icy, greasy sweat was prickling me everywhere under my clothes, and there was a ringing in my ears. Instead I dropped to one knee and crossed myself, then put my hands together and pressed them to my face, breathing out my fury and my guilt into them. *This is my prayer*, I said to myself again and again. *This is my prayer!* But as to what that prayer might be, I had no answer. Except that Simon de Montfort patted me on the back and knelt beside me. We stayed there while the soldier cursed and rolled the grain sacks off the corpse, and while he dragged the dead *Perfectus* away. We stayed until the bishop came out, clapped his hands, and blessed us.

'God's work is never done, my good Leicester, but He does not begrudge us our rest. Shall we take luncheon?'

May faded into June, which dragged endlessly. I remember little except the hiss of the sea and the endless wheeling of gulls against the blue sky. Horribly bored, I wrote letters to the Captain that contained all the news I had, which was to say nothing, threw stones into the sea and drank too much wine. That morning with Balecester and the Earl of Leicester had left me feeling poisoned, as if I had eaten spoiled meat and could not get the smell out of my nostrils. The ladies in waiting felt it too, for one by one they left me to myself, all but Margarete, who had discovered that, like a good horse, I could be ridden into a better mood. Balecester had called upon me again, and I had had to explain to him my invented theory as to why the existence of the Cathar crucifix did not mean that the *Mandylion* had anything to do with it. I knew, though, that the man who had died that morning had seen the very thing that I had taken from the Pharos Chapel, and that had made a bond between us even in the few minutes that we had spoken. I had killed him, in a way. But then as a *Perfectus* he had wanted to die. I wondered if the bishop would understand that, or de Montfort. And I decided that they would not.

We left Royan in the second week of July, heading north-west through the flat water meadows of Poitou. I had no real place in the great armed column. I was officially a courtier now, I supposed, but no one in the king's party really knew what to make of me, and I was keen to escape any further attention from Balecester, so I trotted up and down the line, feeling like a pet dog, finding all the excuses I could to visit Letice, who was travelling in a lovely silk-lined wagon with a gaggle of court ladies. I had some sport with her, for she could not abandon her pose of the noble lady, no matter how much she longed to lash me with her foul London tongue as I teased her, but she made do with getting the ladies to mock me in their turn, and although they were all as lovely as a bowl of strawberries and cream I will confess their tongues stung like nettles, a needling that was not completely unwelcome, for my tryst with Margarete had been cut short by our departure, as she was riding in the wagon train with the ladies, and there would be no way we could meet without discovery. I was missing her already. If it had not been for the fact that we were riding to battle it would have been a lovely way to pass a couple of days, but there, somewhere up ahead, lay something terrifying. Still, the jolly men and women around me might have been on a summer pilgrimage – the nobles and gentry, that is, for the foot soldiers and camp-followers slogged and cursed somewhere ahead of us, so that we at least trailed the real world, although we seemed to be doing our best to ignore the truth of our situation.

I was part of Earl Richard's retinue, and I rode most often in the crowd of knights and squires that jostled for favour around him, hoping for some of his power to rub off on them, competing in their vanity and obsequiousness. I played the part as well, and Earl Richard liked to talk to me of the places I had been and the wondrous relics I had helped translate. My professional urge to find him something that would take his fancy, should I ever return to my old life, had been dampened by Balecester's murder of the poor Cathar, but I did my best and hoped I was doing my duty by the Captain. As a further spur for my disquiet, Simon de Montfort seemed to have taken an interest in me as well, and revolving against my will between de Montfort, Earl Richard and Balecester I felt their powerful, competing interests bind me ever tighter.

I had played my part at the rectory too well, for de Montfort seemed to think I was some kind of nascent Inquisitor, full of hardness and zeal and yet tender compassion. He was not simply the warrior and con-summate diplomat that reputation painted him to be. He was also a man of deep faith, which I gathered his time in the Holy Land had strengthened. I could talk to him of the scriptures and indeed of the holy places we had both seen, and a bond formed between us, superficial at best, for I was a commoner and a merchant, at that. Nevertheless, de Montfort seemed to find himself alone in this army, for although he and Richard were old friends, there was a distance between them, for Richard had never quite got over the way de Montfort had rather underhandedly married his sister. But I gathered they had patched matters up between them, even that Richard had stood godfather to his sons.

I also gathered that de Montfort had an abiding contempt for King Henry. He did not utter treasonable words out loud – he was far too clever a man for that – but it was plain that he thought of Henry as little more than a buffoon. When I told him of the great fuss the king had made of his newly painted ship at Portsmouth, he pursed his lips in vexation. 'The kingdom will be bled white,' he muttered, and stared at where the king rode at the head of the column, dressed in red and cloth of gold, the banners of England fluttering promiscuously above his crowned head.

As we progressed I had the sensation that we were heading into a storm, for what traveller has not found a wall of black clouds across his path, and has sunk into his clothes, knowing full well that, although he is warm and dry now, in a half-hour he will be drenched and assailed by thunderbolts. The sky ahead was blue, day by day; the perfect blue eye of summer. But somewhere below the horizon a storm waited just the same.

It was past the mid-point of July when we came to Tonnay-Charente, and could go no further in that direction, for the Charente river is wide and deep, and there is no bridge downstream of Taillebourg. At Tonnay we learned that Louis was heading for Taillebourg, for the lord of the castle there had taken the French side in this matter. So we set off again up the right bank of the river, through a sweet land of willows and grazing sheep, until two days later we came to a village called Saint James, which lies in the midst of flat, marshy fields astride a raised road leading to Taillebourg bridge. Evening was coming on, but there was enough light to see that over the castle flew the white and gold banner of the King of France.

Chapter Twelve

Louis had got here before us, but there was no army to oppose us this side of the Charente. If we attacked at dawn, went the talk around the royal tent, we would take the bridge and be treating King Louis to luncheon, for he had plainly outstripped his army in his haste to reach Taillebourg. We were no more than a bow-shot from the river, and it would be short work. All this jolly talk of easy victory made me even more uneasy than I had been. I dearly wanted to visit Margarete, but she was with the throng of court ladies, and so I wandered slowly around the meadow for a while, trying to ready myself for sleep before I took myself off to the tent I was sharing with a party of over-excited gentlemen and squires. I was passing near the spot where the king's tent was pitched when I heard a discreet cough behind me. Turning, I found a freckle-faced, carrot-topped page who I vaguely remembered from Portsmouth. He was wearing the colours of Lusignan.

'Would you come with me, sir?' he asked politely. I thought that perhaps Earl Richard wanted to see me for some reason and had sent his mother's page to fetch me, so I nodded and began to follow him. To my surprise we passed the earl's tent and instead I found myself in front of a small but richly decorated pavilion from which was flying the flag of the Counts of Poitou and the blue and silver banner of the Lusignans. The page slipped through the door curtain and I followed. I found myself in a space that was bigger than it promised to be from the outside, lit by scores of candles so that it glowed pale gold. There were dividers and screens of tapestries, and behind one I heard the low growl of Hughues de Lusignan, whom I had encountered once or twice with Earl Richard but who had never given me more than a contemptuous glare from beneath his lavish grey eyebrows. He was a fearsome man, a dangerous warrior and as fickle as a sand-bar in the Gironde, and I was very relieved that the page did not conduct me to his presence. Instead, he showed me with a bow that I was to go behind a fine tapestry of leaves and roses. I gave him a puzzled look but he was already scurrying away, so I pushed aside the hanging.

'Petrus Zennorius. Please sit with us.' In a chair flanked by two racks of candles sat Queen Isabella. She would have been above fifty years of age then, but even so she was still one of the most beautiful women I have ever seen. When we had first met in Westminster Palace she had been dressed plainly, but tonight she wore a dress of green and silver damask and her face was powdered white. Her eyes were delicately outlined in black and her lips were stained strawberry-red. She looked both young and old, as delicate as a shell but hard as marble. But she was smiling.

'This is a happier meeting than our last. Since then, I have learned that our younger son speaks very well of you,' she said in French, pointing to a low stool at her side. I sat, almost squatting, and she nodded her head.

'You are a Cornishman,' she said. I nodded gratefully, for this sounded like small talk, but no. 'We have never been to Cornwall,' she went on, 'Though Richard is fond of it. Of course, Cornish tin has made him rich.'

'It is a venerable trade,' I said, hoping for some shallow discourse about tin.

'As venerable as yours?' she asked lightly. I sighed inwardly. She was yet another would-be customer, and a rich one, but on the eve of a battle I was in no mood for business. Still I smiled my most professional smile.

'Like a tinner I could be said to bring hidden riches to light,' I said. 'But . . .'

'Quite so.' She tapped the chair with the perfect oval of a fingernail. No small talk after all. 'What are you hunting for now, Monsieur Petrus?'

'I am not hunting for anything, Your Majesty. My company has lately moved into banking. In fact we are at this moment opening a bank in Florence.'

'Speak to us of Constantinople. The Emperor Baldwin is our cousin. You have been a great help to him.'

So I told her a little about the relics of the Pharos Chapel and their translation to France and the possession of Louis Capet, which was a well-known tale by then, and one I had told more times than I could remember. She seemed politely interested until I drew it to its end.

'And the last of those treasures is now in Paris,' I finished, and she leaned forward, eyes narrowed slightly.

'All of them, gone to Louis?' she said.

'Indeed. The piety of King Louis is unbounded – though it does not approach that of your son,' I said diplomatically.

'And his wealth matches his piety.'

'That I could not say.'

'So. Nothing else in Constantinople. There are many stories, however. One has heard some of them. So fascinating, so . . .'

'If there is something in particular, Your Majesty, I would be honoured to discuss it.'

'Oh, no,' she said airily. 'Wondrous things, though, Monsieur Petrus. Saints' heads, the nails of the Cross . . .' she shuddered almost coquettishly. 'And miraculous shrouds.' Her fingers closed over the end of the chair arm, and then let go. There was something almost spider-like in the gesture, but . . . no, it was a lovely hand.

'Alas, that is mere legend,' I said sorrowfully. 'If such a thing ever existed – and we only have the word of one dead Crusader and some schismatic Greeks – it burned along with Constantinople. I will admit that it has been my dearest wish to find it, and I searched long and hard in Greece, but everything I discovered told me that it is lost forever. There were some burial garments of plain cloth, and those are in Paris. But no miraculous image, or face, or any other of the many wonders said to be possessed by the holy shroud.'

'So you have given up the hunt?' she said winsomely, and I thought *she is mocking me!* – but surely not.

'When one deals with the miraculous, one comes to expect miracles,' I said piously. 'I don't suppose I shall ever really give up. But I do not expect to find it.'

'Such a pity. To look upon the Holy Face . . .' She crossed herself, and I did the same. 'How nice to talk to you, Monsieur Petrus,' she said, holding out her exquisite hand for me to kiss. 'May tomorrow bring you good fortune.'

The freckled page led me out to the meadow, and I stood there for a moment, staring at the faint golden light seeping through the walls of the pavilion. I had just received a great honour, and yet I felt strangely cold, and uneasy. But then my mind raced forward to the morrow, and I set to pacing again, and the Queen, and her white hands, faded from my mind.

The river had spun a gauze of mist over the meadows when I finally crawled out of the tent. I had not slept a wink, but now the churning of my stomach had made the wait intolerable. There were plenty more figures wandering about, carrying pails of water or bundles of hay, hunched over blades or bows, or just standing and gazing over in the direction of the French lines, where Venus was hanging, a baleful point of fox-fire in the sky. I tottered on stiff legs over to a culvert and squatted among the reeds. I was not the first to empty my guts here, for the stench was strong even in the cool air of the night. Now I felt a bit better, although if anything I was too empty, a sack of skin filled with nothing but vague terrors.

Before dawn, a slight breeze came and tattered the mist, and then came the half-light. It found me sitting on an old ant-hill, fretting over the binding of my sword-hilt. The wire was loose, or at least my jitters had made it so, but my numb fingers could not fix the problem. The blade was sharp enough, for I shaved my thumb-nail almost to the quick in testing it. And now I must go shit again, for my guts had resumed their liquid churning. At the ditch I met a knight I recognised, a carrot-haired fellow from Ludlow, who was wincing as he pulled up his breech-clout.

''Tis the fucking French water,' he told me, shaking his head. 'God knows why we drink it – there's wine enough.'

'Why indeed?' I grunted. It was not the water, of course, and we both knew it, but men must puff themselves up like gamecocks, never more so than in the grey nothing of a battle's morning.

The horses were coughing and stamping, and suddenly the field was full of stumbling grooms spilling pails of water. They tore the mist to shreds, that swirled and steadied and clung to the cobwebbed thistles like gonfalons of the underworld. That was not a thought I wished to keep in my skull, and to drive it out I drew my sword and swung it at the nearest thistle stand. There was a neat twang and the spiny head hung for an instant and then dropped. I wiped the milky sap from the steel. As I sheathed it I saw that there was enough light to pick out the purple of the flowers I had cut, tumbled now in the dew. Somehow that seemed like an even worse omen, so I cursed and trotted back to the tent.

The gentlemen's servant, a boy with a strawberry mark on his jaw, had kindled a fire and was pulling food from a battery of haversacks arranged in front of him. I smelled ham and swallowed queasily. Letice appeared from behind the tent, scratching her arse absently.

'Good morning, my lad,' she said cheerily, swinging a hank of knotty hair from her face.

'Up so soon?'

'I had to piss. Don't know where the quality are doing it, but there's nettles all over back there. I have a stung bum.'

'Sorry to hear it,' I said. She gave me a crooked smile and I gave her one back.

'There's beer,' she said. 'And wine – want some?'

I did not think I would like the sourness of wine at that hour, so I accepted a clay jar of beer and sank my face to its foam-netted surface.

'Are the quality doing this?' I asked Letice.

'The quality, my boy, are all off their heads. I think that's how it's done – the battle thing. You drink yourself stupid, then wake up and drink some more. That way, by the time they've hoisted you aboard your horse, and you're waving your sword and yelling, it might all be making sense to you.'

'You must be right about that,' I said, trying not to sit on my own sword. 'Wish you'd told me earlier, though. I didn't sleep a wink. And I hate fucking tents.'

'How about fucking in tents? Or are your powers of persuasion on the wane? Little Margarete was pining for you last night, you know.'

So Letice knew about Margarete, and all the others, no doubt. Of course she did. I supposed I had known it all along, and in truth I did not mind, one way or the other. If she was jealous she did not show it, and I found I did not want her to be, for there was no reason anymore.

'Margarete is a flower. Much too sweet for me. I've been meaning to say goodbye, but it turns out I'm too soft.'

'Well, you'll be dead soon, so it won't matter. That was a *joke*, Patch,' she added, seeing my look of utter mortification. 'You aren't going to be in front, lovely man. You aren't important enough. Just make a lot of noise but don't kick your horse too hard. Then you can ride up when it is almost over and kill some poor wounded Frenchie while the king's watching.'

'Bollocks,' I said, reflecting inwardly on how very sound her advice seemed to be.

But in the event I was just important enough to land myself in trouble. I had dragged on my expensive new armour and was beginning to sweat even though the sun was but a hand's span above the earth's edge, when the Royal page cantered up, bowed from the saddle and informed me that I would be riding in the king's party. He left, his horse throwing up clods of earth, before I could even open my mouth. And so I found myself sidling my mount up alongside Earl Richard, under a grove of stuttering, snapping pennants and flags. I recognised some of the men with him: Sir John Maunsell, the king's clerk; Roger Bigod, Earl of Norfolk; Warren de Montchesnil. And there was the Bishop of Balecester, bareheaded, his mace resting upon his shoulder. Half a mile away was the river, the first rays of the sun seeming to make it boil as the mist lifted from the water and hid the bridge. Beyond, the red roofs of the town and above them the purposeful block of the castle. And against the bleached sky, the great standard of France hung slack, its golden lilies sparkling.

'Well met, Auneford,' barked Richard, with a jerk of his perfectly barbered chin. 'No shield, eh?'

'No crest to put on a shield, Your Highness,' I said. 'So I reckon my bare left arm's prettier than a plain bit of wood,' I added, dredging up a crumb of bravado from God knew where. Richard seemed to appreciate it, for he gave a barking laugh.

'Spoken like a true man of Devon,' he said, giving me a stinging whack on the shoulder. 'Your arm may not be bare by nightfall,' he added, but before I could answer this astounding remark, the king trotted up in a cloud of golden silk and horseflies, for the sun was warming the earth now and the numberless host of biting things had already commenced their own battle.

'Ready, brother?' he asked Richard.

'It is but a bridge – let us be done in time for lunch, eh?' I studied Richard's face, but saw nothing but amused impatience, as if we were riding to hounds and nothing else. Meanwhile, the king raised his arm and the trumpeter at his side blew a stuttering call.

To our left there was a sudden clatter and clank, and a part of the army's wing began to move off across the water meadows, a hundred or so mounted men in the lead, another hundred men-at-arms marching behind them, pikes and halberds bristling. Their shadows, long and lean, harrowed the ground before them as they went.

'They will take the French positions before the bridge, and then we shall go across,' said Richard. There was no trace of doubt in his voice, and indeed, now that they had crossed half the meadow, the company began to trot and the footmen to run, loose and easy, as though this were a tourney on some village green. But the air was warming, and as it warmed, the mist began to dissolve from the river bank and, as though a conjurer had whisked away his magic kerchief, a line of soldiers was revealed, and the dull shine of kettle helmets, and a thicket of spears. Our men did not hesitate. The cavalry gave a whoop and broke into a flat canter, their pennants snapping out stiff behind them. The men-at-arms fanned out and began to sprint. There was a commotion amongst the spears that awaited them, a waving of flags and a blare of horns. A horseman appeared and galloped along the French line. He seemed to wheel and launch himself towards the English knights, only to be swallowed at once, for in another instant the leading horsemen had crashed into the Frenchmen.

I strained my eyes to see what was happening. Everyone around me was doing the same, leaning forward, taut and grimacing, like figures carved into a church roof. But there was nothing to see, just a confusion of blurry, undulating shapes and – very faint, for the sound was swallowed by the mist – a hiss and clatter, no more than the whisper of hedge crickets, as men clashed and died. Then the king sat up straight and turned to his brother.

'They have carried it, I think?'

'So it appears. Now then . . .' But Richard of Cornwall did not finish, but instead leaned forward again, eyes narrowed. I could see a haze of figures running for the bridge. That must be the French, for there were our standards chasing them. But all of a sudden there was a piercing call from a trumpet, and the bridge across the Charente filled with jostling shapes that burst like dark water from a gutter into the water meadows. The English standards met this tide at the end of the bridge and I guessed they would drive the French reinforcements back, but instead the brave flags and pennants halted, shivered, and began to go down. There was confusion again, a blur of motion and a rising haze of dust, but still the bridge poured men into the water meadows, mounted men now with flags of their own.

'What's that?' asked the king, pointing. A score of courtiers squinted to see what he meant.

'French counter-attack,' said a young knight with a big red bird on his shield. 'Hopeless, Your Majesty – they'll never get free of the bridge.'

But the king was holding up a mailed hand. 'Oh, I say,' he said, with mild exasperation. Across the meadows, English standards were falling back, and still Frenchmen were pouring across the river.

'Shall we go forward, d'you think?' he asked his brother. Richard held up a mailed hand.

'Look, over there.' A horseman was pounding towards us on the raised track that led to the bridge. He reined in before the king and bowed hastily. He was covered with dust and his horse was drenched with sweat. The creature rolled its eyes as it danced nervously alongside the king.

'The town is full of the enemy, Sire – in great numbers,' said the rider. 'They have secured this side of the bridge and are sending men across in boats.'

'What numbers?' asked Richard. The man – he was a knight, with a pricey mail shirt all floury with dust – wiped the sweat from his eyes.

'Countless!' he said. 'The town has become a city – there are French-men as far as the eye can see, my lord. They have three men for every one of ours, at the very least, and more are coming. And King Louis is with them. He had not crossed when I left, but he was preparing to, I think.'

'And see there!' Richard was pointing, shielding his eyes. 'Louis has raised the Oriflamme. He means to give us no quarter.' I looked, and saw a bright red flag with many streaming tails fluttering beside the blue banner of France.

Henry was staring over at Taillebourg, his face flushed red, one eye twitching. He looked up and down our lines, and turned to the dusty knight.

'Fall back, sir,' he said. 'Fall back on me! Trumpeter, sound recall!' Earl Richard nodded his approval. The horn blared and the knight rode off, his horse spraying white spittle from its muzzle. There was a heaving in the fighting crowd, and then first horsemen, then running figures broke away and began to stream back to the army. The French were not following, it seemed, but every minute a hundred, five hundred more Frenchmen seemed to appear on our side of the river. *Except*, I told myself, *it isn't our side any more.* There was a flurry of hooves and I saw that Hughues de Lusignan had ridden over from the left wing, where the men of Poitou had drawn themselves up. I heard Richard greet him curtly, then Henry's plump voice rose up, choked with anger.

'Where are all your promises now, eh, my lord and father?' Lusignan's choleric features went slack with surprise, then his eyes narrowed to slits. 'When we were back in England you promised us, many times – you sent messengers and letters patent, my lord – that you would gather together an army so great that we would be able to oppose Louis of France without fear, and . . . and you told us we only needed to trouble ourselves about money!'

'I never did any such thing!' said Lusignan, angrily. The men around us were looking on with a mixture of curiosity, embarrassment and fury. Earl Richard had pulled off his mail gloves and thrown them at his squire.

'You did!' he cried. 'You did, and I have your letters with me!'

'They were not written or signed by me,' snarled Lusignan.

'What did I hear you say, father?' said the king, aghast. 'Have you or have you not sent to me and, yes, begged me to come here, both by your many letters patent and your messages, and complained in the meantime of our delay? We are here, my lord! Where is all that *you* promised?'

'By Christ's cuckold father!' yelled Lusignan, his cheeks purple. 'I am to blame for none of this! Blame your mother, my wife – by God's throat, she has contrived all this without my knowledge!'

There was a horrible silence, and in it we heard the pounding of hooves and feet and the rattle of weapons as the advance party straggled back across the field. Henry and Lusignan were glaring at each other, the king white, his mouth working, and his father-in-law an awful, splenetic colour, his jaw jutting and his eyes glaring. Earl Richard broke the silence.

'I will parlay with Louis,' he said, firmly. He looked hard at his brother, then at the count. Turning to Henry again he lifted his chin and gazed at him. Then he gave a brisk nod, called an order to his squire, then wheeled his horse and walked it, very deliberately, through the soldiers behind us and back to the camp, his squire following behind. The army was silent save for the coughing of the sick and the stamp and bridle-clatter of horses. But across the field the French were hooting and mocking us, calling us on, challenging the mighty English king. I do not know how long we stood there as if enchanted, mute, angry and frightened. But then there came a murmur through the army and suddenly horses were being edged sideways to make way for Earl Richard.

He was barefoot, and his head was bare. He wore a plain pilgrim's smock of coarse brown cloth, and in his hand he carried a wooden staff. Silently he passed through the English lines and set out across the thick green grass. When they saw him the French, to my great surprise, fell silent in their turn.

'Do you know the story?' said a quiet voice at my shoulder. It was Simon de Montfort. 'In Outremer, an army of Frenchmen were ambushed by the Mussulmen at Jaffa. Six hundred knights were captured, and my brother Aimury was among them. Earl Richard parlayed with the Mussulman prince called Al Nasir Dawud of Kerak, and had every one of the captives set free. Look: the French honour him.'

It was true. The enemy had parted and made an avenue for the earl that led to the high arch of the bridge. As he approached they began to cheer and to kneel, and as he passed through them it might have been their own victorious king they were greeting. He walked up the steep side of the bridge and vanished down the far side.

It was a long wait. Henry and his father-in-law at last ceased to glare at each other like scorpions in a basket, and a low muttering rose from along the line of men. But no one stirred, save once when a knight's horse bolted out into the field and the foot soldiers let out a nervous cheer. It must have been an hour later, for the sun was up and the day was starting to become very hot, when Richard of Cornwall appeared again at the crest of the bridge. Again the French army cheered him, and their cries rang out as he walked back across the empty field. Moths and grasshoppers flew up around him. He strode up to King Henry and laid his hand upon his brother's thigh. The king bent down to him. I was near enough to hear his words.

'We must get away from this place quickly – *quickly*, brother – or we will all be taken prisoner,' he said. 'Cousin Louis has granted us a truce until tomorrow. Let us do nothing until darkness comes, and then we will escape as fast as we can.'

Hughues de Lusignan was the first to move. He nodded at Richard, his face a blotched mask, and rode back to his men. The king gave an order to the trumpeter, and at his call the army, the whole long bristling line of battle, began to melt and recede, like a wave drawing back from the beach. In a few minutes the camp was full again. As if in a dream I found myself back at the tent in which I had spent the night, the boy with the strawberry mark cooking me something to eat as if nothing had happened. But the camp was fevered. Inside every tent men were packing, preparing, so that as soon as night fell the army could move straight away. We would leave the tents, in case the enemy might be fooled into thinking we had stayed to be butchered. I had not unpacked, so I had nothing to do. I was desperate to take off my armour, but in light of the French host pitching their own tents in such numbers that the river was completely screened by them, their digging of parapets and the loud clatter of arms and men certain of victory, I decided to keep it on.

Letice was nursing a noblewoman who had come down with the flux but did not seem to be doing too badly, for she was sipping on sweet wine and fanning herself.

'Still alive, I see,' said Letice as I walked up.

'Yes. Even I managed to survive this particular battle,' I said. 'Are you ready to move?'

'This lot will take days to pack up,' she said, taking my arm and drawing me away so that she could speak in her own voice. 'And bloody hell, we had been tearing up sheets all night so that we could bind all you wounded men up nicely. Lady Agnes feels cheated. I don't, though,' she added. 'These women think this is all as normal as shopping for chickens in Cheapside. Me, I've decided I'd rather be back there than here, and sod the husband, which they have not found me, I might add.

All this la-di-da and waiting to get our heads chopped off is getting on my fucking nerves.'

'Mine too. I'm glad Earl Richard had the sense to parlay. We would all be dead by now otherwise.'

Letice blinked her blue eyes at me, then rose on tiptoe and kissed me very quickly on the mouth. Our lips were dry but they clung to each other for a moment.

'I am glad you are not,' she said, and went back to her sick friend, leaving me standing like a fool, itching myself where the mail chafed me under the arms.

The sun seemed to take a year to sink behind us. But as soon as it was gone, the mist began to rise from the river and creep towards us, and the French lines vanished into a thick gloom. The moon would not be up until after midnight, and it was so dark that it was hard to see from one tent to another. There was a strange kind of silent purpose to us all, and incredible as it might seem, our great army of almost thirty thousand men had slunk away before the church bells of Taillebourg had rung out the mist-muffled eleventh hour. We were headed due south to the city of Saintes, and once we had found the road we hurried as fast as we could, a river of men, women and animals a mile long all hurrying to reach safety before the sun came up. It was barely eight miles to Saintes, but we soon left the flat lands and the road started to roll up and down until I feared we would be caught in the open. But in the watery light before dawn I saw the white walls of Saintes rise up in front of us, and the pretty chalk hills of that country, all lined and ordered with vineyards, slowly revealed themselves. I was riding just behind the king's party, and so I can say that when Henry saw the city gates in the distance he clapped his spurs to the flanks of his horse and galloped towards them, the nobles and squires streaming after him as though this were a Sabbath-day hunt. With that the whole column lurched forward with a huge clamour of creaking, shouting and horrible oaths from the wagon drivers and muleteers, who were far behind the knights and soldiery. By the time I had reached the city walls the end of the train was just coming into sight through a fold in the low hills. White chalk dust was beginning to rise, for the sun had already driven off the dew. The king had gone through the gates, but most of the nobles had drawn themselves up in the fields on either side, watching the column as it came in. Somewhere down there was Letice. I could see the brightly painted carts of the court ladies. They had fallen behind.

Simon de Montfort saw me and gave me a jolly wave. His helm was resting on his knee, and he was smiling. He called to me, and I trotted over.

'Do you think we will be in time?' I asked.

'It seems so,' he said, and his face fell. 'The king could not control himself, of course, rushing for safety like a . . .' He blew out his cheeks and sighed, exasperated. 'A fine example. Still, Lusignan's men are still with us.' He pointed over to where the blue and red flag of Marche, with its three lions, waved out on the left. 'I am surprised. I thought old Hughues would have slipped away.'

'Has he betrayed us, then?'

'God knows. The Lusignans, and the queen mother, are all mad. They are schemers. If Lusignan has betrayed us, the fault is Henry's, for taking the bait.'

I was thinking that it must be because we were surely about to fight a battle that a great lord could gossip to a commoner like this, when there was a scream, faint but shrill, and then an ugly din. The end of the column was close now, less than a mile, but the road behind them was no longer white and empty. It was boiling with mounted men, and like a serpent they had already swallowed up the last English carts. As I watched, the great serpent, with teeth of steel, devoured the carts of the noblewomen. A pennant waved bravely, and went down.

Chapter Thirteen

'God's bloody hands!' shouted de Montfort. 'The French! The French are here!' He slipped on his great helm and turned the black eye-slits towards me. 'Are you ready to fight?'

I nodded. My stomach felt empty and my blood had left my head, but I still nodded. 'Then follow me. And pick up a shield as soon as you can, or you'll lose your arm,' he barked. 'To me, to me!' he yelled, drawing his sword and waving it high over his head. 'King's men, to me!'

All the English nobles and knights were riding to the road, and in a few minutes a short, thick line had formed, a packed mob of shouting men and the tossing heads of horses.

'The king is here,' somebody called, and there was Henry, looking very young and not half so composed as he had been yesterday at Taillebourg. But he raised his hand and the trumpets sounded. The lions of England snapped out, and a great cheer went up.

The French were pouring down the road now, and were trying to form up into battle lines, but the vineyards were hampering them. The foot soldiers in the column who had been straggling along just ahead of the carts had turned and thrown themselves at the enemy and the cross-bows of both sides were pouring bolts into the air. The sight of the French attacking the women's carts seemed to have enraged the English. Where yesterday men had all been cool and workmanlike, today they roared and shook their swords.

Richard of Cornwall had joined the king, not a pilgrim now, but shining in mail, and with a gold-banded helmet on his head. His horse was dancing from left to right in its impatience.

'Give tongue, brother!' cried Richard. The trumpet blared again. Henry drew his sword and held it high, and with a sound like a great sheet of ice sliding down a stone roof, a thousand swords came out, and my own with them.

'By the Holy Face!' yelled the king, and his own placid face was transformed suddenly into a straining web of sinew and muscle. 'On, king's men!' There was a huge, incoherent roar, and I found myself screaming along, one word, hollow as a plundered reliquary to me these many years but rising now like desperate joy from my throat:

'JESUS!'

My sword was out. Yelling, I stabbed it towards the enemy. With a creaking lurch, as a heavy ship will make when a strong wind catches its slack sail, the English army began to gather speed: my horse was trotting, taking its lead from the mounts beside it, and I was rising and falling in the saddle, left hand tangled in reins and mane. We had the advantage of a gentle slope that was carrying us, faster and faster, towards the French knights where they were hacking their way through the foot soldiers.

'King's men! King's men!' I shouted with the rest.

'*Montjoie!*' the French screamed back at us. '*Montjoie, et Saint Denis!*' And there was Montjoie itself, the Oriflamme, flying above our enemies. No quarter. But I only remembered that much later. As I charged that day I thought of nothing save how strange it was that the blood sang in my ears as if I had seashells pressed to them. I felt no fear. It had left me when I drew my sword. But I have talked to the mad, and those who have fallen in and out of madness, and I think, in those hours in the vineyards before Saintes, that I was perhaps a madman.

I was rushing down a narrow lane between two plantings of vines. Simon de Montfort was in front of me with two other knights. I could see the shield of John Maunsell; and Ralph Fitz-Nicholas, the king's seneschal, was beside me. Then we crashed into the first line of the French.

A man flashed past me on the right. I swung my sword at him but cut thin air. A horse screamed and then another horse ran across my path. I saw black slits in a gold cross, eyes staring from a helmet, and a lance shot past my left shoulder. The wooden shaft slapped against me and I swung at the man, a high overhand blow. A shock jolted my arm but I was already beyond whatever I had done, and a foot soldier was scrabbling at the bridle of my horse. I stuck him in the neck with the tip of my sword and he screamed and flailed backwards, his blood spattering my leg. My horse was plunging in terror. As I fought to calm him another shape rose up and I saw the glint of steel barely in time to parry the man's blow and I thrust at him, striking nothing. He swung again and again I parried, his sword slamming into the hilt of mine and almost knocking it from my hand. He was wearing an open helmet and his eyes were wide and white. I yelled and sent my half-numb sword arm flying at him back-handed, but as I did a lance caught him in the small of the back and went straight through, the point tearing off the ear of his horse. An English knight, still holding the lance, crashed into the back of the impaled Frenchman and all went down in a shrieking boil of horse-legs and bloody chain-mail.

The dust was roiling around us, thick and white like smoke. I heard 'King's men! King's men!' in front of me, and saw the red shield and white lion of de Montfort. 'Devon!' I yelled in answer. A dozen French knights appeared out of the dust, their horses just breaking into a run, lances in a ghastly row levelled at my chest. I slashed at the nearest lance, knocking it aside, and kicked hard, driving my horse between the spears. Hacking to left and right I forced my way through, turned and went at their backs. There was a whizzing in the air – it had been going on the whole time, I realised – and a crossbow bolt plucked at the mail on my stomach. I was already surrounded by chopping, stabbing swords when de Montfort's red shield crashed into a face very close to my own. Maddened by the burning in the flesh of my belly I turned the other way and swept my sword down, and found I had split a man's shoulder down to the breast-bone.

'Pick up his shield! Pick up his fucking shield!' De Montfort was shrieking at me. He had lost his helmet and his face was streaked with blood and spittle. The man I had struck had fallen off his horse and was writhing feebly beneath me. My stroke had split his chest so that it hung open as if hinged by the rent muscles, and the purple bag of his lung worked feebly in the wound. I swung myself out of the saddle, leant down, and clapped my hand to my stomach, for the pain was tearing at me. But I did not find my guts, just chain mail, so I put my foot on the Frenchman's neck, wrenched off his shield and climbed back into the saddle. The shield was heavy and strange on my arm. In a daze I peered over the top of it to see what sign it bore, when a crossbow bolt struck it with a thwack.

'To the carts!' The cry was to my right. I wheeled and charged to-wards it. There were the carts. Two of them were burning – so it was smoke after all, I thought, distantly. By now my thoughts were so buried in the havoc of the battle that they came to me one by one, shyly and delicately, as though I were drawing pictures for myself in the margins of some vast, illegible book. *Letice!* That thought was distinct enough, though. The wagons were empty save for the headless body of a driver. I rode down the line. Nothing. Another driver's corpse, his severed arm still tangled in the reins. The oxen stood and grazed stolidly even as the carts they were lashed to blazed behind them. As I searched, one great white beast took a crossbow bolt in the eye and dropped with a thud that shook the ground.

'Yield!' It was a voice I recognised. A man I recognised, an earl of somewhere or other, had knocked a Frenchman from his horse and was kneeling on his chest. 'You! Help me,' he called, pointing in my direction. I dropped from my horse and ran over.

'Get his helmet off!' the nobleman ordered. I did so. The Frenchman was of middle years, ruddy and full of face.

'Sir John de Barres!' said the English knight. 'Delighted to see you again. We met at the tourney two years since.'

'*Enchanté*,' wheezed the Frenchman. Some English foot soldiers were running towards us so I got back on my horse and galloped down to the end of the wagon line. All were empty. The battle had passed over here, and I saw the shields of Earl Richard and Pierre de Moings dancing in the midst of the vineyards to the east.

'King's men! King's men!' I yelled, and spurred my sweating, almost blown mount back into the fray. The quiet man drawing those careful illuminations in my mind was holding up a concise little painting of Letice lying dead, the finger of guilt pointing at me. The dust had closed around the earl. My horse ripped through a wall of vines into a narrow lane. In front of me were three knights beating upon the shield of a fourth. As I watched, they knocked him from his saddle and, with a French oath, two knights slid from their horses, swords raised. Without thinking, I kicked my beast at them, knocking the mounted knight aside with my shield and thrusting at the nearest man on the ground. I missed, and my blade slid under his armpit, but I must have cut him as I pulled it back for he cursed and tripped backwards into the vines. Meanwhile the other man had grabbed my bridle and was trying to pull my horse down. I smashed at his helmet with the pommel of my sword until he let go. A blow fell on my shield and I had time to swing my sword around and catch the knight with the flat of my blade upon his mailed neck. Yelling, I turned and flailed at the other knight, who seemed to have lost his sword. The Englishman who had fallen was sitting up, his face in his hands. I bent down, grabbed him by his mail hood with my left arm and put spurs to my horse, dragging him down the lane of vines until my arm felt as if it were being torn out of its socket. So I reined in and dropped the man I had rescued, who lay in the dust, his face floured white with it, coughing. The only colour in his face was the red that rimmed his eyes and a smear of dark blood on his brows, but even so I realised that I had just saved the Bishop of Balecester.

I must have seen his shield out of the corner of my eye and followed it, for he would have been near Earl Richard, so this was not the blind chance it seemed, and I saw all this almost at once, but in the instant that we stared at each other wild eyed and panting it seemed that the Devil must have brought me here. That was my first thought. My second was that I could bend down and stab him through the neck, and no one would ever know. But then the bishop spoke.

'Who are you, my son?' he gasped.

'Petrus Zennorius,' I said without thinking. And then I thought: *I am covered in this dust. He would not have known me.*

'Help me up,' he said. I reached out and he pulled himself to his feet. 'My thanks . . .' he began, wiping streaks across his face with the palms of his hands.

'Are you hurt, my lord?' I said. 'No? There are horses down there—' I pointed down to where the carts were burning.

'Where is the battle?' he said, shaking his head stupidly.

'All around us, my lord!' I cried. 'There are no French that way, though. Hurry and find a horse, and get away from here! You are hurt.' It was true. His ears were leaking blood and he staggered like a drunkard, but he could walk, and I was done with him. I should have said *Go!* I could have struck him down, or left him for the French. Would that have been right or wrong? Would it have mattered with a man like Balecester? But instead I saw him totter, an *old* man, his knees too loose. I pictured those same legs striding across the rectory barn. The wolf, the bloody wolf. But it was too late now: I had let him live.

'Get up behind, my lord,' I told him, and gave him my stirrup so he could heave himself up, cursing. I wheeled my horse and went off to look for Earl Richard.

I found the earl in the midst of a small company of knights and nobles at the top of a small hillock. All of them leant on their horses' necks, and all were white and red with dust and gore.

'I have found my lord Balecester,' I called, as soon as I had come up to them. It was quieter up here away from the shrieking of men and the ring of steel against steel, the crash of hooves and the snap of breaking vines, and the whining of the crossbow bolts. I was yelling even so, for I had forgotten how to use my voice any other way, but when they recognised me, two knights yelled back. It was Edmund de Wykham and Gervais Bolam, the boys who I had fought with on the Lych Way. I raised my sword and laughed out loud. Simon de Montfort was there next to Earl Richard, and they were both pointing down the slope I had just climbed. Turning, I saw the battlefield for the first time.

The Taillebourg road was below me and about half a mile distant. The walls of Saintes were on my right. The neat, straight lines of the vineyards ran down to the road and up the far side, divided by other narrow lanes rutted by farmers' wagons. The English charge had struck the French where they had been gathering on the road, and the force of it had shattered both lines, sending shards, splinters of battle out into the vines. There was a confused melée on the road, and like a vast spider's legs, dark lines of combat radiated away up the lanes and rows of vines. Another desperate fight was going on between our hill and the city, and the flags of Marche and Poitou waved above it.

A foot soldier and a couple of pages were helping the bishop down. I found de Montfort and Earl Richard beside me.

'Well, well,' said Richard. 'What are you doing with the good bishop?'

'He drove off ten verminous Frenchmen who were about to take me captive!' rasped Balecester.

'Ten?' said Richard, looking at me incredulously.

'Ten! Ten, I say! Would I have been taken by any lesser number of French lice?' roared Balecester and crumpled in a fit of coughing.

'My lord bishop is hurt,' I said, and they laid him down and gave him wine, although he seemed to be feeling a good deal better.

'Look, Richard! Zennorius killed the Sire de Bourbon,' said de Montfort, tapping my shield with his sword.

'Good God! So he has. Archambaud Dampierre. Well, well.' I studied the shield again: it was red, with two stalking leopards in gold. There were three crossbow bolts jutting from it, and a gash of raw wood from a sword-stroke.

'Well done, sir! And saving my lord bishop from ten . . .'

'To reduce that number would dishonour my lord Balecester,' I said hurriedly, 'But if I said it were true, it would dishonour me.' To my relief, the two earls laughed, as if we were all sitting down in some comfortable hall and not up on this dusty hill with bolts flying about our heads.

'You should make him a knight, Richard,' said de Montfort, jovially. 'He has slain a very notable man, and rescued my friend, after all. Would you allow a commoner to bear Dampierre's shield?'

'Oh, very well,' said Earl Richard. He might have been agreeing to another round of cards. 'Down from your horse, Petrus Zennorius.'

It was no more or less dream-like than any other moment in that day. I knelt on the chalk pebbles, and Richard of Cornwall tapped me on the shoulders with his sword, and told me, 'Be thou a knight.'

'Get him a shield,' someone was calling.

'You can't carry that one any more,' de Montfort agreed. 'An Englishman will kill you. Here: they have brought you a buckler. Can you use it?'

I nodded and accepted the round foot soldier's shield, plain hide-covered wood studded with iron nails. I was glad to be shot of the bulky kite-shaped one anyway.

'What are your arms?' asked Gervais. He and Edmund were crowding round me, slapping my back with their mailed hands. It hurt.

'My arms?' I said stupidly, holding them out.

'Your *coat* of arms, Sir Petrus!' they hooted.

'I don't know. My family . . . were without such a thing,' I muttered.

'He shall have a red shield,' said Earl Richard, mounting again, 'In honour of the one he took.'

'And on it?' Edmund insisted.

'I don't . . .'

'A griffon,' said de Montfort, laconically. 'Sir Petrus is a little of this, a little of that, as a griffon is.' He gave me an absent-minded grin, but I could tell that I was no longer important to these great men. He turned and began to speak loudly with Earl Richard.

'A griffon, Sir Petrus?' demanded the lads. 'A griffon is a mighty charge, to be sure . . .'

'No,' I said, my head clearing for a moment. 'Not a griffon. A dog. A black dog.'

'Like the great dog of Dartmoor!' said Gervais. 'Did we not take you for . . .' But whatever Gervais was about to say was cut short, for there was a clamour of noise from the direction of Saintes, and we all turned to look.

'Lusignan is fighting as if he wishes to be killed,' Earl Richard was saying.

'He has a guilty conscience,' answered de Montfort.

'He does, the brute. My damn father-in-law, God smite him. Well . . . Oh, look there! More of the French!'

We had been fighting only the vanguard of the French army, I saw, now, and our numbers had been almost equal. But now another wave of knights was pouring down the road.

'Fetch Lusignan!' de Montfort ordered Edmund de Wykham. 'Let him draw his men up here, and we will charge their flank.' The lad galloped away. I climbed back on to my horse. I was stiff, and looking down I saw that I was bleeding from under my mail coat. The bolt that had skipped off my belly must have driven some chain links into my flesh. There was a tangle of smashed links on one thigh and blood was clotting there into a glistening jelly. There was blood, too, all over my surcoat. But everyone was splattered and daubed with red, like men in a shambles. I waited, rocking in the saddle, impatient now to get back into the fight, for I was infected with the fever of battle, and we were passing the contagion back and forth between us with every dry, painful breath we drew.

At last Lusignan rode up, his shield with its bands of blue and silver slashed almost to splinters. Behind him came a grim-faced band of knights. De Montfort yelled instructions and pointed, Lusignan nodded matter-of-factly, and that was it. With a great shout of 'King's men!' Earl Richard dug his spurs into the bloodied flanks of his charger and without a moment's hesitation every man on the hill screamed the same words and flung their horses down the hill.

I do not remember the charge, save that my chest was filled with a great and luminous energy that forced its way out of my mouth in the cry I yelled over and over again. It was not courage, nor was it fear. Perhaps it was just the joy of being alive stretched to its utmost as I hurtled towards death. For the French host was very large now, so large that they were having difficulty turning themselves to face us in the confines of the Taillebourg road. They were still wheeling and cursing when we struck, lances still up and wavering. There was a sound like a tall winter wave falling onto a pebble beach, or a thousand axes felling a thousand trees, and a knight I had seen an eye-blink ago, mannekin-small in the distance, was yelling in my face, his tongue out, his golden beard . . .

My elbow smashed into his cheek and instantly another knight crashed into me from the side. My horse reared and almost fell, sliding through a little gap between horse tails. A mace appeared from nowhere and the pommel of my saddle exploded into shards and nails. But I was rushing past and the mace – I never saw its owner – thudded into my stomach and disappeared behind me.

I was battering to right and left with my sword, desperately beating away the forms that rose up through the dust and the sun-glare, swatting at shadows and disembodied yells and cries that danced in and out of my dust-blurred vision. The din was abominable: horses, metal clashed against metal, a tumult from thousands of throats giving voice to ecstatic terror. As in a fever dream, faces came very close and vanished. I felt buffets and blows, but distantly, as though I were wrapped up like an Ægyptian corpse. I could no longer hear my own voice, only the tearing in my throat as it came out of me.

Then I was flailing at thin air. I had burst through the hedge of French bodies, and found myself in another of the narrow lanes between vineyards. All around me, other Englishmen were appearing, their faces, those not hidden behind the blank steel of helms, shining with sweat and blood, looking around wild-eyed for something to cut, to stab. And here it came. For through the vineyards, smashing the fences and rending the nets of vines, a wall of Frenchmen rode down upon us, their horses fresh, their shields and surcoats bright. '*Montjoie! Montjoie et Saint Denis!*' Their cries came before them like a thickening of the air itself. The rest of Louis' army had arrived upon the field.

I saw some English knights wheel and throw themselves back into the fight behind us. I stuck my spurs into the flayed belly of my own horse, but the poor beast gave a sickening groan and staggered sideways. I was be crushed between two lines of steel. Despairingly I screamed at the horse and urged it on. If I was going to die, I would not be rode down. *Go forward! Always go forward*, I heard one of my old fencing teachers say somewhere far back in my head. One last clap of my heels, and the wretched horse leapt ahead on watery legs. It broke into a tottering run, heaving itself up the shallow slope. I could feel its heart slamming against the great ribcage beneath my knees. On came the French, their lances straight and steady, death shining from the points.

'DEVON!' I yelled, trying to crouch behind my shield, its roundness hardly covering me. I picked a French face, black-bearded, distended with rage, and levelled my sword at it. I could feel the muscles of my horse tearing and failing. The head of a lance danced towards me like a shining, speeding bird. Time enough to take a last gulp of powdery air, before . . .

There was a massive jolt: I was a hanged man at the end of his long drop, a woodsman caught by the tree he has felled. Every bone of my body felt clenched by an iron hand which shook them like a lion shakes its kill. Then nothing. And then another crash. There was no air left in my body, so bile came instead. Hooves throbbed and clapped very close to my head. My left arm . . . I could not feel it at all, but it was still attached to me, apparently. I managed to shake off the straps of my buckler, seeing as I did so that it was gouged and cracked from side to side. Using my sword I levered myself onto my knees, the horses rushing past me on each side. My own mount was nowhere to be seen, lost in the blur of yelling, heaving creatures all around. I ducked my head and held up my sword, quavering, one stalk of corn before the scythe, trying to stand, my left arm hanging lifeless. Then the storm was past, and I was still standing, swaying. There was a horrible sound all about me, a keening, moaning drone. All about me, horses lay kicking, and men sprawled or writhed: the drone came from them. The barely-living were singing their own dirge. I blinked stinging wetness from my eyes, and found there was some feeling in my arm after all. I took a step and tripped over something: it was a man's leg, severed at the top of the thigh, still wearing its mail stocking. I gagged, seeing, a little further away, a lower jaw nestling in its beard, one red lip like a fat lobworm, an arc of white teeth.

French voices came from near by. A party of foot soldiers was trotting down the hill, dressed in kettle helms and leather armour. They carried bucklers and some held short spears such as might be used for hunting boar, or axes, or short, heavy swords. As I watched, one of them paused and stabbed down with his spear, impaling a body that lay tangled in the vines. He bent and rummaged, and straightened with a golden chain in his fist. Then they saw me. I managed to get my left hand around my sword hilt and, wrapping my right hand around it, lifted the blade and held it up. The gold chain twinkled, and the men leered. I was going to be butchered. But, Christ! If I were captured by the French . . . Louis Capet was here, somewhere nearby. He would find out, and what would that mean for me? Would he think I had betrayed him? I was an Englishman, so I could not be a traitor to France, but after so many thousands of pounds of French gold had made their way into my company's chests? And Louis had his treasure. He could make me vanish on this battlefield just to satisfy a spiteful whim, and who, really, would blame him? So the trap had closed: so be it. With all these spears and axes heading for me I could get myself killed quickly enough. But then I thought of the burning carts, and Letice, and realised that the madness of battle was seeping out of me, and suddenly I remembered that I . . . it sounds strange to relate this, but in a battle there is no room in a man's head for anything save fear and death, and soon enough only death remains: bringing it to others and waiting for it to come for you, and everything else is like the memories you might have of being a very young child: distant, faint and perhaps not even real. But now I was becoming sane again. Behind me, the sounds of battle had grown dim. The battle must be over. The English had lost: I could not imagine it otherwise. My head suddenly became clear. I turned my blade and stuck it into the ground, and pulled off one of my rings.

'Là!' I cried, holding up the heavy little circle of gold. 'I am an English knight, and I am worth a fat ransom!' The men circled me, spears and swords levelled. Their eyes ran over me as if I were a naked maid in a brothel. Then one of them – his gut pushed over his belt and his face was furrowed and thickly stubbled with grey – hefted his axe and spat at my feet. He reached out and snatched the ring, and handed it to the man on his left, who bit it, nodded, and handed it back. The man spat again, then opened his toothless mouth wide and laughed at me.

'*Alors, mon chevalier*,' he said, wetly. 'We will take you up on that. Follow us, my lord, if it pleases you.' He gave a mocking bow, and his fellows did likewise. Then, with the dull, notched blade of his axe, he pointed the way up the hill.

Chapter Fourteen

Two of the toothless soldier's mates escorted me away from the battlefield. They let me keep my sword, though when they began to search me I feared they would find my purse and so I pulled off another ring and gave it to them, which they seemed to appreciate, for they left me alone after that. I wondered if they were going to take me straight to the king, but shrugged this unpleasant thought aside: nobody knew anything about me, after all. I was just an unknown knight – I *was* a knight, though, wasn't I? How strange. Was it real? I had *earned my spurs*, as the saying goes. Did one become a knight in such an off-handed way? And if Earl Richard and Earl Simon had not come through the battle alive, did my knighthood count at all in any case? I was pondering these questions, and discovering that, although I did not seem to be wounded in any proper way, I was not in particularly good shape, when my escorts grabbed me by the shoulder and pointed towards a tall linden tree under which a crowd was gathered. Further on up the hill, a company of men were putting up a richly decorated tent, no doubt for Louis.

'You go over there,' one of them said. 'On your own parole.'

'What is your name, knight?' the other asked, rolling the words mockingly across his tongue.

'Sir Peter Blakkedogge,' I told him. Ridiculous, it sounded, but not to these men, for they tapped their heads, knocking the name into their brains, for they would be after a share of the ransom later on. I was not even sure if knights had special names or not – I'd never had to think about it before. Perhaps I was Sir Petrus Zennorius. Sir Petrus . . . Sir Petroc. Useless thoughts. Free of my escort I turned around and looked back at the battlefield.

The rich country I had seen this morning as I sat with Simon de Montfort under the walls of Saintes was fearfully changed. The soft hills that had looked so neat and orderly with their rows of vines were churned, the straight plantings smashed as if the sea had flowed in and receded, leaving a hideous tide line of ruin. The English army was nowhere to be seen, but the English lions flew above the city, so perhaps what was left of it had taken refuge inside. If the flag flew, King Henry lived, at least. The land fell away from me down to a low valley and then up again to the walls of the city. In the valley and on the far slope bodies were littered, men and horses. Small bands of men on foot were roaming, searching for prisoners and loot. On the other side of the Taillebourg road the French cavalry had formed up, one wing on the road itself, the centre on the hill where only an hour ago – or more, or less, for I had lost track of the time – I had been made a knight. The Oriflamme flew there next to the blue and silver flag of France, so King Louis was down there. Good – I would not be running into him up here. There were thousands upon thousands of mounted men around the king, a forest of spears and flags. More were coming down the road. And all around them and beneath them, men lay in black drifts. The ghastly sound of the battlefield, the moaning, keening lamentation of bad ends coming slowly, hung over everything, unearthly and chilling. The French had won, there seemed no way to doubt it. But both sides had paid a high price. At the place where our last charge had caught them on the road, a line of corpses and half-living horses lay thick and tangled. A little beyond it, the place where their counter-attack had struck, another blurred line of butchery. A confused jumble of dark shapes over where the English carts still smouldered. Here and there a shape would rise up and stagger away or fall again. Wounded men limped aimlessly through the maze of ruined vines and bodies. I watched as the French foot soldiers cut down a wounded man quite close by, although he held up his clasped hands and begged them. No gold rings on those fingers.

I stumbled onwards towards the crowd, and as I drew nearer saw that the throng was a hundred or more in number, men in armour for the most part, some standing, some sitting, others lying on the ground, hurt or dying. I looked to see if I knew anyone there. A few knights I recognised: the red-haired man I had spoken to before dawn yesterday was lying close by, his face white as the chalk he lay on, his armour hanging from him, a livid gash in his side. I thought I saw young Gervais Bolam, and there was Henry, Lord Hastings, a haughty gentleman I had sat next to at the king's table once. Married to the Princess of Scotland: he'd bring a pretty ransom. Gervais saw me, and limped over. He was grinning as if he'd suffered no more than a rowdy game of football.

'Sir Petrus!' He cried, giving me a great, painful hug. 'Knight of the Black Dog! How goes the day, sir?'

'Tolerably well, Sir Gervais,' I replied. 'Except that I am horribly thirsty. Is there anything to drink?' It was true. I was dry as an embalmed carcass, and now that I had said the words out loud I could think of nothing else.

'I saw you in the charge, man,' the boy went on. 'A mace almost took your bollocks off, by God! And the way you charged the second line . . .'

'I am sorry, Gervais, but I do not remember seeing you at all. Did you . . . are you all right?'

'Fine, fine. A knock on the leg. I cut that French devil clean in twain, though!'

'Jolly good,' I said weakly. 'What happens now?'

'Well, we will be ransomed – I trust!' he added, with a wild laugh. 'Or we will be exchanged. We took a lot of French knights prisoner, you know. So I would guess . . .'

'Are there any ladies here?' I cut in. 'My . . . my cousin Agnes was in one of the carts that the French captured. I looked for her there, but she must have escaped. I hope.' I looked again at the carnage all around us, and at the black smoke rising from the carts.

'Your cousin? Lord! No, I have not seen her. There are some women – perhaps some ladies too – somewhere about. I think they are over near the tents.' He waved a hand towards the hilltop. 'I do hope your cousin is all right. She is a fine . . .' He blushed, poor boy.

'And your friends? What about Edmund and William?' I asked to change the subject, although I was already staring in the direction he had pointed. I could see no women, though.

'They will be all right,' he was saying. 'They were with my lord Leicester and Earl Richard, and their party fought their way back to the gates. No, those two rogues will be drunk already, telling lies about all their great deeds.'

'Good for them. So a few of us escaped?'

'Oh, most of us!' he cried. 'While you and I were fighting down there—' and he pointed to where the bodies lay thick in the valley '—the rest of the army managed to get into Saintes, and Earl Richard led his men, and Lusignan's, back as well.'

'And Lusignan?'

'I believe he was with the earl.'

'So it has not been a complete disaster.'

'No, not at all! A very fine fight – did you not think so?'

I tried to show him a ferocious grin, but God knows what he saw. 'Very fine indeed,' I told him. And for no reason I threw my arms around the lad and embraced him. 'Now I will look for my cousin,' I said, and started off towards the tents.

'You'd better stay here, Black Dog!' called Gervais behind me, anxiously. You're a prisoner, you know!' I waved my arm tiredly and staggered on. My limbs were really hurting now, and the rest of my body was smarting and burning. It felt as if I had been rolled in nettles, thrown through a blackthorn thicket and then been threshed with flails. 'And you're bleeding!' came Gervais' faint voice as if to confirm what my senses were telling me.

I paused to lean on a vine-hung stake. The gnarled wood of the vine was thick with leaves and festooned with bunches of green, unripe grapes. Without thinking I grabbed a bunch and stuffed it into my mouth, letting the grapes pop against my teeth. The juice was thin and terribly sour, but I gulped it down anyway. A shadow fell over me. Looking up, I found a knight looking down at me from his horse.

'*Que faites-vous, Anglais?*' he snapped.

'Thirsty,' I croaked.

'Back to your fellows,' he ordered.

'My friend, I am looking for my cousin, a lady named Agnes de Wharram. She was in the carts that were straggling at the end of our line. Have you seen her?'

'A lady?' The man brightened immediately. 'What does she look like?' I described Agnes. He frowned. 'There are some women up there,' he conceded. 'Ladies-in-waiting, most of them. Noble ladies . . .' He scratched his nose. 'You had better go and look,' he said, and leant down towards me. 'Do not say I let you, though. What is your name?' I told him, and stuffed a few more grapes into my mouth. He shook his head and trotted off towards the other prisoners.

Spitting bitter grape-skins, I had not gone far when I met up with a party of knights on foot. They had been in the battle, for their armour was white with dust and they were daubed with blood. In short, they looked just like me, but for some reason they seemed to know I was English, and hailed me loudly and angrily. There were seven of them. One had a bandaged head, another's arm was in a sling, but they all had their hands on the hilts of their swords.

'French knights,' I said in their language, 'Do not . . . we have all battled enough for one day, have we not? I am looking for my cousin, the Lady Agnes de Wharram. Have you seen her?'

'Ladies?' sneered one man. 'Are the English sending ladies to fight their battles for them? Or are you saying that French knights would fight women?' He was working himself up to fight. A thought, heavy as lead, settled upon me: I would have to draw my sword and give them the satisfaction of hacking me up. Wearily I was lifting my hand, seven sets of blood-rimmed eyes watching it like lurchers following a hare, when a voice I knew, from somewhere – where? – spoke up.

'Wait, my friends, I know this fellow.' One of the men, he of the bandaged head, pushed past his comrades. I recognised something about his face, though it was streaked with his blood: it was a strong face, with a sharp nose and piercing eyes.

'My God,' I rasped. 'Aimery? Aimery de Lille Charpigny?'

'The very same, Petrus!' To the consternation of his friends he strode up to me and, grabbing me around the chest, planted a kiss on each cheek.

'You know this villain, then, Aimery?' said the man who wanted to kill me.

'I do. This is Petrus . . .' He frowned at me, trying to remember.

'Petrus Zennorius – as was. *Sir* Petrus Blakkedogge, or Canis Niger, or . . . Black Dog,' I stuttered, steadying myself with a hand on Aimery's shoulder.

'You are a chevalier now! God's tongue, I . . .'

'I will tell you everything later. My dear man! I am so . . . I cannot believe it. I never thanked you for . . .'

'For letting that girl knock me out? You can thank me now,' he grinned.

'So thank you a hundred, a thousand times! And now it seems you have saved me again, so I will put myself even further into your debt.'

'Why are you wandering around, Petrus? You should be over there with your countrymen.'

'I cannot . . . Listen, have you seen a lady called Agnes de Wharram?' I asked. 'She is my cousin.' Somehow it did not seem right to lie to this man, whom I had last seen sprawled unconscious in the Bucoleon Palace of Constantinople, and who had risked his life to save mine.

'Your cousin?' Aimery scowled, unconvinced.

'If she is not my cousin she is certainly nothing else,' I said. 'She has fair hair, the colour of butter, and very blue eyes. Not very tall. Very . . . comely,' I added. Then I thought of something else.

'Good Aimery, I will never be able to thank you sufficiently for Constantinople. But would you care to ransom me? I am worth a fair amount. I don't think I surrendered officially, but now I surrender to you.'

'And who will pay this ransom of yours?' asked Aimery, laughing.

'I will,' I said.

'Come now, do not mock me, my friend,' said Aimery, looking pained. 'I have had a sorry day of it. I thought to capture a great English lord, but instead I got this—' he tapped his head delicately '—and I am still as poor as a grasshopper.'

'Not so. You have captured the knight who killed the Sieur de Bourbon,' I told him, remembering the man's grinning, yellow teeth as I had torn off his shield. My stomach lurched, but I smiled as I knew a bold knight would smile. 'And I will ransom myself. You may have this armour, which cost me a pretty penny, and the gold in my purse is yours if you do not ask me how I came by it.'

'Gold?' said Aimery, bewildered.

'Aye, bezants.'

'My friend, I will take your armour, for that will satisfy honour all round,' he said. 'But . . .'

'Aimery, do not fly in the face of custom. If you do not ransom me, someone else certainly will,' I pressed. 'I do not intend to be a prisoner. If things were reversed, I would be taking your money, do not doubt it.' We glared at each other, then Aimery burst out laughing.

'Well, you *do* owe me a debt, damn you!' he cried. 'My head swam for weeks after that little Greek wildcat brained me.'

'And now it's happened again?' I pointed to his crusted bandage.

'No, no: that was a bolt. Straight across my forehead. Lots of blood, but 'tis not much. Now then, I accept your surrender, *Sir* Petrus.' He turned to his comrades, who were watching us intently.

'I know this man from Constantinople. He is a very great fighter, and I count him as my friend. Today he met with the Sieur de Bourbon upon the field, and slew him. He has put himself under my protection, and I would ask that he receives all the honour that his rank and valour is owed. All right, friends?'

Grudgingly they accepted, and wandered away in the direction of the city. 'Now let us search for your cousin,' said Aimery. He had seen some women on the far side of the tents, so we made our way slowly past the little palaces of cloth that were rising and billowing like sails while men heaved on ropes and cursed the saints out of heaven.

'What are you doing here, brother?' I asked him straight away.

'I was about to ask you that very same thing,' he laughed. 'My story is simple, and I am sure yours is not . . . I can see that I am right! Well, you have seen Constantinople. There is nothing there for a landless knight like me: no prospects, no wealth, no honour. I love my lord

Baldwin, but I think even he has abandoned the Empire in his heart. I would have stayed even so, but the squabbling of the barons, and their bloody inability to *do* anything save torment the Greek citizenry, sickened me so much that . . . we are supposed to be Crusaders, friend Petrus! We are meant to be defending Mother Church, but every day dawns without hope, and the schismatic Greeks who besiege us have more fire, more – let me say it, and do not think ill of me – more faith. I could not stand it. So I came back to France, which my blood calls home though I had never seen it, and pledged myself to king Louis. And I feel like a man again.'

'Do you have land here?'

'No, I am as landless here as in Greece. My family held a fief in Burgundy, but it reverted to the king years ago. But I intend to serve my king and fight in his wars, and perhaps fortune and skill will bring something my way.'

'And it has, it has,' I said, patting my chest. 'Quite the prize, eh?' I told him the story of my past few weeks very briefly and left out most details, especially my recent visit to Paris, but Aimery was no fool.

'You helped with the translation of the Bucoleon relics, did you not? I have heard, from men close to Emperor Baldwin, that you were with the Crown of Thorns when King Louis took posession of it at Troyes. We missed each other when you last came to Constantinople, but word had it that you were favoured at Vincennes.' He gave me a penetrating look. I remembered the cold, wet day when we had sat in a tavern and I had discovered that, far from the Frankish oaf I had taken him for, Aimery de Lille Charpigny was a man who observed the world around him with sharp eyes and a busy, astute mind.

'It was my good fortune to be given charge of the earthly details to do with the Crown and the other relics,' I said. 'Your emperor has been good enough to put his trust in me, and I have indeed met King Louis on two or three occasions. But as a go-between, nothing more. He is a very noble and righteous monarch,' I added. 'And I have been just a glorified clerk, really, a witness and recorder of transactions.'

'And now a knight,' he reminded me. 'The Sieur de Bourbon – he is a powerful man, you know. Did you really kill him?'

'I did – not deliberately, though.' For some strange reason we both burst out laughing, though there was precious little joy or mirth in it. We laughed, I suppose, because it was not us who were lying, hacked and bloody, growing cold among the vines; and because grown men who wear swords at their belts cannot be seen to weep.

Chapter Fifteen

There was a stand of plum trees a little further on, and between them, white sheets had been stretched to give some shade to the five or six women who sat dejectedly beneath them. They were guarded by a pikeman who leaned on his weapon and regarded the women slackly, sweatily; and a jowly priest, who hailed us and trotted over officiously, his ruddy jowls quaking. Aimery explained our errand, and they stepped aside, though he eyed me suspiciously.

There were three maids-in-waiting, and one of them, to my joy, was Margarete. With her was a young knight's wife I recognised, and an older lady I did not. Letice was not among them, but Margarete, who looked frightened and dishevelled but unhurt, held out her arms to me, a desperate look of relief on her lovely face. Not thinking about scandal any more, I would have held her to me but fortunately for both of us the young wife, who was tear-stained and red-nosed, stepped between us artlessly and seized my hand.

'Master Petrus! How did you come here?'

'Captured like you, Lady Cecily,' I said, gently. 'Are you well, Lady Margarete?' As I was already holding Cecily's hand I took hers as well and gave it a squeeze. It was warm and alive, and I tried to reassure her with my eyes, but she was too rattled. 'There were more of you,' I went on with false gaiety. 'Is my cousin Agnes here? I think you were in the same cart . . .'

'I was,' said the older lady. 'She is over there, with Giliane.' She pointed to another shelter a little further away. At first I could not see anyone there, but then my eye fell on three shapes lying on the ground. I gasped and took to my heels – to my shame forgetting all about poor Margarete – with Aimery muttering and panting behind me. I dodged around the trees, ignoring the cries of the priest. In front of me, very white in the dappled shade, lay a linen-covered body. Next to it a woman lay on her side, and next to her . . .

'Letice!' I yelled. She lifted her head from the pillow of her crossed arms and scowled. 'Oh, God! Letice . . . Agnes . . .'

'Stop shouting, Patch,' she said. She sounded very weary. Her throat was bound up with a bloody length of gauze, and there was blood on her tunic.

'Christ Almighty, my love, you are hurt!' I knelt beside her and helped her lean against me.

'Not really.'

The other woman stirred, and I saw it was the sick noblewoman that Letice had been nursing, Gunnilda de Lucie.

'Have you come to fetch us, good sir?' she said.

'Not yet, Lady Gunnilda,' I told her. 'But the battle is over. Soon everyone will be ransomed or exchanged.' To Letice I said: 'Have they hurt you? What happened?'

'They swarmed all over the carts,' she told me. 'We knew we were dragging behind, but there was a lame ox up ahead and the driver was tired . . . I mean, it was more horrible because I knew they would catch us, and we were crawling along, waiting for it to happen. They charged down the road, and before we could do anything they had lopped off the driver's head.'

'I saw them come,' I said. 'I thought—'

'Agnes . . . tell him what you did, my dear.' Gunnilda de Lucie rolled over and took Letice's hand. But Letice shook her head.

'She took up the carter's sword,' said Lady Gunnilda. 'And she used it, too. My Agnes, you were braver than many a knight in their first battle, I'm sure. If she hadn't, sir, only God in his mercy knows what would have befallen us. But they had some honour, I suppose, and took us prisoner in return for Agnes putting down her blade. I do not think . . .'

'In the other cart, a maid had her throat cut, and another was dishonoured,' said Letice flatly. 'The girl they raped . . . I don't know what happened to her. The other one is there.' She nodded towards the shrouded body. 'Everyone was nice enough to her after she was dead. God bless us all, eh, Patch?'

'Amen,' said Lady Gunnilda, not catching the bitterness in Letice's tone.

'Is this your cousin, Petrus?' said Aimery.

'It is. Agnes de Wharram, may I present Aimery de Lille Charpigny? We knew each other in Constantinople,' I said. Aimery knelt and kissed Letice's hand. She was too surprised to resist. Then he kissed Lady Gunnilda's hand as well, and she blushed.

'You are a gentleman, sir knight,' she cooed.

'But the Lady Agnes is hurt,' said Aimery, reaching out and touching her bandaged throat very tenderly.

'Nothing. Just a scratch,' she muttered.

'Nonsense! Her leg is broken!' Lady Gunnilda put in. Meanwhile, Letice was scowling at Aimery, pale eyebrows lowered. I knew that look, and I wanted to warn the Frenchman to leave her be, for his own sake. But he did not notice, or ignored the look.

'I am horrified,' he said, 'That any countryman of mine would think to harm so fair a lady. Or any maid at all,' he added hastily. So he had understood her after all.

'My leg isn't broken. I have twisted my ankle, that is all. And I am *not* a maid,' hissed Letice.

'She is a widow,' I added hastily. 'Her late husband was a Crusader and died at Venice.'

'My lady, you are alone in the world?' Aimery said in horror. 'How could heaven allow such a state of affairs?'

'Well, what are your affairs?' countered Letice rudely. Aimery drew back his head. *Oh Christ, now she's offended him,* I thought, but instead he bowed rather sweetly and placed his hand proudly on his hip.

'I may not be a man of wealth,' he said, 'But why should that matter? There is a song that says,

If the beautiful lady I want to belong to
Wants to honor me
Just so much that she agrees to let
Me be her faithful lover,
I am mighty and rich above all men,'

he chanted. He had a good voice, but Letice, hurt and grieving, merely scowled. Aimery was not to be put off, however. He knelt down and took her ankle gently in his hands, and she was too surprised to protest. He felt it expertly, and smiled.

'Just a sprain, my lady. It will be healed in a week.'

'What are you on about, Frenchman?' demanded Letice.

'Good lady, I ask you for nothing
But to take me for your servant,
For I will serve you as my good lord
Whatever wages come my way,'

he replied. 'How else might a courtly knight like Sir Petrus or myself live with honour? Without love, what is there? Chrétien of Troyes wrote . . .'

'What do you mean, a knight like Sir Petrus?' said Letice. Meanwhile she had evidently heard quite enough about Chrétien of Troyes, and she was regarding Aimery with something like horror, although there was, perhaps, a touch of amusement as well. I explained what had happened, and how I was now an actual knight, forsooth. I must confess I felt a brush of satisfaction as I watched her gape in disbelief.

'Black Dog – how did you come by such a name?' asked Aimery.

'A pet name from his youth – isn't that right, cousin Petrus?' said Letice. She gave us both a sort of twisted smile. 'I told you, didn't I? But you did not believe me.'

'I seem to remember you saying something about me being chopped to pieces,' I reminded her. And at that moment a great cheer went up from the crowd of prisoners under the linden tree. Shielding my eyes, I thought I saw the white flag of truce. Aimery looked as well.

'I would guess that the prisoners are being exchanged,' he said. 'You had better go, Petrus, and you too, my ladies. I will see to it that your friend is buried decently.' He helped Lady Gunnilda to her feet – she winced, but the flux seemed to have left her – and held out his hand to Letice. She tried to rise, but gave a moan and shook her head.

'My ankle,' she gasped. She had gone very white, and I helped her lie down.

'Here,' I said to Aimery, reaching under my mail coat and drawing out my purse. 'Here is my ransom, and here's for Lady Agnes as well, and this dear lady.' I took two bezants from it and handed the heavy little bag to Aimery, but he held up his hands.

'You will be exchanged,' he protested. 'You need not pay a ransom at all, to anyone.'

'Take it!' I told him. 'A man who does not at least try to pay his debts is no man at all. We are by no means even, my friend, but this is a beginning.' And I took his hand and folded it into a fist around the purse. 'I will send you my armour, and may it bring you good fortune – you'll need to get it mended, though.' I patted the tangled rings that covered my belly. 'Look after Lady Agnes, my dear friend. I am leaving her under your protection, but as a free woman, not a prisoner, yes?'

'No! What the bloody hell do you . . .' Letice was struggling to sit up, but I knelt and put my hand gently over her mouth while I planted a firm kiss on each cheek.

'Aimery *is* a good man,' I whispered to her. 'One of the few people in this world I would actually trust with my life, let alone yours, you difficult wench. You are safer here than in the city. King Louis has enough men to lay seige to Saintes for ten years. Go back to . . . go back to Venice.' Her eyes were slashing at me like razors. 'Very well, go back to London. You will be safe there now.' I gave her the two bezants I had taken from my purse. 'This will get you wherever you wish to go. Trust Aimery.' I took her skull between my two palms and kissed her hard on the forehead. 'I love you. I don't expect you to care, and I don't require your love any more, but I do love you.' Then I embraced Aimery, and with a by your leave took Lady Gunnilda by the arm and helped her away through the plum trees towards where the English prisoners were beginning to form themselves into a line. I left the noblewoman with the party of John de Hastings and set off down towards the Taillebourg road.

It was not even a mile to the gate, but it took me an eternity to reach it. The vineyards had become a maze, and I was so exhausted that I could not bring myself to clamber over the tangles of stakes, vines and the corpses of men and beasts. So I had to cast about to find clear ways through, and by the time I gained the road I was reeling with fatigue and with the horrors I had seen. Already, a rabble of soldiers, peasants and camp-followers was picking over the corpses, plundering and stripping them naked. The chalky ground was blotched everywhere with great dark stains and scattered with severed body parts: legs, arms, hands. Heads lay like grotesque root vegetables, black, distended tongues licking the earth, eyes staring glassily. Corpses lay heaped in butchered wantonness, pale as maggots, French and English knotted together, legs splayed, manhoods lolling. The ravens and kites were already gathering.

As I came close to the city I passed beyond the looters. Here at least the bodies were still clothed. In a daze, half fainting with thirst and the pain from my injuries, I let my eyes drift over the shields and surcoats, looking for blazons I recognised. But I saw none, until I passed a cluster of bodies. Next to them lay a shield of dark blue divided by a stripe of white, a yellow star above and below. I had seen that device not so long ago. It was the shield of William Maynet.

He lay on his back, arms outstretched and eyes wide open. A cross-bow bolt jutted from his breast-bone. Another body was sprawled across his waist, its neck a black stump. Edmund of Wykham's head lay close to his friend's open hand, eyes narrowed, lips pulled back. He must have dismounted when his friend fell, and as he knelt . . . I pulled the signet rings from their hands. William had a chain around his neck with a garnet-studded cross upon it, and Edmund had a gold chain and a worn medal wrapped around his wrist. I took them for Earl Richard, for their mothers and fathers. When I stood up, I saw that they had almost made it to safety, for English voices were calling to me from the walls. In another minute, I had passed inside the gates, a knot of soldiers had gathered round me, and I was taking a long, long drink from a wineskin. The king and his brother had taken over the castle, and I found my way there. I knew what needed to be done, but I needed Earl Richard's permission. The nobles were shut up in urgent councils, I was told, so I let some kindly monks undress me and clean up my wounds, which were many but slight, and as the stinging of the last dressing faded I fell asleep.

I had not slept for two hard days and two long nights, but I woke in time for breakfast, which I fell upon although I was not hungry. I was stiff as a statue but there was no fever, and after I had found my baggage down in the town, arranged for my armour to be repaired and sent across to Aimery de Lille Charpigny, and changed from the linen shift the monks had lent me – it reminded me unpleasantly of grave-clothes – into my normal things, I took myself back to the castle and asked for an audience with Earl Richard. It was past luncheon by that time, for Saintes was in an uproar, stuffed full of angry, defeated Englishmen and preparing for a siege. The townsfolk were scuttling about, boarding up their houses and avoiding the English, who no doubt had already begun to steal and to bully them.

Richard received me in the castle solar. He did not look like a man who had played any part in the last two days, but lounged, clean and groomed, in a high-backed chair.

'Sir Petrus,' he said as I entered. 'Have you come to confirm your knighthood?' I could not tell if he was jesting or not, so I bowed and said, 'If your lord still means to honour me I will be the happiest man in your brother's kingdom . . .' But he cut me off.

'You did kill Archambaud Dampierre, yes? You did save the life of my lord Balecester? You did. There are witnesses. Do not be uncouth, man. A knight you are, whether you like it or not. And now, since we are defeated and trapped, and our precious allies have proved no more use than a candle in a snowstorm, what have we to discuss?' His face had gone cold. I drew back my shoulders.

'My lord, I brought you a message that held no personal interest to me. But nevertheless I did bring the message, and you have acted, in some part at least, because of it. I cannot speak for the man who sent it, except to assure you that, circumstances being what they are, he acted in good faith, for the cause of Raymond of Toulouse is closer to his heart than any other thing in this world. Knowing Jean de Sol, perhaps you will see that this is true.'

'I listened to my dear brother, and that was the cause,' said Earl Richard, clenching the arms of his chair, his face reddening. 'And the lies of my father-in-law, promising a great host of allies that never existed. As for . . .'

'My lord Richard,' I said quickly, risking all to head off his anger. 'You are blameless in this matter, and no man could say otherwise. The whole army saw how your allies betrayed the king. But if I had not brought the message, perhaps you would not have chosen this course. I would make some small amends, if I could.'

'Amends? You are trying my patience, sirrah! I am beginning to wonder what sort of Englishman you are. Do you dare speak of betrayal to me?'

'The English cause is not the only one betrayed,' I reminded him. 'King Louis has gathered a vast army. He will crush Toulouse in a day. News of the battle will reach Aragon and Navarre, and they will not have the stomach for a full-blown war. But some good may yet come of all of this.'

'Do not talk in riddles, man,' barked Richard.

'What if I could still ensure that Sanchia of Provence gave you her hand?' I said, slowly, deliberately. My heart was knocking the words up out of my chest, but I kept breathing, and looked the earl straight in the eye.

'I have not kept my side of our bargain, so why should Raymond?' asked Richard, coldly. 'Toulouse's cause is lost,' he went on. 'He will surrender to Louis, and take whatever the king chooses to inflict upon him.'

'He still needs friends,' I said.

'Poor Raymond,' said Richard, bitterly. 'Do you know what my brother the king has done? He has fled. He left this morning for Bordeaux. Finished with all this nonsense, for which I am sure he has already absolved himself of any responsibility at all. Father Lusignan is off to beg Louis for mercy, and meanwhile I, who knew this was a fool's errand from the start, must sit here like a woman. Do you know what de Montfort said this morning? That my brother should be locked up like Charles the Simple. I could have had his head for that, except that he's bloody right.'

'Well, my lord,' I said. In my profession it is either an extremely good sign or an even worse one to have powerful men tell you exactly what is on their mind. I could not take back what I had just said, and neither could he, so I decided to ignore it and press on. 'Raymond will lose his lands, and the Church will be given free rein to do what it will,' I told him. 'He knows this. He has lost his allies in war, but he will need allies more than ever if he is to survive the peace that will be stuffed down his throat. I will ask, or Monsier de Sol will ask, that he gives up the Lady Sanchia in return for your good will and that of England. It is a promise you can make without any concern, for Count Raymond is a hollow man now.'

I could see the thoughts flying behind Richard's eyes. His knuckles went white, then back to red again. I have you, I thought. Money might have done it, but love . . . The Captain was not mad at all, I realised. And he had possibly just saved my life.

'Come here,' he commanded. 'Kneel.' I did so. 'Raise your hands in prayer,' he said. I did, understanding with a sickening clarity as I touched my palms together what was about to happen. Richard stood, and pressed my hands tightly between his own. 'Say these words after me.'

I intoned the solemn words, those nails, the glue and mortar that bind men to their masters:

'I, Petrus, swear on my faith that henceforth I will be faithful to my lord. I will never cause him harm or lay open to another what he has entrusted to me, and will do my homage to him completely, against every man, with no deceit.'

'You are *my* man now, Petrus,' said Earl Richard, releasing me. 'A knight must have a master.' He was watching me keenly. I forced my lips into a grateful, worshipful smile, the smile the gamekeeper finds on the fox that has died overnight in his trap.

'You have made me a promise, my knight. If you are not lying, and can deliver my lady to me, I will be in *your* debt. Fail, and I tell you now that you will be arraigned as a traitor and meet a traitor's end. I assure you I will not forget, either way. Am I making myself plain?'

'As you command, my lord,' I said. 'I will set off tomorrow, if that is possible.'

'You seem to know what is possible, Petrus, so . . .'

My new lord dismissed me with a wave of his hand. I left and wandered about the castle for a long time, finding myself at last up on the battlements, leaning through an embrasure and staring out at the rolling land. The air was heavy with the sweet foulness of spoiled meat, and amongst the vines the naked bodies were turning black. The sky was filled with wheeling crows and kites. Bands of people were wandering here and there, some looking for friends or masters, for corpses were being carried both to the French camp and into Saintes, and some searching for what little plunder must be left. There was no sign of any preparation for a siege, and I guessed that Henry and his cousin Louis must be engaged in whatever negotiations cousins make after one of them has lost a battle with the other. The flags were flying over Louis' camp, already a large town of tents and rough shelters, the smoke from a thousand campfires rising up straight as columns.

I thought of Letice, and hoped she was all right. Her leg had not seemed to be broken, but Letice was not used to being at the mercy of others. Of all men, though, Aimery would take care of her. I had thought a great deal about him over the years, but though I had returned twice to Constantinople since he had helped me escape from the alliance of Nicholas Querini and the Emperor Baldwin's regent I had not seen him, for he had been away at the wars, and there was always war on the borders of the dying empire. Aimery had been a man of honour in an Empire that existed because honourable men had been poisoned by greed. He had risked his life to save mine, for no other reason, so far as I knew, than that it had seemed to him the right and honourable course of action. Letice could not have a more worthy protector. I hoped she would not make his life too miserable.

The next day I slipped out of the city just before dawn and galloped south through the vineyards, still green and lovely here, beneath a sky that was dark and tattered. I had gone to say goodbye to Margarete but her door was barred by a lady from Shropshire with the arms of a washerwoman, who looked at me as if I were a weasel out to rob the henhouse, and so I fled before I caused more of a scandal. I never saw her again, though more than once I wished, in the months to come, that I had braved the wrath of the court ladies and showed Margarete some honour, as she had showed me love.

The French had not yet bothered to encircle Saintes, and I saw nothing but cattle, and a few tired peasants walking to their fields, to trim the vines and hoe in the cool before sunrise. Overhead, beneath the ragged clouds, flocks of black birds were flying north to where the carrion waited to delight them. Earl Richard had given me a parting gift: a surcoat of red cloth emblazoned with a crouching black dog, a red-eyed Alaunt with bristles like a boar and white teeth. Some swift-fingered seamstress had worked day and night to make it, no doubt. I was bound, now: tied with all the chains of obligation I had spent the past seven years avoiding and mocking, I who had called no one master or lord. The oath I had sworn meant nothing to me, but I was inside the trap now, that cage that men call their world, whose bars are the power of others, and whose key is never quite in reach. I felt the weight of it pressing upon me even as I flew down the roads of Poitou: rank, influence and power, layers and layers of it, heavy as time. Above me now, my lord Richard. Above him, the king, and above him God himself. I believed in none of them, but that luxury afforded me no comfort, for now they all believed in me.

Chapter Sixteen

Raymond de Saint-Gilles, seventh Count of Toulouse, sat at the head of a long table in an empty hall, his greying head sunk into his hands. There was no noise except for the sparrows high up amongst the beams. Finally one hand dropped to the table, two fingers standing, tapping.

'Henry has run away, you said?' His voice sounded terribly weary but somehow unsurprised. 'And Lusignan's word was nothing but empty air. My God, to be ruined is one thing, but to be ruined by fools . . .'

'My lord, you have been unwell,' said Captain de Montalhac. We were standing together before the Count, the three of us alone in the great hall save for the sparrows in the ceiling and an old black cat asleep on a window ledge. 'Perhaps we should not talk of these things now.'

'No, de Montalhac? Then what shall we talk of, man?' The Count looked up at last. He was haggard, for the sickness that had almost killed him three months ago had burned away the flesh beneath his face leaving him hollow-cheeked and aged beyond his years. He was a handsome man, in his fourth decade, broad-shouldered, his long and curly hair just beginning to leave his temples, but the skin below his eyes was papery and bruise-black, and his eyes had not lost the yellow stain of fever.

'King Henry has abandoned us. Hughues de Lusignan, that posturing serpent, has betrayed us. France has a vast legion of men in the field – how many d'you think, young man?'

'There were thirty thousand at least before Saintes, my lord,' I said reluctantly. 'And I heard, while I was a prisoner, that more were joining Louis every day. We faced perhaps five thousand knights and more than twenty thousand foot, and countless crossbowmen and auxiliaries. If Lusignan has gone over to France, then there are another thousand knights and five or more thousand foot.'

'Christ. And England will not fight on?' There was no hope in Raymond's voice, and I could give him none.

'No, my lord. The English barons are furious with Henry. They were forced to pay a shield tax of thirty marks on each knight's fee, and now they have seen him toss their silver into the kennel – worse, for no doubt they would rather have seen it in the shit than given to Lusignan. I am afraid that Lord Cornwall and Lord Leicester will have sought terms with Louis by now.'

'It is finished, then,' said Raymond. 'I have heard nothing from Navarre or Aragon, and I will not. The stupidity of Avignonet has cost me . . .'

'You have been excommunicated before, my lord,' said the Captain. 'That need not concern you. And remember, there is still . . .'

'Still no pope in Rome. Yes, yes, I know that, Michel. That will not matter to Louis. And I fear it will dampen the enthusiasm of my vassals and allies. Roger of Foix has been very silent these past few weeks. I am alone, I tell you.'

'Not entirely so, my lord,' I said. Raymond regarded me, bleary with defeat. 'You may still have a friend in England,' I went on. 'Richard Earl of Cornwall is willing to show his friendship – this I have from my lord Richard himself.'

'That is something,' muttered Raymond. Then he brightened a little. 'Better Richard than his half-wit brother,' he said.

'I cannot answer to that,' I told him, 'But Richard is well-loved by Louis Capet.' I told him briefly how Earl Richard had gone as a pilgrim to parley with the French king at Taillebourg, and how the French knights had cheered him. 'He will not be an ally in war, but in peace you will find him a powerful friend.'

'Why?' Raymond's question was blunt, his eyes sceptical.

'He despises Hughues de Lusignan, and he knows that his brother has abandoned his friends and shamed the crown. I believe he is a loyal man, although I base that on very slight acquaintance. That is the answer to your "why," my lord. But in fact I am authorised to offer you the means by which you may secure an alliance with the earl.'

There was silence for a moment. Raymond inspected a chewed fingernail bitterly.

'How, young man?' he asked me at last. It was very clear that he was not looking forward to my answer.

'It is no secret that Earl Richard has, for two years now, desired the hand of the Lady Sanchia of Provence.' There: it was said. I expected the silence to grow like a thunder-head, but instead Raymond scratched his ear and cackled grimly.

'Sanchia? I am to pay tribute to the mighty Earl of Cornwall with my betrothed, am I? My God. Well – are you Richard's ambassador, young man? What is your *exact* title?' He fixed me with a yellow but piercing eye.

'Petroc has no exact title, my lord. He has been acting on my instructions, and so he is in effect, and in this matter, your agent.'

I glanced at the Captain, but he seemed quite at ease with all of this. He knew about my homage to Earl Richard, for I had told him everything as soon as I had ridden into Toulouse two days before and found him, much to my joy, at the palace of the counts.

'So you are Richard of Cornwall's knight,' he had said, amused. 'Do you intend to keep your oath?'

'I am not certain,' I had said, truthfully, for all through my long ride down the valley of the Garonne I had turned the question over and over in my mind: it meant nothing, just an assortment of words designed to intimidate the weak. But I did feel the stifling weight of obligation, of tradition. All those tombstones of loyal knights I had knelt on in church, all the songs. They involved me now. I had taken off my red surcoat after the first day's journey, but I could hear myself screaming *King's men! King's men!* as I fell asleep at night and as I trotted along the empty roads, and felt again the unlooked for, unwelcome bloom of pride within my chest as Earl Richard had laid his sword upon my shoulders. The Captain laughed, however, and patted me on the knee.

'One should never be certain about oaths,' he said, 'Speaking as one who has never sworn one.'

'Not even to Count Raymond?'

'Good Christians are not required to swear their loyalty,' he answered. 'But I am bound, nonetheless. You have sworn, but are you bound? You have a lord now, if you choose, but you have no king – or did you take a shine to Henry?'

'God, no . . . no, I didn't.'

'Well, then. The problem is that they – the lords of this world, those with the pretty colours and fierce beasts on their shields – do not understand that you are free. They do not understand freedom at all. You do, by now.'

He was right: I did understand freedom, well enough to see that Raymond of Toulouse had almost lost his, and that it filled him with dread. 'Do I take it that you are agreeable, my lord?' I asked him. He drummed his fingers on the table.

'I have been asked this question before. Richard sent a man – a bishop, I think, name of Pierre. He was most impertinent. To him my answer was no, although the fellow was so wrapped up in his own bluster that I am not sure he took it thus.' The count winced, as if his anger had taken a bite out of his innards. He was growing old, and he had no son. The young daughter of the lord of Provence would have given him a last chance to sire an heir. It was no love match, but Raymond was struggling to make his choice, that was plain. Finally he bit his thumb-nail savagely and pointed the ragged end at me grimly.

'Circumstances are somewhat altered now, young man. So I will allow you to achieve what bishop Pierre did not. You may send word to Richard of Cornwall. Tell him he may have his little Sanchia.'

'That I will do, my lord,' I said. So he would forfeit an heir to save his land. It was the braver choice, I had to admit.

'How can I serve you now, Lord Raymond?' asked the Captain.

'You can do no more, Michel. I will have to ride out to the borders and wait for Louis to show his intentions, but we know what those will be. I will have to grovel to him, and let the wolves in to my lands again. Your people will not survive them this time, my friend,' he said, quietly. The Captain lifted his head and watched the sparrows fly from beam to beam.

'You must seek a treaty with France,' he said. 'Send word to Blanche: Louis' mother will do what she can to stop any more bloodshed. You must stop fighting, Lord Raymond, but I cannot. The Good Christians will either fight to the death, or be led to the slaughter. They are your people too, my lord. What would you have them do?'

'You must look to yourself, Michel,' said Raymond, pushing himself upright. 'When France is let in, I will not be able to protect you.' He turned and walked slowly away from us towards the cold hearth, and stared for a moment into its cavernous black mouth. 'You have been a loyal servant,' he said, and his voice echoed hollowly from the fireplace. 'Many years ago you helped my father to win a marvellous victory, and your reward was exile. You have done all you could to help me again, and your reward . . .' He turned to face us, and leaned back against the stones. 'The only reward I can offer you is the truth. Which is that Louis will force the Inquisition upon me and my subjects, heretic or not. I will have almost no power, and that I will use to keep Rome and the Dominicans out of my lands. I must beg for mercy from the king: I shall not bend my knee to the pope as well. The Good Christians are finished. I am an excommunicate. I have no son, and my daughter is married to Louis' brother. If I cannot give my people a son, this country of ours will vanish at the moment of my death. I have fought against that fate all my life. I must be allowed to marry and get an heir. If I have to turn against your people to save mine, I shall, with a glad heart. There. That is my gift, old friend.'

The Captain smiled and drew himself up to his full height. I had not noticed that his back had become a little bowed, but now, in his long tunic of black damask, he stood like a looming shadow, as if the cold fireplace had breathed a black flame out into the hall.

'We all strive, Lord Raymond, and we all fail. Your world will fade, and your place in the memories of men will be stained with that fading, that defeat. I will not be remembered, and nor will my brothers and sisters, but we will leave this world behind, far behind. You and all lords, and kings, and popes, will roam forever through the ruins of your vanity, but we shall walk through the fire, and be gone.' He bowed to Raymond, and held up his hand.

'Goodbye, Count. If you must fight the Devil by joining his army, then so be it. There is no victory in it for you, and that, as you understand, is your curse. But know this, lord. The Good Christians have their victory already.'

Chapter Seventeen

Outside, the sun was blazing down, and there was a breeze coming up from the south, sharp with pine resin and sage. The birds chirped and clattered in their wicker cages. The Captain led me unhesitatingly, silently, through the chaotic tangle of alleyways until we came to the city walls. There was a steep flight of stairs and we climbed them, the Captain's legs as spry as my own. When we were on the parapet, which was crowded with lounging guards, courting youngsters and peddlers, he led me again past a watchtower and then another until we had escaped the crowd. Finally he stopped and leant on the rosy bricks of the wall. We gazed out northwards over the flat, fertile lands that stretched away to the soft hills far in the distance.

'It was here, or hereabouts,' said the Captain at long last. I said nothing, for I had nothing to say. It seemed that the time for idle questions was past.

'When I was something like your age I . . . No, wait,' he said. 'I told you, a long time ago, something of my family, didn't I?'

'In Viterbo,' I said, remembering that strange night in the pope's palace when we had dined with an Inquisitor and stayed up very late, talking of the past and of the future. 'Only that Simon de Montfort . . .'

'I told you everything important, then,' said the Captain, holding up a finger. 'Yes: de Montfort. I escaped him, with some others of our village, but my family did not. And so I took to the fields of my homeland and, I suppose, cheated death not once but many times. So it was with all of us who survived the French. It was a land of refugees and outlaws – who had been the highest folk in the land before de Montfort came. Many died. I found my way to my liege lord, Count Raymond of Toulouse, and became a knight in his army. I was lord of Montalhac – there were hundreds of us, nobles without land. Faydits, they called us, young men in rusty armour, bellies empty, hearts raging. Anyway. I fought de Montfort, killed Frenchmen when I could. There was a great battle, at Muret, when the King of Aragon joined us and we thought we would drive the wolves from our country. De Montfort faced us, and we had twenty men to every one of his. I was in the army that day. I saw his little army all huddled around the red lion on de Montfort's flag. I faced the French charge, when it struck us like a mountainside crumbling into a valley. It was a sound . . .' He touched his ear, and grinned at me, but there was nothing in his face but remembered horror. 'I still hear it. We could not lose, and then that terrible sound, two armies crashing together like a great mountain toppling down into a valley. Thousands of our people died – seven or more thousand. We fled. The pope gave Languedoc to Simon de Montfort, and ordered him to hunt us Good Christians to the death.

'And then came Toulouse. Five years of scrabbling, fighting off the French, who were everywhere, gorging themselves like rats in a tithe-barn on our land and our people. And de Montfort was fighting us for his land – *his* land, mark you, the pope's gift. And in 1217 he was ready to take the prize, which was Toulouse itself, his capital – except that the folk of Toulouse had decided that they did not want the French devil as their lord, for they had one already. He came to terrorise, to tyrannise, but then, greedy swine that he was, he left to steal more land down in the south.

'So we came in disguise, early in the morning, riding like fury through the gateway, and when we were inside we unfurled our banners and Count Raymond threw back his cloak to receive the kisses and tears of his people. "The morning star," they called him, and though he was an ageing man by then he did shine, to me and to all of us, for there was still hope then, and he carried it with him.

'The French were furious, as you might imagine, and de Montfort brought his red lion flying up from the south. He laid siege to the city – *his* city. All through the winter we held him off, and it was terrible, because the French were brave as beasts are brave, and hurled them-selves at the walls until we butchered them. And then we rode out and were butchered in our turn. But the countryside was against Simon, and we were supplied with ease. Then Raymond's son joined us – Raymond the Younger, whom you have just met. Achilles, they called him, fairer than a rose, for he was young and strong, and gave the city new life. We held out through the winter and into the next summer, until Simon's patience snapped. In his vanity he built a great siege engine that towered over our walls, a wooden monster that began to lumber very slowly to-wards the city, a few yards a day. When it reached the walls we would be lost – how we cursed it, the great lumbering thing, covered all over with raw cowhides that stank like a mountain of corpses. So we made a great sally, all the men of the city, and the Wolf met us and hurled us back. But just when he seemed to have bested us, one of the mangonels on the walls behind us let fly, and the stone found Simon's head and crushed it like a ripe fig.

'*The Wolf is dead!* The whole city took up the cry. The French were finished. We attacked them again and again, burned their stinking tower . . . and they slunk away. I tell you, Patch . . . but you look puzzled, my friend.'

'No, sir, no, not puzzled. It is a mighty story,' I said hurriedly. For it was, and my head was fairly spinning with strange pictures: the Captain as a young man, that was odd enough, but charging at Muret? Riding into a besieged city? It was almost as if I had not seen this man properly in the seven long years I had been at his side.

'It is simply that . . .' I bit my lip, then pressed on. 'It is simply that I cannot imagine you as a knight,' I finished, wondering if I had presumed too much. But he laughed, something like a proper laugh at last.

'Aha. Well, I might say the same about you. I told you about the stone that crushed the Wolf's head? It is a famous story, that.'

'I have heard it, of course,' I said. 'It was a woman who cast the stone – that is the tale, anyway.'

'That is so. The walls were manned by women and even girls, children, when the men went forth. Noblewomen, in fact, for everyone was caught up in this great, burning thirst for vengeance, and Count Raymond – well, they called him Morning Star, but also Christ, even the Good Christians; and his son was our springtime. The people of Toulouse, every living soul, were ready to give their life for their lord. But you have heard the story. The stone was thrown by a mangonel crewed by a lady from Béziers and her three daughters. If you know what the Wolf did to Béziers, you will know that this lady sought to avenge twenty thousand souls slaughtered there, her mother and father, her husband and oldest son amongst them.'

'Can you aim a mangonel?' I wondered aloud.

'Hardly. But a quick eye can judge distance, and when a target comes into range . . . No, what the lady from Béziers took was an opportunity. It was chance that brought the Wolf under her machine, but she took his head off just the same. That mangonel was lashed down where you are standing, by the way. Over there . . .' He pointed to where a poplar tree stood at the edge of a field of corn. 'That was where the tower came down. Do you see that tree with the vines growing over it?' I shielded my eyes: there it was, a crossbow-shot away. 'Simon de Montfort fell there. I did not see it: I was down in the fight for the tower. But I heard the cry go up. And I turned and looked back, up here.' He slapped the bricks. 'The next day when I looked out from here, all you could see below were corpses and naked limbs, white like maggots around the carcass of the tower.'

'I have seen that, now,' I said. 'How strange – now I have met two men who were here that day.'

'Who is the other?' asked the Captain.

'Simon, Earl of Leicester. He saw his father go down, so they say, and he could not have been more than ten years old.'

'Strange again,' said the Captain, picking at a yellow disk of lichen on the wall. 'I was ten when his father killed mine.' He flicked the lichen out into space. 'It looks peaceful enough, doesn't it? Much like when I was a boy. But there are invisible chains that bind everyone here to some horror or other. Count Raymond – he is no more free than that tethered goat down there. And now that I have returned, neither am I.'

'What will we do, then?' I asked.

'We?' The Captain turned his face to mine. I could see the lines that were deepening in it, like a dry slope scored by a summer downpour.

'There is nothing left in the Pharos Chapel for Louis to buy. I would dearly love to go back to Devon, but I will not be any man's vassal. And the comforts of Venice will be all the more welcome if I postpone them for a while,' I said. I was thinking of the corpses I had seen in the fields around Saintes, and of the death of fathers, and so I was almost startled when the Captain laid his hand on my shoulder.

'You can come with me, if you like,' he said simply. 'I am going to see Gilles.'

'Very well. Where are we going?'

'To the Synagogue of Satan.' He began to laugh, and the breeze caught the sound and swept it away towards the hills. 'That is, we will ride south,' he said, sombre again, 'to where the Good Christians will be gathering. The Inquisition likes to call it that, but men of reason have always called it the castle of Montségur.'

We left the next morning early, and the Captain led us in a canter across the flat watermeadows. He wanted to shake the gloom of the city and its defeated lord from his bones, I guessed, and we did not look back. Soon we were riding through hilly country, heading south-east. We were heading for Mirepoix, where the Captain had an errand, and we got there at noon the next day. It was a market day, and we found ourselves struggling against a tide of cattle and oxen coming into the town to meet their fate. The whole place smelled of dung, but it seemed rich and content. We put up for the night in a good inn near the covered market, and as soon as we had thrown our packs onto the bed, the Captain patted me on the shoulder.

'Let us go out. There is someone I want you to meet.'

We made our way across the square, past countrywomen with wind-scoured faces hawking chickens and geese, through herds of stolid cows, confusion in their gentle eyes. The Captain led me along the side of the church and into a narrow alley between old and leaning houses. It was alive with gossiping women yelling to each other from their doorways in thick Occitan dialect, and though the Captain did not look left or right he was smiling. Then he halted before an archway, glanced up and down the alley and stepped through it. I followed him into a dim court-yard filled with geese and reeking of their turds, and up a worn flight of stairs at the far end. There was a door studded all over with rusty iron bosses at the top, and he rapped a quick rhythm with his knuckles on the stained wood. The door opened and an old man stuck his head out, recognised the Captain and beckoned us inside.

Straight away I knew we were in a Cathar house. I had been inside one once before, in Venice, and it had the same sparse furnishings, the same whitewashed walls, the same calm hanging in the air like incense. The old man, who was dressed all in black and whom I guessed was a *bon homme*, led us into an inner chamber and bade us sit on one of the benches that lined the walls. He left, and returned with another *bon homme*. At once the Captain sprang to his feet and embraced him warmly, planting a kiss on both his cheeks while the man patted his back joyfully.

'So you have returned to us!' he said, and his voice was low and rich – a priest's voice, or I missed my guess.

And I did not. 'Petroc, this is Bertrand Marty, bishop to the Good Christians of Toulouse, though his diocese stretches over all these hills and mountains.'

So this was Bertrand Marty, the heretic bishop. If the Good Christians had such a thing as a leader, it was he. I knew of Bishop Bertrand, for it was to him that the Captain and I had sent the *Mandylion*, three years ago now. Now I found that he was a very different bishop to any I had met before. Prelates – and by now I had known many – tend to be haughty, self-serving beasts who love to see the laity cower and kiss their amethyst rings. Ranulph of Balecester, vile though he might be, was by no means unusual in my experience. But Bertrand Marty was exactly as he seemed: a stocky, pewter-haired man of sixty years or so, burned nut brown by the sun; warm, bustling, filled with energy that seemed inseparable from the love he bestowed on everyone around him. He had spent his whole life pursued by the Church, roaming this land and sleeping in barns and hedges. And yet he had managed to keep himself a free man, and even thrive as the anti-prelate of the Languedoc.

The bishop held out his arms to me and folded me in a strong embrace. 'You are Michel's friend who has been working for us in far-off lands!' he cried, and kissed me on the cheek. 'Welcome, dear man! Are you bound for Montségur?'

'It seems so,' I said, laughing. So this was the man whose cause I had been serving. Suddenly my trials almost seemed worthwhile.

'Now then. Let me tell you what has been going on here,' he said, inviting us to sit. The older man brought out a brown loaf of bread and three horn cups of water, and the bishop divided the loaf between us.

'Pierre-Roger is assembling a force to garrison Montségur,' he said, munching. 'He has already gone down to the castle. I am going out into the country again to bring in as many of the faithful as I can. War is coming, I can feel it. But how soon? Can you tell me, Michel?'

'Sooner than we would have liked,' said the Captain, and he told the bishop of our words with the Count of Toulouse. 'He will not defend us again,' he finished. 'Once more we find ourselves alone.'

'Alone? How can we be alone in the company of our friends, our brethren?' laughed the bishop. 'No, no, I take your point, Michel. The storm is racing down from the north. But it will break against the rock of Montségur as it has before. The French will give up when harvest time comes, and Raymond will realise that his own people are his truest friends. Despite his words, he will not desert us for ever.'

'So you say,' said the Captain, doubtfully. 'But you are right: no one can take Montségur. Perhaps, if Raymond can make his peace with Louis and keep the Inquisition at bay, it will all blow over. Raymond hates Rome more than he hates the French.'

'Meanwhile I have been preaching," said the bishop, folding his hands across his belly. 'We had a close call at Avignonet: the Inquisition was a day away from catching us. But what happened then . . . I doubt it was worth the tempest it has brought down upon us. Pierre-Roger went too far. But he is still young, and very hot headed. I should have restrained him. Do you know, he called for the Inquisitor's skull as a wine cup? He did not get it, I am glad to say. His blood has cooled a good deal since then, and that is fortunate. He is a more sober man, and his preparations have been careful. I am proud of him. And while butchering the emissaries of Rome would not have been the course I would have chosen, it has rallied the country to us. I have been show-ing . . .' he paused, and glanced at me. The Captain raised his eyebrows.

'Ah. As it happens, you have young Petroc to thank for the crucifix,' said the Captain. 'It was Patch who found it in Constantinople and filched it from the Emperor.' I shrugged, modestly, for the bishop was looking at me with new warmth. 'You have it here?' the Captain asked.

'I do,' replied the bishop.

'Then guard it well – I am beginning to wonder if perhaps it should have remained secret. All sorts of rumours are abroad of some lost wonder that has been found again.'

The bishop suddenly looked uncomfortable, like an overgrown child sitting upon a secret too large for him. He rubbed his hands together nervously and cast his eyes about the room. They found a battered leather satchel in a corner and he rose and brought it over to us. After some ferretting around in its depths he drew out a dirty sheet of parchment.

'One of Pierre-Roger's men brought away the Inquisitor's papers. They ended up with me, for Pierre-Roger thought they might contain some clue as to Rome's intentions toward us.'

'What did you find?' asked the Captain, leaning forward, alert.

'Pious, self-satisfied claptrap, and the depositions of our bretheren, given under torture. And this.'

He held out the parchment. It was pale and new, dappled with dark brown blood where gory fingers had snatched it up. 'A letter that will never be sent,' the bishop was saying. I let the Captain take it. He opened the letter, read it quickly and then again, more slowly. Then he handed it to me, his face expressionless.

From Garsias d'Aure to André de Longjumeau

    My brother in Christ, greetings.

    We have but lately set out on our new Inquisition through the thicket of heresy that is the County of Toulouse. We have spent a week in Saissac hearing confessions, and before that Laurac, and other towns the sinful names of which you will find in the official report but which I have already put from my mind. We are bringing souls back to God, but in pitiful numbers that speak eloquently of the Enemy's hold over these benighted lands.

    As to that with which you have charged me: there are many rumours and more than rumours. At Laurac a woman described the heretic crucifix, stating under question that she had seen it with her own eyes.

Three more men and a woman expressed their desire to see it. At Sorèze an old man declared that it was being taken about the land by the Albigense's so-called bishop and displayed to the credulous. It is variously described as a painted image of Our Lord, an image painted in blood, and a miraculous imprint of Our Lord himself. When questioned as to the nature of the image, the heretics claimed that it was an object of dread or fear. The woman of Laurac told us that, as the image clearly showed a dead man, and was composed of the blood of the corpse, it proved beyond doubt that Christ was a being of flesh and blood and therefore not the Son of God, in accordance with their blasphemous creed and indeed proving the truth of that creed to her satisfaction.

We have put several to the question in this town to which we have come this day, which is called Avignonet, and where the Albigensian bishop has lately been seen. As you instructed, I have conducted my questioning in private. And God has granted my prayer that I might find out some news that will delight his gracious and pious majesty. One man, a half-simpleton, the son of some knight with holdings to the south, I pressed harder, and from his addled mouth came gold. For the cruxifix, he swore, rests in the hands of the heretic bishop, one Bertrand Marty, who is at this moment the guest of the lord of Mirepoix, a day's ride from here. This lord, Pierre-Roger, is a known friend of the heretics. The so-called bishop intends to show the relic in the villages round about Mirepoix. With our strength, modest though it is, we may be confident of taking this rogue, and rest assured that our secret matter shall be

The letter ended abruptly. The breath I had been holding whistled out between my teeth.

'Brother André,' I muttered. I ran my forefinger over the parchment. Some of the blood was still faintly tacky. I scraped at it and it clung to my fingernail like tar. I did not know who Garsias d'Aure had been, though I could guess; but I knew that man for whom he had gathered his news.

I had not seen Andrew of Longjumeau since he had delivered the Crown of Thorns to Louis three years ago on a hot August day at Troyes. I had grown to like the polite, gentle Dominican, who I had first met when escaping from Constantinople with Letice. Clearly he had grown in the king's affections since then, for it seemed I had not been the only one charged with finding the *Mandylion* of Edessa. Plainly, Andrew had made some guesses as to what the rumoured heretic crucifix might be, and had placed one of his men in the party of the Inquisition. Well, he would never know how close he had been to the prize.

'Is the . . . the crucifix safe, Bishop Bertrand?' I asked, handing back the dead man's letter. He nodded, gravely.

'Where do you reveal it, and how often?' asked the Captain.

'Only to believers, at our most secret gatherings,' said the bishop. 'Although I have shown it twice up in the mountains by the light of day, where all the folks are believers, more or less. It has great, great power. All who see it are bound to our cause like iron to a lodestone . . . but it does not bring joy. The people weep and quail before it and I must confess that it fills me with something of an unnatural dread. But so it should. It is the record of a man's suffering, almost as if Death himself were giving a sermon. No better proof could there be of Rome's lies, but I might wish that would bring joy instead of fear.'

'I would advise you to bring it to the fortress as soon as you can,' said the Captain. 'And yourself along with it, Bertrand. These fields will be full of wolves in a few weeks, and the flock must not be out when they come.'

'So be it. I will come after the harvest,' said the bishop.

We stayed a while longer, and I listened while Bishop Bertrand told the Captain of his work and the converts he was still making, and how the people were torn between their love of the truth and their fear of Rome. There was fear everywhere, he said, and some believed that the end was coming for the Good Christians. I wondered if their crucifix cheered them or made them more frightened. The *Mandylion* was not a cheerful portent, I thought to myself. It was spreading more than rumours: ripples of its dreadful attraction were fanning out, catching the Inquisitors at Avignon and the wretched heretic in Royan – and poor Stevin, too. And the avarice in the faces of Bishop Ranulph and all those royal cousins: Louis, Richard and Queen Isabella. It had power, all right. And now an embattled faith was making its last stand around it. But Bishop Bertrand was a good man, and his belief was as pure and true as anything in this world. Would that be enough to save him, though? As we made our way back through the market square I pondered that question. Despite what we are all taught from the moment we draw breath, is the truth enough to save any man? I found no answer within me, and outside there was nothing but the hissing of geese in the butchers' pens.

Chapter Eighteen

We came to Montségur on a drab afternoon at the end of September. The top of the crag, which rises like a vast, corroded tusk from the valley of the Lasset river, was hung with a grey gauze of cloud. I could not see the castle at all, and it was with a stomach full of misgivings that I said goodbye to my horse in the village that clings to the crag's skirt and set off beside Captain de Montalhac to climb the path that led, almost sheer in places, up to the gate.

Montségur was not a large place, for there is very little room on top of the crag, or *pog* as they call it in those parts, and the castle was fitted to the summit like a helmet of cut stone. We reached the gate after a long, lung-tearing slog up through three curtain walls that ran across the steep face of the *pog*. Beyond the castle, the mountain top formed a sharp ridge that sloped away gently to the north-east before ending in a sheer cliff, and at the brink of that precipice stood the castle's barbican, the Roc de la Tour. And cliffs fell away from the ridge in every other direction. If we had just come up the easy way, it did not seem to me as if the Good Christians were in much danger from their enemies, no matter how zealous they might be. It was bleak and harsh, and seemed as high and remote as the heaven of some bitter faith. The mist was sliding across the arrow-slits as we walked inside.

There was an open space between the towering walls, and it was crowded with people, all busy doing what people do on a September evening: starting the cooking fires, which smouldered drably; gossiping, mending clothes, scolding children who in turn ran about, chasing their little brothers and sisters. It was not at all what I had expected, and not what the dour welcome of the mist-beaded gate had promised. The Captain was known here, for he was greeted from all sides, and he waved all about him with a great smile on his face. We did not linger, though, and made our way across the courtyard to the keep. This was a stark though well-built tower, still new-looking, for at that time the castle was not even forty years old. We were welcomed inside, and without any ceremony a guard showed us into the solar.

The *seigneur* was not at home, and instead we were greeted by Pierre-Roger de Mirepoix. This was the man who had led the attack on the inquisitors at Avignonet. He was quite short, but lean and quick in his movements. He had coal black hair cut surprisingly in the latest fashion, and his jaws were deeply shadowed with stubble. He had high, jutting cheekbones, a nose canted slightly to the left, and dark eyes that flicked from here to there as he spoke, as a hunter's eyes do as he walks through his woods. It seemed the Captain knew him, for they greeted each other cordially, although there was caution behind their words. The seigneur of Montségur, Raymond de Perella – who I discovered was Pierre-Roger's father-in-law – had been summoned to Foix on business that he did not impart to us, but which seemed to be of grave importance.

But we were welcomed, and given a room that we found already occupied by three *perfecti* who greeted us with much joy, although we were making their already cramped living quarters even more cosy. They fell to talking with the Captain, for they were hungry for news of the world outside, and because I did not want to see their gentle, eager faces fall when he told it to them, I went out to look for Gilles.

But I did not find him in the castle, although I searched until darkness had come – and up here in the mist it fell like a headsman's axe. Gilles and I had not seen each other for more than a year, and I had begun to miss my old friend badly. So I made my way through the folk out in the courtyard, still cheerful despite the damp which had grown cuttingly chill now that the sun had gone, and asked if anyone had seen him. Of course they had! Brother Gilles was here – not *here*, I was made to understand, but here. And the plump woman who had spoken pointed up and over the walls.

'Oh, Lord!' I exclaimed, assuming that he had died and been buried somewhere beyond the castle. But I was wrong, and the woman seemed to find it quite hilarious. Apparently there was a village outside the castle, though where I could not imagine, for I had seen nothing but a sheer drop. No, no, said the woman. There was just enough land for folk to cling to. It was where the *perfecti* lived, and those who wished to learn from them. And there were more folk coming up every day, for something must be going on down in the land of poor Count Raymond, but then, wasn't there always something? There was, there was, I agreed: always something. I asked her for directions, but she shook her head and wagged a plump finger at me. No man in his right mind would venture along that edge after dark, and in such a thick night as this . . .

So I bid her farewell, foraged up a little dinner, for the Captain was nowhere to be found, and curled up in the corner of our room. The three *perfecti* were still deep in some quiet debate, and a mother and her young daughter had taken up the floor in the opposite corner. The girl was sobbing uncontrollably and taking in great shuddering breaths, but I hid my frown from the mother, who looked to be exhausted, and by and by the child let herself be comforted and fell silent. The gentle whispering of the *perfecti* soon had me drowsing, and when I opened my eyes again it was morning.

The Captain was not there, though it was barely past dawn, and the air was sharp. I lay on the straw for a minute, watching the steam of my breath gather and fade, then I roused myself. Our room had grown much fuller while I had slumbered. The other sleepers were bundled up or crouching in various stages of awakening, and the young girl who had been so upset last night sat giggling and prodding her mother, who seemed to be keeping her patience with difficulty. I wiggled my fingers at the girl – who hid beneath her mother's dress – stretched, and got up.

Outside, the cooking fires were lit. There were bread ovens some-where, for the smell of hot bread curled like a vein of gold through the frosty air. 'Master Petroc!' It was the woman from last night, beckoning me over. She had a fat slice of fresh bread for me, with sweet butter melting into it, and a cup of milk warm and frothy from the goat. As I was chewing, she told me how to reach the dwellings beyond the walls, and it did not seem as impossible a feat as it had last night, for the sky was as clear as a diamond and the castle's pall of mist had gone with the night. Behind me, high up on the eastern wall, a woman began to sing. It was a song to the rising sun, and to a lover – and perhaps they were one and the same. She stood in an embrasure, outlined against the pale gold luminance, a small figure made at the same time more and less substantial by the aura of light that surrounded her. She could have been a seraph, a being of pure radiance, except that her voice was achingly human. It was high and clear, with a crack, a flaw that ran through it like a seam of despair that hollowed out the beauty of the words.

> *Sweet friend, the morning star*
> *Has risen in the east,*
> *And all the greenwood birds*
> *Fill the air with song*
> *For the dawn is coming.*

Sweet friend, turn from the window.
The stars fade from the sky:
Soon the watcher on the walls
Will sight his prize,
For the dawn is coming.

Sweet friend, the flowers open
And await the sun,
But love's pale rose, that blooms by night
The sun must kill,
And the dawn is coming.

I shivered. There was something final in the beauty of that voice. It was implacable, not quite of this earth, as if the singer had seen beyond the vainglory of the world and found a merciless purity there.

'That's Iselda,' said the woman who had given me breakfast. 'Doesn't she sing lovely?'

'She does,' I said. 'She surely does. Does she live here?'

'She sings here, so she must live here, my darling. Lucky for us! She's sweeter than nightingales.'

The song had reached its end, and when I looked up at the wall the singer was gone. But her voice followed me through the courtyard. Outside the gate I paused, gazing over at the mountains across the valley in their clothing of autumn. The river below was a trickle of mercury, and the terraces that scored the lower slopes looked like ripples in sand. Snow had already bleached the teeth of the high peaks. Up there, I thought suddenly, the wind would sound like Iselda's voice: glorious, without pity.

I had thought it would be an easy matter to find Gilles, but I was mistaken. There was a path, well-worn and wide enough for two men to walk abreast, that led away from the gate and vanished around the curve of the wall. At first it was easy work to follow, but soon the looming wall on one side and the sheer drop on the other began to prey upon my mind. There were the first huts of the *perfecti* just ahead of me, and behind me, I knew, the sun-drowsed guard was only a few paces away. So by keeping my eyes on the dusty pathway and planting one foot before the other like a rope-walker I managed to stifle my sense that I had stumbled out of the world, but the flash of sun on black wings made me start and I saw a flock of choughs wheeling below me in the great emptiness of the air. Straight away my legs wobbled and for a moment I felt as if the birds were urging me to step into the abyss. The wall, implacable, seemed to be leaning over me, edging me off the path. Then I heard the sound of a woman's laugh and caught the scent of cooking, and with a grunt of effort I forced myself to stumble on and another few agonising steps brought me to the village of the hermits.

I had heard it called that, the hermit village, but what manner of hermit seeks the company of other folk, let alone that of other hermits? Perhaps I had expected a silent place, but it was not silent here, this confusion of huts that hung like a colony of those wheeling, red-legged choughs who still turned and called in the air below. There was a gentle hum of discourse, the ring of spoons in iron pots, the thud of mallet upon stake as someone anchored his home a little more securely to the clifftop. There was a stout wooden palisade across my path, but the gate was open and unguarded. As soon as I was safe amongst the huts I looked about me. An old woman in a shabby dark robe was seated on the ground outside her hut, which perched at the very brink of the drop. She was staring out at the birds, but hearing me approach she turned her head and nodded a greeting. Her hair was long and dirty white but her face was serene, almost young, until she smiled and revealed toothless gums. I waved, and she waved back as if I were her favourite grandson, and turned her head again to the choughs. I walked on, following the path through a thickening copse of huts and shelters. Some of these were older and quite well-built, with foundations of cut stone that might have come from the wall of an older fortress. Some were little more than piles of staves and faggots thatched with furze, nestled into scraped-out hollows in the stony ground. Some were bigger than others, in that a small man could perhaps stand up and turn about, arms outstretched, without knocking down the walls. Here and there the ground was terraced and level, but most of the dwellings around me were clinging to the bare rock like the houses of mud-daubing wasps.

Some of the inhabitants, like the old woman, sat or knelt beside their homes, praying or contemplating the play of sun and clouds upon the far mountainsides. Others read or worked upon books with pen and ink – and it was a strange sight indeed to see wagging quills in this wild place. Still others sat surrounded by groups of men and women who nodded and murmured – these were teachers and their pupils, I realised. Before me, an almost young woman with a crooked shoulder and wiry red hair struggling out from a plain white coif stirred a pot of beans. She beckoned me over and offered me a ladleful, for plainly strangers were welcome here, but I declined politely.

'Good sister, do you know Gilles de Peyrolles?' I asked her. She did, and raising her bad arm, shattered in some long-ago fall and ill-set, she pointed out a hut that leaned against an outcrop of rock beneath the wall. Thanking her, I scrambled up the steep bank.

Gilles was sitting in the sun, leaning back against the warm rock. He wore a long smock of white flax, and his feet were bare. He had lost weight up here in the thin air, and his flesh was stretched tight across his cheekbones. I had not seen him look so gaunt since we had crossed the Sea of Darkness together, but now, instead of the gnawing of fatigue and scorbutus, it was as if the sun had burned away all the soft living of Venice and released a younger, happier man.

'Hello, Patch,' he said, opening his eyes. He did not seem in the least bit surprised to see me. His eyes, shaded from the sun by his hand, were more piercing than I remembered.

'The same to you,' I told him. 'I have risked my neck to seek out this horrible perch of yours, and that is all you have to offer me?' I squatted down in front of him, and then we were hugging, and his beard was scraping my new-shaved cheek.

'Michel told me you were here,' he told me, patting the rock beside him. I sat, and felt the warmth of the rock seep through my clothes.

'Where is he?' I asked.

'He has gone down to the village with Pierre-Roger. Making plans.'

'Plans for what?'

'You know that better than I,' said Gilles, laughing. The knowledge that dwelt within those words was heavy as lead, and yet he sounded as if we were lounging in the prow of the *Cormaran*, watching flying fish shoot across our path.

'You have heard, of course,' I said.

'Of course. Such a great and wonderful plan, broken into ugly shards. Vanity, Patch, is a terribly poor craftsman – his work is always shoddy, don't you think?'

'Vanity? Desperation, more like.'

'To think we can order the affairs of man and write the chronicles before anything has actually happened – pure vanity. You've had a time of it, I hear. A battle. So you understand me.'

I thought of King Henry in the field before Taillebourg, and his expression when the French army had begun to pour across the bridge, and then the muddled, butchered corpses in the vineyards outside Saintes. All Count Raymond's hopes were shattered on the reef of a king's frozen smile. And if we had beaten the French, then what? A hundred, a thousand more pitfalls, accidents, cruelties of fate were waiting their turn. Yet Raymond must have thought he had at least a decent chance of success. Vanity? Plain old delusion, perhaps . . .

'I see what you mean,' I told Gilles. 'So is that what you do up here? Meditate upon Man's vanity?'

'I am still wrestling with my own,' he chuckled. 'I don't think I'm quite ready to tackle the whole of mankind. But tell me everything. It is very quiet up here, and very far from the world.'

'That is why you are here, Gilles,' I said. 'The Captain told me you have taken the *Consolamentum*. What do you care about the world?' I was teasing him, though I wondered whether I should. But he just chuckled again.

'I suppose I am waiting for the world to end,' he said. 'But it can be a little boring. If you think I have turned into some strange beast, or a mad zealot, you will be disappointed. I am still your friend Gilles – or rather, this is who I have always been underneath it all. Nothing . . . no, everything has changed, I will grant you, but while I still inhabit this flesh and blood I can still, apparently, be bored. If you can bring yourself to entertain me, you will put yourself on the path to your own sainthood.'

'I doubt that,' I said. 'But if stories can get a man beatified, I'll be Francis of bloody Assisi by the time I've done telling mine.'

'Ah, good,' said Gilles, stretching out his legs luxuriously and arching his back against the rock. 'Tell away, Patch, tell away.'

I had just finished describing the audience with Count Raymond when there was a skittering of loose stones and the Captain dropped down beside me. He was breathing hard, and beads of sweat were glinting on his brow, but he was grinning.

'You found each other, then!' he panted. 'Excellent. So, Gilles, has he told you everything? He has? Well, if that is so, nothing I can say will dampen your spirits further!'

Perhaps it was the thin mountain air, for what other reason could there be for these two grown men laughing in the face of the end of all their hopes? But the Captain was tucking his rolled cloak behind him, and Gilles was pointing out an eagle that floated, huge but weightless, half a mile out in the void.

'We were talking, earlier, about the Inquisitor's letter,' said the Captain. 'It was strange, was it not, to see the name of Andrew of Long-jumeau?'

'Maybe not,' I said. 'Before I left Paris, Louis commissioned me to find the *Mandylion*, whatever the cost. And meanwhile, it seems that now everyone has heard of the Cathar crucifix. Louis, and Queen Isabella, and the bishop of Balecester – and the Earl of Cornwall, of course. I'm not sure what they know or what they think they know. Louis brought up Robert de Clari.'

'So far as I know, de Clari is the only Frank who ever wrote about the *Mandylion*,' said the Captain. 'There may have been stories brought back by Crusaders . . . but my guess is that Louis, who is no fool, heard of our crucifix, remembered de Clari, put two and two together . . .'

'And told Brother Andrew,' I finished. 'So the rumours found their way into the church gossip mills, and now every collector has heard of a miraculous image at large.'

'Strange are the workings of the world,' said the Captain. He did not sound all that worried. 'The one relic we gave away is the one everyone wants.'

'Typical, eh, Michel?' Gilles stretched again and sat up. 'Are you thinking that we should have sold the thing to Louis and had done with it?'

'Of course!' he laughed. 'We would have become richer than . . . well, even richer than we are.'

'Were,' Gilles corrected him. 'Yes, and there's so much to spend money on up here, eh, Patch?'

I shrugged. 'It would have been simpler,' I told him.

'I know,' said Gilles, suddenly grave. 'This is very strange to you, isn't it? All this?'

'You mean finding that you've both renounced everything and turned into believers? Yes, it's a little odd. The way I feel about this – the *Mandylion*, Louis, all of it – is the way you both taught me to think. Opportunity. Find where greed and credulity share the same purse, and go to work. I learned that from you. But it isn't that . . .'

'I know. It's that we are believers after all. That is what troubles you.' Gilles put his arm around my neck and hugged me to him. 'We always were, Patch. We always were. Do you know what we believed in? This.' He swung his free hand to take in the valley, the mountains, the drifting eagle. 'We believed in the homes we left, and our faith – the faith of our fathers and mothers, who died in this land because they believed in something other than the pope's lies – our faith has been our home as we wandered. We have stopped wandering. We are still, we are home, and we believe.' He slapped the rock on which we sat. 'This is my home.' Then he laid his hand on his heart. 'And so is this.'

I remembered how the sweet breeze from Dartmoor had wound itself like columbine around my soul as I had rode towards Buckfast, and how I had found that I desired nothing more in this world than to find myself a home in one of its deep green valleys. But I did not believe in

185

anything, except perhaps the thick, cloying scent of haythorn flowers hanging in a Devon lane, or the clear yellow of primroses, or the cuckoo's chant. Perhaps . . . perhaps that was enough. I stared out at the white blades of the mountains, and the singer's voice came to me again.

'Will you ever leave?' I asked.

'Why would I?' answered Gilles. The Captain nodded in agreement.

'The French will come,' I said.

'Of course they will. But that means nothing. No one could take this place – angels, perhaps, but they do not fight for Louis.'

'He thinks they do. No, you are right: your Montségur is invulnerable. So what should I do?'

'Must you do anything?

'I mean, the business.'

'Oh, the bank will run without us,' said the Captain calmly. 'It is growing. Roussel has Florence grasped tight in his fist. Our agents are trustworthy, and even if they are not, they will not plunder us while there is the promise of yet more wealth. While our star is rising, we will be fine.'

'So, my good men, what should I do?' I asked again.

'What does your heart tell you?' asked Gilles. He raised himself into a crouch and brushed the dust from his white robe. He seemed . . . he seemed at home, within his own flesh as much as on this otherworldly crag.

'Perhaps I will stay, for a while,' I said. 'What is winter like up here?'

'Dreadful!' said the Captain, leering.

'Horrifying!' echoed Gilles. I looked at them both – transformed for a moment, it seemed, into their young selves – and burst out laughing.

'I'll leave in the spring,' I said.

Chapter Nineteen

aving made up my mind to stay, I spent but one more night on the *pog* of Montségur before I was off again, for the Captain, after spending a long day shut in the castle solar with the castellan and Pierre-Roger, asked me if I would be agreeable to riding, with all speed, to Marseilles. The company had an agent there, and the Captain and Gilles had resolved to withdraw the last of their funds to pay for supplies and men. I agreed, somewhat reluctantly, for although I did not particularly enjoy sleeping in a room full of *perfecti* who, though they were the kindest souls imaginable while awake, snorted and snuffled like a sty-full of hogs as they slumbered, I was sick of being propelled by the plans of others across the face of the earth.

And there was the singer. I woke early, picking my way through my wheezing roommates, and went outside. I leant in the doorway, buckling on my sword, and ran my eyes around the battlements, but the only silhouettes were those of the guards slumped in their embrasures. The courtyard was just coming to life: damp wood was smoking, a knife was being sharpened, a baby was crying as its bleary, red-faced mother rocked it with the jerky rhythm of absolute exhaustion. I looked around for Iselda – was that her name? – and realised that I had never seen her face. Never mind. But what a sweet voice. Maybe when I returned I would hear it again.

Stepping through the gateway I almost dropped my bag in shock. Montségur was marooned in a sea of white mist brushed with the burnt umber of sunrise. Instead of a mile's drop to the valley floor a gently undulating shoreline lay only a hundred or so yards beneath me. I started off down the path towards the village. To make the almost sheer side of the *pog* climbable, the path, no wider than two men standing abreast and made of nothing more than loose stones and gravel, zigzagged sharply. Even so the slope was almost as hard to descend as climb, and my knees were already aching by the time I reached the first defensive wall. This was no more than a rough dry-stone affair, and it did not need to be anything more fancy, for a defender would hold every possible advantage over any exhausted man struggling up from below. The gateway was not guarded, and I stepped through to find that the ocean of clouds began only a couple of paces beyond.

Now comes winter, the thief
To rob us of leaves and buds and blooms.
And snow and ice and mud
Are all the earth can give.
And how will my love keep warm
When the fire trembles in the hearth
And the birds will not sing?

The mist was reaching for my boots as the words caught me. I turned, and there, leaning against the wall, stood a woman. She was in shadow, and I could not properly see her face which was no more than an impression of eyes, nose and mouth all framed by the heavy tresses of her dark hair, which hung down in two thick ropes almost to her waist. She wore a long tunic of plain linen, a dark ivory, almost the colour of the mist. How long I watched her I do not know, but I did not stir until her song was finished.

'I did not seek an audience,' she said. Her voice was deep, even, and warm, not the desolate instrument that had given life to her song. But it was not friendly. Confused, for I felt as if a fever had just passed from my head, or an enchantment, I stepped back and found the smokey rags of the mist-sea writhing about my chest.

'Your pardon, my lady. I did not mean to offend. I think your music has turned me to stone . . .'

'To stone? Like a curse? I am sorry I petrified you. You are released.' I stood there, stupidly, feeling the damp fingers of the mist searching through my clothes. 'I release you: please go,' she said, her voice honed fractionally, an edge now where no edge had been before.

'I am going, my lady,' I said, hurriedly, bowing and sending the mist swirling. 'I am unmannerly. Petroc of Auneford . . . is my name. I am a companion of Michel de Montalhac. I . . . I am going to Marseilles,' I finished, holding up my arms in confusion, in supplication.

'Then I wish you all speed,' she said, and not knowing what else to do I bowed again and stepped back down the path. Instantly the mist closed over my head, and for a moment, through the grey wetness, I saw the singer sink down onto her haunches and clasp her hands around her knees. I turned, and let the murk swallow me up.

The gloom hung over me until midday, by which time I was almost at Mirepoix, for I had set off hard, spurred on by a lingering sense of mortification and of an opportunity squandered that had been with me since I had left the *pog*. I reached the town before nightfall, and next day started again in driving sleet. In less than a fortnight I was at Marseilles, in the cool sunshine, signing papers in the counting-house of Don Bonasasch. I knew this gentleman from a week he had spent in Venice, and as I scratched with my pen he regarded me over steepled fingers. He was a Jew of Valencia, and therefore one of the most mannerly and cultured beings in all Creation. So he did not enquire how it came to be that Michel de Montalhac and Gilles de Peyrolles were, in effect, leaving the company of the *Cormaran*, and I did not offer an explanation, for I had none that would make sense to a businessman, a scientist and a man of reason, all qualities I knew Don Bonasasch possessed in abundance. Gilles, along with myself, Roussel and Isaac of Toledo, were the last remaining partners in the company, but Michel de Montalhac was its master, its owner and its creator. The Captain must have a plan, I reasoned uneasily, and not for the first time. There was always a plan. I read over the papers he had prepared while he poured us some excellent pink wine in silver cups, and scratched my name and initials where appropriate.

As I worked I could see a distorted image of myself in the silver of his goblet, which had been polished until it shone like the full moon. Although my tiny reflection bulged and curved I could tell I was not the easy young fellow he had met amidst the finery of the Ca'Kanzir: my cheeks were hollow, and I had let a dark brush-stroke of beard grow into a point beneath my chin. My hair, the height of fashion three months ago, was a lank ivy-tangle of long ringlets that had receded somewhat from my temples. Half an eyebrow was struggling to grow back through a dark red scar. As my face had thinned so my eyes had apparently grown, so that it seemed for all the world as if some feral night-creature had been trapped in the glossy meniscus of the silver cup. How old was I? Christ, it escaped me. Ink splattered from my quill as I tried to work it out. Twenty-five years? Twenty-six? Was that what a man of twenty-six years should look like? Nudging the goblet from my line of sight I concluded my business and left, to Don Bonasasch's concerned but evident relief.

I went and stood on the seafront, staring out at the shimmer. *Akdeniz*, the Turks call it: the White Sea, and today it was the white of polished metal. But the wind was ruffling the surface and I could not see myself, thank God. How I missed this sea, which I had crossed so many times. I had seen the sun rise and set in her, turning the waters golden, purple, black; and I had learned her moods and endured her fury. With a sailor's eye I plotted a course out of the bay, past the islands of Frioul and out into the Gulf of Lions. In my head I drew a line across the cat's paws: slipping between Elba and Corsica, dropping like a stooping hawk to the Straits of Messina, around Spartivento and Capo d'Otranto and into the icy teeth of the Bora gales, to beat a way up the Adriatic until the dark line of the Lido of Venice came into sight and then, at last, the golden domes of San Marco. I could do it now. There was nothing keeping me here, and the business needed me back in Venice or perhaps in Florence.

But no, it did not need me. And while the Captain had never once commanded me to stay at his side, or even, if I thought about it, asked me, I seemed to have made my choice. This sea, which lapped so politely at my feet, would wait. I picked up a warm disk of chalky stone and sent it skipping out into the harbour. A silvery spray of tiny fish leapt over its wake. A little way away, an old fisherman yelled at his bothersome grandchild in the name of Jesus, Joseph and every fucking saint to make himself a bit fucking useful. I would be useful too. I knelt down, dabbled my hand in the water, smelled its brine on my finger-ends, and went off to fetch my horse.

The Captain had told me to seek out the White Dove hostelry in Narbonne on my way back. It was owned by a family of Good Christians, and was a place where heretics left messages for one another. If the Captain had any other tasks for me, he would leave word with the innkeeper. And indeed there was a message for me. If I chose to, I could ride to Toulouse, for Count Raymond had some words for the garrison of Montségur. It was a long detour, to be sure, and the weather was growing worse, the cold breath of the mountains meeting the damp of the north and making thin, chilly rain which seeped into my bones and surrounded me with the reek of wet, miserable horse. But the dogged beast kept his feet on the rutted, muddy roadways and on the last day of October I rode into the city.

The Count was not there after all, for he was at the town of Lorris, signing a treaty with King Louis. So it was all over, as Raymond had known it must be. I scratched about to find any information I could about the peace terms, but no one knew anything, save that Louis' mother Queen Blanche had brokered the treaty and that could mean only one thing: for the Queen Mother and her son were both ardent defenders of the Faith, and any treaty with Raymond must hinge upon him ridding his lands of heresy for good and all. But there were indeed words from the Count for Montségur, that I could make no sense of, but that were whispered to me by Raymond's chamberlain: *wait for my affairs to prosper*. That was all, and the chamberlain had no explanation, just tight lips and narrowed eyes.

My horse had grown lame within sight of the city walls and so I rested him for a week before setting out again. The weather had cheered up but I had to go carefully, for suddenly the countryside was full of soldiers: the Count's men returning home from a war they had not had to fight, and French adventurers trying to steal a march on the flood-tide of their victorious countrymen which, no doubt, was about to engulf the Languedoc. So I did not climb the path up to Montségur until three weeks had passed, December had come, and winter had descended upon the *pog* and wrapped it tightly in a pall of snow and ice.

That evening I clutched a mug of hot wine in my chilblained hands and told what I had learned. The Captain was there, and Pierre-Roger, and the castellan too, Raymond de Perella, a calm, handsome man in his late middle years, going grey about the ears, with sandy eyebrows and beard and grey eyes. He was the inverse, it seemed, of Pierre-Roger, for he was thoughtful, indeed fatherly. And as I was to learn, his family lived at Montségur with him: Corba his wife, his daughters Arpaïs, Esclarmonde and Phillipa – who was married to Pierre-Roger – and his little son Jordan. Corba's mother, Marquésia, lived there as well, and she was a *perfecta*. Now Raymond looked grave as he heard the odd words of the Count of Toulouse. Pierre-Roger tugged at his short beard and rapped on the table-top with his fingernails.

'*My affairs*? Nothing more?' he asked, the tension sharp in his voice. I nodded.

'I could get nothing more from any soul in the palace,' I said. 'But I am sure that those words were delivered just as Count Raymond intended them.'

'But what can it mean? His affairs are in the midden! They are being trampled as we speak by the King of France, trodden into the shit . . .'

'Nevertheless he means us to heed them,' said the castellan, thoughtfully, and put his hand on his son-in-law's arm. Immediately, Pierre-Roger inclined his head almost sheepishly and patted the castellan's hand. There was a real affection between these two very different men, I saw to my surprise.

'Well, my good Petroc,' said Pierre-Roger. 'Thank you for this news, vexing though it is. If my lord the Count has indeed made peace with

Louis, I fear that we will not be peaceful here for long. I will begin to ready the garrison – what do you say, Raymond?'

'Let us look to our provisioning, and to the state of our defences. Thank you, young man—' and he took my hand and clasped it warmly. Then he turned back to Pierre-Roger and the two fell into a rapid discussion of stores and supply-lines. The Captain stood and beckoned me from the room.

'Even if you wanted to leave – and I could not blame you – you will have to wait awhile,' he said, nodding towards the open doorway. Snow was driving, thick white snowflakes by the thousands, straight across the opening, and it was beginning to drift against the door posts. The wind moaned, hollow and hungry.

'I am not planning to leave,' I said, gently, and the Captain smiled and said something about dinner, and the greedy wind took away my next words, which were:

'*I will not leave you here.*'

The singer was gone. I asked the folk who lived in the courtyard – in crude huts and tents and lean-tos that took up every inch of wall around the yard – but they had not seen or heard her for a month or more. So she had left before the weather closed in. That had been sensible of her. The jolly woman who baked good bread, who had told me the singer's name that first morning, could give me no more information than that her name was Iselda, which I knew, and that she came from Rosers, though she did not know where that might be. Another woman thought she was a dispossessed noblewoman, a widow or a *perfecta*, but not all three, and a girl said she had heard, from another, that Iselda was a *trobairitz*, a woman troubadour. I had never heard of such a thing, but it seemed reasonable to suppose she was some sort of lady driven from her lands, and was it not likely she had found herself widowed in the process? I asked the Captain about her, but he hurrumphed and gave me a look that suggested my time might be better used by addressing more pressing matters. Gilles, of course, gave me a blank look. He had not been inside the castle for months, and in his present state of mind I doubted he would have even heard her had she raised her voice next to his ear.

And the Captain was right: there was much to do. The castle was not large, but it did not need a big garrison to defend it: the land itself was its armour. Food began to come up the *pog* from the country all around: sacks of wheat, barley and oats, hogsheads of flour, of salt pork and lard, kegs of olive oil, wine and beer. Men were recruited: crossbowmen mostly, soldiers who owed some allegiance to Pierre Roger or Raymond. They trickled in when the snow paused, or on warm days when the wind came from the sea, and when spring at last showed its face they came in earnest, toiling up the slope with their weapons over their shoulders, sweat blotting their leather armour.

One day the evening brought Bertrand Marty, who came tramping into the castle followed by nine *bons hommes*. He passed through the courtyard and many of the people there gathered round him and touched his robe or knelt as he went past. That first evening the bishop held a service in the keep for the faithful, which Gilles told me about the next day. After he had blessed and prayed, a box had been opened and the *Mandylion* itself had been taken out and showed to the congregation. At the time I felt nothing but a sort of professional relief that the thing I had stolen from Constantinople, and that half of Christendom seemed to be lusting after, was still safe and intact. But Gilles was troubled. 'The believers fear it,' he said. 'We thought it would show them that the Christ who died at Golgotha was a ghost, an illusion, but those who see the shroud see something different.' Contrary to everything they had held sacred all their lives, the Good Christians now found, in the ancient shape on the cloth, proof that Christ had indeed suffered and died as a man, and my friend had begun to worry that it had brought a new and troubling desire for death to the faithful.

'And what do you think of it?' I asked him.

'Old bedsheets,' he said. 'Good work, very good – but I wish, though, that we had sold it while we had the chance. It seeps death, somehow, but with no promise of reward. What a pity it isn't making King Louis miserable instead of us.'

It had worked its way into me, into my bones, this odd place – not the place so much as the people who lived here, I should say, but even the castle itself had begun to feel like my home long before the snow had started to melt from the mountains to the south. Winter had indeed been savage, the wind slicing across the top of the *pog* like a great scythe blade day in, day out, snow piling man-height in the courtyard, fire seeming to lose its power to give warmth. The sky would change day by day: pressing down upon us, yellow and heavy with freezing fog like a vast, sodden fleece, or glaring, high and impossibly blue, the gaze of someone's merciless god – not mine, and not the god of the *perfecti* either, but perhaps the God to whom I used to pray, the God who had brought the French down to the land of the Good Christians.

At first I had stayed to be with my two friends – they were not my employers any more, somehow, and though they were officially my business partners, that had come to seem a very dessicated way to describe our friendship. We were the *Cormaran*'s last crew, we were comrades in arms, we were, as we had always been, friends. I spent most of my days with Gilles or Michel, out beyond the walls in Gilles' hut. He had built himself a sturdy little dwelling out of the remains of some previous hovels that had stood nearby, for the village of the *perfecti* had waxed and waned with the fortunes of the lands below, and as brothers and sisters left or died, so their huts were taken over or were brought down by the wind and snow. Gilles had provided himself with four walls of carefully laid stone and a roof of timbers overlaid with faggots of broom, over which he had stretched a large piece of sailcloth – he would not say where he had got it, but all manner of things came and went from the *pog* in those days – which was lashed down with rope and sailor's knots. It rustled and crackled in the slightest breeze, which is to say always, but kept him warm and dry, though when a fire was burning in the hearth the smoke did not always find the hole that passed for a chimney, and I would stagger out feeling like a smoked ham. I did not make a fuss over it, though, because Gilles only lit the fire when the cold was too harsh to be kept at bay with skins and blankets, and even then it was for my benefit alone.

For Gilles de Peyrolles, always the dandy, always quick with his tongue and swift with his blade, had passed through a profound transformation. I drew the story from him slowly, not that he was reluctant, but time had slowed inside his head as it had, seemingly, for all those who lived out here on the cliff's edge. Gilles had heard the summons that had brought the Captain to Toulouse, and at first he had intended to enlist as a knight in the count's army. But somewhere on the way – on the road from Montpélier to Toulouse, I gathered – he had been caught in one of the brief, savage thunderstorms that sweep across the southern lands as he was passing through a little village, and a *perfecta* had taken him into her cottage. She had a fire going in the hearth, and as he knelt in front of it to dry his clothes, she threw a piece of wood into the flames. A shower of sparks flew up, like red stars against the sooty chimney, he told me. 'See those sparks, my son? That is you, and I, and every poor soul,' she had said, for that is what the Good Christians believe: that this world is the devil's creation, and to people it he stole light from God and trapped it inside the flesh that is our bodies. If a man or woman becomes perfect, is perfected, as they say, at the moment of their death the spark of God's light is released and joins Him. For the rest of us, we are doomed to be reborn and reborn again, to drag our fleshly prisons around with us and to pay, with the suffering of our bodies, the Devil's rent for occupying his creation.

Gilles knew that, of course, for he had learned the Cathar creed at his mother's breast. I wondered if the old woman had reminded him of that long-dead mother, but he had shaken his head. 'Nothing so grand,' he had told me. It was simply that he was squatting, drenched, chilled and shuddering, the crashes of thunder still piping in his ears, and the sparks . . . each one had been so warm, a tiny fire all to itself, and there they were, tiny conflagrations whirling up into the black. He had felt it inside him, the heat of his own spark, for the first time since he was a little boy, since before his memory had even begun to set down the story of his life. 'It was as if someone or something had opened me up like a lantern and blown on an ember inside, until it burst into flame,' he said. The old *perfecta* had held him until he stopped shaking and weeping, and had given him the *Consolamentum* there and then.

'I was light, all light after that,' he said. 'I gave my clothes and my sword to the people of the village, who were very poor, and followed the hidden paths of our people until they brought me here.'

I would study him sometimes, for we often sat in silence, looking out over the void or staring into the little fire in its ring of blackened stones. He had the hollow-cheeked look of a mendicant, the slightly loosened limbs of one whose bonds to the earth have grown frayed beyond repair. You may see men like him in any town. They are the madmen who are fed and cared for, though they do not ask for it, the thin, ragged men who stand in marketplaces or in the shadows of church doors, whom country women will shyly touch for a blessing. They are different from the beggars and the zanies who get only stones and blows for their pains. Gilles was not mad, I do not believe, but after I had spent a month in his company I began to question what madness might really be. Even as a monk, when I had spent every waking minute supposedly in the service of the Holy Spirit, the strange figures, touched, as some called them, whom the Spirit seemed to have entered, repelled me and filled me with a superstitious dread. Now I wondered how many faces madness wore, and if we all put on its mask sometimes. He was not mad, this man who was my dear friend, but he was not entirely sane either, but somehow that did not matter, especially when I remembered the hollow-cheeked creature with the dark, haunted eyes I had glimpsed in the worthy Don Bonasasch's polished silver; and as time slipped past us on the scoured top of that mountain I let myself join him, as much as I dared, in the luminous calm with which he had clothed himself.

Chapter Twenty

Montségur, May 1243

'Fucking idiots,' grunted Marc le Forestière, spitting a thick gob out into space. We watched it drop towards the French, almost a mile below.

The French army had arrived the day before, a dark stain creeping up the valley from the north. As they had arrived at the village at the foot of the *pog*, I had seen the commander, flanked by his standards. He was only a black dot, but I knew he would be craning his neck, looking up at the castle he had been ordered to capture. Hughues des Arcis was his name, the seneschal of Carcassonne. Was he feeling cocksure or deflated as he stared up towards the sky? The garrison was yelling down at the French to *give up* and *go away*, to *surrender*, or to *come on then, get up here!* They could not hear us. Instead they took over the village, all but empty, for the inhabitants had either fled or joined us up here. A hut had gone up in flames as dusk fell, no doubt a warning to us, but all in all, for the beginning of a siege it was all very dull.

'They couldn't take Montségur with ten thousand men, let alone that poxy lot,' Marc went on. He slapped the stone of the embrasure. 'I don't know why they even bothered to build these walls. Those swine won't ever get up here.'

Marc, a crossbowman from the valleys around Mirepoix, was cheering himself up with a bit of bravado, but he was absolutely right. That army could not take Montségur. They were clearly planning to starve us out, but our storerooms had enough food for ten years of siege, and there were a score of men, and women too, among the garrison who could make their way up and down the mountain by day and night. There were not enough Frenchmen to seal off the bottom of the *pog*. If they tried to climb up the path, we would kill them. If they tried to climb the cliffs, they would kill themselves. That morning, my only worry was how long it would take for Hugues des Arcis to get bored and give up – and it was hardly a worry. Marc, like most of the fighting men in Montségur, was a vassal of the lord of Mirepoix, and had left their families and their harvests to defy the French invaders. They were used to fighting, these hard, creased men. Marc had two daughters and a pregnant wife waiting for him, but he did not seem to think he would have long to wait before he saw them again. It was a warm day, and I allowed myself the luxury of a stretch, and to ponder, lazily, why we had all worried through the winter if this was the extent of our enemy.

The soldiers were yelling and waving cuckolds' horns at the almost invisible army below, but the Good Christians were quiet, either going about their business or peering, expressionless, from the walls. Below on the cliff-edge a crowd of them had gathered, very still and quiet. The little black specks swarmed around the village, spreading outward, intent on surrounding the *pog*. But how could you surround a mountain? It was absurd. To take the path would be certain death. We had mangonels aimed at the knife-sharp ridge that led to the Roc de la Tour, and no man would last five minutes in that dreadfully exposed place. I peered out again. A flock of ravens was drifting slowly past, two hundred feet down. One of them broke off and tumbled, rolling over and over before opening its wings and soaring up to its companions, who whistled and croaked in appreciation. From the parapet of the keep, little Jordan de Perella, perched on his father's shoulders, was screeching in his little boy's voice at the French. He shook his fist, and then hurled something – a small stone or perhaps a toy – out over the edge. It described a puny arc and dropped into a broom shrub that grew at the brink of the cliff. The ravens had found a current of rising air. They rose slowly, wings still, the great black feathers at the tips fluttering. There were ten of them, twelve perhaps. Silently they rose and rose, so close I could see the sun reflected in the jet beads of their eyes. Up and up, until the sun's glare swallowed them all.

For five long months nothing more happened. The French specks in the valley seemed to be busy, but what it had to do with us up on the *pog* was less than clear. They had cut us off from the world outside – but they had not quite managed even that. Men whose families had lived in the valley beyond the reach of memory knew that a web of pathways covered the mountain, all of them secret, most of them impossible for all but the most fearless mountaineer. They came up and down at will, bringing us food, letters and news – in July, we heard that Rome was at last rejoicing in a new pope, one Sinibaldo Fieschi, who was calling himself Innocent the Fourth – and if one of the garrison needed to leave – and Pierre-Roger sent messengers regularly to call for arms or men – there were one or two tracks that an ordinary soul could manage without the fear of certain death. They moved at night, and if I was awake before dawn on sentry duty I often saw the small groups of dark-clothed men, stout boots on their feet, emerge through the postern gate, shepherding a blinking, ghost-white messenger who was still coming to grips with the fact of his survival.

It was on one such morning, a cold one in early October, when hoar frost was already crusting on the stones of the parapet, that I heard the challenge at the postern and, looking down from my place on the walls, saw a woman's head amongst the shaggy locks of the mountaineers. She was untying her braids, and when she was done she glanced up at the sky and I saw that it was Iselda de Rosers. She bid farewell to her guides and disappeared inside the keep. For a moment I wondered if I had imagined her. But the mountaineers were cackling and leering in loud whispers, and even through the jabber of their dialect it was not hard to guess what they were talking about. I went back to my post and waited for the dawn with a lighter heart than usual. The siege had been nothing but boredom for the garrison, of which I was now a member, for as a knight I was supposed to know how to handle myself. When I was not on duty I spent my time with Gilles and Captain de Montalhac, and so I had a foot in the two worlds of Montségur: the dull, duty-bound life of the soldier, and the deep, calm waters of the *perfecti*, in which time was suspended and events wavered in and out of view like river weeds in a lazy current.

The sergeant, Bernard Rouain, relieved me after sunrise, and as I was walking stiffly down the stairs, for hoar frost makes lovely patterns on chain-mail while it is freezing the flesh inside, Pierre Ferrer, Pierre-Roger's bailiff, called to me from the doorway of the keep. I was summoned to a meeting with the castellan and the commander. That was unusual but not unheard of: the Captain, who was very close to the two leaders, had been putting in a good word for me, and I had found myself in the inner circle of the garrison, somewhat to my surprise. After so much time under siege, and in such a small group of men – the garrison was no more than a hundred and fifty souls at its fullest – the boundaries between master and servant become frayed, and the influence of the Good Christians made that even more true. Still, the earthly power of Montségur lay with the commander, Pierre-Roger; Castellan Raymond; Bailiff Ferrer; the Captain; and Imbert de Sallas, the sergeant-at-arms.

There were plenty of other knights on the *pog*, most of them Pierre-Roger's men. But no doubt Captain de Montalhac had presented me as a man with friends and influence in exalted places; and he had been telling the truth, so far as that went. In any case I was occasionally consulted or given important jobs to do, and that made the time pass very slightly faster.

'The lady Iselda has brought us some news,' said the bailiff as I walked into the solar, blowing on my fingers and wiping the dewdrops from my nose. Pierre-Roger sat at the table next to Raymond de Perella. The Captain sat next to Pierre-Roger, and next to the castellan Bertrand Marty sat bolt upright, his hands placed carefully on the tabletop in front of him. It was unusual to see the bishop here, for he tried not to interfere with garrison matters. I bowed to the commander and the castellan and then to the singer, who gave me the politely blank look of someone who has not slept in days. She had great dark circles under her eyes, and her hair was full of furze twigs. And she was beautiful, I saw again, although I forgot it as soon as I sat down and the freezing metal of my chain-mail shirt began to gnaw at my backside.

'She has come from Narbonne. *Domna*, would you tell us again what you heard there?' Raymond de Perella pushed back a lock of thinning hair from his forehead. He looked more tired than usual. Pierre-Roger leaned back in his chair, gaunt and tight-lipped. I glanced at the Captain, but he was studying the singer's face and I could not tell what he was thinking.

'I heard this news two days ago. It was announced in the cathedral by the Archbishop. Pope Innocent has lifted his ban of excommunication on Count Raymond.'

'That is the ban placed on him by the Inquisitor Ferrier as punishment for Avignonet,' said the bishop. Pierre-Roger's lips went white for a moment, but then he shook his head wearily.

'So we are forgiven,' he said coldly. He did not seem to welcome the prospect.

'Raymond is forgiven,' the bishop corrected gently. 'There is another ban, that imposed by the Archbishop of Narbonne himself, but if Innocent has lifted one he will soon lift the other.'

'What does this mean?' asked the castellan.

'It means that Count Raymond has made friends with Rome,' said the Captain. 'He is trying to outfox the Inquisition. The pope will not inflict his Inquisitors upon a friend, or so Raymond hopes.'

'But are we not here because of Avignonet?' asked Pierre-Roger.

'*You* are here because of *us*,' said Bishop Marty. The castellan laid his hand over the bishop's.

'We all know why we are here,' he said, and Pierre-Roger nodded. 'Amen,' he said.

'That is news enough,' said the Captain. 'But is there more?'

'None, save that the French are making very bold in our lands, they are calling this siege a Crusade, and that Sanchia of Provence is marrying the King of England's brother.'

The Captain met my eyes and our eyebrows went up in unison. So my duty to Richard of Cornwall was discharged. But the others were talking in low voices about Count Raymond and the pope.

'I have asked him twice since the French invested us about his affairs,' Pierre-Roger was saying. 'And always the answer is "they prosper." Is this what he meant? He is mocking us.'

'Not so, not so,' said the castellan. 'It may be that he has been parlaying with Innocent, getting Rome to call off the dogs, so to speak. Raymond does not wish us ill.'

'He does not wish you ill or good,' I said, and repeated what we had heard in Toulouse. These men had heard them before, but now the words seemed to fall, leaden, to the tabletop for us to examine. 'Count Raymond wants the Church out of his lands,' I went on. 'He knows he must be France's whipping-boy, but he can keep Louis at arm's length. He can't keep Rome out, though, unless he stamps out heresy *himself*. See how good a son I am, he is saying to Innocent. And so far, the pope has believed him.' I turned to Iselda. 'My lady, what is the mood in the countryside?'

'It is black. The Good Christians are trying to get across the mountains to Aragon or Navarre, or take ship for Italy, but they are not wealthy, those who are left down there.' She glanced towards the window. 'They believe that the Count has turned against them, that he blames the Good Christians for everything that bedevils him. Louis is his master now, he has no bride and no heir, and the only power he has left is the power to snuff out heresy. That is what they are saying. Are they right?'

She turned and studied us in turn. She was pale and perhaps fevered. Somehow I knew she was getting a headache, that kind which starts behind the eyes when you are exhausted. The bleakness I had heard in her song was in her face, as if she were weary of loss, of carrying the shadowy burden that people and things leave when they are taken from us against our will – weary, but determined.

'Yes, they are right,' Bertrand Marty said quietly. 'Raymond is doomed to play off his tormentors one against the other for the rest of his days. But as he is a man full of faults – on that we can all respectfully agree – the sin of pride is very strong in him, and to lose Montségur, with two of his most famous knights—' and he smiled and nodded to Pierre-Roger and the castellan '—would perhaps seem intolerable to him. If he has won some sort of pardon for himself regarding Avignonet, is it impossible to believe that he will try to extend that to . . .' He lifted his hands and encompassed us, the room, the mountaintop. 'In a sense, we are all that is left of the County of Toulouse,' he said. 'That is something he will wish to save.'

That was the end of the discussion, for there were no answers, either good or bad. Pierre-Roger jerked to his feet, propelled as usual by the coiled anger within him. The castellan exchanged a few whispered words with Bishop Marty, and the two left together, I guessed to visit Lady Corba, whose reputation as a holy woman had recently been growing. The Captain, with a rare display of gallantry, bent and kissed Iselda's hand before leaving. That left the singer and me, at opposite ends of the table. She was slumped, almost asleep, and I was tempted to leave her there in the quiet of the room, but as I stood up my mail shirt clacked against the wood of the chair and she startled and turned her face to me, her eyes confused. They were green, those eyes, the colour of moss seen through the golden water of a Dartmoor brook. And they were bleared and rimmed with red, and her nose was running worse than mine. She sniffed loudly and sighed.

'My lady, I have been meaning to apologise for my rudeness,' I said, to break the tension I was beginning to feel in my chest and to allow me to leave gracefully.

'When was that?' she said, frowning at me, not really listening.

'Last year,' I began.

'Last year?' She asked, sceptically. Her frown had deepened. She blinked at me, trying to focus her tired eyes. I gathered that I was either an irritation or a madman.

'Yes, in the autumn. I was leaving the *pog*, it was morning – foggy – and you were singing outside the second gate. I said you had turned me to stone.'

'What did I say?'

'That you had not meant to petrify me.'

'Oh.' There was a long and prickly silence. Then suddenly she brightened. 'Oh! A man sinking into a cloud. That was you?'

'It was. Petroc of Auneford is my name.'

'That was a lovely morning – the last warm day. Winter came after that.'

'Winter was already there. I found it beneath the mist.'

'Ah. So it was an illusion, my beautiful day?'

'Your beautiful song was no illusion,' I said. She frowned again, and I made a pretence of stretching. 'You are exhausted,' I said. 'Do not let me keep you from sleep, my lady.' I edged between the chairs, but she fluttered her fingers at me, distracted.

'Wait a minute. Are you a knight? You don't look like a *bon homme*, and you aren't Occitan. Are you in the service of my lord of Mirepoix?'

'Yes, I am a knight, and I am called Sir Petrus Blackdog by some, and I am English, but I am in no man's . . .' I paused. It was an easy and tempting lie, but the truth was complicated and stung me where I kept my pride and illusions of freedom. 'I do not owe homage to Mirepoix,' I said instead. 'I came here with Captain de Montalhac. We are colleagues – partners.'

'Why, then? Why here?'

'Why did I come? I was on a mission to the Count of Toulouse, Captain de Montalhac was also there, and I came here with him to see my old friend Gilles de Peyrolles, who lives as a *perfecti* beneath the walls.'

'But then you stayed.' She was studying me as intently as her fatigue allowed.

'Not quite. I came back. When you saw me I was leaving for Marseilles. Then . . .'

'You could have left. Captain de Montalhac came from Venice, I've heard. And you: you have a foreign look to you. Not English – something else. So why didn't you just go back to Venice? Much nicer there, I should think. I . . . I'm sorry,' she said brightly, and sniffed again. 'I am talking too much – I'm asleep on my feet. Do not let me keep you.' The edge – which was self-control and perhaps not coldness, I wanted to believe – had left for a moment, but now it was back.

'No, you are not – talking too much,' I said. 'I am going to find my breakfast.' I walked past her and then paused in the doorway. 'But to answer your question: yes, in fact I did think of leaving. Of going home to Venice. But alas, when I thought about it . . . I have four walls in Venice, and my own country that I still dream about, but as to a home, I came back to be with my companions, for the only home I possess is, it seems, with them. Now *I* have talked too much, so I'll bid you good morning, Lady Iselda.'

I went off and got stiffly out of my chain mail. I shared a room – it had been intended as a stable, and gave out onto the courtyard – with six other knights. Two were sleeping and another was mending a shirt. I threw a log onto the fire that burned in a makeshift hearth and squatted down before it, gazing at the sparks as they flew. I could never find, in their twinkling ascent, even a hint of the epiphany that had struck Gilles, but I had taken to studying them anyway, for keeping warm was serious business on the *pog*, and everyone tried to spend as much time as they could in front of fires. Sometimes I saw firebirds such as are said to dwell in the mountains of Persia, sometimes souls ascending to Heaven, and other times souls writhing in Hell. But I found no answers. Now I wondered why I had said so much, and so unguardedly, to the singer. I prodded the embers with the cooking spit and the sparks whirled and eddied against the soot-black stone. The sparks made the black more absolute. I watched a point of orange light as it hovered and went out. That is why we watch the sparks, I said to myself: so we do not have to look at the darkness between them. That was why I had come back to Montségur. That was why I had told the singer what was in my heart.

My mail shirt needed oiling. I went off to find the tallow pot, step-ping over William de l'Isle, a young man from the mountains near Foix. I wondered, as I did every hour of the day – and as every man in the garrison did, I knew – how long I would have to stay up here in this cold, smelly little castle, and how in the name of Joseph's blue bollocks I was going to leave it. I liked my comrades-in-arms well enough and we all got on in a way I understood, for it was not unlike a huge ship, this place – becalmed, of course. But I had heard all their stories about chasing country girls, and the little skirmishes they had fought against their rivals across valley or mountain, and though I loved to listen to Gilles and the other *bons hommes* I did not, in the end, understand what kept the fires of conviction alive in their souls. The only pretty women up here were Good Christians or the wives or daughters of the import-ant knights. There were a couple of tarts, big, brisk and with arms like bakers, who were tolerated by the garrison and the heretics alike because they kept the soldiers from getting out of hand, but I could not bring myself to visit them, even though my roommates had, secretly and with a good deal of shame after the fact and, no doubt, the drip as a reward for their lust. So I found myself thinking of Letice, very often, as she had been in the happy days in Venice, and sometimes of Iselda de Rosers who, although we shared the same crowded little castle, I almost never saw and who did not sing as the sun rose any more. And some-times I thought of Anna, when the sky was the blue of Greece or when the stars were bright. At night I often dreamed of Margarete, and of the women of Venice, and the girls of Paris and Florence and London, and it brought me nothing but aches in the crotch and in the head. As is well known to the men who lead others to war, if a man needs to fuck but cannot, the next best thing is a fight, and with our enemy a mile below us and showing no signs of coming up, that was as distant as clean sheets and a cunning, willing lover.

It will soon be Christmas, I told myself. The Crusaders will have had enough by then. They will want to be home. They will leave, and it will be over. I was not trying to see the future, that morning as I rubbed tallow across the rusting mesh of my armour, but as it turned out I was half right. The Crusaders ran out of patience. And then everything changed.

Chapter Twenty-one

If you want to know about the battle for Montségur, more than I can tell you, go to Rome. The details are stored in the library of the Inquisition. Ask a Dominican to see them should you ever find yourself there. If you put on a holy enough face, or pull out a properly bulging purse, no doubt the good brothers will be happy to find the pages for you with their dates, confessions, the names of the dead, of the burned.

I wonder if the name of the traitor is among them. I do not know it, but, perhaps I once knew his face. For our story – you know how it ends, of course you do – must have a traitor, as how else could the impenetrable castle of the heretics fall? I will not take long to tell it, for in a sense the whole tale is told by the black ground at the foot of the *pog*, where the grass, so they tell me, has never grown back. If you wish to learn more, read it there. The oily black soot that stains the rocks all around the burning place, the wisps of charred bone, the smell that is not there but yet hangs like a corpse-grimed shroud over the whole valley – that is where you will find your tale. The Church set down the history of the Good Christians in ink at Rome, and in blood at Montségur.

I remember the morning that the first Crusaders appeared on the ridge. They were Gascon mercenaries, we would discover, who had dragged themselves up goat paths and fissures all night. There they squatted, and as we watched they stood up and attacked, a long file of men trotting along the spine of the *pog*. I was on the wall next to a crossbowman called Guillaume Delpech, ready to hand him his bolts, for a knight who cannot shoot a bow is not much use when the enemy is at a distance. There were two dozen Crusaders, their white flag with its red cross straining out in the wind that blew from their backs carrying a hissing burden of ice fragments. The ice was lashing our faces but the crossbowman shook his head.

'Let them come on,' he muttered.

The French had come within a spear's throw of the walls when we let fly from the walls. Not one of them lived longer than five minutes, as arrows and bolts sent them spinning down the precipices on either side. They did not try that again right away, but try again they did, and we cut them down. Handing bolts to my busy crossbowman became as mindless as threshing wheat. Sometimes a few brave souls got close enough to loose off a bolt or arrow of their own, and twice our men were hit: one got a clean wound in the shoulder, the other was nicked in the throat by an arrow and bled to death on the parapet. We had not lost a man to the enemy until then, unless you counted the three or four old folk who had died for want of care that perhaps they would have found in the outside world, or the girl who had died in childbirth, or her little boy, who had not lived to see his third sunrise.

It was around Christmastide. I had been on guard at the Roc de la Tour, our barbican that stood at the other end of the *pog's* sharp ridge. It had been a day of beautiful dullness, for the day was dazzlingly clear and thick, diamond-bright pelts of hoar frost clung to every blade of grass and curl of bramble. I had chatted to my companions, the sergeant Bernard de Carcassonne, Raymond de Belvis, and my mess-mate William de l'Isle, and listened to the snow buntings chirp among the stones. Our relief arrived just after dusk and as was our habit we stayed with them for a while, sharing our supper, such as it was. The night watch was eight men strong. I cannot recall every name, but one of them was Marc le Forestière, who had mocked the French on that first day when they had swarmed impotently around the foot of the mountain. Bernard and Raymond were believers but the rest of us were not, so no doubt we talked longingly of women and what we had done and would do again in tavern and brothel, when we finally got down off this freezing *pog*.

When my watch got up to leave the hunter's moon, no more than a wisp of silver hair, was slipping behind the mountains and Orion was loosing his dogs across the sky. We bid our mates goodbye and held our hands as close as we could to the brazier before pulling our mitts on fast to trap the heat. Wrapped in plumes of our own white breath we set off crunching through the frost. It was stunningly cold and we were silent, each one of us clenched in every muscle against the chill, thinking of nothing but the dim orange lights of the castle not far up ahead.

All at once there was a rattle of stones behind us. We all turned, expecting, perhaps, to see a fox or even a wolf, for those creatures skulked around at night, feeding on the dead and on the rubbish of the living. But instead we saw a tall shadow, then another and another, rising over the lip of the sheer cliff that dropped down a yard from the walls of the barbican. Like ripples in the darkness they seemed, but then came a flash of something thin and pale, and in the next moment there was a scream from inside the tower and then another and another, and then a crash and a shower of sparks boiling from the window as the brazier was kicked over.

We had all drawn our swords, and with a wild look at each other we dashed back down the stony ribbon of the track towards the tower. We were seven or eight paces away when the air filled with whirring, whining shapes. A quarrel struck William in the face and he dropped with a grunt in mid-stride. Something had caught fire inside the tower and by its light we saw that men were pouring out of the door, dropping to their knees as they aimed their crossbows. There were at least fifteen of them, and more shadows seemed to be pouring over the cliff-edge, but our own momentum was carrying us towards them. Another quarrel hit Bernard in the left arm and he yelped in pain and rage.

'Stop! Stop!' I screamed, grabbing at him. 'Too many! Back to the walls, for God's sake!'

The three of us skidded to a juddering stop, turned and ran for our lives, hunched over as the quarrels hissed around us. I found myself leaping over William's still body. Ahead, the lights on the castle walls bobbed. There was an ugly clamour of voices behind us, mocking us as we fled in some harsh dialect. From inside the tower, a last scream.

'They've taken the barbican!' Raymond was yelling. 'To the walls! To the walls, men of Montségur!'

It was not far to the postern gate, but that desperate run across the edge of the mountain, surrounded by a void of dark and freezing air through which quarrels flew like maddened bats, might have been the longest of my life. By the time I crashed into the wall and hung there, panting into the mortar, my lungs were racked by the cold air I had forced into them and sweat was steaming up through the neck of my mail shirt. Determined hands grabbed us and pulled us to safety as the quarrels smacked and chinked on the stones and the thick oak planks of the door.

The rising sun showed us a banner flying from the little tower, and it was not ours. The watch had not stood a chance, it was easy to see that now. They had been overpowered by at least thirty men, Basques, who must have been led by one of our guides up the almost sheer face of the cliff. By now they had dowsed the fire and were pulling out the bodies of the watch. One of those dark shapes had been Marc le Forestière, who would never see his new baby. They dragged them to the precipice and kicked them over the edge, and as each body fell a great cry of anger, of horror, went up from our walls.

The name of the traitor who had shown the Basques our secret paths might be found, I would guess, in the ledgers of the good Bishop of Albi, whose deep pockets were keeping the Crusaders' zeal alive. He had not been keeping idle down in the valley, but drawing up plans and working the Crusaders into a fury of hatred for the garrison of Montségur. And once they had their claws in, the French went to work. All those thousands of swarming ants in the valley, that vast legion of helpless and frustrated men finally had something to do. Like maddened spiders they threw a great, ugly web of ropes, ladders and pulleys over the north-eastern cliffs and up this devil's lattice they heaved a puzzle of beams and blocks and ropes that we could just see, those of us with young-ish eyes. They worked by day and by night, torches edging, like burning snails, up and down the cliffs. And all the time they poured arrows and quarrels into the castle, which we picked up and shot back at them.

The sun came up three days after that, and we saw what the French had been making. It was a trebuchet, bought by the ever-generous bishop of Albi, and they had scratched out a platform for it a good stone's throw in front of the tower. They fitted the arm and counterweight as we watched helplessly. A little after midday the arm swung and the first stone flew high above the ridge, to land with a harmless thud thirty yards from the barbican wall. The second and the third fell short, but the fourth struck the parapet, careened off and smacked into the wall of the keep. A shard of stone as big as a crow sliced off the arm of the *bon homme* Sicart de Lastours, and he died an hour later in the solar, watched over by the castellan's wife, Corbara. That was when we started to die.

I was sitting with Gilles in his hut a few days after that. The village of the Good Christians was quite safe then, for even though it was undefended, all the danger was on the other side of the castle. It was a strange fact of life in Montségur that, although there were almost as many able-bodied men amongst the *bons hommes* as there were soldiers in the garrison, the soldiers did not begrudge them their life of prayer. Gilles was a warrior. I had fought alongside him, and he had taught me many tricks of war, some subtle, some brutish. But I could no more imagine the Gilles who sat cross-legged in his thin robes wielding a sword than I could see the castellan's little son Jordan pulling back a crossbow string. I went to talk to him because he made me feel lighter, somehow, and indeed many, even most of the garrison would seek out a favourite *perfecta* or *bon homme* for the comfort and strength they seemed able to give.

'What do you see, Gilles?' I asked him that evening. The sun was dipping below the mountains, and we were standing beside his hut. All around us, men and women were going about their quiet business, greeting one another, exchanging the day's news or asking some obscure question about their strange doctrine, which seemed to grow deeper and more complicated the more it was examined; and their voices made a strange sound, almost like leaves in an oak wood, reverent and soothing. Gilles was gazing over at the crest of Planas that towered above us on the far side of the valley.

'I see the mountains and the end of the day,' he said. 'What else is there to see?' He looked at me and smiled.

'You know what is happening on the eastern side,' I said. 'The French can get up onto the *pog* at will. There are thousands upon thousands of them, and . . .' It was not worth finishing my sentence. Gilles sat down on a stump of broken wall.

'Are you afraid?' he asked.

'You know what will happen when they take the castle – 1 can say *when* out here, although I would hardly dare utter *if* inside. They came here for one reason alone. They will not let any of us live.'

'But are you afraid?'

'Yes! Of course I am afraid. Not of being shot or stabbed, which is funny, but I have come to understand that. What I'm afraid of is being taken, and judged, and led to my death like an ox.'

'That is not your fate, my dear friend.'

'Can you see the future now, Gilles?' I was jesting – at least I hoped I was.

'Yes.' He waved his hands mysteriously, comically, in the air before him. 'We are all going to die,' he said hollowly. 'At some point, I'm afraid,' he added, patting my leg reassuringly. 'No, I have not been given second sight, but Michel has told me of some to-and-fro between Count Raymond and Pierre-Roger. I guess – and it is Michel's guess as well – that Raymond, who do not forget has been pardoned for Avignonet, has bargained some sort of pardon for Pierre-Roger and his men, which means the garrison, and which would also mean you.

Without a doubt he used us heretics as his gaming pieces. The death you fear is mine, not yours, and I do not fear it.'

'You will let the Inquisition kill you?'

He shrugged. 'I intended, from the minute I became *perfect*, to spend the rest of my days here. My wish will be granted.'

'And the others?'

'Have you been listening to me, Patch?' His words were abrupt, but his voice was kind. 'This is not life, it is all a dream wrought by our captor.' He pointed over at the ominous bulk of Monts d'Olmes. 'All this . . . all this great, terrible weight of matter is an illusion. Just that. The Devil has decorated our prison for us, and he has done it well, but once the bars have been glimpsed, they cannot be forgotten. Can you not feel it, Patch? There is so much lightness here. It pulls you up, ever up, even as the world seeks to pull you down. I will be set free, dear friend. I am glad. Be glad for me.'

After that, there are only fragments of memory, gouged into my mind like the desperate drawings scratched by condemned men on their dungeon walls. I have tried to forget some things and remember others, but these are all that remain.

I am on the ridge in front of the barbican. We have made a sally to try and wreck the trebuchet. It is appallingly cold. I am screaming through the thick woollen scarf I have tied around my face, and the hand that swings my sword cannot feel the hilt. The blade strikes the helmet of the Frenchman in front of me and slices into the metal as if it were an apple. The blood that pours out over his face smokes. I wrench out my sword. We are falling back. Three of my friends are dead, chopped up like mutton, and their blood smokes as well. A quarrel-shaft *tocs* against my arm. I run, while the scarf grows thick with ice. By the time I reach the postern gate it is frozen against my lips.

I am waiting my turn to dip my bowl in a cauldron of thin soup. It is thin, and I know what it will taste like: turnips and cabbage. The steam is rising, thick and white, and gives the soup a promise that every one of us knows it cannot live up to, but we are grateful nonetheless. There is a persistent knocking against the outer wall: the French trebuchet is out of action today, and the mangonels cannot find their range. But two people are already dead this morning, a crossbowman with a slight wound who went to bed cheerful and did not wake up, and a *bon homme* from Limoux who has been sinking for days into fever and then delirium. I have a low fever, and my nose is crusted and yellow. All my joints ache, and I have weeping chilblains on my hands. It is past the turning of the year, at least. The sun is coming back to us, slowly.

Through the steam I glimpse the long dark braids of Iselda de Rosers. She has her arms around a *perfecta* I recognise as Saissa de Congost. The older woman says something and Iselda smiles and shakes her head. She catches sight of me and waves a friendly hand. I have seen her every day since her return but we have not spoken. I have often wished to hear her song, but there is no singing in Montségur, only the croak of the ravens.

Two vultures are hacking at a French corpse out on the ridge. From the walls we can hear the *chack, chock* of the great beaks as they strike, hatchet-like, at the frozen meat.

Guillaume the baker is carrying a tray of loaves across the courtyard. It is balanced on his head. A spent crossbow quarrel drops into the courtyard and hisses across the cobbles towards him. He skips over it, and the tray stays up. A ragged cheer goes up from the walls.

A man stands, exhausted, in the solar of the keep. It is Matheus, the man who had bought me sausages in Paris. People still come and go, those who can face a terrifying scramble in darkness. Messages, letters, even hams and chickens get through to us, but rarely, for the paths still open to us were the most dangerous ones on the *pog*. Matheus holds out a letter to Pierre-Roger, who tears it in his impatience. He reads it, bites his lip, hands it without a word to Bishop Marty.

'Count Raymond wishes us to hold Montségur until Easter,' the bishop tells us – the Captain, the Castellan and myself. I am only in the room as Matheus' escort. 'So says the author of this note, a *bon homme* whose brother is a secretary of the Count's chamberlain. Not the most direct of routes. He goes on to say that the Count's affairs continue to prosper.'

'The Count and his affairs,' mutters Pierre-Roger grimly. A ball from the trebuchet hits the wall of the keep with a thud that rattles the empty trencher on the table, and crashes down into the courtyard. 'We will hold out.'

A sergeant called Raymond de Ventenac has taken an arrow in the groin. He is lying in the shadow of the wall, very still, very white. Blood is pouring from him in gouts as if from a cup spilled again and again over the stones. A *bon homme*, Pierre Robert, is cradling his head in his lap while a *perfecta* speaks the words of the *Consolamentum* to the dying man.

This holy baptism, by which the Holy Spirit is given,
The Church of God has preserved from the time of the apostles until this time
And it has passed from Good Men to Good Men until the present moment,
And it will continue to do so until the end of the World.

Iselda de Rosers is holding his hands so that he cannot pull out the arrow, and crooning something under her breath. Perhaps it is a lullaby. I am hurrying past with a bundle of arrows I have been gathering from the yard. I step over the stream of blood. The cobbles are white with frost, but where the blood has bathed them they shine like garnets. Raymond says 'Oh, my mother!' He twists his head in the *bon homme's* lap and dies. I hurry off to my archers.

Bertrand Marty holds a service in the courtyard, standing in the door of the keep. The Good Christians stand tensely, listening for the whoop of balls from the French stone guns. They have three more mangonels now, and the balls, those that we have not shot back with our own puny machine, are beginning to pile up under the walls, and to live inside Montségur is to live inside a great bell that is constantly ringing with the smash and boom of stone upon stone. Our ears hum and we go about hunched, always ducking and bobbing as the stones sail in. Now the bishop raises his hand. His assistant, old Pierre Sirven, nudges Pons the miller and the two men stoop over the long wooden box at their feet and draw out a sheet of white linen. The watery sunlight is almost too strong, but every eye can see the dark outline of a bearded man, his hands crossed over his chest. Something passes across the crowd, cat's-paws of unease, and three or four women cover their faces and moan. The figure upon the shroud flutters slightly, a ghost, a shade painted in blood, a patient guide awaiting the end of the world.

A trebuchet ball sails over the parapet four paces from me, whistling faintly, and hits the wall of the stable where I am quartered. There is a crash and a clatter as the fragments of stone spray out, and then a man's cry, surprised and angry. I look down out of habit, and see a figure in black sitting on the cobbles, his legs straight out in front of him. He clutches at his upper thigh with bloody hands, and raises his head, for another ball is flying in, and I see it is Captain de Montalhac. I run down the stairs and join the *bons hommes* who have helped him up and are examining his wound. There is a blade of stone the size of a priest's blessing fingers jutting from his thigh but not much blood, so the artery is safe. The Captain's lips are white but he laughs when he sees me and lets me help him into the keep, where Corba de Lantar will help him. It is the last Sunday in January.

I am summoned from the walls, where I am shooting at a band of Crusaders who are trying to dig an entrenchment. I have learned to use a bow, not well, but skill does not matter any more. It is twilight, and the moon is rising in a strip of clear sky between the mountains and the clouds. I am sore, because a mangonel stone struck the embrasure I had been standing in the day before and sprayed me with shards. My wounds are not bad, but there are many of them, and I ache all over, most of all from a deep gash under my left arm. I follow the sergeant into the keep. In the solar I find Pierre-Roger and Raymond de Perella, Bishop Marty and Captain de Montalhac. He is sitting, uncomfortably, looking white and drawn. It is less than a week since his wounding, and he has not healed yet. A dark-haired man with no front teeth is leaning on the table.

'This is Arnaud Teuly,' says the Captain. 'He has come from our brothers in Cremona. There are many Good Christians from our country living there, and they have written, begging the faithful to abandon Monségur and seek refuge with them. I am afraid that they do not quite understand our predicament, however.'

'There are rumours that . . . all sorts of rumours, you know,' says Arnaud Teuly, the air whistling through the gap in his teeth. The loss looks recent, and I wonder what he has endured to deliver his pointless message. 'The community in Cremona is convinced that Emperor Frederick is coming to your aid.' He flicks his eyes ceilingward to show that he does not believe this for a moment.

'We have heard that as well,' the castellan tells him. 'Also that Count Raymond will have the Crusaders gone by Easter. And indeed that Prester John is on his way from India to rescue us. Each as likely as the other, to my way of thinking.'

'We sent our good brother Matheus back down the *pog* to hire as many mercenaries as he could find. He returned last morning with two – *two* – crossbowmen, all he could persuade to come with him, and he scoured the countryside and the towns.' Pierre-Roger is tapping the pommel of his sword as he speaks.

'There is one more thing,' says Arnaud. 'The Bishop of Cremona asked me – entreated me, in fact – to bring Bishop Marty back to Italy. You would put great heart in our people there, brother,' he goes on, turning to the bishop. 'Exiles are crossing the mountains every day, it seems, and now that Raymond has made peace with Pope Innocent, there is no safety in Languedoc. Strange that our safe haven might be in the very garden of Rome itself . . . Bishop, will you come?'

'I cannot, my brother,' says Bishop Marty, sadly. 'The gold of our Church, such as it was, has already left here, and my desire was that it should be sent to Cremona. I trust brother Pierre – he is a stout-hearted and clever man, and he will do his utmost to make sure my wishes are carried out. But the real treasure, my friend, is nothing less than the brothers and sisters who have taken refuge here. They cannot leave, all ten score of them! And I will not abandon them, do you see. I have known, since I came here, what my fate would be, and I welcome it. Tell your bishop that he has treasures of his own to guard.'

'My bishop, I am not leaving again,' says Arnaud. 'If I cannot bring you or my brothers and sisters into exile, I will go with you, gladly, to the light that awaits.'

'So be it,' says the bishop, and took Arnaud's hand. 'It is almost upon us, never fear.'

'And the matter we have been discussing, Bertrand?' says the Captain. He sits up straighter and it makes him wince, but his voice is strong.

'On that, Michel, I do agree. Our crucifix must be saved, so that the faithful in Italy may put it to good use. It seems you must go back after all, brother Arnaud.'

'He does not need to leave if he does not wish to,' says the Captain. 'In his stead I would like to recommend Sir Petroc.' He waggles his fingers in my direction. 'He is experienced in such matters, and has spent several years in Italy. And as I also have a bequest that I wish to put into the hands of the brothers in Cremona, which Sir Petroc can take care of as my proxy, I would very much like him to be our man.'

'We cannot really spare any fighting men,' Pierre-Roger says, frowning at me. I stand there, embarrassed. I have almost forgotten my old life. For the past months I have thought mainly about warmth and sleep. I am a soldier, after all. I study the Captain. He is bone-white around the edges of his nostrils and his mouth, and the skin under his eyes is papery, blue. His hair, I notice suddenly, is almost silver.

'Michel,' I find myself saying, 'It is you who should take the crucifix. There is no one alive who can be of more help to the Good Christians – do they have a diplomat? Someone who has the friendship of the Emperor? They do not. Your wealth will be of more use if you direct how it is spent.' Seeing his eyebrows lift and his mouth tense, I turn to the bishop. 'Sir, Michel de Montalhac would best serve his people as a living man and not a martyr. If you wish to keep your church alive, send him away.'

The bishop opens his mouth, but Pierre-Roger's voice cuts through the room.

'So be it,' he says. 'Michel will carry your crucifix to safety, wherever that might be, and the rest of your gold. You, Sir Petroc, will go with him. It is a long way to Cremona, and he will need an escort who can use a sword. Michel,' he continues, silencing whatever the Captain is about to say with a glare, 'You are hurt, and will not be mended, no doubt, for a while yet. Petroc, I recommend that you take him as far as Montpellier and put him on a ship. Then you can be of use to us again. Go to Toulouse, and find out from my lord Count Raymond exactly what these fucking affairs of his are, and what in the name of God's boils they have to do with us!'

Bishop Marty clears his throat, but he is smiling doggedly. 'So be it. Michel, I entrust our crucifix to you. There could be no better custodian. I have not authority over Sir Petroc . . .'

'. . . Therefore I command him to escort Michel,' says Pierre-Roger. 'You will need a guide. We will have to wait . . .'

The Captain sighs so deeply that Pierre-Roger shuts his mouth abruptly.

'I will find us a guide,' says Captain de Montalhac. 'If you will permit me, that is. I thank you for the great responsibility that you have entrusted to me, but . . . it was never my intention to abandon my friends, and brothers, and sisters.'

'You are a good man, Michel,' the bishop replies. He uses the French, *bon homme*. 'And yet you are not yet a *bon homme*, if you will forgive my pun. You have given over your life and all the fruits of your toil to your church. And yet you have not taken the *Consolamentum*. Don't fear – I am not doubting your faith, far from it. But the fact that you have not, even now, chosen to become *perfect* seems to tell me that you have not finished serving the faith from your place in this world. Go back to Italy. Tell the faithful what has become of us, and shore them up against the storm that will be coming to them. Then you will have fulfilled your destiny, perhaps.'

'Bertrand, would you give me the *Consolamentum* now, immediately?'

'I would, and I will. Nothing could give me greater pleasure. Shall I, then?' The space between the two men seems to shiver as they stare into one another's faces. The Captain grits his teeth and shakes his head.

'Ach, you are right. I wish it were not so, but . . . Very well. I will take Petroc, and a guide, and anyone else who wishes to come, or whoever else you think should go to Cremona. We should leave tomorrow, as there will be very little moon.'

I listen, slightly dazed by it all. *Who is the guide*, I wonder. *Could it be Gilles? The Captain would want to save his friend as he is saving me. But Gilles will never leave, I know it.* I look around the solar at the faces before me. It has been a year and three months since I first stood here. How time has savaged us. Castellan Raymond's hair is almost gone. Pierre-Roger's beard is grey and his face is weathered and etched from days and nights spent out in the slashing winds. The Captain is thin and hollowed-out. Bishop Marty's skin has the ivory transparency of death, and yet his eyes are bright and flicker with strength and purpose. I wonder what I look like. I feel ancient, and the only purpose I have left is to keep myself alive – and why do I do that? To help my comrades, as they help me. The comrades I am leaving behind tomorrow.

Pierre-Roger sticks his head out of the room and calls for his wife. Lady Corba comes in with another *perfecta* and two serving girls. They bring rough bread and pitchers of water and the sour beer that we brew in the castle. The *perfecta* tends to the Captain's thigh. I give him a nod and he furrows his brow at me and smiles vaguely, mirroring my own uncertainty over what has been decided for us. I make my excuses and leave, for I have to explain matters to the garrison. Outside it is pitch black and silent save for the exhausted weeping of a baby, and the thud, thud of stones against the walls.

I went out to the huts beneath the west wall and said goodbye to Gilles. We were two old friends parting before a long journey, as we had been many times before. And as before, we knew where our paths would lead us.

'I won't see you again, will I?' I said. We were sitting in his hut, and the wind was whimpering under the edges of the roof.

'Not for a very long time,' he said. 'We are going to different places, you and I. My dear friend, you are staying and I am leaving – though it seems to be the other way round.'

'Really?' I said. Gilles' pronouncements, delivered as they always were with a wry smile, had ceased to alarm me. But then I saw that his face was solemn. 'What do you mean?'

'That I am leaving the world and going to God's light, while you, without the *Consolamentum*, are doomed to return, and return . . .'

'Until when?'

'Until you become *perfect*. Only then does the soul leave its prison.'

'Oh. I come back, then? As me?' I was pretending the whole thing was a joke, but I was beginning to feel unbearably sad.

'No, Patch. One of you will be quite enough.' He was smiling again. 'The soul enters another body at the moment of birth, with no memory of its former lives. And so it goes, until the soul is released by the *Consolamentum.*'

I wanted to say, *But that's bollocks, Gilles!* But I did not. 'So that is what you really believe?' I said instead.

'I do. And so do all Good Christians. We are leaving, Patch. You, the castellan, the soldiers, even those who have died here: all are staying.'

Can I come with you? I did not say it, but what else could I think? Gilles was my friend. No, he was my older brother.

'Yes,' he said, startling me. 'You can leave as well – that is what you are thinking, isn't it? Become a *bon homme.* Take the *Consolamentum.* I can give it to you.' He reached out and took me gently by the shoulders. 'But you don't want that, do you? I do not blame you, Patch. You are not ready.'

'No?'

'No. You are young. Live well – live *properly,* is what I mean to say; remember what I have taught you and what you have learned here, and if you are ready, you will find your salvation.'

'It . . . I am sorry, Gilles. You saved me once already. Do you remember?'

'The Swan at Dartmouth? When you walked into that room and pulled a golden hand out of your tunic, I thought, this boy is either a simpleton or a magician. And then I wondered, as you were telling us your story, *what will become of him?* Now I have my answer.'

'Lord, I dread to hear it,' I said, trying to jest us out of sorrow, but my words were no match for the stillness that had fallen on the little hovel now that the wind had died down.

'You are here. That is my answer. You had the world to roll in like a great soft bed, and you chose Montségur. I did not: this place chose me, and my faith led me here. Nothing brought you to this place and induced you to stay except love. Perhaps we will not be parted for so very long after all.'

I could find no words to say, so I took his hands between mine, and he kissed the top of my head, softly. Then I stood and stooped under the lintel. I looked back for the last time, and saw Gilles kneeling in front of his little fire. The faint orange glow lit up his face and his eyes glimmered faintly. He was staring into the heart of the flames, and whether he saw things past or things to come I cannot say. I turned and started off along the narrow path through the other huts. I was not the first man to weep on Montségur, and I would not be the last, and by the time I had reached the gates my tears had frozen on my cheeks and left nothing but briny dust.

Chapter Twenty-two

I did not see Captain de Montalhac again until nightfall the next day. I had thought to spend what was left of my time saying fond fare-thee-wells to the men I had come to know so well in the past year, but the Crusaders had launched one of their attacks along the ridge and this time had succeeded in digging a trench and bringing up a small mangonel, for we hardly had the strength, or the arrows and quarrels, to keep them back. A sergeant I knew well had his ear sliced off by a quarrel, and three Good Christians were killed when a trebuchet ball landed on their shelter. So I was busy fighting and pulling smashed limbs out of the wrecked hut, which seems enough for a lifetime when spoken of thus, but at the time was as ordinary as going to the market for a bushel of apples. I hurt in my limbs and in my head, for my various wounds were far from healed, and some had festered, though not badly. A few men wished me good luck, and some others clapped me on the back while complaining about my good fortune. But for most it was as if I had already gone, for wartime has its own leaden rules, and because I would not be on the walls tomorrow, I was as good as dead today.

So I tied up my clothes from times of peace, which I had not worn for a year and more, and rolled them into a blanket. I greased my mail shirt and trews so that they would not rattle as I climbed, slung my shield over my back and said goodbye to the little stable room with its smoking fire. The Captain was waiting inside the hall of the keep, standing next to a man whose face was hidden by a black cowl. Our guide, I supposed, though he looked more like an Inquisitor. The ill and the wounded covered the floor, lying on pallets or on the bare flagstones. The furniture had long since gone for firewood, and the tapestries cut up for blankets, and the walls were sooty from the smoking hearth, in which nothing burned but bundles of furze-twigs. *Perfecti* were busy everywhere, giving comfort and dressing wounds. I saw Corba the castellan's wife, and her daughter Esclarmonde, barely able to walk, who had propped herself in a corner and was tearing up linen into bandages. And there was Phillipa, wife of Pierre-Roger, and Arsende, wife of the sergeant who had lost his ear. The Captain saw me and picked his way through the prone bodies to the doorway.

'Are you sure you can do this?' I asked, for though he had got his colour back and was standing straight and firm, his wound had been ugly, and could not have mended so soon.

'I can do it,' he said. 'I don't want to, mind. My leg is stiff as an oar. But I came to place my life at the disposal of the faith, did I not? I cannot really complain. And we have not had an adventure, you and I, for a while.'

'An adventure, is it?' I said, laughing. 'What fun. You have the . . .' I saw that the Captain had a small, bulging satchel over his shoulder. 'Is it in there?'

'It folds up quite neatly,' he said. 'Our guide has volunteered to carry my other things.' The man had come up behind him. He was slight, and under his cowl he wore a thick black tunic and leggings that were tied tight to his legs. I knew most of the mountaineers by sight, and I did not recognise this one. He must be a *bon homme*, for a few of them, like the tireless and brave Matheus, knew their way about the *pog* as well as any mountaineer. I was sticking my hand out to introduce myself when the Captain took my shoulders and steered me out into the corridor.

'I am not looking forward to this night's work,' he said. 'So let us get it over with.'

'Amen to that,' I replied. Out in the courtyard torches flickered by the postern gate. Bishop Marty waited for us there with the castellan. The bishop kissed the Captain on both cheeks and embraced me, and then the castellan held out his hand and bade me God's speed.

'You have another companion,' he told me. 'This is Bertranz de Quidhers, whom the bishop is also sending into Italy.' I recognised the man, a young-ish *bon homme* who lived out on the cliff-edge near Gilles.

'Are you in the mood for a climb?' I asked him, giving him my hand to shake. He took it: his grip was hard.

'If it serves our church,' he said briskly. A ball from the French trebuchet thumped against the wall nearby, and a sleepy pigeon tumbled into the air behind us. 'I would rather . . .'

'Stay here? So would we all, and is that not an odd thing to say?' I told him. 'Let us go. They are waiting.'

Out on the narrow lip of rock the dark outline of the Captain stood leaning into the wind, his head close to the guide. We had left the torches behind, and the only light came from the stars and the flow of the Milky Way. I was fiddling with my sword, which I had lashed to my shield but which seemed to be loose – or perhaps it was only my imagination.

'Ready?' said the Captain. Bertranz nodded. I gave an errant knot a final tug and grunted a *yes*.

'Good. Now let us pay attention,' he said. The guide pushed back the heavy fold of his cowl. There was just enough light to see by, very faint, like the moon reflected off burnished silver, but in the spider-web glow I made out the face of Iselda de Rosers.

'Where is our guide?' I asked, loud with surprise.

'This is she,' said the Captain.

'But . . .'

'We have to hurry,' said Iselda tersely. 'Since you seem to be curious, I know these paths better than any man up here save Matheus. I have been up and down them eight times since the French arrived, but no one gives a thought to the comings and goings of women. Pierre-Roger is sending me to Toulouse to plead with the Count, and good Captain Michel thought to make use of my knowledge. If you are coming, come now.'

I heard Bertranz' teeth clack shut, and I swallowed down my own words, whatever they would have been. I knew the singer had climbed the *pog* at least once, which was more than I had done. I felt uneasy about this whole enterprise, and I realised, as I walked gingerly towards the brink, that if putting myself into the hands of a woman did not make me feel especially happy, it made me no more worried than anything else. Iselda took a step and suddenly only her head and her shoulders were visible above the edge of the cliff. She held out her hand for the Captain, and he sat down and pushed off. Bertranz and I looked at each other. I gave him a tight nod. 'After you,' I rasped. He dropped down, and I followed.

At first it was not so hard, merely a scramble on steep, narrow paths of loose scree. I was not as quick as I would have liked to be, for my injuries were bothering me. They were starting to heal, all but the one under my arm, and as they knit were making me very stiff and sore. Even so, I began to wonder if the mountaineers had not been exaggerating their bravery. But very soon we came to a sheer drop, or so it seemed. Iselda cast about for a minute, stooping and peering out over the edge, then beckoned us over. The cliffs dropped straight down into darkness, but just below us the rock bulged slightly, like dried tallow from a candle or a frozen waterfall, and this cascade of solid rock was riven by a dark crack, a notch of darkness no wider than a man's body.

'Down here,' Iselda whispered, and lowered herself feet-first into the black fissure. One by one we followed. When it was my turn I dangled my legs above Bertranz' head and pushed off. For a nasty moment I was caught by my shield and twisted myself in a growing panic until suddenly I came unstuck. I found that if I wriggled I slipped and scraped downwards, the jagged stone biting at my knees and elbows, my wounds protesting. A vein of faint light showed where the crack opened onto the void, and as we descended the crack became wider until I found myself suspended, as if in a window. Only the pressure of my arms and legs against the sides of the crack kept me from falling forward into the black nothing. I took my parchment-dry lip between my teeth and eased myself down again. Suddenly a boulder appeared, wedged somehow in the crack, and Bertranz was squeezing himself behind it. I followed and popped out onto a narrow ledge. The Captain was sitting down, resting against the rock wall, and Iselda was crouched over him.

'Is he all right?' I hissed.

'Yes,' grunted the Captain.

'I think his wound has opened, but it is not bleeding too badly,' said the woman. The Captain was retying his bandage, and when he was done he levered himself upright and shook himself like a great grey dog. He grinned at me encouragingly. Iselda stepped around him and beckoned us onward.

We edged along the narrow shelf of stone, which wavered and grew wider and more narrow by turns. In one place it vanished altogether for an arm's breadth, and we had to reach up and grasp a twisted root of some tree that clung there, and heave ourselves across the gap. Then we were in another fissure, angling like crabs first one way and then another. I felt my nails split and my fingers begin to bleed as I scrabbled again and again for a handhold. Once, Bertranz slipped and, with a strangled howl, dropped, flailing, onto the Captain's shoulders. By pure good fortune the Captain's feet were firmly set and his body braced and the *bon homme* was brought up short and managed to cling on with his hands, but I heard his boots strike the Captain and winced. My friend was all skin and bone, and his wound weakened him even more than cold and hunger had already managed. We stayed, trembling, for an eternity.

'I am secure,' said Bertranz at last. The Captain coughed and shifted his weight.

'Let us go on,' he said, and his voice sounded choked. Iselda was already far below. I heard the Captain's feet searching for a hold, and then with a sudden hiss of loose stone he fell. There was a surging and a clattering that echoed up the rock walls, and for a moment a thin wail, as if a scream had been bitten down upon. Then silence.

'I'm all right,' came the Captain's voice from very far down. 'I slid.' There was another silence. When it came again, his voice sounded strangled, but it was at least strong and loud. 'You can come down on your arses, my lads, but be more careful than me.'

We found him on another ledge, leaning against the cliff. His clothes were white with dust, and Iselda was kneeling at his side. She looked up as we came out of the fissure.

'He slid down on his bad leg,' she said, her voice soothing. 'It has opened, but I've bound it tight, and he says he will go on. Ready?' She looked up at the Captain, and he nodded.

'How does it go with you?' I whispered, a hand on his shoulder.

'I am fine. I thought I was falling into nothing, but 'twas just a little hard on my backside after all. Let us get on now.'

Iselda started down once more and the Captain followed, and Bertranz – whose breath was coming in shuddering gasps, for he had clearly not mastered the fright he had taken when he fell – and then myself.

'Now we have to jump,' said Iselda. 'There was a rope here, but it has gone. It is not far – three times my height, if that. The landing is hard but flat. Watch me.' She sat down and twisted herself around until the pale oval of her face was towards us. Then she vanished. There was a soft thud.

'There is an overhang,' she called up. 'Let go and bend your legs when you land.'

'You go next, Bertranz, and then me. Captain, we will catch you.' I motioned Bertranz to the brink and he sat down, somewhat reluctantly, I thought. Then he dropped, and I followed. It was not dreadful, but I made sure that we broke the Captain's fall just the same. As he landed I took his weight, and felt his fingers squeeze my shoulder.

'Still faring well?' I whispered.

'Ach. This is delightful, isn't it?' he muttered back.

There was a path after that, and one more scramble down a steep ramp of scree, and then we were in the trees. The bare, stunted oaks rattled their branches at us, but we were almost down. The path under our feet was made by sheep or goats, and we were back in the realm of the living, at least. So we marched, down and down, until we came to the course of a frozen stream thickly overhung by leafless rowans and willows. Iselda led us along its narrow bank for perhaps three miles, until the sky was beginning to grow light. Then we sat down under the lean of a huge boulder to rest. I felt the frozen grass crackle beneath me, laid my head back and closed my eyes. There was a slide and a rustle beside me.

'Don't get too comfortable, sir knight. We must be at our journey's end by dawn.'

'Christ. And where is that?' I said. Iselda wriggled herself comfortable against the stone.

'Not far. It is a farm where the family is loyal to Mirepoix. They will have horses for us.'

'Where are the French lines?'

'We already passed through. Do you remember when we came down out of the trees? The sentries should have been there. But they are boys from Camon sur l'Hers, and their fathers farm their land at the say-so of Pierre-Roger, and so at certain times of night they make sure they are investigating suspicious noises on the other side of the wood.' She leaned closer. I felt myself prickle with something I had not felt for months, and though I caught only the sourness of hunger on her breath, the scent of the beseiged, my blood began to warm a little.

'Your Captain is not well,' she whispered, and I went cold again. 'His leg is still bleeding, and it does not smell right. And he is old.'

'I don't know about that. He was . . . he was my age at the siege of Toulouse, he said. So he is fifty-five or thereabouts.'

'As I thought, near enough. He is too old to be here. I fear for him.'

'What can we do?' I asked after a long silence.

'I have some skill with herbs and such. They may have something at the farm. If we can get to Montpellier in time . . . He was strong, before all this.'

'He was.'

'So much waste. How thin us hunted beasts become, and how frail. And now our country belongs to the huntsmen.'

I said nothing, but leaned back and stared up at the sky. The great swathe of the Milky Way was fading, and just above the ragged jawbone of the valley hung a spark of green light.

'*Sweet friend, the morning star has risen in the east,*' I murmured. Iselda turned to me. She closed her eyes, and when she opened them again they held a ghost of reflected starlight.

'That song does not end happily, my friend,' she said.

We slept through the day that followed in a barn, covered in sweet hay. The farmer's wife brought us warm goat's milk and knelt for a while at Bertranz' feet, for she was a believer. Horses were found, and at nightfall we took the road north. It was strange being on horseback again, and my arse had become lean and bony, so at first the jolting gait of the horse was agony. But, by the time we had passed Le Peyrat, my arse had gone numb while the rest of me began to come alive. We were free.

We rested for a few hours before dawn in an old tower, woke up before noon and set off again. We were far enough away from Montségur now that there was no reason for a watcher to take us for anything but ordinary travellers. And as Iselda told me as we shared out the bread the farmer had given us, everyone knew that the heretics and their guardians were all locked up on the *pog*. To all intents and purposes we were an English knight, a wealthy merchant and their two companions. All at once the appalling dead-weight of threat that had lain across my shoulders since the day the first Frenchmen scrambled up onto the ridge had vanished.

The Captain was feeling better that morning, and was straight and sure in the saddle. We rode close together for a while, but after a while the Captain and Bertranz crept to the front, leaving Iselda and I together a few lengths behind. It was a fine day, and as the miles passed by and Montségur grew further and further away, I found myself growing lighter inside. And here beside me was the woman who had been haunting my thoughts for so long.

Iselda de Rosers. It had been many, many days since I had first heard her voice, and she had drifted in and out of my life since then, and neither of us had paid much attention to the other, for in the roar of the French bombardment and the howling of the wind there had never been time. I had seen her every day, I suppose, and we would smile at each other when we chanced to meet in the courtyard or in the keep, and perhaps exchange some pleasantry. I wished, always, to tarry with her and speak more, to open my heart a little more, and hers likewise, as we had done that morning in the solar. But then the grinding toil of the siege would scrape those feelings away, for I would be back on the walls or in the armoury, and she would be with the women in the keep, tending to the sick, the wounded and the dying. But what never left me, in all those long months, was the desire to hear her sing once more, and it hid inside somewhere deep and dark, like a tortoiseshell butterfly sleeping the winter through, tucked away in some crack in a wall. Now here she was, at my side. There were many things I wished to ask her, but one thing above all, and as I jogged along I gathered my courage like a bashful youth, until the words could stay in my throat no longer.

'Will you ever sing again?' I asked her finally, after we had ridden together in companionable silence for the better part of an hour. She looked at me with something more than surprise, and I winced inside, hoping I had not broken the spell that had created some warmth between us today. But at last she gave me a wan smile and shook her head.

'What's there to sing about?' she asked. It was a statement, but also a challenge.

'We are alive . . .' I began, but found myself sighing as I said it.

'We are alive because we have left our friends to die. Shall I sing about that?' she snapped. But she hung her head, and her next words were more gentle. 'Forgive me. But both of us know we shall not see them again.'

I had been thinking of little else since we had left Montségur, and I was about to blurt out the words that I was clinging to as guilt tossed me about with its cold teeth: that when the castle fell, those who were not heretics would be safe, more than likely, and the Good Christians had already resolved to die and would welcome their end when it came. But however true that might be – and there are no certainties in war, especially when matters of faith are the cause of it – I had left my post. A soldier would have told me that I had been so commanded and therefore had no choice in the matter, but though I had learned the skills of war in the long months since I had ridden up to Taillebourg, I had not learned the soldier's habits of mind.

'You are right,' I said. 'I feel like a deserter. I *am* a deserter.'

'Is that really what you think?'

I looked at her in surprise. 'Yes. Of course it is.'

'You, a man from another land, with no master – you told me that, remember? – who owed nothing to any man on Montségur, a deserter? You aren't subject to Pierre-Roger, and you aren't a Good Christian. Who, my friend, are you deserting?'

I closed my eyes for a moment and saw Gilles, serene, gazing out over the valley. Could you abandon someone who had already left the world and you along with it?

'The *perfecti* knew their fate when they climbed the *pog*,' said Iselda, as if hearing my thoughts. 'And the soldiers? They are there for their lord, and because they hate the French. Do you hate the French as well?'

'Not particularly,' I muttered. 'No more than . . . no, I don't. I have been filled to the brim with hate for one sort of person or another, for the whole world, even. But not any more. What's the point? We are all fools, we shall all die.'

She shuddered. 'Lord! Is that what you believe?'

'I've had enough of believing,' I told her. 'I used to believe in Holy

Mother Church, and nearly died because of it. I believed in power, but what a midden that turned out to be! And I have lost a dear friend to belief, and though he is happy, I only see that he will die for nothing. All those wretches back there – the sergeant, Raymond? Remember him? What did he die for, with his blood coming out all over the stones?'

'You rail at belief because you have none,' Iselda replied gently. 'I think you saw the peace that the Good Christians found, and it showed you the turmoil inside your own soul.'

'Listen. My friend Gilles – he lives out in the village of the *bons hommes* – used to stare out into the distance and see nothing but illusion. This is a man who saw beauty in everything, or worth, at least. He would pluck a beetle from a tree and show you the patterns on its back, or pull out an ancient stone and marvel at the way it had been carved so that the eye at its heart shone through, until you would marvel with him. His belief, it turns out, took all that away. So for all those years, when he was looking *at* things, should he rather have been looking *through* them? Life was not an illusion then . . .'

'And was he right?'

'About what?'

'About things. Beetles and stones. The world. Is it all the Devil's dream?'

I laughed emptily. 'Up on the walls, at night, with the ice and the quarrels coming at me out of the dark, how I used to wish it was all something I would wake up from. Alas, the world may be the Devil's work, but it is real enough. But what about you, my lady? You don't believe the *perfecti* either – or do you?'

It was her turn to laugh. 'No. I am no believer. My grandmother, God rest her, was a *perfecta*, and she died up on the *pog* . . .'

'Oh! I am sorry. I did not mean to be so scornful.'

'Don't worry. She was old, and it was a year or more before the siege began. She taught me most of the songs I know, so you see that Good Christians can find joy in the world, before they say farewell.'

'Your songs aren't altogether joyful,' I said, though I was pleased, for at last she was talking of the thing I so dearly wished to learn about.

'But they are about love,' she pointed out. She was looking at the road ahead, so I could not see what look was on her face, but I knew that, somehow, she had decided to be gentle with me.

'And yet you do not sing any more,' I said. 'What happened to love, then?'

She turned to me, and her mouth was tight with sudden anger. 'You ask too much, sir!' she growled.

'Peace, Lady Iselda. I did not mean to sound so callow. And I do know something of love, to my misfortune. Here: I will tell you, and put myself in your power.' She scowled but said nothing, so I went on hurriedly. 'My first love died in my arms with her beautiful face in ruins. My second love saw me grow cold and greedy and so she left me, and now she will not have me back, though I am a good deal changed. Not enough for a great song, perhaps, but a verse or two?'

'Tss. You do feel sorry for yourself, don't you?'

'I did. Not any more. She was right to leave me. I had become the kind of man I have always despised.'

'And she who died?'

'The longer we live, the more dead we leave behind us. For a long time I wished I had died with Anna, but she would have thought me a great fool, had she known. Still, I did not care much for life.'

'You would make a good *bon homme*,' she said, a little slyness creeping into her voice.

'Yes, I suppose so!' I admitted. 'Strange, though. I have been around death far too much these past two years, and at times perhaps it would have been easier just to let go. To renounce everything, like Gilles. But here I am. I'm still alive, and I don't want to die any more.'

'You've found something to live for, then?'

'I don't know. But I haven't found anything to die for.'

'Or any*one*.'

'And you?' I asked again.

'I make my own way,' she said, and I thought I saw her set her jaw a little.

'Come on, my lady. I showed you the scars on my heart. Show me yours.'

'Not much to show.'

'I doubt that. No one could sing of love as sweetly and as coldly as you do and not have . . . not have . . .'

'Lived? Very well. I loved a man, and he betrayed me. I loved my country, and it died. Are those the qualifications you sought?'

'Ah, Lady Iselda. We are not trying to hurt each other, are we? Tell me about your life. You are a *trobriaritz*. I know nothing about your art, for you are not mere entertainers, are you? I've heard my Occitan friends talk about the troubadours as though they were poets and prophets rolled into one. You must have sung for some worthy audiences.'

She shrugged rather prettily and rolled her eyes. 'When I was a girl there were still courts that welcomed the troubadours. And yes, I sang for the lords and ladies.'

'And your lover – was he one of them? A lord?'

She gave me such a look that I thought she was about to attack me, but instead she threw back her head and laughed.

'God, no! He was a lawyer, a Genoese lawyer. Of noble birth, I should add – oh, salve my pride! A pretty man, and charming as a jackdaw. The surprise was not that he betrayed me, but that he took so long to do it. I do not sing for him, as I think you suppose. My songs are for my . . . if you can understand, for my grandmother's world, the things she saw when she was a girl, that I will never see. This land when it was the fairest in the world, with the most gentle and wise rulers, courts full of poets and scholars from across the seas, songs and poems and deep talk of God, and how the world is made . . . All that is gone. That is what I grieve for.'

'You could have died with it,' I said. 'You have chosen to live too.'

'There you have it. But I won't sing any more.'

'I once had a friend, a Moor,' I said, just to keep us talking together. 'He sang well, and at night – I used to sail on a ship, and hardly ever walk on the land – at night we would sing and tell stories over our meal, and my friend would sing his Moorish songs. I could not understand the words, of course, and I would ask him what they meant. He told me they were love songs, but really about God, and how to find him in this world.' This was only vaguely what Nizam the helmsman had told me, for we had spent many long hours talking of his faith, and of the teachers he had called *Soof* but whom Isaac, the ship's doctor and a Jewish scholar from Al-Andalus, called Sufis. I tried to explain some of this to Iselda. 'Anyway, some of the troubadour songs I have heard sound like the ones my friend sang. I always thought that was curious.'

Iselda furrowed her brows. She no longer looked as if she wished to knock me off my horse, which was a good sign, I supposed. 'My mother used to say that our songs – not the songs, but the form of them, really – came from Al-Andalus. Can you sing one of your friend's?'

'No!' I shook my head. 'But I remember the tune of one.' I began to whistle it, and though the sound fell flat in the wide valley we were riding through, Iselda smiled, and even the Captain and Bertranz, up ahead, turned in their saddles and grinned.

'That could be two dozen songs, but you are right. I would like to speak to your friend.'

'Alas, you cannot. He went off into the east to look for a master, for he wished to become one of those Sufis himself. It is strange: he was a great giant of a man, a blackamoor from beyond the Egyptian desert, and the rudder of our ship looked like a twig in his hands, though it was the trunk of a young tree. But he was calm inside, calm as a millpond. I hope he found his teacher. I miss him, though.'

'So in these songs the loved one was God Himself?' Iselda was interested now, and her horse had drifted closer to mine. 'It is the same in our songs, though vulgar folk don't wish to hear that.'

'Yes. They were all about the lover, and drunkenness, and heart's desire. You say vulgar folk and I am speaking of sailors . . . but that was why I loved the songs. One meaning for those that listened with their ears and . . .' Iselda understood, for she grinned knowingly. 'Anyway, another meaning if you listened with your heart. Not your head: your heart.'

We let ourselves sink deep into a discussion about all this, in which I was very much relying on my heart to guide me, for my head had no idea, really, what we were talking about, and after she had told me of the troubadours and their songs, and I had told her about my life and made her tell of hers, the sun had started to roll down into the west. At last there was a shout from up ahead, and the Captain called to us that there was a likely-looking barn just off the road where we could spend the night. We trotted up to join them, and that was all we spoke that day, for Iselda set to tending the Captain's wound and I went about gathering wood and cooking dinner, the last of our eggs and some herbs from the deserted vineyard behind our shelter. Later I fell asleep without meaning to, for the day had been long and the fire was warm, and the next day Iselda rode with the Captain, though every now and again she would turn and smile back at me, and when we stopped to take our luncheon of cracking, yellow cheese and dried out bread, she let me share my portion with her.

Since we no longer needed to ride under cover of night, we made camp that evening in an abandoned house, for war and famine had emptied out this corner of the land. The place had been long since been plundered, but there was a roof and a fireplace, and we made ourselves as comfortable as we could. I was tucking myself into a corner on a pile of old broom twigs I had gathered outside, and Bertranz had already fallen asleep by the door, when the hiss of a cold log on the fire made me look up. The Captain was lying on his side, propped up on one arm, and Iselda was settling herself down beside him. They were very close, and then she bent down and seemed to be whispering into his ear, her long braids brushing the floor on either side of his silver head. I could not hear what was said, but the soft shush of their voices sounded warm and happy. I realised that I had not heard people so at ease for many, many days. And then I began to wonder what I was seeing. The curve of the singer's shoulder as she leaned, the way her leg was curled under her, and the easy way the Captain was lying, despite the pain I knew he was suffering from his wound: if it were not impossible, I would have said I was spying on two lovers.

Well, that was impossible, but . . . was it? Yes, impossible. The Captain had no interest in women, nor in boys. I had never really given it much thought, for since I had known him his life beyond the *Cormaran* might as well have been that of a priest. He was the warmest and kindest man, but on the inside you might see a silence in him, an austerity that I had always thought was part of his faith and of the horrors that lay in his past. Captain de Montalhac lived his own life, in so far as it was ever separate from that of the *Cormaran*, as if he were a *bon homme*, and while he never frowned upon the romantic or lusty attachments of his crew, and was always the courtliest man to all women, he spent his nights alone.

We met a party on the road who told us that Montpéllier was full of rowdy French soldiers, and so we decided to head for Marseilles, where we had a better chance of finding a Pisan or Genoese ship. We rode north and east, skirting Narbonne and Béziers, and by the time we had the fens of the Camargue on our right shoulders it felt like springtime. It seemed, as we rode, that the Captain had Iselda at his side, and I rode alone, for Bertranz was proving to be a moody fellow: not ill-natured, but withdrawn. Boredom got the better of him sometimes, and I discovered that, before he had turned *bon homme*, he had been one of Pierre-Roger's sergeants-at-arms at Montségur. He had been in the party that had gathered outside Avignonet, and had burst into the house where the Inquisitors and their retinue were sleeping or praying. He thought he had killed the Franciscan monk called Stephen de Saint-Thibéry, but it had been a butcher's shop. *We killed them with axes*, he muttered, *like swine. I was a soldier; I had seen blood before. But not like that: running down the walls, and hair and bones all over us.* By the time he had ridden back to Montségur he had thrown his sword into a ravine, and by the summer he was a *bon homme*. I almost envied him his conversion. All the butchery I had seen had only turned me more cold inside, and more weary of my fellow men. Bertranz had not found peace, but he knew his face was towards the light, and I could find no such comfort.

Captain de Montalhac did not seem to be in pain any more. His wound had not been grave, and perhaps would have been healed by now if we had not left the *pog*. But when he had fallen as we struggled down the mountainside, he had torn it open and the dressings had become soiled, and by our second night of liberty it had begun to throb and ooze yellow pus. Iselda, though, had more than a little knowledge of herb simples and the workings of the body, and her ministrations seemed to have driven out the infection. But the Captain was impatient to reach the sea and we spent far longer in the saddle each day than he was truly capable of bearing, and when we would stop for the night, in abandoned barns or houses, or hostelries in out-of-the-way villages, he would look drawn and almost transparent with fatigue. But he was beginning, despite that, to seem like his old self again, and when we chanced to ride together we would laugh at our old stories and remember voyages and places we had seen together. Still, every night, he would stay awake late into the night with the singer at his side, the two of them murmuring in low, fond voices, their bodies close and easy with each other.

Now that we were free, and even, perhaps, safe, I found myself becoming quite consumed with the need to be at Iselda's side. I wanted her to sing, but I also wanted to learn where the unearthly wonder of her voice came from, and what she carried within her that could bring forth such beauty. But every day it was at the Captain's side that I would see her, a few paces in front or behind me, and always there was a warmth in her voice that I did not seem to hear when she talked to me. One day, though, I had let my horse lag behind the others, for my own wound, the deep one under my arm, had not yet healed properly and the constant throbbing and darts of pain it sent down to my hand and up into my neck were making me tired and lightheaded. I had wrapped myself in silence, in expecting nothing but the next hoofbeat, when Iselda appeared beside me.

'How is it with you, Petroc?' she asked. She was looking at me closely, concern in her eyes. I stretched, embarrassed, and tried to shake off my lethargy.

'I am fine,' I assured her. 'Daydreaming.' I smiled, hoping to reassure her, and she smiled back. Reaching across the space between us, she took hold of my hand, tangled as it was in reins and horse-hair, and squeezed it, not gently.

'If you are hurt, come to me,' she said. 'And we can talk. I would like that.'

'I will,' I said, pain and startled joy rendering me all but dumb. She let go of my hand and laid hers on my breast just above my heart.

'Is it here? Your arm has been stiff, hasn't it?'

'In the armpit. It is not bad: a good sharp piece of stone went in and I took it all out. It is clean, but stubborn. Annoying, more than anything.'

'Come to me and I will see . . .' Her hand hovered above my shoulder, then she smiled almost ruefully and closed her fingers. 'I will see what I can do.' Throwing another smile behind her she trotted back up the track to the Captain, and I took a deep breath and watched her as she leaned in to tell him something – no doubt how I was faring. I would take her at her word, I told myself. I wanted, more than anything at that moment, to feel her soft but definite touch, to see, if only for a few moments, her face grow tender, the way it did when she bathed the Captain's wound.

But somehow that did not come to pass. My own wound began to heal after that, and by the next day was paining me so little that I would have felt foolish in seeking Iselda's help. So instead I worked harder, making sure it was I who gathered the evening's firewood, fed the horses, bought, scrounged or snared our meals, and as my master seemed to grow stronger, so I became almost happy. For as I told myself, it was not my place to envy the Captain, and I drove such thoughts from me as best I could. But as his strength returned, so Iselda drew ever closer to him. She kept his wound clean and mending, and the pain seemed to be gone, though as he was a brave man it was hard to tell how much it troubled him, for he would never say. I could not stop my thoughts from turning to the two of them, though, however much I tried. Above all, I wanted to know what it was they whispered about, so late into the night, and where their warmth – nay, I will call it what I knew it was, and that was love – where their curious love had come from.

Then one day, with the walls of Nîmes in the distance and thin rain sheeting down out of a high grey sky, the Captain raised his arm and we halted.

'Iselda is leaving us,' he said, abruptly. I turned to her in amazement, but she just nodded, her face a mask.

'Where are you going?' I cried, with more heat than I perhaps intended. She lifted her head and narrowed her eyes at me, for the rain was blowing into her face.

'I have to look for something,' she said.

'Will you be coming back to us?'

'No,' said the Captain. 'Not now. We will be at Marseilles in a day or so, and then on board a ship. Iselda cannot come to Italy, so she may as well leave now.' And he walked his horse up to hers and, leaning in his saddle, he took her in his arms and held her tight, wrapping her slight form in his old black cloak. Then he let her go and without a word he turned his horse and began to amble up the road without a backwards glance. I gave Bertranz a look and he nodded and set off after him.

'Iselda, how can you leave like this?' I said, for she was still sitting there, the rain dripping down her face.

'One parting is like another,' she said. 'Have you not become used to saying farewell?'

I knew she meant the dead back on Montségur, but somehow I also knew she was talking about all the other farewells I had said, all the others who had gone into the dark.

'Too used to it. I did not think we would be parting so soon.'

'Spring is on the way. The birds will soon be coming back to us across the sea, and the flowers. Or that is what the world promises us. I'm not sure if I believe in spring, though. I need to find it.' She wiped the rain from her eyes.

'You are going to find the spring? Dear Iselda, it will find you!' I protested. She gave me a look as if I were the dullest of fellows, then half a smile.

'Will it, though?' she said.

'My lady, I do not think that spring will come for all of us,' I told her, and I knew I was letting too much sorrow into my words, but I did not care. 'Man seems to desire winter these days, have you felt it? There is an ending of things, and steel is as cold as ice and as merciless. I wish for spring more than anything in heaven or on earth, but I do not know if it will find me. But it will find you, Iselda, for it will always have need of a nightingale. I would wish you Godspeed, but I do not want us to part.'

'Oh, Petroc,' she said, and the smile she gave me was full of pain and, at last, that tenderness I had so wished to find in her. 'Go with the Sieur de Montalhac. He needs you now.'

'Do any of your songs end well?' I asked bitterly, 'For this one does not.'

'I have been singing them all my life,' she said, 'and they are all sad. Save for one,' and she smiled again despite the rain lashing at her, a real smile such as was not seen on the *pog* of Montségur. 'Only one. Now fare thee well, Petroc, Sir Black Dog. I pray that the spring does find you, wherever you are going.' And without another word or a backwards look, she kicked her horse and cantered off into the curtains of rain, towards the line of black mountains that rose in the west.

That night the Captain rolled himself in his blanket and went to sleep before Bertranz and I, and when he awoke his leg was stiff. He was quiet all that day, and when he dismounted at its end he was baring his teeth in pain. It was plain that he was missing Iselda, so I tried to leave him to his thoughts, though I was sorely tempted to pry, just a little, into what exactly had passed between them.

The next morning the Captain limped to his horse, and when he began to pull himself up into the saddle his leg gave away suddenly and he dropped onto the stony ground, his heel still trapped in the stirrup, the black bag which held the *Mandylion* across his chest. He began to struggle and I saw he was desperately trying to push the bag away. I ran over but he tried to wave me off, the bag now lying a yard away in the grass, and indeed for an instant I thought he was more embarrassed than hurt, but as I bent over him I saw a damp patch spreading across the thigh of his leggings, and a faint but unmistakeable reek of corrupted flesh crept into my nose. With the help of Bertranz I got him back on his feet, but standing on the damaged leg made him turn pale and, ignoring his almost angry protests, I made him show me the wound.

The shard of stone that had struck the Captain had cut a gash almost the length of my hand before burying itself in the meat of his thigh. When he had slid down the rock wall he had torn off the scab and opened up the place from which the shard had been pulled. It had begun to heal again – at least the superficial edges of the gash, which were now scabbed and pink. But at the centre of the wound the scab had turned to an oozing crust that came off with the bandage, revealing a black, welling hole surrounded by a raw welter of wet flesh mottled in shades of pink and sulphrous yellow. A dark, almost black bruise was spreading across the skin surrounding the wound.

I knew little about healing, but I had to do something. With Bertranz I gathered handfuls of thyme, which was just beginning to put out new green shoots from the dry clumps that grew everywhere among the rocks of this land. We boiled some water, cleaned the wound as best we could and made a poultice from steeped thyme leaves. It smelled sweet and seemed to drive off the smell of decay, and though the Captain kept silent, jaw clenched, when it was done and his thigh bound with the cleanest linen I could find in our packs, he looked more comfortable.

'You missed your calling, Patch,' he said. 'I am amazed.'

'I used to watch Isaac at work – he cleaned me up often enough. But I know nothing. Your leg smells better, nothing more. Why did Iselda leave? She knows far more than I. Could she not have stayed until we reached Marseilles?'

'I sent her away,' said the Captain firmly.

'But why?'

'To keep her safe. She did not need to follow us. Where I am

235

going . . .' He paused, and laid his hand on my arm. 'I am leaving. And it is to serve my faith. Iselda's place is here. She has done enough for the cause.'

'Very well. But we must get you to a surgeon,' I replied sullenly.

I was telling nothing more than the truth. By the end of that day he was shaking with fever. We bathed the wound morning and evening with hot water and thyme leaves, but the infection was seated deep within the muscle, and I feared there was a well of corruption that was spreading inside faster than I could salve the outside. We tried to draw out the suppuration with a hot compress, and that at least broke the fever for a while.

'Patch, take the bag. With the . . . the Cruxifix. I cannot carry it any longer.' I nodded.

'Of course,' I said. His eyes had gone unfocussed with pain.

'Get me to the sea,' he muttered, as the compress steamed against his blackening flesh.

'Soon,' was all I could say as I dabbed the sweat from his forehead. 'Very soon.'

I thought of lancing the wound, but that was just something I had heard said, and I was not going to stick a knife in my dear friend's leg if I had no way to deal with whatever happened next, not when there was a chance we might still reach Marseilles in time. At least the rain that had followed us for days finally lifted. But while the sun had come out again and we were now passing through olive groves, dappled by their miraculous green, the Captain's pain had grown so bad that he could hardly speak, and for every hour that passed he seemed to age another year. And if spring was coming, we did not notice it.

Chapter Twenty-three

We came to Marseilles the day after Ash Wednesday, to the house of Don Bonasasch. The Captain was very weak, and could barely keep himself in the saddle. Bertranz and I had taken turns riding at his side, to make sure he did not slip and fall. He had a fever again, and his wound was seeping through the bandages and leggings and making a faint but foul reek. Bonasasch greeted us calmly, although we were no doubt shattering the peace of his home, and took charge immediately. He had the Captain carried to his own bedroom, and sent for the only physician in Marseilles worthy of the name, as he said bluntly, who turned out to be another Jew from Valencia. He was an old man with a beard the colour of old ivory, and he looked at us all with grave suspicion, until I began to blather at him of things that Isaac the *Cormaran*'s surgeon had taught me over the years, and then he softened somewhat, especially when he heard I knew someone who had studied at Toledo. He sent us out of the room while he made his examination, and he stayed inside for a long, long time. There were mumblings and at one point a ghastly sound, a sob mixed with mirthless laughter, rang out. When the doctor came out again, wiping his hands with rosewater, he was muttering to himself.

'How long has he had this wound?' he snapped. I told him a brief version of our tale, and he began muttering again.

'Gangrene. Do you know what that is? Of course you do. And there is nothing to be done. I have cleaned it, cut out as much of the infection as I dare, but the rot has its teeth too far into his flesh. If the wound were lower on his leg I would take it off, but it is much, much too high up.'

'What will happen?' I asked, feeling ice cold from my neck down to my toes. I suppose I had known. I had seen many people die of infected wounds: men, women, even a child hit by a little splinter from a stone ball. It is not a smell one forgets.

'He will die. Not immediately, for he is a strong man, though he appears to have been denying himself food. I have, as I told you, cut out the necrotised flesh and packed the wound with clean linen and various unguents. He will prefer the smell of myrrh to that of his own rotting meat, and that will help his spirit. If he stays here, and I attend to him every day, he will live a week, perhaps more, though he will begin to sink much sooner than that.'

'And if he does not?'

'That, my boy, is an unnecessary question. Two days, three at the most. I have left medicines for the pain. If he wishes to leave his bed, make sure he takes more of those, rather than less. He is sleeping now. Leave him. I will come back in the morning.' And he left, giving Bonasasch a disappointed look, as if in reproach him for involving him in this nonsense.

Captain de Montalhac was indeed asleep, his head on a dazzling white pillow, a white counterpane pulled up to his chin. My heart gave a lurch when I saw him, for he looked diminished somehow, small and lost on a snow-drift of linen. His mouth was slack and a thread of spit was running down his cheek. I wiped it away and felt his brow, which was hot but not burning. I kissed it, and left him to his rest.

The next morning I stole through the sleeping house and put my head round the Captain's door. To my horror he was sitting up, and had managed to swing his legs over the side of the bed. They looked very thin and white, and there was a great winding of cloth around the top of his thigh, but when he looked up his eyes were clear and the room smelled like crushed rosemary. I ran over to him and caught his arm as he was trying to stand.

'Help me up, Patch,' he said firmly.

'No. You must stay in bed. The doctor has commanded it,' I told him sternly.

'The doctor is a fool. No, he is a kindly man, and . . . just poking about in my thigh must have taken a good year off his life – and alas, a little more off my own. Help me up, Patch. I want to sit near the window. I have something I must tell you, and it appears that time is not our friend.'

I could not refuse his order, and so I slid my arm under his shoulder and heaved him up. He gave a throttled hiss but managed to settle his good leg under him, and we half-dragged, half-hopped ourselves over to the bench that stood beneath the room's only window. He sat down heavily, and I saw that there was a weakness in his eyes, a kind of softly gripping fear, that I had never seen there before. He was looking through me as if I were thin air. 'Are you all right, Michel?' I said, for I feared that my dear master was suffering an apoplexy. So I reached out and touched his sleeve, and he shook his head again and this time saw me sitting before him. He took a deep breath.

'I have to go,' he said.

'To Italy? We shall wait,' I said, trying to calm him.

'No. I will not . . . that bed is soft, but I will not say farewell to the world in it. I am going. Bonasasch is looking for a boat. You are not the earliest riser, my boy. But there is something weighing me down, and . . .'

'The *Mandylion*? I will carry it. Please don't worry.'

'Not that. Something much heavier.' He paused, and, leaning his elbow against the windowsill he stared out through the olive leaves. 'I cannot leave this way,' he said at last. 'There is something you must hear.' He shook his head, as if a fly were bothering him, but there was no fly. His eyes had lost their focus again. The room was quiet save for a sparrow scratching on the window ledge. He seemed, in that moment, quite lost.

'Have you had some news, from Don Bonasasch perhaps? My God, is it the Ca'Kanzir?' I blurted, for the Captain seemed like a man whose home has been destroyed, and if Michel de Montalhac ever had a home, it was there in Venice.

'No,' he shook his head and gave a me tiny, haunted smile. 'Very good, Patch. But it is not my home. It is my family.'

'The company?' I began, frowning, puzzled. He gave his head another weary shake and looked down into the trough.

'I have a daughter,' he said, so softly that I thought I had not caught his words properly. 'A daughter,' he said again, and looked up.

'Then . . . my God, sir, you have lost her?' I said, softly, for in his stricken face I could find no other explanation. I hardly dared to breathe, not knowing what was the more shattering discovery: that my master had a family that he had never once spoken of, even made the smallest hint of, in all the years I had known him; or that he was suddenly bereaved.

'Lost her? *Lost* her? Yes . . .' I took a step back, fearing I knew not what, but knowing the earth was shifting beneath my feet. 'I had lost her,' said the Captain. 'And I then I found her.'

'Sir, I do not understand.'

'Nor did I, Patch,' said the Captain, and sighed painfully. Then he gave me a tired smile and patted the bench next to him. 'Come,' he said kindly. 'I will tell you.'

'When I was something like your age I . . . No, wait,' he said, and, folding his hands in his lap, he winced and leaned back against the wall. His eyes had gone soft again. 'I told you about the siege of Toulouse, didn't I?'

'You did. About the tower going down in flames, and your charge, and de Montfort's head stove in by the ball from a mangonel.'

'It is a good tale, is it not? Better if one had not lived through it. And now you know something of that, of course. Yes, I saw de Montfort go down. And it was a woman who let fly with the stone. The mangonels were manned by women – ha! By ladies, rather, so that the men could fight. That particular machine was commanded by Domna Assenda de Gaja, and Domna Assenda had two daughters, Alayda and Gazenda, who worked the mangonel with two of their kinfolk. Gazenda was pretty, twenty-two years old, almost my age; but Alayda . . . Ah! She was twenty and as lovely as a field of wild iris. Their father was dead, of course, like mine, and . . . Well, we fell in love. It was a strange time, a war, and we fell in love.'

'Nothing strange about that,' I said.

'No. It didn't seem strange. Domna Assenda was a *credenta*, like me, so she approved of the match. And like all Good Christians she did not believe in marriage, but considered us man and wife. Alayda and I lived under her roof . . .'

'Wait, Michel . . . you were married? I . . .'

'Not married.'

'Then what?' I was pressing him, and I knew I must seem rude, but I could not quite take in what I was hearing.

'Our love was like . . .' He fumbled for my hand and held it tightly. His own fingers were cool and trembled as if with an ague. 'I do not mean to unearth things that time has laid to rest, but we were something like you and your lady Anna.' He squeezed my hand reassuringly. 'Did you never see how I watched you? How I tried to smooth the way for your happiness, the both of you?' I could do nothing but gape at him. 'Good. Then I did as a *credente* should – as Domna Assenda did with us. We do not believe that the race of man should continue itself, as the Church of Rome so delicately puts it, through the marriage bed, for by doing so we merely create another prison in which the Evil One will lock up one more soul. But while the *bons hommes* tell us that the flesh is not good, they also tell us that it is not so very bad, for as all sins can be washed away by the *Consolamentum*, the doings of the flesh do not matter very much. Which is a lovely thing to tell two young lovers,' he added. 'And as you have realised, that which we had tried, not very dilligently, to avoid, came to pass. When Alayda was heaving on the arm of the mangonel that day on the walls, she was already carrying our child, though we did not know it then.'

'And you had a little girl.'

'Yes. She was born in January. Tiny, as the babies of that year were, for their mothers went hungry in the siege. I could hold her so . . .' He held out his hand, palm up, cupped it gently, and touched his other hand to his arm just above the wrist. 'She came to here. I have a scar – see? That was our measure for her.' He curled his fingers up into a fist and led out a ragged sigh. 'Though I never saw her grow past it.'

'She . . .'

'No. She lived. It was I who died, at least to her. The Crusaders would not go away, you see. De Montfort's son tried to take back his – *his* – lands, as he thought of them. We fought him, one little skirmish after another, and he slipped away and burned another village. In the spring he turned and fought, at a place called Baziège. We were led by Raymond, who was young then and went through the land like a flame, and we destroyed them. But I was knocked from my horse and kicked in the head, and when I came to I was a prisoner. They were fleeing, the Crusaders, and when they stopped to see if they could ransom me they realised I was a *faidit*. I had no lands, no wealth at all. It was customary to slit the throats of wretches like me, but I suppose they needed to rescue something from the ruin they had brought on themselves, and so they sold me as a slave. Not so boldly as that, of course, for Christians cannot sell other Christians, and because I wanted to live, to see my Alayda and my baby girl, I did not tell them I was a *credente*. So I was forced to sell my labour to a rich trader from Boulogne, and my contract bound me to him for two score years. He put me to work in his warehouses, and that first year I was beaten half to death every other week. But this is not the story you need to hear, and I will tell it to you another time, eh?'

'I will give you no peace until you do,' I told him, gritting my teeth against the sadness that rose up in me. It seemed, meanwhile, as if the blood were draining from his face drop by drop, for his pallor was growing more ashen, and he had slipped his hands between his knees to stop the palsy that was shaking them.

'My boy,' he smiled. 'Yes. After two years I was given to a monastery to settle a debt, and they discovered I could read and write, for in those days the sons and daughters of Languedoc were not brought up in darkness and sloth like the fools of the north. And so I made myself useful, and then indispensable; and then I stole their most precious relics and all the silver I could find, and my course was set. But in the meantime I had written again and again to Alayda, bribing messengers with money I stole from the abbot. I did not know if any of my letters had reached Toulouse, but I never stopped writing, and then – four years had gone by, I think – I had a reply at last.

'The writing was Domna Assenda's, and I knew at once – I cannot explain it now, save to tell you that the ink itself seemed to leach misery onto the page – that Alayda had died. There had been a contagion in the city and it had carried her off. But not Flower.'

'Flower?'

'My . . . our daughter. She was safe with her grandmother, who raised her as her own child. Now Domna Assenda was well known, in her younger days, as a singer, indeed she was a *trobriaritz* in her own right and exchanged songs with many a famous troubadour. No doubt her skill as a singer of stories helped the world to know who had killed Simon de Montfort. Anyway . . .' He broke off, coughing, and a shudder went through him.

'Do you mean to tell me that she didn't kill de Montfort?' I said, to distract him. He chuckled weakly and raised his chin, the southerner's shrug.

'It was a good story, though,' he said. 'Perhaps she did do it, at that. There was more than one mangonel on that stretch of wall, and you cannot really aim those things. And besides, they were flinging great chunks of masonry, which go whichever way they please. But let us say she did. And that famous old *trobriatitz* raised my little girl in her own image. She taught her the songs she knew, and how to make music and dance. And . . . Patch, you are all slack-jawed. Have you not caught on yet?'

'Caught on . . . Oh, dear God. Iselda de Rosers. Oh, Christ almighty!' I buried my face in my hands, overcome – with what, I could not have said, but it began as burning shame at my own grimy suspicions, and after that the floor seemed to have melted beneath my feet.

'Iselda. We found each other at last. How strange it has all been. I have been watching over her all these many years, you know. When I began to make my mark in the world I sent Assenda a little silver, and then some more, whenever I could. And I have seen to it that Iselda never lacked for anything, except a father. But I never dared come home for fear . . .'

'You were an outlaw,' I said, gently.

'Yes . . . No, not really. I did not come home – and of all the things I have told you, this is the hardest to admit, but I must – I did not return

242

because I had set myself up against Rome, and everything the Church did I tried to corrupt, to undermine. I heard what had befallen my Languedoc when King Louis forced old Count Raymond to kiss his boots, and how the *bons hommes* were hunted again, and dead bodies dug up and burned, and old women taken from their deathbeds and thrown onto bonfires – and how my people starved and had to bow their necks to the French. I did not dare return for fear that my anger would destroy me, but worse, that in destroying myself I would somehow bring destruction down upon my child.

'So I let her be, and, is it not the strangest thing? She has grown beautiful, and within her, like a lovely walled garden, she carries every-thing that was good about this land as it once was. When she sings . . .'

'I heard it,' I whispered. 'The first day I spent on Montségur. I thought, then, it was as lovely as almond blossom and as cold and pure as the north wind.'

'Beautiful and yet desolate,' he murmured, nodding his head. Then he turned and gazed out of the window. 'I believe the desolation is what little she has of her father. I would give the earth itself to be shown I am wrong. But she is like me enough to have grown up hating the French, and though she is not a believer she chose to follow her people to Montségur. Assenda died there, you know, two years before we arrived. And Iselda had become a *trobriaritz* – not as famous as her grand-mother, but no troubadour can live without fear or suspicion these days – and went from castle to court, singing the old songs and her own, and passing news and messages among the believers and those loyal to Count Raymond. When Assenda went to the *pog* to live, and then to die as a *perfecta*, Iselda became one of the . . . I would say *spy*, but that has no honour to it. She went out into the world and saw, and listened, and brought things back to the faithful. Gilles saw her and wrote to me, quite unknowing, of the singer who carried messages, and I knew who she must be. It took me almost a year to . . . to summon up enough courage to tell her who I was, and to convince her. And – she will tell you.

'Listen, my boy,' he said, and reached for my shoulder. 'I have to leave you. I will be on the sea very soon. Out on the silver sea. This journey . . . I have plotted my course, do not fear. I am ready at last. Now, good Bonasasch has done two things for me. He has given the affairs of the *Cormaran* entirely over to my children.' He reached up and I felt his fingers run through my hair and come to rest, cradling the back of my head. I thought of his hand that I had seen so many times, and of the baby he had held cupped in it, all the life I had never guessed at.

'I do not know what you mean, sir,' I said, blinking something hot from my eye.

'I mean Iselda, and I mean you, Petroc. My daughter and my son. Why are you weeping? It's I that should be weeping: all at once I have not one child but two, and I am such a dullard that I have only just discovered it. And now I must leave. So listen: I will ask your forgiveness, for you had a father and lost him, and now I am giving you another whom you must lose. I would not dare ask to be your father, Patch. But would you like to be my son?'

'Sir, I have been your son since you found me at Dartmouth! You have cared for me, taught me . . . you have shown me this whole wide world, and how to find myself in it, in all its vastness and shadow. And I never knew the world was so wide until you showed me.'

'So you will do me this honour?'

I caught his hands and, pressing them together, put my own between them and pressed my forehead to his fingertips.

'I will serve you for ever, sir. I have forgotten how to be a son, though, I fear.'

'And I have never known how to be a father, until now.'

The evening had turned everything the warm, pale orange of a tabby cat's dusty fur when I went back to the house of Don Bonasasch. I had spent the hours wandering along the beach, trying to empty my mind of everything, of all the thoughts that filled it like a million dark little pearls, but I did not have much success. I wandered through the door and up the stairs, but outside the Captain's door the hushed sound of voices coming from within stopped me with my hand on the latch. It was the slow, careful measure of the *Consolamentum* that I had heard so many times, easing the ripe soul from the shackles of the world. *Hate this world and its works*, Bertranz was saying, *and the things that are of this world.* I sat down on the top step and waited for him to come out, and when he did at long last he gave me a tired, faded smile.

'He wants to see you,' he said.

The Captain was lying in his bed, propped against the bolsters. He was in a black robe, and it made his face seem all the more pale.

'Now you are a *bon homme*,' I said. He nodded.

'The last great change in a day of changes,' he said. 'Sit here.' He patted the bedcover. 'Bonasasch has a ship for me. It leaves at dawn for Pisa.' He drew in a breath carefully and let it out again, a long shuddering sigh. 'I am leaving this with you.' He pointed to the chest at the foot of the bed. On it lay the plain old satchel that held the *Mandylion*.

244

'You are taking it to the brothers and sisters in Cremona!' I protested.

'No. It is nothing but an icon of torment. It stinks of death – have you never smelled it? The Devil dipped his brush in agony and despair to paint it. I believe it filled Bertrand Marty and the *credenti* with a madness of some kind. How they would beg to see it, but then shrink before it as if it caused them pain . . .' He took another wavering breath. 'Do whatever you like with it. Louis Capet will give you a ship full of Moorish gold for it, and you have other customers. Burn it. Use it to bind your leggings. But do not believe in it, Patch. Do not.'

'I won't,' I said.

'And Iselda. I sent her away because . . . because I did not want to force a long and sad farewell upon her. But good Master Bonasasch has some some papers she ought to sign, and some letters. She does not want what I am giving her, but I would like you to make sure, if you can, that she accepts . . . no, that she finds some good in all this. You will not be able to force riches on her, and she would make an appalling banker.' He laughed, shallowly. There was a rasp in his throat that had not been there before. 'Bring her something good. Promise me, Patch: bring her light. There is some left in you.'

'I promise, of course. And I will bring her to you in Italy.'

'Ah. Italy. I will be there,' he said. 'The ship leaves at first light. I would have liked to sail with you again, Patch, but not this time, not this time.'

I slept on the floor at the foot of the bed. My blanket was thin and sleep came only lightly, and many times I found myself awake, listening to the in and out of Captain de Montalhac's breath, an ebbing tide leaving a pebble beach. We were both waiting. There was a ship. Bonasasch had found the Captain a berth on board a wool trader's vessel bound for Pisa, and as the stars began to dim I got up and went to find Bertranz and the servants of the house. The Captain was awake when I returned. He was too weak to stand, and so we dressed him carefully in his tunic of fine black damask, very worn now from Montségur, and his travelling cloak. I buckled on his belt with its purse and knife, and then we carried him downstairs and out into the blue half-light.

We carried him through the cool alleyways, and before long we turned a corner and there was the sea, still as a mirror, just beginning to glow from the light of the barely risen sun. As we came out onto the waterfront, the Captain lifted his head.

'Is that the ship?' he whispered.

She was a Genoese galley by the looks of her, not very big and needing paint and polish. Dried salt crusted the waterline and she sat low in the water, fully laden, but she was a ship, and I ached to go aboard her. The master was a bow-legged Majorcan who greeted us solemnly in the Lingua Franca. He eyed the Captain for a little too long, and I wondered what Don Bonasasch had told him, and how much he had been paid, but then he stepped forward and greeted his passenger with gruff respect.

'Men, come up! Carry this good man aboard,' he called to his crew. But the Captain shook his head.

'Put me down, Patch,' he said. We helped him stand, and he held me fast around the neck, but he was upright, though his one good leg shook.

'I'm going now, my son,' he said. 'This good ship is casting off for Italy. Wish me Godspeed.'

'I know where you are going, sir,' I answered, as best I could. 'Gilles told me. I can't come along, can I?'

'Not now, Patch. Do not cry.' He kissed me on the forehead, and his lips felt like dry leaves. I hugged him tight, feeling the bones of his back, the pyramids of his shoulderblades, the hard path of his spine. 'How strange, though. I will be free soon, and I have waited so long for it. But now I find that I am free already. There is light everywhere. The sun is rising. And look: they are waiting for me.'

I kissed him on his cheeks and on his lips, and stared for a moment into his grey eyes.

'Captain de Montalhac will come aboard now,' I said, and helped him step over the side and down onto the deck. Bertranz and a crewman caught him under the arms, and he showed them that he wished to lean upon the mast. But his legs could no longer hold him upright, and seeing he was about to fall I lunged and caught him around the waist and gently, clumsily lowered him to the deck. He was sitting, back against the mast, head tilted back a little. All of a sudden he seemed hollow. He blinked, and his eyes sought mine.

'Are they making sail?' His breath was shallow and harsh, and when he spoke there was nothing left of his voice, and yet it was still Michel de Montalhac. I gave him a sip of water from his flask and took his hand, all bones and papery skin, and fitted my fingers gently around his knuckles. Then I levelled my eyes at Bertranz and gave him the slightest of nods. He understood, and loudly bade the seaman show him where to stow his belongings. Then I saw him mutter something in the master's ear and press something into his hand. The master looked over at me and then at the Captain, pursed his lips and glanced up at the sky. Then he clapped his hands, and all was work and the noise of ropes hissing and thudding and oars starting to churn the water. It was a good crew, and in a few minutes the galley was swinging its nose towards the harbour's mouth and gathering speed, and the water fell in ropes of captive sunlight from the ends of the oars. The breeze caught the Captain's hair, and he smiled and closed his eyes.

The master was bending over us. There was concern in his face, and pity, but the Captain was a stranger and there were matters of ill-luck to be considered. I knew that well enough.

'Take us out to sea,' I whispered to him. 'Out beyond the islands. Let him ride on the deep water. Then . . .' The master shook his head faintly, tugged at his ear and then nodded.

He stared down at the Captain for a long while. Then he crossed himself.

'God grant him rest,' he said quietly. He crossed himself again and then hurried back to the stern.

The hills with their white houses had already slipped past, and now the breezes coming down from the mountains caught the sail and we began to hiss across the barely ruffled water. Gathering speed, the mast creaked and the Captain opened his mouth. I bent close to listen, cupping my hand to my ear, for the headwind was getting stronger. His tongue was working dryly against his teeth, and I held the flask to his lips and forced a trickle between them. His hand fluttered against mine.

'Did I sleep all day?' he said. 'Night is falling.'

'There was no need to trouble you, so we let you rest,' I said. He blinked slowly, and his eyes wandered, following things I could not see.

'What a long time we have been at sea,' he whispered. 'But there will be land in the morning, and sweet water.' His hand gripped my sleeve, hard, and his eyes cleared and found mine.

'It is not far, Patch!' he said strongly. 'Not far at all.'

I let his head fall back gently upon the salt-jewelled wood of the mast. Water was falling in ropes of captive sunlight from the ends of the oars. The breeze caught the Captain's hair. The Isle de Pomègues was slipping by on the starboard side, and the seagulls had all woken up at last and were wheeling and shrieking in the galley's wake as we slid out into the great silver sea.

Chapter Twenty-four

I stayed in Marseilles for a while, drinking too much, staring out at the horizon. I thought of following the Captain, and twice I went looking for a passage to Italy, only to stop myself at the last minute. The water was calling, but something was holding me back. But the weeks went past and I remained trapped between the land and the water, for the truth was that I had nowhere else to go.

We had gone out, far out into the Gulf of Lions that morning, and then the sullen crew had rowed us back against the wind, muttering about the Evil Eye, and we had carried Captain de Montalhac ashore. Bertranz wanted to take his body to Italy, but the master of the galley would not wait and I took my leave of the solemn *bon homme* that evening. I could not bring myself to lie to a priest and have my friend, my master – my father – laid to rest in a Christian burial ground, so I had him borne to the charnel house and paid a dour brotherhood of glorified tanners to perform that rite called *mos Teutonicus* upon him. For the next four days I paced the alleyways, knowing that somewhere close by, the Captain's body was being boiled in wine and his bones stripped of their flesh. The bones were clean when I collected them, white as clouds and reeking of vinegar and some cheap facsimile of myrhh. I put them in a Saracen bag of silk that Bonasasch had given me, and took them back to my lodgings.

I supposed that I owned the Ca' Kanzir now, or half of it at least, and I called no other place my home. But the Captain and Gilles would never come there again, and I knew that now it stood dark and empty, as I had first seen it: wrapped softly in cobwebs, reflections from the canal dancing on the ceilings for the ghosts to enjoy. I could not return to that, not now. I thought often of Devon, and of the deep valleys that bit into the flanks of Dartmoor, where a man might measure his years with nothing more troubling than the coming and going of the bluebells in his woods. Devon, though, was Richard of Cornwall's domain, and I would never be free there.

I was a rich man now. What did half the company of the *Cormaran* mean? I had no idea, but I would never want for money again. The very thought of money was strange to me now, after so long in the ascetic world of Montségur, and I would find myself turning silver coins over in my hand, weighing them, as if I were some barbarian from beyond India who had never heard of such things.

One night I drank myself into that strange state where the body is numb but the soul is flayed raw, and in my confusion I laid my hands on the bag that held the Captain's bones and beseeched him for help, as though he were an oracle. There was nothing but silence and the wine ringing in my ears, and then my eyes fell on the dark bundle of the *Mandylion*. I grabbed it up and unwrapped it, flicking it open so that the phantom man suddenly appeared in the room, and let it settle upon the floor. A man outlined in blood. So much more blood had run since I had first seen it. Those I had never met, the Inquisitors and their men at Avignonet; every corpse carried out of the gates of Montségur, frozen by death and by winter, to be stacked beyond the walls; and now my master, brought to agony and vile decay. Perhaps I would have destroyed it then. There was wood in the cold fireplace, and a tinderbox. I thought of it ablaze, of the bearded face haloed in flames and being swallowed by its own darkness. I had the tinderbox in my hand. But I thought of the Captain, and of the calling he had taught me, and how I had learned to fear nothing on earth and in heaven. So I threw the tinderbox into the hearth and, my legs starting to grow soft as my stupefaction grew, I sat down on the floor beside the shroud, then lay down and stretched out on the boards, my hands crossed over my body.

'Teach me about death,' I said to the image. 'Tell me where they go. You are looking at me from there, aren't you? So what have you done with them, you bastard? Tell me where everyone has gone.'

But the shroud was silent, and the bones kept their peace, and soon the wine closed my eyes. When I woke, much later, the night was thinning outside, and the floorboards had pressed their grain into the side of my face. I lurched to my feet and gulped down a pitcherful of water to slake my horrifying thirst, and only then did I notice the shroud laid out on the floor and remember last night's one-sided conversation. I lit a lamp and began to fold the old cloth until only the face was left, nothing more in this poor light than a collection of rusty stains. I knew it was there, and I ran my finger over the smooth, brittle tissue of the linen, shuddering a little as I did so, as one does when one stares into the face of a dead friend. Here is the mouth, here the eyes; this is the beard, and these are the bloodstains on the brow. *This was a man,* I thought. *This is how you'll end up: stains, nothing more.* But as I traced a strange but very clear realisation struck me: this was not a relic of the dead. I shuffled on my knees over to the chair where I had set the bag of bones. I put my hand on it, and felt the smooth, chalky shifting of the things inside. Here was a dead man: my teacher, my friend. My father. And here was what the dead feel like: they are dead, nothing more. I have held many, many dead things in my life: people I have loved and people I have hated; withered corpses and bits and pieces of them, saintly and other-wise; bones, the hard tar of ancient blood; the honey-tinted vellum of human skin. But none of them have horrified me beyond their clear message: *we are gone, we are not here.* There is no artifice to the dead. They have no power, save to remind us of our own certain end.

The *Mandylion,* though, had power. I could feel it now, still tingling in my fingers, the gaze from its face stroking the hairs on the back of my neck even though, in the flickering light from my lamp, it was no face at all. It was a feeling I had had before, but I could not place it. I bent my head and laid my forehead on the bag. The limestone breath of the bones brushed my nostrils. The Captain had only been dead a fortnight, and already his remains smelled like an ancient cave, a tomb, a . . . a chapel. That was it. In the Pharos Chapel, where the shroud had lain hidden, there had been a great mural of Christ crucified. Our Lord had hung, a pallid, wrecked giant. The painter, some Greek from the days of Constantine, no doubt, had managed, with nothing but plaster and pigment, to saturate the image with pain, despair, horror. Death seeped from it like it never does from a corpse or a relic: death as a presence, despair made tangible. It was artifice – a miracle, of sorts, but the work of man. And now I saw, as somehow I had not in all this time, that the *Mandylion* too was something made.

Whoever it had been – and I would never know, for he was lost down the black well of a thousand and more years – had painted a man on a winding sheet, and had done it so well that he had given it life. He had raised the dead: with paint, and blood, and linen, he had made a ghost.

A chill ran through me like the first grip of an ague and I hastily fumbled the thing back into its box. It was a curse. However it had been created, it was a curse. Somehow, the world – or so it seemed – had come to wish for nothing more than to worship this thing that reeked of agony and despair. Even the heretics, who sought the light of truth, had been seduced in the end, and they had longed for the baleful horror of the shroud even as it gave them pain. Now it was mine, if it could belong to anyone. And though I did not want it, there was no one left alive who could tell me what to do with it. I lay down on the bed and wrapped myself tight in the blankets and lay there shivering until sunrise, the relics of death gathered around me like my family.

So time passed, but when I had been idling for a month or so I chanced to meet Don Bonasasch in the street one day, and as we exchanged pleasantries, and he gave me some business news and told me of some papers I should sign, I caught him regarding me with a look in which pity and embarrassment mingled. He hid it well, and I promised to visit him the next day, but I heard the Captain tell me, as he had hundreds or even thousands of times, *pay attention*. Bonasasch was a good man and all his cool efficiency could not hide the vein of kindness that ran through his character, and it does not pay to ignore the warnings of the good. So I made up my mind then and there in the narrow street that it was time I carried out the Captain's last order to me. I would find Iselda and try my best to make her accept her father's legacy.

I picked up a sheaf of papers from Bonasasch, bought myself some decent clothes from the traders from Outremer who sold fine and rare stuff from their wharfs, had my shield repaired of the gouges it had received coming down the *pog*, and packed the Captain's bones at the bottom of my saddlebag, and the *Mandylion* on top of it where it would look like a soiled nightshirt if anyone bothered to look. Bonasasch had found me a good horse, and I rode out of the gates of Marseilles on the sixteenth day of March. I decided to start my search in Toulouse, for the city of Iselda's birth was as good a place as any to hunt for her. It was an easy ride, and in a week I was there at the pink brick gates, looking up at the walls from which women had once shot stones from mangonels. There seemed to be something smothering the alleys of the city, some gloom that had not been there in Marseilles or as I rode through Provence, but which had begun to build when I crossed over into Languedoc. I found myself an inn and went to bed early, thinking I would begin my search in the morning.

I was woken by a peal of bells, which was strange as it was not Sunday. At first I thought it was an alarm, but it sounded triumphant, and I stuck my head out of the window to see what might be going on. Of all the spires in Toulouse, though, only one was sounding, and down in the street people were looking angry and muttering amongst themselves. I got dressed, and for the first time in a long age I unwrapped Thorn from the greasy cloth where she had been imprisoned, deep in my pack, and hung her from my belt. I put the *Mandylion* in a new satchel I had bought, such as a lawyer might carry, and went out. I found a stall selling slices of bread and goose-fat, and I bought one and a mug of cider. As I chewed I asked the woman why the bells were ringing.

'You're not French, so I'll tell you,' she said bitterly. 'A messenger came last night from the south. Montségur has surrendered, and they've burned all the *bons hommes*, every one, even the castellan's wife and our own Bishop Bertrand. Eight days ago, it was. You could see the smoke from twenty miles away, or so the man said. I'm not a believer, mind, but the *bons hommes* were kinder and made a lot more sense than all these greedy pigs from Rome, with their greasy hands in our pockets and their beady eyes in our houses.'

'Oh Christ,' I said. 'So the bells . . .'

'One priest, one fucking French priest, thought he'd celebrate. I suppose he thought we'd all join in. Didn't notice we all have our faces in the mud. Curse them with the red plague, every one.'

I found a shadowy spot under the walls and sat down in the cool dampness. I could see the greasy smoke rising behind my eyes, rising above the valley with the sharp *pog* and the little castle rising at its end. Gilles was dead. Escaping, he had said, but it did not seem like escape, herded into fire. I thought of farmers swaling their fields back home, how the rats would come out of the stubble as blaze marched across the furrows, and how the children would beat them back into the fire where they leapt and twisted and became dancing coals. That was not escape. There could be no escape. Beside me, the *Mandylion* sat in its bag. *The good people who gazed on you with such fear, but yet begged to look again, are all dead*, I thought. *Did you prepare them to meet their death? Or did you bring it upon them*, I asked it, remembering how its face, sketched out in ancient blood, had seemed to regard the crowd of believers that day on Montségur. *If you are Christ, then bring them back*, I told it silently, and then I grabbed the bag and began to cast around for the way up onto the walls.

'If you are Jesus Christ, who brings the dead back to life, bring back the Good Christians, who loved the words you spoke to men, and whose only prayer was the prayer you taught the world!' I said aloud. In my head I saw myself standing on the southern wall, unfurling the shroud into a gonfalon. I was almost on the parapet when I slipped and landed on my elbow, and the pain cleared my thoughts. Christ, I am going mad, I thought. And then, because I was bursting with rage and grief, I decided what I would really do. I would go to Count Raymond and make him tell me what he had meant with all his cryptic talk of *affairs,* and why he had dragged out the agony of Montségur only to turn his back on its defenders at the end.

'Who is prospering now?' I muttered as I marched through the alleys towards the palace. 'All the Good Christians are dead, and Gilles and your old friend Michel de Montalhac, while the Roman priests ring their bells.' I had no plan, but strode into the Palace of the Counts, evidently looking rich and grim enough that the guards did not challenge me, and not until I was demanding, through clenched teeth, to see Count Raymond, and the chamberlain was gently but expertly steering me to a chair in the antechamber, did it occur to me how feckless I was being. But I did not care. I sat there fuming, jiggling my leg with a fury I could not keep tamped down, rudely hailing the secretaries and officials who scurried here and there, ignoring me.

A good hour had passed, and I was beginning to wonder if I should just walk in on the Count, and what was likely to happen if I did, when there was a tramping of shod feet, and a sound I had not heard for a long time, that of English voices, rang out far too loudly in the corridor. A moment later, and three knights entered the room, chatting amongst themselves, and to my horror I saw that one of them was a man I knew from my time with King Henry's army. I willed myself invisible, but his eye fell upon me and he exclaimed in surprise.

'God's teeth! It is . . . it *is!* Sir Petrus! Good God, man, what are you doing here?'

I rose, reluctantly, and nodded hello. 'Geraint?' I hazarded. 'Well, what are *you* doing here, then?' I said, somewhat rudely.

'Jeffrey! Jeffrey of Abbot's Dene. I have come on an embassy from Earl Richard to the Count. Still finalising some things relating to the earl's wedding, you know.'

'Oh. Did he marry Sanchia, then?'

'You should know, my dear fellow. Was it not you who brought the thing off? Where *have* you been? The wedding was last November. And Earl Richard has been looking for you, before and since. Any man coming into France was given orders to keep their eyes out for the Knight of the Black Dog. And, strike me dead, I have found you!'

I was sorely tempted to take him at his word and strike him down there and then, but I gave him a wince disguised as a smile instead.

'What could be so important that all these good men have been looking for me?' I enquired coolly.

'You are to be entreated to come back to England. No doubt the earl has some reward to bestow upon you, dear man. But when my party left, he asked us to leave word wherever we went that you were very earnestly enjoined to come to a wedding.'

'I thought you said that the earl's marriage had already happened.'

'No, no, not the earl's! It is his ward who is being wed – your cousin, the brave Lady Agnes de Wharram. I am amazed you did not know of it.' He stared hard at me, as though he had just realised that I was a simpleton or a mooncalf. 'To one Aimery de Lille Charpigny.'

'Good heavens,' I breathed. 'I . . .' Casting about desperately for something to say, an image came to me of Aimery holding Letice's ankle after the battle, and looking up her so tenderly, as if she were a wounded bird. 'There could be no better match,' I said at last. 'Please send my congratulations.'

'You must come!' they all cried, gathering round me. I began to feel uncomfortable.

'Alas, I have urgent business in the east.'

'But you are here to speak with Count Raymond, even though he is not here.'

'I beg your pardon?' I was beginning to think that these English buffoons were some manner of vision sent to try me.

'He is in Narbonne. We are here to deliver something to his equerry. Where *have* you been, Sir Petrus?'

'On a very long journey.'

'It looks to have been arduous. 'Tis only a year and a half since Taillebourg, but you are somewhat altered, my friend.'

'I have been in strange lands. When is this marriage? Where?'

'In London, a month next Tuesday,' chimed the youngest knight.

'I will not be able to attend, in that case. My affairs will keep me . . .'

'In the east,' said Jeffrey. 'So you said.'

I made my excuses as politely as I could and hurried out of the antechamber while they gaped, astonished, at my back. Almost running down the hall I all but collided with the Count's chamberlain, and before I knew what I had done I took him by the shoulder and all but shouted at him, all the confusion and anger of the day pouring out into the bewildered man's face.

'So the Count is not here, eh? Has he heard the news from Montségur? Does he know the end he has made of the Good Christians with his affairs?'

'Take your hands off me!' squealed the man, outraged. But I held on.

'Week after week we had word from here, from this palace! Hold on, wait for Easter, wait for the Last Trumpet! Why, for God's sake! Why?'

The chamberlain had gone pale. 'Stop, stop,' he said, his voice dropped to an urgent hiss. 'You were there? Who are you?'

'Petroc of Auneford, companion of Michel de Montalhac and sergeant of the garrison of Montségur,' I told him.

'De Montalhac . . . Is he here?'

'No, he is not. He is very far from here.'

'Ah . . .' He pinched his nose and gritted his teeth. 'Did they burn him? Curse them all.'

'No, he was not burned, but he is gone nonetheless.'

'I am sorry. I truly am: I knew Michel years ago when de Montfort was outside these walls. Did he take the *Consolamentum*?'

'He did,' I said, letting go of the man's shoulder. 'But what is it to you?'

'Nothing, save that I knew the man, and we spoke when he was here last.'

'When the Count said he would abandon the Good Christians.'

'Yes. I am . . . again, I am truly sorry. Some of us here did try to help, you know. But what could we do?'

I remembered that some of the messages that Iselda and Matheus had brought were from someone close to the Chamberlain. 'It was the Count who could have helped us, but he did not.'

'He wanted to, and he did try. The garrison has gone free, did you know? Your comrades, at least, are safe.'

'They were all, all of them, my comrades,' I said, swallowing down a bitter surge of grief.

'Listen to me. You must leave the palace, and do not come back. The French are everywhere now, and the Inquisition as well. If they sniff you out . . .' He gave me a haunted look. 'If it means anything to you, Count Raymond has lost everything. He has bowed his knee to the pope, and the bloody king of France, and in return for his freedom he will see his lands overrun by every sort of foreign louse, and sucked dry. Toulouse is finished. Languedoc is finished. You have seen the end of a world, young man. Now go, and if you have a story to tell you must tell it, but do so when you are far from here.' He took my hand and patted it hurriedly, and with a glance over his shoulder at me he hurried away.

'Wait,' I ran after him, and he paused, looking harried. 'Do you know Iselda de Rosers? The daughter of Assenda? You do, I see it in your face. Is she in Toulouse?'

'Iselda the *trobriaritz*? I gave . . . that is, I believe she took a message there some months ago. No, she is not here, and her friends, some of whom are mine as well, have not seen her. I fear she will have been at Montségur.'

I left the palace and went out into the city. I made my way up on to the walls, to the place where Domna Assenda's mangonel had stood. Once again I did not know what to do. Somehow I believed the Chamberlain: Iselda was not in Toulouse. So where was she? Narbonne? Montpellier, Foix? The thought of roaming through Languedoc suddenly filled me with dread. I did not wish to see this land die. I looked through the embrasure, out over the fields to the spot the Captain had pointed out. Simon de Montfort had died there, his head knocked off by a mother and her pregnant daughter – or perhaps not, but it made a good story. A story that no doubt a granddaughter would be glad to sing. Christ, there had not been enough songs lately.

Then and there I made up my mind. I would go to London and see Letice Londeneyse wed. I had meant what I had said to Sir Jeffrey. Rarely had I met a better man than Aimery de Lille Charpigny, indeed I could not say that I knew anyone else who acted entirely out of fairness and honour. I would always owe him my life, no matter how I repaid him, and besides, Letice Londeneyse and I had said goodbye to one another years ago. I had thought of her often, very often, during the siege. By day she had come into my daydreams as my dearest companion, and by night as lust incarnate; and many times I had sworn to myself that if I ever came down from the *pog* alive I would seek her out and win her love as I had won it before. But I had slowly forgotten the real woman as life itself became less and less real, and when she had gone the phantom girl of my dreams faded as well. Now here were two people whom I could wish well with all my heart, and it would be a fine balm for my battered spirit if I did exactly that.

And then I would rid myself of this dreadful thing I was carrying with me. I had thought many times of what the Captain had intended me to do with the thing, and now I guessed that he had meant for me to get rid of it, for it was a curse. I could not fulfil his last wish and find Iselda de Rosers while I still possessed it, for if I did so I would be bringing the shadow of death with me, and I was sure – suddenly, there on the walls of Toulouse, as the bells of the city still tolled defiantly for the dead of Montségur – that the Captain had meant me to bring life. Richard of Cornwall would give the mountains of the moon for the shroud, and I would make him dissolve the bond between us into the bargain. And then I would come looking for Michel de Montalhac's daughter. All at once I wanted, more than anything else, to hear her sing once more. Remembering my jealousy, I scratched at the lichen on the warm brick in embarrassment. At least I could make it right again. I would find her – I had tracked down far more elusive things, had I not? – but first, London. Feeling lighter already, I picked up a crumbling chunk of brick and flung it hard towards de Montfort's dying place, watching as it flew and dropped, lamentably short, into a stand of dry reeds. It would be good if someone could put the last year of Montségur into song. Perhaps, if the story were told, true and clear, in a voice as pure as the wind that blew down from the January mountains onto the *pog*, it might make sense. Perhaps it would even bring me rest.

I returned to London a day early for the wedding of Letice and Aimery. The road to Bordeaux had been crowded with soldiers, but they had all been going the other way, down into the southern lands, and no one bothered an English knight, for the French and the English seemed to be friends again. It was a vile crossing, stormy and wet, and twice we came in sight of the South Downs before the weather blew us back to Cherbourg, but at last I stepped ashore in Portsmouth, in rain so thick the town seemed to have slipped beneath the sea. It took me a week on England's vile and muddy tracks to reach London, but on the twenty-eighth day of April, as the afternoon was waning, I rode into the Borough and threaded my horse through the melee on London Bridge. I took a room at the Three Coneys and went to bed early, though I lay there for a long time, listening to the clip and clatter of footsteps in the alley below, and the London voices.

Next morning, early, I sought out a haberdasher that I remembered the courtiers mentioning, while we languished in Royan with nothing better to do than compare clothes. His wares were dowdy compared to the best of Venice, but I found some good sakarlat leggings and a tunic of fine bronze damask and paid over the odds for them. At least I would go unremarked at Westminster, for I would be as badly dressed as the rest of them. With Thorn on my belt and the fancy satchel with its secret cargo across my shoulder, I left the city by Lud Gate and rode across the meadows towards the Palace of Westminster. The tide was out, and the Thames mudflats looked like dirty pewter in the sunlight, but the rushes were putting out their spring shoots, and catkins hung from the hazel thickets. I thought I heard a cuckoo, though it was just a child calling his dog, but by the time I had come to the palace I was not so sunk in gloom as I had thought I might be. No: I was happy. I had not been to a wedding since Zianni, to everyone's amazement, had got himself married to a pretty, plump Tiepolo cousin, and that had been

257

four long years ago now. And as Letice had just left me and I was still cancelling my own wedding plans, I had never been likely to enjoy it.

I knew nothing about today's marriage save that I had got the date right. So I thought I would make my way to court and ask. Presumably it was an important occasion, if Earl Richard were giving away the bride. As I knew my way around Westminster after my fruitless week there, all of two years ago now, I wandered through the throng of courtiers, all as peevish and unfashionable as I remembered them, making for the hall where supplicants waited for their audience with the king. I was in sight of an archway I recognised when a loud, rich voice boomed out behind me:

'Zennorius! Zennorius! Hold, man!'

I whipped round to see Bishop Ranulph of Balecester, bedecked in the full regalia of his office, striding through the crowd towards me. God, no! Of the many people I did not wish to see, Balecester was the very least welcome at that moment. I lifted an arm in reluctant greeting, but as I resigned myself to his loathed company a swarm of clerics separated from the throng and began to assault him like horseflies, each jabbering and waving their arms, trying to outdo the other in forcing their petitions into his ears, and even plucking at his dalmatic. As he tried to beat them off I slipped behind a pillar and, hurrying along the wall, soon found myself at the hall of waiting. The door-keeper was the same thin and foxy fellow who had made my life miserable before, and he leant on his gold-knobbed staff and gave me a withering look, though he could not have recognised me. Somewhat elated by my fortunate escape from the bishop, I gave him a beaming smile that deepened his frown instantly, as lemon juice curdles milk the instant one touches the other.

'My good man, I am here for the wedding of Lady Agnes de Wharram,' I said. 'I am invited.'

'And who are you, sir?' he asked grudgingly. I had not impressed him yet: it must be a big wedding, then.

'Sir Petrus Zennorius,' I said, 'lately back from distant lands.' That always sounded impressive, but I was not prepared for the transformation my words brought about in the odious doorman.

'Sir Petrus?' he said, plainly amazed.

'I am he. I may have given the impression that I would not attend, but I was in London, so . . .' I said airily. The man was not listening.

'Please wait here, sir,' he said in an unctuous tone I had not heard in all that long week I had spent at his mercy. He showed me to a seat in the inner waiting room and disappeared through one of the doors. I had always assumed that beyond this room the king was waiting in all his glory, but now I thought about it, there wasn't anything grand about this room. There must be a dozen more beyond it, I mused as I sat there alone, all occupied by poor sods who know they are more favoured than the man in the room before, but who have no idea that the doors are endless. Much like life itself, I was thinking, when the doorman returned. He bowed most convincingly and indicated one of the other doors.

'This way, sir,' he said, silkily. I followed him through another door, bracing myself for the dazzle of the royal presence, for I seemed to have hit squarely in the red today. But instead I found myself in another corridor, down which the doorman hurried, his claret-coloured tunic fluttering behind him. The door at the end was shut, and the man rapped on it with the end of his staff. It was opened from within. The doorman bowed again and ushered me inside.

It was rather dark inside, but it seemed to be a small chamber. *You see? Another waiting room,* I said to myself. Someone held a lighted lamp very close to my face and the flame dazzled me. *How rude.* For a waiting room it seemed to be quite full. Perhaps these were the other wedding guests. All these thoughts went through my head as the door was closing behind me and my eyes tried to blink away the flare of the lamp.

'Sir Petrus Zennorius?' It was a voice I knew, a woman's voice, though I could not say whose it was. But all of a sudden the hairs stood up on my neck.

'Down on your knees, man, before your Queen!' barked one of the soldiers. I stiffened, for who was this fool to tell me what to do? But then I remembered where I had last heard that voice. The silver stain had faded from my eyeballs at last, and there, a few steps in front of me, Queen Isabella sat, dainty but coiled, in a high-backed chair. She raised a long, ring-weighted hand and tapped the arm of her throne.

'You have kept us waiting, Sir Petrus,' she murmured. 'And that, sirrah, has not improved our temper.'

Chapter Twenty-five

Queen Isabelle raised her long and elegant hand, and my arms were seized from behind. I knew enough not to struggle. I had been struggling for a long time now, years in fact, and it kept getting me nowhere.

'Put him in that,' said one of the knights whom I saw were standing around the walls. I was shoved down into a low chair with my lawyer's bag behind me. I felt the ancient cloth inside it crepitate softly.

'Now, Sir Petrus. It is a long time since we last saw you.'

'At Royan, Your Majesty,' I said politely. The men beside me held ropes, and I did not want to give them the excuse to lash me down.

'Exactly. Do you recall the conversation?'

'We talked of treasures as I recall, Your Majesty. My recollection is a little dim, however. I trust I have not missed my cousin's wedding? I was rather urgently requested to be here, and if I am too late I humbly apologise.'

The Queen's face did not move. It was as beautiful as it had been two years ago, though it had aged – we had all aged, of course, but Isabella's skin seemed to have transformed into ancient ivory: smooth, white and webbed with fine dark lines. 'Now then. We have been looking the length and breadth of Christendom for you.'

'Might I ask why, Your Majesty?'

'You are the expert in various matters. And there is one thing in particular that we desire to ask you about. One thing in particular.'

'I am at your service,' I said earnestly.

'No you are not,' snapped Queen Isabella. 'You are decidedly *not* at our service. You have been in France all this time. You have been in the employ of our cousin Louis. Not content with delivering up to him the holiest relics known to the mind of man, you have plotted with him to find that most holy of all things, that secret thing . . .'

'My dealings with the King of France are well-known,' I protested feebly. 'We have spoken of this before, surely?'

'Do not toy with us, creature.' The Queen had one hand on her hip and the other caressing the air malevolently in front of her. No wonder old Hughues de Lusignan did what he was told. 'The Crucifix of the Cathars. That is why you vanished after Saintes, and abandoned my son's army into the bargain. Do not try to deny it. We will have the thing one way or another.'

'I can assure you – nay, I will take an oath on the holiest relic in the kingdom – that I was not searching for that so-called crucifix,' I said, which was indeed the truth so far as that went. And all the while, *I'm sitting on it!* I was screaming to myself.

'Let me put it more plainly, because we seem to be at cross purposes,' said the Queen. 'If you have supplied, or have even attempted to supply that thing to Louis of France, we would regard it as treason. Our interest in it was well known to you – you, a vassal of my younger son! Villain, where is your loyalty?'

'Your Majesty, I believe the Cathar Crucifix, or the rumoured miraculous image, whatever it may be, is nothing more than a myth, and – you must believe me – I know a great deal about such things.' All this time I had been studying the Queen with every quivering nerve, every corner of my intellect. *Surely they will search me*, I thought, but I had dealt with monarchs before, and a horrid realisation began to dawn on me. They would not search me. It would not occur to her to do so, for she did not have the smallest knowledge of life's practicalities, or any interest in those things whatsoever. Other people did those things. To her I was nothing but . . . an ape, an uncouth vessel of either convenience for her, or inconvenience. I began to see that my fate, without a doubt, had already been decided. Still, I persisted, if only to bring out some little spark of humanity. 'If there is something else you would like me to find for you . . .'

'Be quiet. It is distasteful to us to be bandying words with a *tradesman*. Oh, my son was generous in making you a knight, but where are you really from, Sir Petrus? We could find out.' The Queen leaned on the arm of her chair. 'Did you by chance see the building works outside? My dear son is rebuilding the old abbey, for the greater glory of Our Lord. It will be the finest church in the kingdom.'

'I did not, Your Majesty. I will make a point of admiring it as soon as . . .'

'Our cousin Louis is making a miracle out of stone in Paris,' she went on as if I had not spoken. She was beginning to sound angry, and it was almost a relief to find some emotion in her. 'Why could we not do the same thing here? The finest masons, artists, all have been found. Louis built his Sainte Chapelle around the wonders you brought him – traitorously, to be sure – and we will do the same.'

'That is wondrous news,' I said brightly. Sweat was running down my back and pooling under me. My satchel was strangely comfortable, pressed against my tailbone. I had the wild fancy, all of a sudden, that the ghastly image would somehow betray me, perhaps rising of its own will to stand in judgment, and I eased myself back against it. 'What, though, do you believe this . . . this heretic crucifix to be?'

'The *Mandylion* of Edessa,' hissed the Queen. 'Lost and then found again, first by the heretical beasts who brought it out of Greece, then by you or your company. Produce it. Produce it, or I will watch as your guts are pulled out of you inch by inch, and cooked under your nose. Do you know how traitors die in England? In public their death is as slow and as agonising as the hangman can make it. In private, where the audience is not so impatient, I can assure you that your torment will proceed at a much more leisurely pace.'

At that moment I would have given her the *Mandylion*, I think, reached behind me and pulled out my satchel. I would have opened it and shaken out the stained old cloth within. It was not worth my life, surely. But it had claimed many other lives, so why not mine? In the instant those thoughts took to form out of the desperately whirling smoke inside my brain-pan, the Queen clapped her hands, and I knew that, no matter what I did now, I would not live to see another morning.

'Oh, Lord. We think you must be a heretic yourself, Sir Petrus,' said Queen Isabella. She was passing sentence: I could hear the calm in her voice. 'A heretic and a traitor. We do not like the way you grin at us. Certainly you understand that we can find out the truth. And now, enough. Take him downstairs. Make him talk, and be sure to leave enough of him to suffer a traitor's death.' She tugged at a stray lock of hair, thin-lipped, narrow-eyed, and winced. My heart was beginning to slam against my ribs, but I knew, in every muscle, that nothing I did now would make a difference. This was a creature who decided the fate of countries over luncheon. The life or death of a verminous brute such as myself . . . The Queen picked her nose distractedly, as if to prove my point. I was already dead. A year under siege had made me understand, as I never had before, what it means to be helpless, and so I closed my eyes and tried to make my thoughts go blank, as I remembered Gilles had tried to teach me once, long ago on his sunny cliff-edge. I took a deep breath, and as I did so, riving through the silence that had fallen on the chamber, a door handle rattled, hinges squealed and footsteps clacked. Somehow I sensed that the balance in the room had shifted, and I opened my eyes to see Bishop Ranulph of Balecester and two other men standing between me and Isabella. One of the men was Richard of Cornwall. The other, to my complete amazement, was the king.

'What in God's name can you mean by this?' cried the Queen. I felt the guards cringe, but the men stood their ground.

'I ask the same of you, mother!' Richard of Cornwall snapped. 'This man is my vassal. This is yet one more outrage against me. And please inform me, dear brother, how it is that you feel able to abduct a knight who is under my protection?'

'I had nothing to do with it,' protested Henry. His voice had grown a little higher, a little weaker than when I had last heard it. 'This is another of Mama's cursed schemes.'

'This man is a traitor,' said the Queen, looking somewhat affronted, but nothing more. 'He has been conspiring with Louis Capet to over-shadow Henry's great plan for the abbey by delivering to him the heretic crucifix, or *Mandy lion*, or whatever it is called. If that is not a crime . . .' She was growing more animated again. '. . . It is a crime against God himself! Indeed it is clear to us that this Sir Petrus, so called, is nothing more than a Catharist heretic.'

King Henry turned and found me sitting behind him. He seemed mildly surprised. The last two years had been kind to him: his hair cascaded down on either side of his head in lovely golden curls, and he had grown a beard that hid his weak chin.

'We remember you from the battle in front of Saintes,' he said mildly.

'I was there, Your Majesty,' I agreed.

'A dreadful mess, a dreadful, dreadful mess,' he murmured. 'And you did well. Well done.'

'If he is conspiring with cousin Louis, he is hardly likely to be a heretic,' said Richard, dry as dust.

'Is this why you have grown so interested in the abbey recently, Mama? To spite Louis?' Henry was standing his ground, despite the look his mother was scorching him with.

'Your Majesties, Sir Petrus proved to me beyond a shadow of a doubt that the *Mandylion* of Edessa is a myth,' said Bishop Ranulph. 'Not one soul has seen it since the burning of Constantinople. If your royal cousin wishes to squander what is left in his coffers on a fruitless search, does that not serve the interests of Your Majesty?'

'How can it be a myth?' snapped Isabella. 'Louis believes it is real, and *he* is not a fool.' It might have been my fancy, but she seemed to fix her eyes on Henry as she spoke.

'That does it, Mama. The abbey, do you hear me, is *my* business, or do you and honest Hughues de Lusignan wish to befoul it with your schemes, as you have fouled so much else? Do you know what our war in Poitou cost us, Mama? Apart from the scorn of the Continent, and the contempt of my barons, and the pleasure of seeing my own father-in-law turn his coat and toady to Louis? Apart from the shame, which I have not yet put a price on, it cost an ocean of silver, dear Mama, and the commons are not best disposed to fill it again. Now if you have some other evidence that this man is a traitor, I will hear it.'

'I will vouch for Petrus Zennorius,' said the Bishop of Balecester, drawing himself up to his full height, which was still impressive, though he had aged in the two years since I had seen him among the broken vines. 'He came to my aid at Saintes and carried me to safety when I was hurt. He is no friend of heretics, as I know from our . . . our investigations together. And he has fulfilled a solemn and difficult promise to your son Richard. These hardly sound like the actions of a traitor.'

'*Balecester?*' hissed the Queen. 'How dare you challenge us so? You owe your favour to . . .'

'He owes it to me, mother,' said Richard abruptly. 'Ranulph opposed your fantasy war in Poitou with all his power. I should have listened to him. If we are bandying *traitor* around, meanwhile, you have never properly explained either to Henry or myself why exactly you drew us into a war it seems you never intended for us to win. My brother and I have been thinking about this a great deal.'

'I did it for England!' the Queen shouted.

'Nonsense!' Henry yelled. Something within him had evidently snapped. 'Nonsense, I say! You did it for Hughues de Lusignan! You conspired to draw us into a profitless battle with Louis, and mother, your husband told us so himself: *blame no one but your mother*, he said at Taillebourg. I cannot . . . mother, I will brook no more interference from you. I command you to return to France as soon as you are able, and to keep your affairs, and those of your unlucky husband, separated from those of my kingdom!'

'I will not,' she said, an icy, dangerous smile parting her rouged lips. A mother and her two powerful sons – and she had given them their power. 'I will not,' she said again.

'My honoured mother,' said Henry, and he sounded stronger, all of a sudden. 'I have lately been forced to sign a treaty with Louis Capet, and while he was kind enough not to make it an occasion for humiliating the crown I wear, nonetheless England is the laughing stock of Christ-endom. Your beloved husband has submitted utterly to Louis, and my brother will never reclaim Poitou now that Lusignan is a loyal vassal of France. And we know, mother: we know that it was you who urged Lusignan to rebel.'

'That is a lie!' Isabella stood bolt upright and a ripple of unease went around the room. But her sons stood firm.

'By the Holy Face, mother! I find you here, about to have my brother's man condemned as a traitor, while the only traitor I find in this room is you yourself! It was your vainglory that lured one Christian monarch to attack another,' Henry continued, his voice rising. 'God is my witness that I bear my cousin Louis no ill-will. I cannot even bring myself to hate my step-father, for he has shown that in the end he was weak and a dupe. No, it is you, mother. You have proved yourself to be a canker in the bosom of our kingdom, and that cannot be tolerated. You will be escorted back to your lands in France and there you may do what you will. And be sure that it is only because you gave me life that I am sparing yours!'

Someone tapped me on the arm. It was Bishop Ranulph, looking flushed.

'Come away,' he said. 'This does not concern you.'

'It did a minute ago,' I said, standing up gratefully.

'It did, indeed it did,' he said. 'Now come. We must attend a wed-ding.'

'I will join you,' said Earl Richard. 'Goodbye, mother.' He bowed stiffly, and the three of us marched out between the frightened guards, leaving the king and his mother facing each other like maddened tom-cats on a narrow wall.

'My lord Richard,' I said as we made our way through the private corridors of the palace, 'I do not understand. You have rescued me, and yet I came here at your invitation to find myself . . . to find myself trapped,' I finished abruptly. I was sick of tripping my tongue around the niceties of these grand folk.

'My invitation?' said Richard, sounding puzzled.

'Sir Jeffrey of Abbot's Dene chanced upon me in Toulouse. He told me of your urgent desire to have me attend my cousin Agnes' wedding. And it seems there were people looking for me all over France.'

'Jeffrey of Abbot's Dene is one of Lusignan's English knights,' said Richard. 'I never sent any such invitation. This wedding was . . . my mother took a liking to Lady Agnes after she heard of her bravery in the wagon train at Saintes. She rather pushed Agnes and that Frenchman, that . . .'

'Sir Aimery,' I prompted. 'De Lille Charpigny. An old Burgundian family.'

'*Là*. Well, she is your cousin, so I expect she won't mind me telling you. She brought a proposal to me, a trading matter, the Levant and all that sort of thing . . .' he waved his hand dismissively. 'In any case it prospered and both of us became somewhat the richer. My mother began badgering me about a wedding two months or so ago, and I agreed to sponsor it. But as for you, Sir Petrus, I am afraid that I supposed you dead.'

'No, I did not die,' I muttered.

'Evidently not. I owe you a debt of thanks.'

'Oh! My lord, I forgot! My heartiest congratulations on your own marriage,' I said. 'I heard in Toulouse.'

'Thank you. Now I have things to attend to before this damned wedding. My brother has kicked a hornet's nest, and he will have no idea what to do now.' And he patted the bishop on the arm and loped off.

'So there *is* a wedding then, my lord?' I asked the bishop.

'Of course. In Saint Margaret's Church. Couldn't spare the Abbey for a commoner.' He glanced at Earl Richard's retreating figure, and then caught my arm.

'Now then. Never mind what you told the Queen. Did you find it?'

I blinked at him, feeling as if I had just clawed my body out of a deep well only to lose my grip at the last moment. I had actually forgotten about my satchel and what it contained, though it still hung innocently against my hip. I wondered for an instant whether I should call Richard back and sell him the damned thing on the spot. But I had not given it to his mother, so why should he have it? I saw, very clearly, that I could not sell this thing. It could not go to any man or woman who saw power in it, for as the Captain had discovered, and I had also seen with my own eyes, it seemed to drive men headlong towards death. What would it do to the worldly ambitions of Earl Richard? And even pious King Henry . . . No. I would destroy it. But what if . . . *What if?* I thought of flames eating the shadowy face on the shroud, and shuddered. No. It would have to go to someone who understood what it was but had no desire to use it, no desire for power. I opened my mouth to let out a name, but before it found the air I realised that someone was talking very loudly in my ear.

'What about it? The *Mandylion*? Sir Petrus! I know you were searching for it.' The Bishop of Balecester was staring at me with a mixture of impatience and concern.

'My lord,' I said, 'I was, you are right. I looked . . . I followed the heretics. To Avignonet, where the Inquisitors were killed. To little villages where not one wretched ear has ever heard the true word of Mother Church. And do you know where I finished up, my lord? At Montségur itself.'

'The Synagogue of Satan!' he looked at me with awe and perhaps fear. 'And it was there?'

'They worshipped an old piece of cloth like the one you took off that heretic in Royan,' I said. 'A crude copy, and I realised this at last, of an icon that was once famous in Constantinople. I saw a drawing of it there, and copies of it were quite popular with the heretic brethren called Bogomili, or so an old Greek priest told me. It proved some esoteric point of their absurd doctrine – I never troubled to learn the details. A copy of a facsimile of something half-remembered. We have been chasing a phantom.'

'And the heretic treasure? One has heard about it,' he whispered. 'I guessed that it was . . .'

'No, it was not the *Mandylion*,' told him. 'And besides, all has been destroyed. The heretics went up in flames, and their treasure with them. That is the truth, and the end of it.'

'You were there?'

'Almost,' I said and, catching his incredulous look, managed to grin. I slapped my satchel. 'My Lord, I have a wedding gift to deliver. Let us go and find the bride-to-be.'

Letice Londeneyse was surrounded by a gaggle of bridesmaids and old maids and serving maids, all twittering and clucking. There was a merry hum all through the chamber, which overlooked the abbey precinct and the little church of Saint Margaret's, whose bells had just started to ring, shaking the dust from the beams and sending it down twinkling through the sunlight. When the women saw me they all gasped and threw themselves into attitudes of mock anger or overplayed modesty, and I had the pleasure of seeing Letice's lovely mouth fall open in utter bewilderment.

'I was invited,' I said, striding in, 'So I am here. Pleased to see me?'

Pushing through the women and knocking one of them back on her plump bottom, Letice bounded across the room in a most unladylike fashion, holding up her skirts and bawling something at me in the arcane tongue of Smooth Field. She wrapped herself around me and squeezed until my ribs creaked.

'I thought you were dead!' she yelled in my ear.

'Not yet,' I gasped. 'I'm so happy for you, Letice. How is your leg?'

'Patch, that was two years ago! It is fine, of course it is! Where have you been, you bloody man?'

'Almost to the end of the world,' I told her. 'Letice . . . *Agnes*, I need to tell you . . .' But I could not. The Captain would not have wanted it so. Sad news did not belong in that room, and the tattered clouds of grief I had been trailing had no place in the speckled sunlight. 'I need to tell you that there is no finer man in the world than Aimery.'

'Oh, I know, I know! Even if he does bang on about his precious chivalry. I've read those books, you know. Rubbish!' She was chattering happily. 'God, it's so long ago! The battle . . . it all got puffed up beyond belief, you know, what I did. And then Aimery took me back to Paris . . . Do you know what? With all my money we are going to buy back his lands in Burgundy! King Louis has said yes . . .'

'You had better tell me later,' I said gently. 'The bells are ringing, or have you deafened yourself with all this chatter? Listen, I have a gift for you, but we need to be alone for a minute.'

'Alone? I don't think . . .' She was not really listening, for the women were giving her impatient looks, so I bowed to them, the most flowery Venetian bow I could muster, and took Letice by the arm.

'You must lend me the bride for two minutes,' I said. 'We . . .' I remembered that I had passed a tiny private chapel, its door ajar, just down the passage. 'We need to say a prayer together.' And before anyone could protest I had half led, half dragged Letice out of the door and into the chapel. I shut the door behind me and made sure it was latched.

'We only have a moment,' I said.

'What's come over you, Patch? Praying, all of a sudden?' Letice was put out. Her ears had gone red, a sure sign of disfavour.

'Shush,' I said. 'Take off your dress.'

'Bloody hell! You little bastard!' she shrieked. I put my hand over her mouth and shook my head urgently.

'No, no! I missed my chance long ago. You're safe, my dear. Look: it's this.' I jerked open the satchel and pulled out the folded *Mandylion*, creased and crushed into a tight square from my using it as a cushion.

'Patch, that's the shroud from Constantinople,' she hissed, her eyes very wide.

'So it is. And I am giving it to you, to do with as you will. It is worth more gold than either of us have ever dreamed of, but . . . I would not sell it. You can, but I cannot. The Captain . . .' I stopped, and let the folds loosen and unwrap themselves. The dark impressions of bloodied feet appeared. 'Listen to me. Keep it safe for a while. Many people are hunting for it for their own reasons. Let it become an old myth again, and then, perhaps, take it to King Louis or Earl Richard. Your fortune will be made ten thousand times over. Or . . . please, though, Letice. Please do not believe in it.'

I could see fear and interest working in her eyes, and then something else appeared, a spark I had not seen for many years. She took her bottom lip between her teeth and held it there. Then she nodded sharply.

'Go on then,' she said. She hoiked up her heavy robe of blue Florentine silk and there she was, pale and lithe and naked save for her hosen. I averted my eyes, suddenly feeling indecent, even though I had not seen a woman's body, God save me, since Royan. I took the end of the shroud and wrapped it once around her waist, tucking the end in on itself, and then began to wind it, all fourteen feet of it, as tightly as I dared. She helped me, turning and tucking, and on the third turn we both began to laugh nervously as we wound the dark, stained cloth onto her like a living bobbin, Letice wincing at the feel of the ancient stuff against her skin, both of us trying to avoid seeing the shapes that had been marked there. Soon it was done, and with a sound like snow falling from a roof she let her heavy dress slide to the floor.

'If it is a true relic, may it give you blessings,' I said softly, and still on my knees I put my arms around her waist and laid my face against her belly, though all I felt was the stiffness of the shroud. She laid her hands gently on my hair.

'What do you think it is, Patch?' she asked.

'Desire. Desire for peace, for truth, for death. And love, if you believe the Gospels. I think it is man's desire, painted in blood.'

There was an impatient rustling of gowns out in the corridor. I stood up, and Letice smoothed down her silks.

'We have caused a scandal,' she said, and gave me a peck on the cheek.

'My darling Letice, we have done much, much more than that,' I said, and taking her head in my hands I kissed her hard on her forehead. The sun was filling the room, and the bells were clanging. 'May you have light like this always, my love,' I said, and together we opened the chapel door.

Agnes de Wharram, widow of the City of London, ship-owner and purveyor of pepper, silk and other rarities married Sir Aimery de Lille

Charpigny, knight of France, in Saint Margaret's Church in the Liberty of Westminster on the twenty-fifth day of April in the year of Our Lord 1244. Richard, Earl of Cornwall led her up the aisle and as her protector, gave her away to the groom. She moved a little stiffly, my Letice, and she had gone a little red in the face for lack of air, but she did not burst out laughing, as I had feared that she might, or weeping, for which I would not have blamed her, and nor did any ancient cloth appear from under her shimmering blue dress. I watched until Bishop Ranulph had put her hand in Aimery's, and slipped from my pew unnoticed. I had wanted to see Aimery again, but after the liberty I had just taken with his bride I doubted that I could look him in the face.

I paused in the doorway. They were still listening to the bishop as he sought to bind love with the laws of Rome, and the light was dancing off the crucifix and from all the gold and jewels on the altar. I was thinking of Captain de Montalhac and his Alayda, and of Anna, and how an English priest had spoken over her as she lay, cold and white, not very far from this place. There was a song winding through all this, somehow, a cold but lovely voice bidding us all to take the sweetness of life in both hands and hold it tight, for the dawn was coming, and with it the end of dreams. Bishop Ranulph had taken the chalice and was raising it up over the lovers' heads, and the garnets that studded it caught the light and set a host of tiny red sparks dancing over the congregation. I looked down, thinking one had touched me, but there was nothing. The light danced again and I saw the flames go up from the pyre of Montségur, all those cinders that had been Gilles, and Bishop Bertrand, and two hundred people I had known. All free now, perhaps: all perfect. Gilles had desired that more than anything: to be free from desire.

I did not want that. As Aimery took Letice in his arms and kissed her, embracing the thing that Ranulph of Balecester desired above all things, I knew that I would not be perfect. Gilles had told me, long ago, that when he had become a *bon homme* it had felt as if someone had opened him like a lantern and blown the ember inside into a flame. Something was kindling inside me now. I said a silent goodbye and went out into the burying ground. There, among the ancient dead, the mothers and fathers, enemies and lovers, my own father's words came back to me: *there is some light left in you.* Perhaps I could find it. I had found stranger things. I could try – at least I could try.

Chapter Twenty-six

I went to Paris, to Vincennes, and found myself sitting once more beneath King Louis' oak, watching the brimstone butterflies drift through the glossy leaves of May. I had visited the Sainte Chapelle, growing slowly in the midst of Paris, a filigree of wondrously carved stone strangely at odds with the lumpy, formless buildings that surrounded it, the skeleton of some fabled sea-beast washed up on a crude cobbled beach.

'King Henry is rebuilding Westminster Abbey to rival it,' I told Louis, and he smiled as if it were a great compliment.

'Will he succeed?' he asked, mischievously.

'Without your Monsieur Pierre de Montreuil, I don't expect so,' I said. 'Interesting thing, though, Your Majesty. Isabella of Angoulême has been taking an extraordinarily keen interest in the proceedings. Even to the extent of trying to procure for her son a relic to rival your own.'

'There is none,' said Louis, giving me a puzzled look.

'To be sure. But she appears to have fallen under the spell of the fabled *Mandylion*,' I went on, dismissively. 'Even to the extent of seizing at least one agent of yours, Your Majesty, who was searching for it on your behalf.'

'No!' He sat bolt upright, and a thrush began to scold him from the lower branches.

'Indeed yes. She made it a capital matter, no less. Treachery, to her mind. This is hearsay, of course, Sire.'

'Damn her! That woman has plagued me for too long! First a ridiculous war, and now this. But she has it, though?' Louis had gone horribly white.

'Of course not, Your Majesty.'

'Good. Isabella! I will have to take steps . . . But the *Mandylion*, though?

'Your Majesty, trust me when I tell you that it does not exist. If it ever did – and it may have done, I will admit – it has gone from this world, as is the way with things miraculous,' I added piously.

'And the heretics?'

'An illusion. Daubings on bed-sheets to scare the credulous. I believe the so-called heretic bishop, one Bertrand Marty, was responsible.'

'I remember the name. He was burned.'

'At Montségur. I think that you will find these whisperings, these rumours about a miraculous shroud will fade with the passing of the *bons hommes*.'

'That is a pity,' sighed Louis. He had regained his natural colour, and looked once more like an overgrown boy. 'Of all the great relics . . .'

'Your treasurer will thank you, Sire,' I reminded him.

'And, great heavens, my mother,' he whispered, and we both laughed, as though the things that were said here in this gentle place had no power to harm anything greater than a horsefly.

I rode south after that, down through the soft valleys of Burgundy to the Rhône and then to Avignon. I had no idea how to search for Iselda, so I began by seeking out the town of Rosers, from which she had taken her name. I found a Rosières, and a Roziers, but no *trobriaritz* had ever been heard of in either one. There was a Rosers near Arles, a verminous hamlet of old women and three-legged dogs, and she was not there. By the end of the summer I had gone almost to Marmande in the west and Grasse in the east, picking my way through the sad lands of the Languedoc and keeping far away from the southern mountains, for I did not wish to see those places again. There had been a day of storms that had raced over me one after the other as I rode towards Narbonne, and I had taken refuge in a barn close to the Abbey of Fontfroide. Huddled under my cloak, wet and lonely, I decided that enough was enough. I would go back to Venice and see what waited for me there. But when I awoke the next day that plan did not seem so attractive, so I took a track leading away from the coast towards Carcassonne. It took me through low, dusty hills planted with vines, and some time after midday, when the air was still and the heat was clamped around my head, and there seemed to be nothing in the world but the ageless churr of cicadas, I came to a village that rose in terraces up a hillside above a river. The windows were shuttered and the doors shut tight against the heat, so I watered my horse at the fountain in the tiny square and found some cool shade by the wall of the church. I fell asleep, and when I woke up the heat had eased and there were people walking about.

I bought some figs and cheese, and walked to the end of the main street, which gave out on the bare hillside. There was nothing but wild sage, and rock roses, and bees in the thyme bushes, but it was peaceful, and I looked across the valley at the next shoulder of hills, and the ridge beyond. And far away, dancing in the breath of the hot earth, the mountains. I got up and walked back to where my horse was waiting. I did not feel tired, and I thought, how fine it would be to ride all night and come to Carcassonne in the morning. Then I would be done with this aimless life, and go back to Venice at peace with myself. The little stalls along the street were doing a little business, and the old ladies were gathered in their doorways. A goose was chasing a little boy, who was screeching that it had bitten his arse. Shutters banged. A girl staggered past me with two big pails full of water yoked across her shoulders. And from a window a woman's voice drifted down, pure as the water Moses brought forth in the desert.

My handsome friend,
Brave knight you may be,
But your bright armour and your painted shield
Are no match for the thorns that await
When you go to pick roses.

I looked up, but the window opened onto shadow.

'Iselda!' I called. 'Iselda! Is it you?' The song broke off, and I looked around guiltily, but no one except me seemed to have noticed. 'Iselda!' I called again.

She put her head out of the window. Her long plaits dropped from the sill and hung against the ancient stone. 'Who's calling Iselda?' she said. Then she saw me.

'I've been searching for you,' I said. 'All through these lands.'

'Why?'

'I had to.' People were beginning to look at me – perhaps I was to be the evening's entertainment: a mouthy foreigner annoying the village singer. 'And I have something for you.'

'These are riddles, sir. I do not answer riddles. I am not a sphynx. Go away.'

'I cannot, Iselda. There is too much to say. And I can only tell you.' She was reaching for the shutters. 'No! Listen to me. I told you once that you had enchanted me. Perhaps that was true. How else could I be standing here? I have news for you: sad and strange. I don't know what you will make of it. But you ought at least to hear it, and I have brought it to you across a thousand miles or more.'

'News?' She let go of the shutters and leant her arms on the window-sill. She seemed to be staring at me very hard, and her head fell to one side as she did. I realised she was smiling at me the way she had when we had last said goodbye, in the rain outside Nîmes. 'I will listen to anything and everything you bring me, save the news. I have been hiding from the world, though not from you, Petroc Black-Dog. Do not ask me how, but I knew you would come, by and by. Because you were right: the spring did find me at last. And now you have too. What else have you brought?'

I raised my hands towards her. 'Figs and cheese,' I offered.

'Wait!' She ducked back into the shadows and then reappeared. Stretching out her arm, she opened her fist and something small and black fell towards me. I reached out my arms, a reflex, and snatched a key out of the air.

'You'd better come up, then,' she said.

Epilogue

Montségur, September 1244

There was the *pog*, rising like the stub of a broken tooth in the great jaws of the mountains. We had come up the road and had our first sight of Montségur in the mid-morning. It was a clear day, though a breeze was coming down off the high peaks and breathing cold air in our faces. The oaks and chestnuts were just beginning to turn. Fat sheep were grazing in the pastures, and beside us the river was clucking to itself in its stony bed, almost dry, waiting for the rains of autumn. There were no people about. We had not passed anyone on the road for five miles or more. I sniffed at the cool air for the taint of burning, but there was nothing.

It was Iselda's wish that had brought us here. We would lay her father's bones to rest along with the dead *perfecti* of Montségur. 'He would have sought death there,' she had told me, after I had given her, at last, all the news she had dreaded to hear. 'But he thought he could help keep the belief alive in Italy. I wonder, if the bishop had not commanded him, he would have left? I think his heart stayed on the *pog.*'

'I think his heart had come to rest *here*,' I told her, kissing her brow. I did not want to see Montségur again, or whatever terrible thing the Crusaders' piety had left there, but now Iselda's idea had lodged in some unhealed part of my soul and I knew that, though neither of us wanted to make this journey, this was a thing beyond desire, and we would both return there one final time.

'It looks different,' said Iselda. We were only three miles away now. A buzzard mewed high overhead.

'The castle!' I said, squinting. 'They've pulled down the castle.'

As we rode closer we could see that nothing remained of the walls of

275

Montségur. The bastions that had given the *pog* its austere crown had been razed and the stones scattered, for there was no sign, from down in the valley, that men had ever set their mark on that high place. We reined in and stood in the middle of the track, staring. I turned to Iselda and found my confusion reflected in her eyes. The centre of our world for two years – no, it had been our whole world – might never have existed.

The village at the foot of the *pog* was deserted, doors hanging off, thatch beginning to rot. The French had been quartered here and the villagers had not dared to return, not yet. There were piles of pig, sheep and cattle bones; and heaps of men's excrement, and a dead dog lying in the main pathway, nothing but a bag of dappled white and black hair collapsed over its skeleton. We rode on, ears pricking, but there was no sound except the thud of our horses' hooves. We could already see where we were going. Further ahead, just before the rise of the ground where the *pog* began to jut from the hillside, a shadow lay among the abandoned fields. A great patch of black was smeared from the foot of the cliff and out into the sheep pasture, overgrown now, for all the sheep were dead. Like the pupil of a vast eye it stared up at the blue sky. We could smell the ash even here, see the greasy soot where it had drifted down onto the failing whitewash of the village walls.

It took no time at all to reach the burned field. As we rode up I saw where they had built their monstrous pyre, and how every tree and bush for half a mile around had been hacked off at its base to feed it. A soot stain like the frozen shadow of flame lapped up the face of the cliff, higher than a church steeple. The grass was burned right up to the track, wildfire that must have taken off the dry grass of winter. Lush new grass and late flowers grew happily through the dark crust of ash, but at the heart of the field nothing grew at all.

Silently, reluctantly, we swung our legs over our horses and slipped down onto the ground. The burned layer gave a breathy crunch. We stood at the edge of the devastation – but it was not that, nothing more, really, than a farmer's swaling, a day's work to make the grass grow stronger next year. Except that no farmer had done this, for nothing would be growing here when spring came. Towards the centre of the field, the fire had burned so fiercely that the earth itself had been consumed, and white rocks were shoving through the cinders. But at the very middle a low mound rose, no higher than a man's knee, and the things that were jumbled there were not stones.

Two hundred and more people lay here, turned to powdery ash, to grey clinker, to blackened chips of bone. Here and there the fist of a knee-joint or the bowl of a skull-top poked through the desert. Here were two eye sockets, burnt to coal and without the rest of their skull. I reached for them, but they crumbled in my hands. I stuck my fingers into the ash pile and thought for an instant that the ground was still warm. But it was not.

'Raymonde.' Iselda's voice rang against the sooty cliff. A spark burst into life on the mound of ash, the white petals of a daisy.

'Bruna.' Another flower dropped beside me. 'Ermengarde. Rixende. India. Braida. Arsende.' Every name was the tolling of a clear bell. And with every name, a flower. 'Maurina. Esclarmonde. Rixenda. Marquesia. Oh, God . . .'

I took her in my arms as she folded. 'She sewed our clothes . . . Poor old Marquesia! How could they burn her? How could they do this? How could they do it?'

'I don't know, my love. I don't know.' I could smell the daisies in her fist, crushed into white and yellow crumbs. Her tears were hot against my neck. I pressed my thumb against my own eye to stop the tears, so my grief took my voice instead and we clung together in the great silence of that desert place, dumb, shaking. At last I took her hand and brushed the damp mash of ruined flowers from it onto the ground.

'Gilles,' I said.

'We cannot leave him here,' I said. We were sitting on the other side of the track, over where the path began to rise steeply up towards where the castle had been. 'He always wanted to be free, and he had his wish. But here is the end of hope. I cannot imprison his bones in this wasteland.'

'I know,' said Iselda. She leant against me, her hand in mine, resting in her lap over the sack of bones. We rose, and made our way over to the mound. The sun was slanting towards the high mountain tops, and the shadows seemed to be gathering in the blackness at the heart of the field. I set down the bag, and the contents brushed against each other, a sigh and a scratching. Then, as if a great, soft hand had touched me between the shoulder blades, I found myself kneeling in the ash, which yielded with a tiny hiss. Under my knee, the blunt pressure of splintered bone. With the bowl of my cupped hands I gathered up a heap of the ashes and held them up to my face.

'Gilles?' I whispered. 'Gilles de Peyrolles.' Then I tipped them gently over the jumbled bones of his friend.

The *Cormaran* nodded its head to the south, to where the dark brush-stroke of Crete would soon be rising. There was a gentle wind out of the East, and we were dropping down slowly across the Aegean, Milos just sunk behind us, the waves flashing from blue to silver, to quicksilver, to flying spray. A porpoise had shadowed us from Milos, but now he had gone, back to the island or away on some errand. We had our relics with us, and our own errand to perform. Here, over the deep waters, cradled by a hundred unseen islands, we had all come home.

Most of the crew were strangers, Venets and Croats hired off the Molo in Venice for a trading run to Alexandria. Of the Captain's old crew only Isaac the doctor and Dimitri, the *Cormaran*'s old master-at-arms, now older and a little fatter, with the damp of Venice turned to rheumatism in his knees, were aboard. The others were far away, or like Zianni, further still, for he was dead of an ague, and Istvan had been taken by an apoplexy at the turn of the year. The sailors hung back around the stern castle or tended to barely needed chores, giving us some peace. I stood with Iselda in the prow, where I had often stood with the Captain and Gilles. The rail was worn and smooth where our hands had gripped it year in and year out as many seas had passed beneath us. Isaac leaned nearby with Dimitri, silent, staring out over the water. The old master-at-arms cradled two swords in his arms, the Captain's old fashioned, heavy blade with its iron handle, and the newer sword that Gilles had been so proud of. They had taught me to fight, these men, here on this deck, while the crew jeered and clapped.

'Are you ready?' I asked Iselda. She nodded, and lifted the plain sailcloth bag from where it had been resting in a coil of rope. She cradled it for a moment, then handed it to me. I held it against my chest, and felt the smooth bones within move against each other, the long bones, the ribs, the jumbled spine and fingers and toes shifting with the ashes, the gentle orb of the skull. I held out the bag to Isaac and Dimitri, who laid their hands on it. Dimitri crossed himself, and Isaac began to murmur the words of the Kaddish. I turned back to the sea, and Iselda helped me open the mouth of the bag, our fingers fumbling with the cords. When it was open, Dimitri slipped the two swords inside, hilts first. I drew the cords tight and knotted them around the worn leather of the scabbards.

'Here,' said Iselda. Together we leaned over the side, the cloth of the bag in our fists, our arms in the sea spray. I cannot recall who let go first.

'Pray God made you good Christians, and brought you to good ends,' said Iselda, her voice cracking. Salt was sparkling on her cheeks. I took her hands, cold from the sea.

'Amen,' I said.

The End

Author's Note

This is fiction, but the main events – battles, the massacre at Avignonet, the plots and intrigues of England, France, Toulouse and Poitou – are matters of record. The rest is a coarse weave of what-ifs and why-nots, but the loose ends I gathered are also based on fact:

The *Mandylion* of Edessa disappeared in the sack of Constantinople in 1204, and has not been seen since.

Geoffrey de Charny, killed fighting the English at Poitiers in 1356, is the first recorded owner of the relic that we know as the Shroud of Turin. An ancestor of Geoffrey, one Hugh de Lille Charpigny, was present at the sack of Constantinople, however, and the de Lille Charpignys, and the Charnys, as they later became, ended up as one of the most renowned noble families in all of France. How the Shroud came to be in their possession has never been established.

The Sieur de Bourbon was killed at the battle of Saintes in 1242, but the name of his killer has not been passed down to us.

All the Good Christians who survived the siege of Montségur perished in a huge bonfire prepared for them at the foot of the *pog*. The place where they died is still known as the *Prat dels Cremats* – the Field of the Burned.